Praise for *Collision of Lies*

"Excellent pacing and surprising twists will keep readers guessing and engaged until the end. This is Threadgill's most intricate, propulsive novel yet."

Publishers Weekly

"Threadgill plunges a detective from the San Antonio Property Crimes Division into a deep-laid plot involving murder, kidnapping, and myriad other crimes above her pay grade."

Kirkus Reviews

"I didn't want to put this book down . . . *couldn't* put it down. I absolutely adore Amara Alvarez and her relationships with her co-workers, friends, and her iguana! Now I want one. She was a heroine who made me laugh and one I could really relate to. I can think of a few words to describe this book: amazing, incredible, intriguing, mesmerizing, unputdownable. . . . I could go on, but I need to stop so I can go buy up the entire backlist of my new favorite author."

Lynette Eason, award-winning, bestselling author of the Blue Justice Series

"This book is a journey, drawing its readers and characters onto a path that is both curious and intelligent."

More Than a Review

"The plot flows at breathtaking speed as the clues become more bizarre."

World Magazine

NETWORK OF DECEIT

ALSO BY TOM THREADGILL

Collision of Lies

NETWORK
OF DECEIT

TOM THREADGILL

Revell

a division of Baker Publishing Group
Grand Rapids, Michigan

© 2021 by Thomas D. Threadgill

Published by Revell
a division of Baker Publishing Group
PO Box 6287, Grand Rapids, MI 49516-6287
www.revellbooks.com

Printed in the United States of America

Library of Congress Cataloging-in-Publication Data
Names: Threadgill, Tom, 1961– author.
Title: Network of deceit / Tom Threadgill.
Description: Grand Rapids, Michigan : Revell, a division of Baker Publishing Group, [2021]
Identifiers: LCCN 2020024916 | ISBN 9780800736514 (paperback) | ISBN 9780800739720 (casebound)
Subjects: GSAFD: Mystery fiction.
Classification: LCC PS3620.H7975 N48 2021 | DDC 813/.6—dc23
LC record available at https://lccn.loc.gov/2020024916

This book is a work of fiction. Names, characters, places, and incidents are the product of the author's imagination or are used fictitiously. Any resemblance to actual events, locales, or persons, living or dead, is coincidental.

Published in association with the Hartline Literary Agency, LLC.

21   22   23   24   25   26   27   7   6   5   4   3   2   1

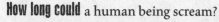

How long could a human being scream?

Three times through the video so far and Amara's appreciation for the woman's lung capacity grew with each viewing. No sound on the recording, but there was no mistaking the outburst. The wide eyes, gaping mouth, and panicked attempt to be anywhere else other than there. Not that the shrieking had any relevance whatsoever. The woman's reaction was entirely normal. People tended to scream when dead bodies appeared beside them.

On the monitor, an older teenage male, his chin against his chest and face hidden with a baseball cap, drifted on the water park's lazy river. The deeply tanned boy floated on a huge yellow inner tube with each hand, palms up, tucked under one of the black handles. His knees were propped on top, allowing his feet to dangle in the water. During the seven-and-a-half-minute video clip, a series of rapids and a few collisions with other riders jostled him enough that his hands and feet moved, making it difficult to determine if the teen was dead or passed out. Either way, the other park visitors were too absorbed in their own day to notice. That would change.

A short way ahead, the not-yet-screaming woman and her three kids—two boys and a younger girl, all under ten or eleven by the looks of them—linked their floats together in an ovalish circle. Each member of the family held the foot of their neighbor as they meandered through the twists and turns of the attraction. The distance between the teenager and family narrowed, and Amara leaned closer to the monitor as her heartbeat accelerated. This was like one of those nature videos where a lioness stalks her victim. Creeping up on the unsuspecting wildebeest until . . . now.

The teen caught up to the family and his left leg bumped against the back of the young girl's head. She jerked, turned to see who'd nudged her, mouthed something to him, and pushed his tube away. Barely a dozen clock-ticks later, he collided with her again, sending the mother into mom mode.

She grabbed his inner tube, pulled it to herself, then heaved it away with all the strength she could muster. Doing so flipped the boy's head toward her and his ball cap fell into the water. His open, unmoving eyes were all it took. The woman screamed. And kept screaming. She paddled furiously for several seconds in a futile attempt to flee the corpse's gaze. The adrenaline kicked in and—still shrieking—she rolled off her inner tube and pushed her three children aside as the corpse continued its slow, rambling journey.

"You can turn it off," Amara said.

Dr. Douglas Pritchard, the medical examiner for Bexar County, clicked his mouse and the recording paused. "I requested the footage from the Cannonball Water Park after doing the young man's autopsy. I trust it will be useful in your investigation, Detective Alvarez?"

Her investigation? Would Zachary Coleman be her first case? Not unless Dr. Pritchard could convince her there was something worth looking into. Truthfully, he wouldn't have to show much. Her current routine, while interesting and necessary, wasn't exactly stimulating.

After the Feds took control of the ongoing probe into the Cotulla aftermath, she'd been granted a transfer from the San Antonio PD's Property Crimes Division to Homicide. Her first month in the new position had consisted of reviewing old files, shadowing other detectives as they worked, and keeping her mouth shut as much as possible.

When the LT had hollered her name an hour ago, she figured he had more files for her to review. She was wrong. Lieutenant Rico Segura was sitting behind his desk, an unlit cigar hanging from his mouth. Every morning the man pulled a new stogie from his drawer and planted it between his teeth. By the end of the day, most of the cigar would be gone, whether from absorption or chewing or swallowing or spitting or . . . She managed to restrain a shudder.

Get to the ME's office ASAP, he said. Find out what Pritchard's got. Suspicious death. See if it's worth investigating.

After a quick yessir, she'd hurried over and caught the doctor between autopsies and meetings. Douglas Pritchard worked with her on Cotulla, and at the time he'd been dating Sara Colby, a Texas Ranger who'd also been involved in the inquiry. The two were no longer together, a fact Amara knew from her increasingly infrequent conversations with the woman.

The ME cleared his throat. "Detective?"

"Sorry." She shifted in the red leather armchair. "Yes, the security video will be helpful if we move forward with an investigation. But there's nothing on there that even hints at a crime. When the tox screenings come back, the department may take another look if warranted."

He scanned his desktop. "How's Sara? Do you two speak often?"

"Um, last I heard she was doing well."

He shuffled through a stack of file folders. "So that's a no?"

"We talk on occasion. She's fine."

"Give her my best, would you?" He looked up and stroked his goatee. "Now that's an interesting saying, isn't it? My best. My best what? Intentions? Makes no sense. Wishes? I suppose that might work under the right circumstances, but I—"

"You have more evidence to support your suspicions regarding the death?"

He nodded. "Zachary Bryce Coleman, seventeen-year-old Caucasian male. I have his file ready to, um, it's right, well . . ." He moved his hand over his desk twice, then pounced on a folder. "Here we go. The young man expired in rather peculiar circumstances."

"Yeah, it was on the news too."

He shrugged. "Perhaps. I'm afraid I don't spend much time watching television." He dragged his finger down a sheet of paper. "The death happened two days ago. Exceptionally hot, if you'll recall. The decedent and a group of friends planned to escape the heat at the water park. Have you ever been there, Detective?"

"Uh, no. Not that I recall."

He tilted his head. "Is that something you'd forget? Of course, if you visited before the age of three, it's unlikely you'd remember, and recent studies regarding Freud's childhood amnesia theory indicate that most events occurring before a child reaches seven or eight fade as—"

"No," she said. "I've never been there. You were saying the victim and his friends wanted to spend the day at the water park?"

"Yes, along with thousands of others. He had a blood-alcohol content of point-zero-eight. The final toxicology report may show a variance from that number, but he definitely consumed alcohol. Our initial theory was the combination of excessive temperatures and alcohol consumption led to heatstroke. The autopsy, however, showed no signs of petechial hemorrhages or—"

"English, please."

"There was no indication of bleeding in the membranes surrounding some of the body's organs. No congestion in the lungs or swelling in the brain. None of the symptoms we'd typically identify in a heatstroke victim. And before you ask, alcohol poisoning would exhibit many of these same indications, as well as others which also were not detected during the autopsy."

She planted her elbows on the chair's armrests and inched forward. "How did he die, then?"

"We don't know. It will be four to six weeks before the toxicology tests are completed, so as of now, the cause of death is undetermined."

"You told Lieutenant Segura it was suspicious. Just because you don't know how he died doesn't mean it's a potential homicide."

His eyebrows scrunched together "What in the world?" He leaned back in his chair, pulled off his left shoe, and removed a tea bag from it before tossing the thing in the trash.

Don't ask. Don't do it. No wonder Sara broke things off. "I was asking why you think this might be a homicide?"

He slid a large photograph toward her. "Take a look at this. That's from the water park's security cameras. First image of Coleman on that ride. I requested video of him from the time he entered the water until he was pulled out. This is all they had. Something about camera malfunctions, but they estimated he'd been on the attraction for somewhere around two minutes at that time, based on the distance between the last working camera and this one."

The cropped photo focused on the teen, though numerous people were visible in the water around him.

Amara glanced at the doctor. "Is he alive or dead here?"

"Hard to tell, isn't it?"

"No video of him getting in the water?"

"What you saw is everything I received, but my request was extremely limited in scope. Beyond that, you'd have to ask the park."

She scooted back in her chair and crossed her legs. "I get why you think this could be suspicious. Trust me, I'd love to look into this, but so far you haven't said anything that makes me believe it might be a homicide."

"I thought not." He pulled another photo from the folder and passed it over. "Tell me what you see."

She held the picture higher. "Bottoms of his feet? Nothing unusual as far as I can tell."

"No? Think about it."

Guessing games. What fun. "Dr. Pritchard, I'm not a medical expert. If there's something here that might—"

"Do you ever shower? Take a bath?"

How did Sara last so long with this guy? "Now and then."

He waved his hand in a circular motion for her to continue. "And your toes and fingers . . ."

She knocked her fist against her forehead. "They wrinkle. Pucker up. And Zachary Coleman's toes didn't."

"Precisely. Our central nervous system triggers an involuntary reaction when we interact with water. Our capillaries shrink, causing the skin to furrow. As to why this happens, there are several theories. My favorite is—"

"I'll cede the point," she said. "So why weren't his toes wrinkled?"

"It usually takes less than five minutes for the body to initiate the reaction to water. That didn't happen with Mr. Coleman because his nervous system ceased functioning before the response could begin."

Amara licked her lips. "You think he was already dead when he went in the water."

"No, Detective. I'm certain of it."

2   **Amara kept her head down** as she walked through the Homicide department. Her reception had been tepid at best. Starsky said not to worry about it. They treated all the new ones this way. Maybe. Sure seemed to be an edge to the looks from the other detectives, men and women alike. Unspoken, but not hidden, bitterness or resentment. Alvarez hadn't paid her dues. Got all the publicity and attagirls because of Cotulla. The chief had no choice. Had to give her what she wanted. Plenty of others waiting to move over to the department but, well, better luck next time. Never mind that she was on the verge of a transfer even before Cotulla.

Starsky said it was all in her head. That she was seeing things that weren't there. Overreacting. Yeah? Then why didn't she have a desk yet? The LT told her on three occasions that he'd find a permanent home for her soon, but his voice had a distinct "whenever you ask, I push it back a week" vibe to it. Every morning, she toted her belongings to any open place she could see and arranged her makeshift office. At first, she'd tried to share desks with detectives who were out, but quickly decided it'd be easier to settle into a spot no one wanted. Fewer not-so-subtle hints about choosing somewhere else to sit.

Her latest semi-regular work location was a folding card table, clean when she'd left for the ME's office but now covered with the remnants of pizza or nachos or pretzels or all of the above. She clenched her teeth and brushed the crumbs into the palm of her hand before realizing her garbage can was gone. Again.

After a quick glance behind to make sure no one was watching, she flicked her wrist toward an open area off to the side and sent the food bits scattering through the air like a sprinkler. Cleanliness may be next to godliness, but God didn't have someone constantly stealing his trash can.

"I saw that."

The familiar voice came from across the room. Amara closed her eyes and shook her head, then spun her chair around. "You didn't see anything."

Detective Jeremiah Peckham, though everyone she knew called him Starsky, shrugged before ambling over. "I know what I saw. You threw crumbs on the floor. That's how we get mice."

Amara crossed her arms and smiled. "Witnesses are notoriously unreliable and I'm living proof. Twice I've been chosen out of line-ups. Shortish Hispanic female. That's me."

"Well, so far no tall, thin, exceptionally good-looking redheaded males have committed a felony around San Antonio, so I've been spared lineup duty."

"Gingers don't commit crimes, huh?"

He grinned and nodded. "Nothing other than stealing the hearts of women."

She rolled her eyes. "Your CI is giving you bad information. And two dinners. That's all it was."

"Hey, don't trash my confidential informants. And it's three if you include this coming Friday."

"Don't count your chickens," she said. "You know the only reason I go out with you, right? So people will whisper and wonder what *she's* doing out with *him*."

"Don't sell yourself short, Alvarez. Short. See what I did there?"

"I'd rather see you bringing me a cup of coffee."

"No can do," he said. "No favoritism at work. I wouldn't bring anyone else coffee, so why should I—"

"Because last time I brought it to you. And make sure it's fresh," she said. "Make a new pot if you have to."

He lowered his voice. "Back in a few."

She plugged in her laptop and waited for the device to finish booting. Lieutenant Segura had given the okay to proceed with the investigation for now but said he might bump her up in the rotation if she didn't discover any evidence soon. And no overtime without his approval. Her plan was to spend the rest of the afternoon online digging into the deceased's life and the Cannonball Water Park. Tomorrow, she'd visit the scene of the death to see what she could learn.

Starsky returned with a steaming Styrofoam cup. "Here ya go," he said. "Saw your name on the assignment board. Who's Zachary Coleman?"

"A teenager found dead at a water park. Dr. Pritchard thinks it's suspicious."

He peeled the wrapper off a Twinkie and bit the snack in half. "Yeah? Saw that on the news. Good luck."

"You don't want to know the details?"

"Nah. Your case, your investigation. You know what to do. At some point, you might need a second set of eyes on things. If that happens, don't be afraid to ask for help."

A surge of heat flashed through her. "You don't think I can do this?"

He pointed the half-Twinkie at her. "Easy there, champ. We all need help. What, well over a hundred murders every year? And all the cold cases on top of that? Not many of us fly solo. All I'm saying is it's your case, but it's ours too, if that makes any sense?"

She settled back into her chair. "You didn't answer my question."

He laughed and shoved the rest of the snack in his mouth. "Of course you can—" He coughed several times. "Sorry. Twinkie crumb got me. Killed by a snack cake. That's the way I want to go. Not yet though. Anyway, yeah, I think you can do the job, and anyone who doesn't, didn't see your work on Cotulla. You don't have to prove anything."

She smiled. "You're just saying that so I won't back out of Friday night."

He returned her grin. "Whatever it takes."

"Starsky!" Lieutenant Segura's booming voice echoed across the room.

Amara turned her face so the LT couldn't see and whisper-singsonged, "Somebody's in trouble."

"What else is new?" He strode away. "Coming, sir."

She turned her attention back to the laptop. Gone out twice, with another dinner coming up Friday. Dutch both times. And no idea where things stood. Friends, yes. No question they enjoyed spending time together. But they were going out, not dating. Weren't they? Did he understand the difference? There was a distinction, right?

She rubbed her palm on her shoulder and searched online for Zachary Bryce Coleman. The only results pointed to the recent news story. Nothing helpful there. She deleted his middle name and searched again. No new links. She leaned back and tapped her finger on her bottom lip. Was Coleman not on social media? Seemed odd for a teenager, but maybe not. She'd erased her own accounts after the privacy headaches outweighed the usefulness. Of course, some of the sites only identified people by their usernames, so Coleman could be there and she wouldn't know. She made a note to ask his friends, then did a search for the Cannonball Water Park.

Page after page of links appeared. In addition to the official website, there were untold blogs, pictures, and videos posted by visitors. Over several decades, the place had grown from a few slides and pools into a resort mecca. With over forty rides and attractions, it now covered an area approaching sixty acres. On any given day, thousands of people visited for a chance to cool off in the spring-fed waters. Each year, the Cannonball received multiple awards from vacation websites and magazines around the world for its value and state-of-the-art water rides.

The park's website focused on their family-friendly environment and their excellent safety record. The most recent news articles zeroed in on improvements to the facilities and employment opportunities. No ride-oriented fatalities had ever occurred at the Cannonball, though several civil suits regarding accidents had been settled out of court. As far as the state of Texas was concerned, the place had a clean history.

After an hour of uninformative surfing, she phoned the park and asked to speak to the head of security.

"This is Eduardo Sanchez. How may I help you?"

"Hi," Amara said. "I'm Detective Alvarez, SAPD Homicide." Felt weird, but good, saying that. "I wonder if I could stop by and speak to you?"

"Of course, Detective. You said you worked Homicide? May I inquire as to what this concerns? If it's one of our employees, HR might suit you better."

"Not one of your employees. At least I don't think he was. I'm looking into the death of Zachary Coleman."

A long pause followed. "My assumption was that Mr. Coleman died of heatstroke. The medical investigator who came here thought that would be the most likely cause. Is that not correct?"

"I can't comment on that, other than to say I'm looking into all possibilities. Would you be available this afternoon to meet with me?"

"Could we make it tomorrow morning? My schedule is full for the rest of today. If that will be a problem, I can try to shuffle some things around."

"Tomorrow morning will be fine," she said. "Eight o'clock?"

"Perfect. Park at the main entrance and I'll meet you there."

She thanked him and glanced at the clock while shutting down her computer. If she left now, she could beat rush hour traffic and get in a good workout at the gym before heading home to Larry, her three-foot-long pet iguana. Over the past month of training, one consistent message echoed from every detective she worked with. At least the ones who were civil. Once she got in the rotation, they said, any concept of normal hours would disappear. When the opportunity for me-time presented itself, take it.

Running in this heat was out of the question, but a few rounds of Muay Thai, a combat sport distantly related to kickboxing, sounded good. The activity cleared her mind and boosted her confidence. She'd used the training on the job only once, when she'd been undercover and captured in Mexico during the Cotulla investigation, and could remember the adrenaline rush that came from using her own body as a weapon. She didn't seek conflict. Didn't shy from it either. If someone wanted to underestimate her because of her size, that was their problem.

She scooped up her belongings and headed for the car. Tomorrow, the investigation into Zachary Coleman's death would begin in earnest. Should be done long before the tox reports came back in a month. Either she'd run out of leads, determine it wasn't a homicide, or catch the killer. The last two options suited her.

And if she couldn't resolve things, there was always the chance the tox report would close it for her. Her only fear was leaving "undetermined" as the cause of death. The boy's parents would never know. His friends would wonder. And her first case would remain in limbo forever.

"Undetermined" meant failure.

3 The next morning, Amara tossed her jacket into the back seat of her car and headed toward the water park's entrance. Barely eight a.m. and the temperature already broke ninety degrees. Welcome to mid-July in San Antonio. She paused and glanced to her left at the structures towering over the flat terrain. Several colorful rides, each vying to be taller than their neighbor, waited for the gates to open and the brave guests to let loose their whoops and hollers. She shook her head. Have fun with all that. A lawn chair and kiddie pool to soak her feet would be just fine.

She dabbed at a bead of sweat on her forehead and resumed her walk to the park's entrance. To the left of the ticket booths, a man in khaki pants and a blue polo shirt waited. He shaded his eyes, then raised a hand and waved. Either she looked like a cop or, at the least, not a typical visitor. She hoped it was the former. As she neared him, he broadened his smile.

"Detective Alvarez?" he asked. "I'm Eduardo Sanchez, head of security."

He appeared to be in his late thirties, only a few inches taller than her, with a stocky build. "Sí. Thank you for meeting with me. I'll try not to take too much of your time."

He waved his hand as if swatting at gnats. "It's no problem. I suggest we meet in my office, if that's acceptable? Afterward, if there are areas of the park you wish to visit, I'd be happy to escort you."

"Sounds good. Lead the way."

She trailed him along a path separated from the rest of the park by a wooden fence. Even out of sight of the public, the area was clean and well maintained. The concrete walkway still had arcing wet spots in places, an indication of the early morning sprinkler system doing its best to protect the surrounding plants. Some summers, it didn't matter how much water you poured on the greenery. Texas temperatures could be relentless.

As they rounded a corner, a cluster of administration buildings came into view. Heat waves shimmered off the asphalt parking lot and gave a faint mirage look to the one- and two-story structures.

Sanchez gestured ahead. "The employees have a separate entrance to the park. They come in over there and"—he pointed off to the right—"go to their assigned work areas through a gate over there."

"Do they go to the same place every day?"

"It depends," he said. "Sometimes yes and sometimes no, but I couldn't tell you how that's determined. If you want, I can ask one of our HR managers to join us. They could explain it better."

"Not necessary, at least not yet. As I said yesterday, I'm just trying to get a feel for the environment here. See how the victim spent his last hours."

Sanchez stopped and turned to her. "The victim?" He shifted on his feet. "Have you confirmed the young man's death was a homicide?"

"Sorry," she said. "Habit, I guess." *Habit? It's your first case.* She glanced away to reset her thoughts. "To answer your question, no, the death has not been ruled a homicide." She dropped her voice a notch. "If it is determined to be a murder, I trust the park's desire to avoid bad publicity won't affect your cooperation?"

"It will not. My background is in law enforcement. I can state without hesitation that Cannonball will provide any and all support it can."

She nodded. "I appreciate that. Just wanted to make sure we were on the same page."

They resumed their walk toward the buildings and within minutes were basking in the air-conditioned comfort of Sanchez's office. A bank of monitors filled one wall off to the side of his desk, and an array of computer equipment rested on the credenza behind him. No personal effects were visible. No photos in sight. And no wedding ring.

Why had she felt the need to check his ring finger? She fake-coughed into her fist. Checking was part of being observant. Standard procedure. If that was the case though, why did she rarely follow that process when talking to other women?

She liked Starsky, but did *like* ever become *love*? Would there be anything to discuss besides death? *How was your day, honey? Eh, stabbing over by the quarry. And yours? Gunshot over in Alamo Heights.* Not exactly the downtime she'd need.

Sanchez twisted the top off a water bottle. "Can I get you one?"

"I'm fine, thanks." She flipped open her notepad. "Let's see . . . the body was found here three days ago, and the video you gave the ME didn't offer much. I assume you reviewed the rest of the security footage? The parts we didn't see? Is there anything that might help with my investigation? And the ME mentioned something about malfunctioning cameras?"

He took a long swig of water. "As you can imagine, there is a considerable amount of video of the young man and his companions. I have personally reviewed every frame, and my staff has made copies for you as well. However, you must understand that our cameras do not cover every inch of the facility. We focus on high-traffic areas. In addition, yes, we have recently experienced, er, hiccups with our system."

"Hiccups? Meaning what?"

"Sporadic outages for the last month or so. Never all cameras at once, but a few here or there. And never enough to cause any security or safety issues. The vendor believes it's a software problem, and we will upgrade to a newer version within the next week."

She sighed and scribbled in her notepad. "Always something, right?" Something either very unlucky or very convenient.

"The young man entered the park with a group and spent his time here on several rides, often alone, sometimes with his friends. Until other guests discovered he was deceased, there is no sign of any problems."

"Any idea where Zachary got in the water?"

Sanchez shook his head. "I'm afraid not. There are multiple locations where a person can enter Crooked Creek, but we were unable to identify exactly where he went in. We do know the first time he appeared on the cameras, so we can make an educated guess as to the general area, but we cannot pinpoint it beyond that."

He walked to a large colorful map mounted on the wall. "Here is where we believe Mr. Coleman went into the water. At Day's End Cove." He used his finger to draw a decent-sized circle.

"No way to narrow it down? That's a big area."

"The only option at this point is to interview employees who might remember something, though with the thousands of guests here that day, I wouldn't expect that to be fruitful. Still, I will gladly make them available for you."

"Um, thank you. If you could put a list together of workers who were in the area and hold on to it, just in case, that would be great." She studied the map for a moment. "Are there parts of the park that are, for lack of a better word, quieter on crowded days? Not so many people around?"

He sat again and planted his forearms on the desk. "What you mean is, if I wanted to kill someone here, where would I do it, correct?"

She tapped her pen on the notepad and smiled. "I thought my question would be more tactful."

"Of course. There are areas that are less traveled and also have no video coverage. Our guests would not have that knowledge though. We do our best to keep the cameras camouflaged so they don't interfere with the themes and designs of the attractions. Committing a crime here is a very big, and I would think unnecessary, risk. If I wanted to kill someone here, I wouldn't. Far easier to do it somewhere without so much security or so many people."

"Fair enough." She jotted another note.

Where would I kill someone at Cannonball? & why do it here?

Sanchez was confident, but his familiarity with the park's layout could be a weakness if he'd grown accustomed to seeing the same thing day after day. Or if he had something to hide. "Can you explain how your screening procedures work? I mean, you don't allow alcohol, yet Mr. Coleman definitely drank shortly before his death."

"Cannonball allows guests to bring in their own coolers for picnics and snacks. We inspect them all to ensure they contain no glass containers or alcohol." He half frowned and arched his eyebrows. "If someone is determined to sneak it in, they will find a way. Vodka and water look the same, after all. And we don't frisk our guests to see if they've hidden alcohol on their person. However, our security team is trained to recognize the signs of impaired activity, whether it's due to alcohol, drugs, or the heat."

"But they failed to spot that with Zachary?"

His frown deepened and he narrowed his eyes. "We can't watch everyone, Detective. Ultimately, people are responsible for their own actions. We try to provide a safe environment for all our guests. I'm sure you understand. The SAPD is no different. *Protecting the Alamo City.* That is on your police cars, no? If they fulfilled their mission perfectly, you'd be out of a job, wouldn't you? Like your employer, we do the best we can with what we have."

Well, this turned ugly fast. She stood and slipped the pen and notepad into the back pocket of her pants. "Thank you for your time, Mr. Sanchez. I don't think I have any other questions right now. You said you had copies of the video footage for me?"

He stood, opened his desk drawer, and handed her a USB flash drive along with an envelope. "That's every image we have of Mr. Coleman and his three friends from the time they arrived at the park. If you have time, I would be happy to show you around."

"Not necessary. If I need anything else, I'll be in touch."

"The envelope contains an entry pass to the park. It's good for the rest of the season. Feel free to come out anytime, whether to continue your investigation or enjoy a day off."

She glanced at the pass before returning it to Sanchez. "Thank you, but I'm afraid I can't accept. Against policy and all that. I do appreciate the offer though."

He slid the envelope back into his drawer. "Of course. I hope you will keep me informed. If something did happen here, I would welcome the opportunity to review our procedures and see how we can prevent such occurrences in the future."

She slipped the USB drive into her pocket and gave a noncommittal smile. "I'll see myself out. Have a good day, Mr. Sanchez."

She reflected on the meeting as she wandered the path toward the main entrance and parking lot. Sanchez had been helpful enough but either didn't have much information to share or was holding back. His sudden slam against the SAPD seemed to come from nowhere. Her insinuation that maybe his people hadn't done their jobs could've caused that. She'd have reacted the same way.

But it was the park pass that bothered her the most. Sanchez had to know she couldn't accept gratuities. Not that plenty of cops didn't. Was he really attempting to be helpful and friendly, or trying to set her up? There was a third possibility too. One that raised her suspicions. The pass had a bar code on it.

If she used it, Sanchez would know when she was there.

Amara's next stop was the one she most dreaded. Zachary Coleman's parents. When she'd phoned the father, his raspy, monotone voice penetrated her heart and sent an ache through her chest. The man's joy was gone. Back in Property Crimes, she dealt with her share of angry and frightened people, but that paled in comparison to this. The Colemans lost their son. How did a person deal with that? When Amara's dad died, the pain had been deep and overwhelming. How much more at the loss of a child?

The death of Benjamin Reyes, the five-year-old boy who triggered the investigation into Cotulla, at least had a silver lining. Nearly fifty other children saved because of his bravery. Had that eased the pain for his parents? Could it?

And the Colemans had nothing like that to cling to. Their son died and nobody could tell them why. Natural causes or OD or bad luck or homicide. Would any of those reasons be better or worse than the others? Zachary was gone, and he wasn't ever coming back.

Dr. Pritchard had texted last night to let her know the boy's body was being released to the parents. The funeral was scheduled for tomorrow, with visitation at the home today. The family would be swamped with phone calls, mountains of food, and outbursts of crying.

And a detective who wanted to pry into every aspect of the dead teenager's life and dig up all the dirt she could find.

She pulled behind the row of cars lining the street in front of the Colemans' address. The residence sat on a huge lot—had to be at least two or three acres—on the outskirts of Helotes, a small city on the northwest side of San Antonio. Mature trees obscured most of the house, a testament to the home's age.

She donned her jacket and strode up the driveway, her stomach fluttering and fingers jittery. What to say wasn't the problem. Knowing what *not* to say was. She'd watched other detectives go through this, and there was a fine line between getting what you needed and not creating additional pain for the victim's family. Usually, there was no way to do one without the other.

Three teenagers—two boys and a girl—came out the front door of the sprawling one-story brick home and passed her on their way to the street. None of them spoke or made eye contact. A man stood off to the right of the house beside the garage, smoking and watching her. He nodded and flicked his cigarette to the ground, then crushed it with his foot.

"SAPD?" he asked.

"Yes." Her cop aura must be strong today. Or she was the only Hispanic he expected.

He walked toward her. "I'm Zach's father. Paul Coleman."

She shook his hand. Her heart ached at the sight of his bloodshot eyes and facial stubble. "Mr. Coleman, I'm so sorry for your loss."

"Thanks. I, uh, I hope it's okay if we go in the back door? My wife . . ." He cleared his throat. "Lori's inside with everyone and I'd rather she not have to go through this right now, if that's okay."

"Absolutely," Amara said. "Lead the way."

They walked through the grass and circled behind the house to a large patio. A huge swimming pool, complete with diving board and slide, glistened as the sun reflected off the tiny waves created by the robotic cleaner. A few people clustered near the back door and the pair passed through the group. One man patted Mr. Coleman's shoulder as he walked by. The rest averted their eyes and stopped their whispering.

He opened the screen door and held it for her. "It's just in here to the left. My office."

She stepped inside and caught a glimpse of the crowd in the front. The hushed talk and symphony of sniffling told her all she needed to know about what it was like up there. No laughter. Everyone afraid to make noise for fear they'd somehow interrupt the sanctity and somberness of the moment. This day was all about pain and suffering, tempered with the brief joys of a shared memory or long-unseen family member.

"Right here," Mr. Coleman said.

She walked into the room and stood until he motioned toward a fabric-covered recliner. She sat and waited until he closed the door and sank into the chair behind his desk.

"Can I get you some water or something?" he asked.

"Oh, no, sir. Thank you. I only need to ask a few questions, then I'll be out of your way."

"You're not in our way." He pulled a tissue from a box on the desk and dabbed under his eyes. "To be honest, I appreciate the distraction. At least it makes me feel like I'm doing something, you know?"

"Yes, sir. Can you—"

"You're from Homicide, right? Do you think my son was murdered?"

She shifted in her seat. "I don't know. There's no evidence that points toward that, but anytime we have an unexplained death, we investigate."

"So you don't think the toxicology report will tell us why Zach died?"

What's the right answer? "There's every reason to believe the lab results will provide answers. In the meantime, though, we want to ensure we've been thorough in our investigation."

"Just in case?"

She nodded. "Just in case. Now, can you tell me a little about your son? What he was like, how he was doing at school, stuff like that?"

One corner of his lips turned up. "Zach is . . . was a teenage boy. Going to be a senior in high school this fall. I'm sure you know what they can be like. He had his share of girlfriends. No one serious as far as I know. Above-average grades. Could've been near the top of his class if he tried harder." His half smile disappeared. "I suppose every parent thinks that. No sports or anything. Spent most of his free time playing video games online or glued to his phone."

She rested her hands in her lap and paused for a moment before speaking. "I understand these questions can be difficult, but it's important we ask them."

"No apologies. Please. We have to know what happened."

"Mm-hmm. Was he popular at school? Any best friends?"

"Popular? No. He wasn't much of an extrovert, but Zach had a few friends he hung out with on what I'd call a casual basis. Nothing regular."

"Yes, sir. Would it be possible to get a list of those friends?"

"Of course." He scribbled on a sheet of paper, then handed it to her. "Those three are the ones he spent most of his time with. You passed them on your way in."

"Thank you." She folded the paper, slipped it inside her jacket, and stared at the blank page of her notepad. "Did Zachary have any enemies?"

"Anyone who'd want to kill him? I can't imagine he did, but these days, who knows? I mean, you see it on the news all the time, right?

Some high school kid shoots up the place because a girl turned him down or a teacher laughed at him."

"I understand. Did Zachary have a job?"

"He worked part-time at Target as a stocker. Maybe twenty or twenty-five hours a week. Enough to get some spending money and pay his car insurance, but not much else."

"What kind of car?"

"Ford Mustang. Racing red with black leather interior. Zach loved that car." He chuckled. "Lori and I fought over that one. She wanted to get him something safer. Said I only wanted to relive my youth. Can't say she was wrong, but . . ." He scrubbed his hands over his face. "Can you imagine? If he'd died in a car wreck instead? I'd, uh, always have the guilt on top of everything else."

She jotted a note to give him time to recover. "Sir, was your son planning to continue his education after high school?"

"Planning? Seventeen-year-olds don't plan things. Computer science. That's what he wanted to study. Zach loved anything to do with technology, but computers were his thing. We were deciding on a college over his Christmas break this year."

"Got it. Did you see your son the day he went to the water park?"

"Yes." He pointed at a drafting table. "I'm an architect. Do as much work from home as possible. Zach shuffled in here early that morning looking like he just rolled out of bed. Probably did. Anyway, he said he was going to stop by and see Grandma—my mother—at the retirement home after he left the water park. Wanted to know if I had anything that needed to go to her." He grabbed another tissue. "That's the kind of boy he was."

"Sounds like a sweet kid," she said. "Your mother lives where?"

"She's got a little cottage over at Green Horizons. We tried to get her to move in with us, but she wouldn't have it. Do you need to speak to her? I haven't told her about, um, you. I didn't want to upset her more than she already was."

"No, sir. That won't be necessary. That morning when Zachary stopped in here, was there anything unusual? Did he seem upset? Worried?"

He concentrated on the ceiling for a few moments. "Nothing I can remember."

"Okay. Did he go to the water park often?"

"Not really. As far as I know, this was his first time this summer. He wasn't much of a water guy. He'd hang around our pool with friends sometimes, but not often."

"I understand. Mr. Coleman, I need to ask a few questions that are a bit more personal. It's important, and I'll do my best to keep them to a minimum."

He gestured for her to continue.

"Was Zachary your only child?"

"Yes. We wanted more"—he scratched the back of his neck and looked away—"but it never happened."

"I'm sorry," she said. "Was there any tension in the home? Either between you and your wife or either of you and Zachary?"

"Nothing between Lori and me. With Zach, the usual, but nothing serious. Money, grades, staying up all night and sleeping all day. Same as every other teenage boy."

"Has anything out of the ordinary happened lately? People you hadn't seen before? Missing work? Stuff like that."

He hesitated as the door opened and a blonde-haired woman with smudged mascara poked her head inside the room. She glanced at Amara, then turned to Mr. Coleman.

"Honey," she said, "can you come up front for a while? I need to lie down for a few minutes."

He nodded. "Be there in just a sec. Lori, this is Detective Alvarez."

Amara stood and clasped her hands in front of her. "Ma'am, I'm so sorry for your loss."

The woman's *thank you* was distant and rote. She turned and disappeared from view.

Amara pulled a business card from her jacket pocket and slid it onto the desk. "I don't have any more questions now, but I wonder if I could see Zachary's room before I go? If you'll just point me in the right direction, I'll be out of your way as soon as possible."

He massaged his forehead and sighed. "Could we do that another day? My wife, um, when she said she needed to lie down . . ."

Amara's throat tightened and her shoulders sagged. *His wife is on Zachary's bed.* "Of course. Would it be okay if I called you on Monday?" With the funeral tomorrow, a Friday, that would give them the weekend to rest.

"That would be fine," he said. "Thank you for understanding."

"Yes, sir. Thanks again for your time. I'll show myself out." She exited the house the same way she'd entered and wandered toward the street. At the garage, she stopped to peek through the side door. Zach's red Mustang sat there, flanked by a white SUV on the far side and a black sedan near her.

Should she have asked for permission to check the sports car? See if there was anything in there that might help? No, not today. That could wait until Monday. She'd intruded enough for now.

If there were clues to the teenager's death, they'd be in his car or his room. Nothing about his parents seemed suspicious, but if they *were* involved somehow, they'd already had plenty of time to clean up things. Let them bury their son.

She sat in her car for several minutes and debated whether to attend the funeral tomorrow. If she played the odds, there was a good chance the killer would be there. The vast majority of murders were committed by people who knew the victim. But spotting the perpetrator at a funeral was the stuff of TV shows and movies. Besides, if today's visitation was any indication, there'd be a big crowd at the service.

She pulled away from the house and headed for the office. With no official need to attend the funeral, she'd skip it. Avoid the danger of the investigation becoming too emotional. Personal.

Instead, she'd spend the day doing something that sent trickles of dread through her body. She knew it made no sense. She worked out. Stayed in shape. But that didn't erase the fear. Going after a possible murderer was nothing compared to the anxiety tomorrow would bring.

She'd be in a very public location surrounded by throngs of people.

And she'd be wearing her bathing suit.

5

Amara tugged the floppy hat lower on her forehead. The security cameras at the Cannonball's entrance would have a tough time seeing her face. She wore an almost knee-length black-and-white-striped cover-up over her one-piece swimsuit and had a tote draped over her shoulder. Flip-flops and oversize sunglasses completed the look.

She merged with others strolling toward the ticket booths. Nearly eleven o'clock Friday morning. Zachary Coleman's funeral would begin in three hours, but after discussing it with Starsky last night, she stood by her original decision. Today, she'd investigate the water park, then check out Zachary's room and car on Monday.

Late yesterday, she'd reviewed the video provided by Mr. San-chez to get an idea of where to spend her time. As the man said, nothing pointed to any potential problems. Zachary entered the park with three friends, the same ones she'd seen at the Coleman house, and didn't seem nervous. The recording had large gaps, apparently when he'd not been in view of any security cameras. Frustrating for her. Convenient for anyone who might have com-mitted a crime.

Her phone rang and she dug the device out of her tote. Starsky? "Hey," she said. "About to go in the park. What's up?"

"Just checking in. Seeing if you wanted any company today."

"You not working?"

"Yeah, but I can take the day off. Nothing major happening and I've got comp time to burn."

35

"No point," she said. "I'll only be here a couple of hours. Wait. Is this an excuse to see me in my swimsuit?"

"There's no right answer to that, is there? But I'd go with a strong *maybe*."

Her face flushed and she pressed the phone closer to her mouth. "No. Absolutely not. If I see you here, no dinner tonight. No dinner ever. You listening, Starsky? I mean it."

"Just trying to help," he said. "A tall, pasty redhead in a Speedo would do a lot to deflect attention from you. Let you look over the place without being bothered."

She snorted, then lowered her voice. "Tell me you don't have a Speedo. Please."

"Fine. I don't have a Speedo."

"You do, don't you?"

"Bright yellow with green accent stripes," he said. "Fits like a glove too, if a glove could somehow vacuum seal itself to your fingers. I tried it on last night and couldn't feel anything below my waist."

She laughed and rubbed a hand over her chest. "You're an idiot, you know that? And I'd better not see you here. I'm serious."

"We're still on for tonight then?"

"Only if I can scrub that image from my mind."

"Good luck. I can send you a selfie if you want?"

"Bye, Starsky. I'll call you when I get off work, okay?"

She disconnected the call and dropped the cell back into the tote. Seconds later, a beep told her she'd received a message. She glanced at the display, saw it was from Starsky, and buried the phone under her beach towel. Not gonna look. Not now. No way he'd actually send a photo of himself in a Speedo. Too easy for her to share it with other detectives.

At the ticket window, she paid cash, buzzed through the security line, and strode toward the people gathered at the wave pool straight ahead. The sooner she lost herself in crowds, the better she'd feel. If Sanchez was hiding something, a possibility that nagged at her, she needed to avoid detection as long as possible. Even if he and the park had nothing to do with Zachary Coleman's death, she didn't want anyone else's input right now. Time to form her own opinions.

A brightly painted post festooned with arrows pointing every direction caught her attention. Honolulu waited 3708 miles to the left. Nassau 1330 miles to the right. And Crooked Creek 160 feet ahead and to the left of the wave pool.

She skirted the edge of the sandy beach, its area already blanketed with a rainbow of towels, and paused to watch a wave elicit screams from the doused swimmers. Fun? Maybe, but getting rocked by a mountain of water wasn't on her agenda today. Or ever.

A shaded path led to the Crooked Creek overlook, and a wooden bridge arched over the water, allowing access to other attractions. Palm trees dotted the landscape, and she spotted security cameras in a few of them. Off to the side, a map, its bright colors reflecting behind the plexiglass, provided an overview of the area. You could float from here and go most of the way around the park. Two islands, each covered with shops and rides, were surrounded by cartoon people drifting past on rafts and inner tubes. The spot Sanchez identified was on the second island.

Two options. Try to walk around the entire river or float along and see things from that perspective. If she got in the water, she'd be able to identify areas with limited access and fewer people. Exactly the kind of place someone might slide a person, or body, into the river unnoticed. She dragged the back of her hand across her forehead to erase the sweat gathered there. The water *did* look inviting.

She wandered farther down the path until it veered away from the river. Ahead was a cluster of food vendors, rental shops, and restrooms. The smell of hamburgers drifted on the air and her stomach grumbled. She had snacks in her tote. Granola bars, bottled water, an apple. All of which totaled less than a hamburger. A long line of customers snaked from the dining area and she sighed. Float first, eat later.

She spotted a building lined with rows of lockers, dodged a cluster of kids, and scanned her options. At the end of each row, a monitor beckoned her to touch the screen to begin. She complied, selected the size she wanted, swiped her credit card, and keyed in her four-digit number. 1104. November 4th. Larry's, her pet lizard's, birthday. Technically the day she got him, but they always celebrated it as his birthday. Down the row, a locker door popped open and she shoved her tote inside. After a moment's hesitation, she removed her cover-up and hat and strode back the way she'd come. She crossed the wooden bridge, turned left, and stepped into the warm ankle-deep water that sloped to the river. A park employee stood there watching the guests and shoving abandoned inner tubes back into the water.

He bent over and grabbed the handle on the next one that came by. "Need a tube?" he asked.

"Sure."

"Gonna sit in it?"

"Um, no." She stepped inside the tube while he held it, then raised it to her waist. "How deep is it?"

"Deepest part is three feet. Here it's about two and a half."

She nodded her thanks and walked into the river. The water became cooler and sent a brief shiver through her body. She took a deep breath, squatted to get wet to her armpits, and waited a moment to adjust to the temperature.

Another tube, this one occupied by a boy who looked to be

around ten, bumped into her. She smiled at him and he kicked against her tube to push away. The splash sent water into her face and dotted her sunglasses. Her grin faded and she lifted her legs to join the current before others got too close.

Sitting in the tube would be easier and more comfortable, but this way kept her body in the water. She'd never been self-conscious about her appearance, as evidenced by her minimal use of makeup, but being in public in her swimsuit crossed an imaginary line. The gene that allowed her sisters to wear anything without being self-conscious had skipped right over her. Based on some of the people she'd seen so far today, the gene should've bypassed them too. Not much left to the imagination.

She drifted around a corner in the river and gained speed as underwater jets shot ice-cold streams along the route. From here, she could see several rides, including one of the slides she'd spotted from the parking lot. A line of people climbed the circular path to the top for their chance to shoot downward on a thin layer of water. Three sharp turns were completely covered, an indication that riders went high on the walls. At the bottom of the ride, guest after guest shot out into a small pool, clambered out of the water, and hurried back to go again. No thanks.

As she rounded another corner, she gained quickly on a group of teens, each with a hand holding someone else's tube. After glancing behind to make sure no one was close, she planted her feet on the bottom and duck-walked to the edge of the river. Let them get farther ahead. On the opposite side, a high bamboo fence, doubtless hiding chain-link, lined a thin strip of land that defined the park's boundary. A pole reached above the barrier and secured two cameras, one pointed at the park and the other at whatever was hidden back there. She peered farther down the river and saw the setup repeated at regular intervals. If nothing else, Cannonball believed in protecting their perimeter. Their insurance probably demanded it.

As she merged back into the current, several people entered the river between her and the teen flotilla. As the day wore on and the crowds increased, any hope of avoiding contact with others faded. Nothing she could do about that. Another reason she preferred a lawn chair and kiddie pool.

She completed her semi-loop of the first island and drifted toward the second. This one was larger and newer, with more open spaces for future attractions. A large beach lined this side of the land. People, coolers, and noise abounded. This was the section geared to younger kids. Smaller versions of the tamer rides oriented themselves around a lake in an attempt to corral the children in a central area so the parents could maintain their view without having to constantly relocate. Based on the amount of running and yelling going on, the concept might be good, but someone forgot to tell the kids. With distractions like this, you could slide a dozen bodies in the water here and no one would notice.

She rounded another corner and continued on the loop for a few minutes before the chaos faded behind her. None of this looked familiar, meaning either Zachary didn't come here or, more likely, the cameras weren't working that day. Hordes of guests could've traveled this way and remained unseen by the security system.

On the other side of the bamboo fence, steel beams stretched into the sky. A sign with an architect's drawing of the park's under-construction ride promised guests new heights and bigger thrills next year. Another underwater jet propelled her forward and the ambiance shifted. A few more rides beckoned the adventurous, but the island grew quieter and the crowd sparser. Cabanas dotted the grassy expanse. Clusters of palm trees provided some shade and a wide beach separated land and water. This was where Sanchez suspected Coleman went into the river.

She stepped out of the water and nudged the inner tube back on its way. The sun soaked her skin and brought warmth to her goose bumps as she wandered the area, casually searching for a hint of wrongdoing. Nothing. Several security cameras hugged their trees, but none of them had the right angle to have taken the first known video of Coleman in the water. A thatched-roof building sheltered restrooms and more lockers.

Plenty of secluded spots existed, but only if no one happened to wander past. On a busy day, there'd be no guarantee of privacy. If the teenager *had* been murdered, the killer was either extremely lucky or had planned the death. Plotting his actions wouldn't eliminate the danger of being caught, but it would greatly reduce the chance of that happening. If Zachary didn't die from alcohol poisoning or an accidental OD, the method of killing had to be fast, quiet, and internal. The tox report would answer that question. Hopefully.

But the problem still remained. If, as she assumed, the death was intentional, why do it in such a public location? Didn't make any sense. There had to be a gazillion better places that didn't have the risks.

She walked to the nearest palm tree and stared at the camera. Pretty convenient that the system wasn't working when the death happened. She made a mental note to follow up on the issue with the vendor who supplied the software. See if they'd had the same problems anywhere else. And if not?

The crystal-clear waters at Cannonball might hold a very murky secret.

6 **Amara and Starsky** slid their menus to the edge of the table, the universal sign they were ready to order. The waiter, properly attentive to such cues, hurried over. The restaurant, an old pub with dingy, dark decor, had struggled with its dive bar identity ever since it had been featured in the *Best of San Antonio* annual awards. What used to be a low-key spot popular with locals was now crowded, noisy, and trendy. Three things she hated.

"What can I get y'all?" the waiter asked.

"Fruit salad for me," Amara said.

Starsky arched his eyebrows. "That's not much dinner."

"I had a burger this afternoon at the water park. Bad call. Good burger"—she tapped her sternum twice with her fist—"but bad call."

"Gotcha. I'm gonna have the burger and chips with everything. Oh, and do you have chili? Put that on it too."

The waiter glanced up from his pad. "No, sir. Sorry. No chili."

"Okay," Starsky said. "Add one of those brat rolls then. And some beef nachos for an appetizer."

Amara covered her mouth and stifled a burp. "I hope you're not counting on me eating any of that."

"Nope," Starsky said, "but I can get a double order of nachos if you want some."

She shook her head and the waiter moved away. Starsky's ability to eat enough food to choke a mammoth and yet remain pencil thin was a thing of wonder. And envy.

He shifted and rested his arm on the back of the booth. "When did this place get so crowded? Have to scratch it off the rotation. You have a fun day at the Cannonball?"

"I was working, not playing." She smiled. "Yeah, it was okay. Oh, and thanks for the picture." The dreaded photo was indeed Star-sky in a yellow bathing suit but no Speedo, and he wore a sleeve-less T-shirt. "Strange how much you looked like a young Arnold Schwarzenegger."

"Get serious. He wishes he looked as good as me."

"I'm sure. You do anything exciting today?"

"Nah," he said. "Caught up on some paperwork and reviewed a couple of cold cases to see if it was time to take another look."

She nodded and doodled circles on the table with her finger. Third time going out, and so far all they'd talked about was work. Realistically, they had nothing in common other than their jobs. Was that enough? Yep. For now. Not like she was looking to get married or anything. But was *he*?

He waved his hand in front of her face. "Hello? Anyone home?"

She straightened and cleared her throat. "Sorry. Lost in my thoughts."

"Yeah? Everything okay? Anything I can help with?"

She rubbed the back of her neck. Tomorrow night was the weekly Saturday get-together at Mama's. She could take him to meet her family. See how he reacted in a group setting. What he talked about when it was more than the two of them. Could be fun. Educational too.

But would she be the teacher or the student?

∎ ∎ ∎

Amara kicked off her flip-flops and tried to relax in a lawn chair in Mama's backyard. Most of the family was already here and plates and cups lined the large picnic table under the mesquite tree. In a few minutes, the parade of food from the kitchen would begin.

Her knees bounced rapidly and she rested her hands on them. Starsky should be here any minute. Mama had oddly hesitated when Amara asked if it was okay to bring a visitor. No problem, she'd finally said. But she hadn't asked about the guest. Amara was the only unmarried child. Mama always wanted to know if it was a man coming with her. Always.

"You okay? Seem nervous."

Amara turned to the man beside her. Wylie Dotson, retired cop and coworker back in Property Crimes, sipped his cold drink and stared at her. Not so long ago, she'd brought him to one of these family dinners, and he and Mama had become somewhat of an item. "Yeah," she said. "I'm okay."

"He'll do fine."

She propped her elbow on the armrest. "Who?"

"Starsky. That's what you're worried about, right?" He wiped beads of condensation off the can and flicked them at her.

"You ever growing up?" she asked.

"Hope not. Anyway, he seems like a good guy. You know how cops are with rumors and gossip. Never heard nothing bad about Starsky."

"He's just a friend, Wylie."

"Yeah? Not what I hear."

She leaned closer and lowered her voice. "What does that mean?"

He shrugged. "Just because I'm retired doesn't mean I don't hear things. Rumors and gossip. Only things that keep cops sane."

"Who exactly are you hearing these things from?"

"Heard that you and Rutledge are best buddies too."

She grimaced. Travis Rutledge, a longtime Homicide cop with a habit of wearing jackets that might have buttoned two decades ago, had gone out of his way to make sure she knew where she stood. At the bottom of the pecking order. She'd already pegged him as the class bully and cautioned him to back off. So far, he hadn't. Fine by her. His face fit perfectly on the Muay Thai bag. A new imaginary target to aim at during her workouts.

The backyard gate swung open and Starsky paused to get his bearings before walking toward Amara. Her chest fluttered and her mouth dried. He wore khaki pants, an olive-green long-sleeved dress shirt that set off his eyes perfectly, and a cream-colored tie. Overdressed for the occasion? Absolutely. Did that bother her? Absolutely not. Really seriously emphatically not.

"You look nice," she said.

"Thanks," Wylie said. "I do my—"

She swatted his hand. "You know I wasn't talking to you."

Starsky grinned and sat in the lawn chair beside her. "Thanks. Couldn't decide between this or the Speedo."

"You made the right decision," she said. "You hungry?"

He tilted his head downward and arched his eyebrows.

"Right," she said. "Stupid question."

The weekly procession of food from the kitchen to the picnic table began as Amara's siblings marched across the yard.

Starsky sat taller so he could get a better peek at dinner. "Looks delicious," he said.

Wylie patted his belly with both hands. "It is. Just as good for breakfast the next day too."

Her mother stepped out the back door and the trio stood.

"Mama," Amara said, "this is Starsky. Starsky, this is Maria, my mother."

The woman smiled and shook his hand. "So nice to meet you. That is an unusual name. Pleasant, but different."

"Yes, ma'am. It's a nickname. My real name is Jeremiah."

Her mother shook her head. "You are not a Jeremiah. Or a Jerry. Starsky fits. Why do they call you that?"

"Yeah," Amara said. "Why *do* they?" Starsky held the secret close. The story was that a few people in Homicide knew the origin of the nickname, but they weren't talking.

"Later," Wylie said. He gestured toward the mass of food. "We have more pressing matters to attend to."

The group joined the rest of the adults while the children sat at two card tables nearby.

"Everyone," Amara said, "this is my friend, Starsky."

A chorus of *Holas* and *Bienvenidos* greeted him and he smiled in return. Mama said grace and insisted on describing each dish to Starsky, who nodded politely as she worked her way down the list. When she finished, she cautioned that some of the food might be too spicy.

Amara pointed at him. "Not gonna be a problem, Mama. Cast-iron stomach."

Wrinkles appeared on the woman's forehead as her eyes narrowed. "*Que?*"

Starsky grinned. "I can eat anything. The hotter, the better."

Wylie pulled a casserole dish of enchiladas over and plopped two on his plate. "We talking or eating?"

Given their cue, the others dug in and began the weekly free-for-all. As dusk faded into darkness, the multicolored strings of lights hanging overhead broadcast their festive atmosphere. The slightest of breezes rustled the mesquite's leaves, and the clink of knives and forks gave way to laughs and boisterous talk.

Starsky pushed his plate away and leaned to Amara. "I can't believe I'm saying this, but I'm stuffed. I don't think I'll ever eat again. Or at least for another hour or two."

"Glad you enjoyed it. Mama's been doing this for as long as I can remember. We've offered to take turns fixing everything, but she won't hear of it. Says that watching her family eat her cooking is one of life's biggest joys."

He puffed his cheeks and let the breath slowly escape. "She brought about two pounds of joy into my belly."

Amara glanced away. She'd never had any desire to learn to cook, but had she lost out on something? Was the time invested worth the payoff? The contented look on her mother's face said it was. Maybe she should ask her for lessons one day.

Wylie tapped a knife against the side of his glass several times, then whispered to her mother, whose smile faded as she stood.

"I have something to tell you all," she said.

Conversation hushed. Squeals and laughter echoed from the far side of the yard as the kids played tag. Her mother watched them for a moment and the smile returned. "I didn't want to say anything, but Wylie insisted." She reached for his hand and clutched it to her chest while he dabbed at his eyes and sniffled.

Amara's heart froze and her lips parted. This was not going to be good. Something was wrong with Mama.

"A little over a week ago," her mother said, "I went to the doctor. There is a lump under my arm. He did a biopsy and I have breast cancer."

Several gasps sounded and Starsky placed his arm around Amara's shoulder. Her mother held up her hand to still the commotion. "I go back next Thursday and they will do a scan of my body to find out if . . . to make sure we know what we're dealing with. I asked Wylie to go with me, and he agreed. When we have more information, I will share it with you."

One of Amara's sisters stood. "I can go too, Mama."

Her mother shook her head. "No, Selina. Thank you, but no. I will not allow this to interfere with your lives."

"Mama," Amara said, "I can—"

"I said *no*. I understand this is difficult for all of you, but if you want to help me, the best way is to continue to live your lives as normal as possible. If you will do that, I promise to keep you informed of everything. That goes for all of you. Now, no more questions or talk of this. Not tonight. There will be time later. *Comprende?*"

Amara and the others nodded.

"Good," her mother said. "I apologize to everyone, especially our guest, for bringing somber news on such a pleasant evening." She picked up her glass of sweet iced tea and held it high. "Will you join me in a toast?"

The group stood and raised whatever they were drinking.

Across the yard, screams of "got ya" and "did not" cut through the silence as the kids chased and tackled each other.

Her mother closed her eyes. "To family."

Glasses clinked and "To family" echoed.

Amara leaned her head on Starsky's chest and wept into her napkin.

7

Amara eased away from the drive-thru window and opened the coffee lid to let the drink cool. Hot was good. Lava was not. Monday morning traffic wouldn't kick into high gear for another hour, and she wanted to get to work early. Anything was better than sitting at home.

Sunday had been a blur. She'd hit the gym for a workout, trying to clear her mind. Even picturing Travis Rutledge on the bag did nothing other than exhaust her body. No sense of accomplishment or rush of energy. All thoughts had remained fixated on her mother. Her one-two jabs were combinations of fear and frustration. She'd always tended to jump to worst-case scenarios in situations. How could she not? Mama had cancer and Amara could do nothing about it. And until the diagnosis and treatment options were known, there'd be no plan of attack. No way to deal with things.

Starsky had been wonderful. Called Sunday morning to check on her and tell her that if she wanted to talk, he'd be there. He asked if she was okay with him checking on her later, and she'd thanked him but said she needed to be alone with her thoughts for a while. "Alone with her thoughts" turned into a day of drowning in emotions and a second night of little sleep.

She'd reviewed the video footage from the water park four times yesterday, each go-through focusing on a different teen. It was like watching a movie with the major plot points cut out. The teenagers bounced from ride to food to ride, sometimes together, oftentimes not. At no point did anything appear out of the ordinary. No sign of any danger. No indication that Zachary Coleman would be dead at the end of the movie.

She tested the coffee with the tip of her tongue, decided it was cool enough, and replaced the cup's lid. The brew was more potent than the stuff at the office and jolted her taste buds awake. The rest of her remained drowsy and dreading. Not a great start to the day.

She arrived at the office early enough to stake her claim on the card table. A few weekend stragglers remained, catching up on paperwork or continuing their investigations. A series of murmurs were exchanged between all, the best anyone could manage.

She booted her laptop and sketched out her plans. First thing was to contact the Colemans. She needed to get a look at Zachary's room. See if anything suspicious was there. That could take most of the morning. Afterward, she'd track down the teenager's friends to interview, or she'd chase whatever clue she found.

A deep, gravelly voice across the room interrupted her solitude. Lieutenant Segura was in early too.

"Good morning, sir," she said.

He nodded. "Alvarez." He walked closer and nodded toward her laptop. "Anything happening with the Coleman case?"

"Not yet. I'm going by the home today and checking out his room. Maybe something there will clarify things."

"Maybe. More likely you'll find his stash of drugs or whatever. When you do, close the case. The tox report will confirm what we already know. The kid died of an OD."

But we don't *know that. Not yet.* "Sir, it could be four or five weeks before we get the report back. By then, any evidence or suspects will be long gone."

He stared at her without speaking.

She glanced away. "I agree. Unless I find something suspicious, it might be time to put this one in the file."

"Just because there aren't any new murders doesn't mean there's not plenty of work to do. Check out the boy's room. See what you find. We'll determine how to proceed after that."

We'll? How long before he trusted her?

The LT shook his head. "Don't give me that look. You have your job and I have mine. We stay on track and on budget. When the time comes that I think a case needs to be put on hold, you'll have a chance to change my mind. Any detective here will tell you I do the same thing to them. Doesn't matter if they're a thirty-year vet or a rookie. No one wants to let loose of an investigation until they've solved it, but the reality is sometimes we have to wait for someone to come forward or new information to turn up. Until that happens, your time is better spent elsewhere."

She pressed her lips into a thin line. Tell that to the victims' families. "I understand, sir."

He sighed and stepped closer. "Understanding and accepting aren't the same thing, but I get it. Two pieces of advice for you, Alvarez. First, focus on the victim, not the family. You're paid to solve a crime, not to bring people closure or relief or whatever you want to call it. That may sound harsh, but that's the way it is. You work for the deceased, or more specifically, the *next* victim. Your job is to make sure a murderer isn't around long enough to kill again."

"And the second?"

"Human nature is your best friend and worst enemy. People are predictable. They kill for the same reasons. It almost always comes back to love or money. Problem is"—he pointed at her—"your nature, all of ours at first, is to want to believe what people tell us. Don't. Everything and everyone is suspect unless the evidence confirms their story."

Starsky said the same thing. Everyone lies, intentionally or not. The only truth was whatever you could prove.

And right now, that added up to a big, fat nada. A lack of wrinkly toes wasn't persuading a grand jury. Didn't really convince her either. If this hadn't been her first shot at a case, if she'd had other *real* homicides on her plate, she'd probably have passed on this one. Wait for the tox results, she'd have told Pritchard. Call back then.

But, just like Cotulla, the itch had grown, demanding to be scratched. Insisting there was more. Always more.

Zachary Coleman. Seventeen years old. Dead. Too young.

Like Mama.

Far too young.

Mama would get her answers. Doctors would diagnose. Suggest options and treatment plans. Give her the odds.

Zachary would get no answers. Too late for him.

Amara scooped up her belongings and headed for the car. She'd get the answers. For his family and friends. For the public. For the other Homicide detectives.

But mostly, for herself.

No other way to make the itch disappear.

Amara pulled into the driveway of the Coleman residence. The garage doors were open and Zachary's Mustang remained where she'd seen it last Thursday. Both of the other vehicles—his parents' cars, she assumed—were also there. No indication that anyone else was at the home, meaning the heavy silence that came after a funeral would hang over the house like a shroud.

She stepped outside and walked toward the porch, eager to dig into Zachary's life but hesitant to intrude. Best case would be for the Colemans to leave her alone while she poked around the boy's room and car. The father seemed like the kind of person who wouldn't have a problem with that, but the mother could be a different story. With Zachary's death so recent, she might not want anyone messing with his stuff.

The front door opened and Paul Coleman half waved. "Good morning, Detective."

She increased her pace and hopped up the steps onto the porch. "Good morning, Mr. Coleman. I appreciate your cooperation. I know this is a difficult time."

He motioned her inside without responding. "Lori is still asleep." He sighed and scratched at the stubble on his face. "Prescription sleeping pills."

Her heart sank. The woman was trapped in a nightmare of anguish. Amara had taken a semester of psychology back in college. The professor said everyone dealt with sorrow differently. That the so-called five stages of grief were meant to apply to terminally ill patients, not to those left behind, and people might go through all the steps or none of them. Ms. Coleman had opted to postpone the process with medication.

"Yes, sir. I'll be out of here as soon as I can. If possible, I'd like to take a look in his car before I leave?"

His expression remained flat. "Won't be a problem. Zach's room is this way."

She followed him down a narrow hallway, pausing as he pointed out a bathroom she could use, and walked inside Zachary Coleman's room. The space was huge, with a full-size bed shoved against one wall and opposite it, a desk smothered with computer equipment. A walk-in closet was off to the right, its open door revealing a pile of dirty clothes on the floor. The short-shag beige carpet, well-worn and dotted with various colored stains, covered the entire area. A triangular path had been permanently etched into the flooring's fibers. Door to bed to computer to door.

Mr. Coleman's voice had a new scratchiness to it. "This used to be two bedrooms, both small. We took out a wall and combined them."

She nodded. "Has, um, has anything in here been touched? I mean, since Zachary passed?"

He shook his head. "Lori rests on his bed sometimes. Everything else should be the same, as far as I know."

"What about his cell? Do you have it?"

"It's in our bedroom. Do you need it? We were hoping to get some pictures off it, but it's locked. I thought one day I'd take it to the phone store and see if they could help."

"It's okay. You can hold on to it for now." She paused. "Mr. Coleman, if you have other things you have to take care of . . ."

"No. Nothing else except another cigarette. I'll be out by the pool. Take your time."

"Thank you." She pulled on a pair of latex gloves.

"What exactly are you looking for?" he asked.

Drugs, weapons, or money would be a good start. "Not sure," she said.

"Do you think it will make things better or worse?" he asked.

She turned and peered at him. "What?"

"If Zach was killed. Is that better or worse than an overdose or natural causes or whatever?"

The same thing she'd wondered when she was here last week. "I don't know."

"Yeah. Me neither." He dragged his finger down the doorjamb before pulling a pack of cigarettes from his pocket and wandering away.

Amara surveyed the room and planned her search. No posters or photos on the walls. Did teenagers not do that stuff anymore? On the desk to the left, computer equipment was surrounded by empty energy drinks and colorful figurines. Save that for last. Move along the wall on her right, check out the dresser and small bookcase, then into the closet. Next, the bed, area around the window, and end up at Zach's computer setup.

The dresser looked like one of those IKEA deals. Clean lines with a modern look. Everything comes in a box that's about two inches thick and weighs eight hundred pounds. Nothing fancy but plenty functional. An assortment of loose change, some candy wrappers, and small bundles of pocket lint dotted the top. She opened the first of four drawers and shuffled through a pile of underwear and wrinkled T-shirts. Nothing out of the ordinary.

The next drawer contained a few pairs of socks, a couple of swimsuits, and some shorts. She squeezed everything to be certain nothing was hidden inside. The next two drawers held various items he'd accumulated in his short lifetime. Concert ticket stubs, plastic and metal figurines from video games, some superhero comic books. She riffled through everything else, confirmed there was nothing of interest, and ran her fingers along the bottom and outside back of each drawer without discovering anything.

She tugged the dresser away from the wall—validating her eight-hundred-pound IKEA theory—and inspected the space. No secrets here. She eased the furniture back into place, planted her hands on her hips, and arched her back. A tablet or two of aspirin might be in order tonight.

The walk-in closet turned out to be mostly empty. The pile of clothes on the floor appeared to be clean. Dumped straight to the ground. She squatted and went through each item but found nothing. Three pairs of shoes and as many flip-flops were semi-organized along the wall, and she inspected them before standing to survey the rest of the closet.

Shirts and pants, jeans mostly, hung along the white wire-rack shelving, and she ran her hands down each item. Nothing. A couple of baseball caps had been tossed on the top shelf, and she stretched for them. Her fingertips brushed the hats, but her height, or lack thereof, made reaching them impossible. She frowned and glanced around for something to stand on.

Unwilling to disturb the Colemans and with no other options, she settled on the rolling chair at the computer desk. After ma-neuvering it into the closet, she placed one palm against the wall and stepped up. The seat swiveled slightly and she grabbed the shelving to keep her balance. Wonderful. Couldn't wait to fill out the on-the-job injury report. She steadied herself and inspected the hats. A bit of dust in each and nothing else.

She pressed her palm against the wall again and eased her right foot toward the floor. As she did, the chair spun and she balanced precariously, left foot planted midseat and right foot dangling in the air. Her heart pounded in her ears as she slowly sank to the ground.

The seat edged a millimeter toward the closet door and disturbed the delicate balance, sending her tumbling to the floor. At least no one was here to see it. Nothing hurt but her ego. She scooted onto her hands and knees and glanced around to make sure she hadn't put a hole in the wall. Everything appeared to be as it should.

Almost everything.

From this low perspective, she could make out the hint of another carpet trail. This one led to the back far corner of the closet. No clothes, boxes, or anything else stacked there. She crawled over and inspected the wall. No sign of any secret hiding spots. She scrunched lower and found the trail again. It led right to her. Had to be old. At one point something was here, maybe back when it was two separate bedrooms.

She ran her hand along the indentation in the shag. The rut stopped short of the corner by about a foot. She rapped her fist on the floor, unsure of what she was listening for. It sounded like wood under there, but weren't all floors wood? Besides, there were no visible cuts in the carpet. She grabbed a handful of fibers and tugged.

The carpet came up a little, maybe more than expected, but nothing major. *Nothing.* How many times had she thought that word in the short time she'd been here? She released the flooring and it settled back in place. A bump remained and she smoothed it in all directions in a futile effort to eliminate the evidence of her work. Old carpet, loose padding, whatever. She sighed and pushed herself off the floor, then squinted at the back corner. The carpet there wasn't under the baseboard. Had it been like that before?

She bent forward and gripped the edge, then pulled the flooring back. After staring for a moment, she grabbed her phone and snapped a couple of photos. There, in the plywood panel supporting the carpet, was a perfectly cut rectangle, roughly a foot by a foot and a half. Scattered crumbs of dark sawdust bordered the cuts. On the side closest to her, thin gouges indicated where a knife or screwdriver had been used to pry up the rectangle.

She closed her eyes for a moment and forced herself to focus. No assumptions. Whatever was under there might not have anything to do with Zachary or his death. Don't jump to conclusions.

She pulled her keys from her pocket, chose the thinnest one, and wedged it into the crack. The board came up easily and she peered into the space. The plywood subfloor rested atop a series of two-by-fours turned sideways and mounted on what she assumed was a concrete slab.

It was hard to know for sure, considering the entire area was filled with bundles of cash protected in plastic wrap.

"What are you doing?"

Amara jumped at the voice behind her. "Ms. Coleman?"

The woman's anger radiated from her. Her disheveled hair, baggy eyes, wrinkled pajamas, and bare feet validated her husband's information about the sleeping pills. "Get out of my son's room."

"Ma'am, I'm Detective Alvarez from the—"

"I don't care who you are." Ms. Coleman took a step forward and pointed at the door. "Get out. Now."

Amara froze. "Your husband said—"

"I don't care what he said." The woman moved another step closer. "I want you gone."

Amara extended her left arm and planted her feet. "I understand, but first, I need you to back away. Please, Ms. Coleman. Neither of us wants a confrontation."

"This is *my* house."

"Yes, ma'am, and I'll be happy to leave as soon as you give me some space. Please. For your safety and mine."

She squinted at the hole in the floor, seemingly noticing it for the first time. "What did you do?"

Amara lowered her arm. "Would it be all right if we got your husband and the three of us talked? About Zachary?"

"Zachary's gone."

"Yes, ma'am, he is. And I'm trying to figure out why."

The woman's shoulders slumped. "Nothing you can do will help."

Amara shook her head. This was the part where she was supposed to talk about getting answers and bringing closure. Justice too if that was needed. But none of that mattered to Ms. Coleman. "No, ma'am," she said. "I can't give you what you want. Nothing I do is going to fix this." She wanted to hug the woman. Tell her how sorry she was that Zachary was gone and that sometimes things just happen. Things like murders and overdoses and breast cancer. Instead, she clasped her hands in front. In her new job, sympathy worked. Empathy destroyed. "Let's go find your husband, okay?"

She nodded once and Amara followed her as the woman shuffled out of the room, down the hall, and to the back patio.

Paul Coleman sat at a table, the ashtray beside him overflowing with cigarette butts. He glanced at them but remained seated. "Honey, you shouldn't be up. You need rest."

The woman squinted against the sunshine, then walked to the table and sat beside him.

He covered her hand with his and squeezed. "Finished, Detective?"

"No," Amara said. "I have to show you something and then I was hoping we could talk."

He raised his eyebrows. "What did you find?"

"There's a, um . . . I found a compartment under the floor of your son's closet. Inside was money. A lot of money. Do you have any idea where he could have gotten it?"

Ms. Coleman looked up. "Zach worked at Target. He probably just cashed his checks and put the money there. You know, to keep it safe."

Amara gestured toward the home. "Could we go inside and I can show you? That might help."

The Colemans trailed her into Zachary's closet, and Amara stood aside while they stared into the hole. What was going through their minds? Cash like that didn't come from working at Target, and they knew it. Mr. Coleman squatted for a closer peek.

"Please don't touch anything," Amara said. "Perhaps it would be best if we talked somewhere else?"

"My office," Mr. Coleman said. He wrapped his arm around his wife's waist. "It's okay if you want to go back to bed. I can fill you in later."

"No," she said. "I want to hear this. Or I don't. I'm not sure how much more I can take."

Amara turned her gaze away from the couple. How much worse could it get? Would anything she said be harsher than Zachary's death? At this point, what difference could it make if their son was a drug lord or an overpaid Target employee? The only thing possibly affected would be his reputation, and was that so important?

"Sit with us," Mr. Coleman said to his wife. "I'll fix some coffee, okay?"

She nodded and the group moved to his office. Amara sat in the same chair she used last week and pulled out a notepad and pen. Mr. Coleman flicked on a coffeepot behind his desk while his wife sank onto a love seat and curled her feet up under herself.

"It looks bad," the husband said. "Doesn't it?"

Amara scooted forward in her chair. "It doesn't look good or bad. It just is. Of course, we need to determine where your son got the money so we'll know whether it had anything to do with his death. Can either of you think of any explanation?"

"No," Ms. Coleman said. "Zach never really spent a lot of money on things. You saw his room. Other than his computer stuff, there's nothing to amount to anything."

"What about banks? Did your son have a checking account? Credit cards?"

"Joint checking with me," Mr. Coleman said. "I told him that when he turned eighteen, we'd set him up on his own. And no credit cards that I'm aware of."

"Would it be possible to get copies of the statements for the last year or two?"

"I can do that," he said. "But you're not going to find anything. I looked at it every day. Wanted to be sure he didn't overdraw the account."

"Thanks," Amara said. "I'm sorry, but there are some difficult questions I need to ask. Did you ever witness Zachary using drugs of any kind? Pills, marijuana, anything? Did he ever act like he might be under the influence of something?"

Both shook their heads.

"Okay. How about visitors at odd hours? Or maybe he'd go out in the middle of the night?"

"No," Mr. Coleman said. "Like I told you, Zach mostly stayed at home. If anything, we encouraged him to get out more."

She flipped back a few pages in the notepad. "The three friends I saw last time I was here. Did they come to the house often?"

"Not really," Ms. Coleman said. "Why? Do you think they had something to do with all this?"

Amara ignored the question. "You said Zachary spent a lot of time on his computer. Did you ever see what he was doing online?"

Wrinkles appeared on Ms. Coleman's forehead. "Spy on him, you mean? He was practically an adult, Detective. It's not hard to imagine some of the, uh, things he might have been looking at, but to answer your question, no. We didn't monitor his online activities."

Her husband stood, poured a cup of coffee, and handed it to his wife. He held the pot higher. "Detective?"

"No, thank you. Mr. Coleman, the last time I was here you mentioned your son wanted to study computer science."

He switched off the coffeepot and returned to his seat. "That's right. I was just glad he picked something that would make him easily employable, you know?"

If Zachary Coleman's life revolved around his computer, there was a good chance his death did too. The bundles of cash might be tied to something online. "I wonder if it would be okay to bring a couple more people out here this morning? Specialists who could examine Zachary's room and maybe help clear up a few things. I'd like to check out his car too."

Ms. Coleman set her untouched coffee on the desk. "They won't make a mess in his room, will they?"

"They'll be as careful as possible. I promise."

She shrugged toward her husband. "All right with me as long as they're quiet. I'm going back to bed."

10 Amara searched Zachary's vehicle while waiting for the crime scene techs to arrive. The Mustang was spotless inside and out. Nothing unusual in the trunk or glove box. No old french fries or straw wrappers stowed away under the seats. No evidence pointing to illegal activity. She'd have the techs do a once-over, but the car was a dead end.

The two crime scene analysts arrived shortly after and got right to work. The first, Barb Freemont, specialized in computers and data recovery. Her focus would be on Zachary's online activities. The second, Gregory Griffin, would document the discovery in the closet and inspect the bed, the car, and other unexplored areas.

Griffin snapped photos of the opening in the floor from every conceivable angle, then placed a large cardboard carton next to the hole. After lining the box with new plastic sheeting, he began pulling the plastic-wrapped bundles of bills from the cavity and stacking them in the container. The visible cash was of various denominations and all appeared to have been in circulation. "Might need a second box," he said.

Amara grunted. "Any idea how much we're looking at?"

"No clue. Lots of tens and twenties showing, but everything inside could be ones. Won't know until we get it back to the lab and count it."

"How long will that take?"

He glanced up at her. "To count it? Ten or fifteen minutes. We'll feed the cash into a bill counter. To get time to do that? Somewhere between a couple of hours and a couple of months. All depends on where the case falls on the list of priorities. Who's yelling the loudest."

"So if I—"

"Uh-uh. You don't matter. Someone over you."

Rude enough? She smiled. "Understood. Let's say a few pizzas happen to show up tomorrow around lunchtime. That buy me any favors?"

He turned back to the hole and continued retrieving the money. "Might, but think about it. We're way behind as it is. If we bump you forward, that means something else gets bumped down. Is knowing the exact amount of cash that important right now?"

"No, probably not. Unless there's something there that will tell me where it came from."

"Which is a whole 'nother thing. If you're wanting the money tested for drugs, we can do that, but not anytime soon. Pizza or no pizza. Tell ya what. When I get to the lab, I'll open one of these packs. Confirm the bills are legit and nothing unusual about them."

"Thanks," she said. "You'll call me and let me know?"

"Only if something's not right. Otherwise, assume they're good." He placed the last stack of bills in the almost full box, pulled the plastic sheeting over the top of the money, and taped the lid closed. Next, he stuck his head in the hole and shined his flashlight to confirm nothing remained, then popped a new filter into a handheld vacuum and ran it through the space.

"Done here," he said. "Off to the bedroom."

She nodded and left to check on the technician responsible for Zachary's computer. Barb had positioned all the equipment so she could see the serial and model numbers. The woman—midforties, too thin or too tall or both, and brunette hair piled into a bun—glanced her direction.

"Anything interesting?" Amara asked.

"Pretty nice setup. The monitor and modem are newer models. Odd that there's no Wi-Fi though, either from an external router or the modem."

Amara checked her phone. "I'm showing a Wi-Fi network. It's locked, but it's there."

"Homeowner said he's got two separate internet accounts through the cable company. The Wi-Fi's coming off the second modem in their living room. The kid wanted a dedicated line, probably for his gaming."

"That unusual?"

"Little bit. The hubs and I do some online gaming and even at the connection's slower speeds, it should be plenty fast for most uses unless someone else is hogging your bandwidth by streaming high-quality video, downloading stuff, or worse, uploading huge files, anything that might take up a chunk of your pipeline."

"So if his folks were watching Netflix, that could affect him when he played a game?"

"Lag is the enemy, my friend. If he could talk his parents into a dedicated line for himself, why not? Then use the Wi-Fi from his parents' modem to surf or download while gaming on the direct line so they didn't interfere with each other. That would mean his computer had to be connected to two different networks at the same time. Not hard to do with the right equipment and software."

Amara crossed her arms. "Could his computer handle that?"

"Haven't dug into it yet, but it's custom built. Entirely possible he designed it to cope with both networks."

"Custom built? Is that relevant?"

Barb shook her head. "Means he didn't want a stock unit off the shelf. I wouldn't read anything into that. Building your own PC isn't hard. Lots of folks do it."

"Including you?"

"Yep. I figure why buy a preconfigured machine when it's easier to do it myself and get exactly what I want? Plus, not have to deal with all the bloatware they shove on them."

"Bloatware?"

"Programs you don't want or need. Can't even uninstall some of them without reformatting your drive."

Amara pointed to the figurines scattered about the desk. Brightly colored humanoids holding an array of futuristic weapons. Mythical characters wielding giant axes and swords. Wizards and orcs and barbarians. Flying horses and robots and werewolves. "Those mean anything? There are more in his dresser."

"Collectibles from the games. Not limited-edition stuff, but cool to have."

"To each his own, I guess."

Barb glanced at her. "I've got several of these at home."

Amara winced and heat flooded her ears. "Sorry. Didn't mean . . ."

"No problem."

"Any idea what games these are from?"

"Those are *Planetary Orcs*, these over here are *Warrior Clans* and *Tango Murked*. There are some from *Two Weeks at War*, *Worlds of Wrath*, a few others. If you want a full list, I'll have it all documented in the next, oh, decade or two."

"Thanks. Would it be safe to assume the figures in the dresser are from games he didn't play anymore?"

Barb nodded. "Probably. That's what I'd do." She grinned. "They're old friends. Can't throw them away, right?"

"Sure. You turn on his computer yet?"

"About to. If it's password protected, I'll have to take it back to the lab. You get permission from the parents?"

"Not yet. We'll cross that bridge if we come to it."

Barb pressed the power button and waited as the computer went through the boot process. "My guess is he's got SSDs in there. Solid state drives. A whole lot faster than traditional hard drives." She stared at the monitor, blank except for a single line of text. "Huh."

"'Boot device not found,'" Amara said. "What does that mean?"

"Hold on." She hit a key to restart the process, then punched the F12 repeatedly until a different screen came up. "Boot order looks fine. If he was starting the PC through the network or a flash drive, he'd most likely have rearranged things here."

"And he didn't, so that means what?"

"Standard operating system startup. The computer would get the information it needs off the internal drive. For whatever reason, that's not happening. Could be corrupted files, damage, any of a dozen other things." She pulled a small screwdriver from her pocket and worked her way around the back of the case, removing the tiny screws. "Let's see what we've got inside here."

She lifted the case, peered at the components, and snapped several photos. "Hmm." She held one end of a cable out so Amara could see it.

"I take it that's supposed to be attached to something?"

"The drive, or drives if he had more than one, are gone."

Amara frowned. "Is it possible there were never any in there?"

"Sure, but like I said, he'd have to boot another way. Most logical manner would be through a flash drive, but honestly, what's the point? If he's playing games, he's going to want the SSDs. And if he's downloading a lot of files, he'd want enough hard drive space to store everything. A flash drive won't do much for him, other than maybe add a layer of protection to the start process. But once you're logged on, it's more of a pain than it's worth."

"So what are you thinking?" Amara asked.

Barb pulled a penlight from her pocket and shined it inside the computer. "Take a look here. That's the slot where the drive would normally sit. Along those ridges."

Amara bent forward and squinted. "Yeah?"

"Now look at the empty slot under it. Notice any difference?" She moved the light between the two areas several times.

"Dust," Amara said. "There's dust on the ridges of the bottom slot, but none on the top."

"Precisely. He had a drive there at some point."

Either Zachary removed it or someone else did. If Zachary, why? What was on that drive? Did he know his life was in danger? And if not Zachary, who? His three friends had been here last week, but so had untold others, any of whom could've come in here. But Ms. Coleman had been in and out of the room multiple times too. Was she or her husband involved?

"I think there's enough here to get a warrant," Amara said. "After that, you can take it to the lab and see what else you can find. Make sure it gets dusted for prints too, okay?"

"Not a problem," Barb said. "But I can already say that without the drive, there's not a lot more I'll be able to tell you. I suppose you could backtrack and try to figure out where the kid got all his parts and see what's missing, but that won't provide any useful info for us. And if he was using an SSD, chances are it's sanitized anyway. No way to recover data."

Wonderful. More circumstantial evidence that piled suspicions on Zachary's death. The money, the missing computer drive, the possibility he was dead when he went in the water.

She didn't know why the boy was killed. Didn't know how he was killed either. She couldn't even pinpoint the spot *where* he was killed.

But he *was* killed.

Even if there wasn't enough evidence to convince anyone else yet, she knew someone had murdered Zachary Coleman.

She flexed her fingers as energy surged through her body. Three days since the boy had been buried. A week since he'd died. She was just getting started but already way behind. She grunted and moved toward the front door. Her first case wouldn't be easy.

Bueno. Muy bueno.

Best way to prove herself.

11 **Amara knocked** on Lieutenant Segura's open door and waited for him to motion her in. Interrupting his morning ritual of muttering profanities while signing the stack of paperwork from the prior day would not be a good idea. Not unless she wanted to be kicked back to a training detail for the next couple of weeks.

It had taken the rest of Monday to get Segura's approval for the warrant, finish searching Zachary's bedroom, and watch as the crime scene techs logged everything into the system. The box of cash, all the computer equipment, the boy's cell, a few items of clothing with tiny stains that may or may not be blood, and the sheets off his bed. The money, the PC, and the cell were good. The rest of it probably wouldn't add up to anything. Mr. Coleman had promised to go online and print out all calls to and from Zachary's phone for the last six months. Said he'd do it soon. If he didn't, she'd have to subpoena the records from the phone company, a process that would take considerably longer.

The LT glanced up. "You need something, Alvarez?"

"I can wait until you finish, sir."

He clicked his pen and dropped it on the desk. "Apparently not. You're still standing there."

Her heart palpitated and her left eye thought about twitching. "I was wondering if you—"

"Alvarez, get to the point."

A tiny bead of sweat trickled down her upper lip. "Yes, sir. I'd

71

like the cash we found yesterday prioritized in the lab. How much money, any drug residue, anything useful."

He frowned and nodded. "That all?"

"Yes, sir."

"No."

"Sir?"

He plopped his head on the back of the chair and stared at the ceiling. "No, I will not move your evidence to the front of the line. Clear enough?"

She wrinkled her forehead. "I understand there are other urgent cases, but this won't take long and—"

"Let me explain something to you. See this stack of papers I have to sign?"

"Yes, sir."

"It's the least enjoyable part of my job. Hate it. That's why I do them first thing. I sign until I start to get irritated. Don't want to ruin my day, right? This morning, I got annoyed earlier than usual. Why do you think that is?"

"Uh, me, sir?"

He sat straight. "What a detective. Every day when I stop signing, I figure I can come back and finish it later. But I never do. The next morning, the pile is higher. And then one day, oh, I dunno, once a month or so, I'll get a call from a senior officer wanting to know when I'm getting this or that piece of paper turned in. That's when I close my door and sign everything. The following morning, the process starts all over again."

She remained silent, but in her peripheral vision caught sight of Starsky sitting on his desk, his arms crossed and smiling from ear to ear.

"Now then, *Detective*, where do you suppose the requisition for your desk is in this stack?"

"No idea, sir."

He shook his head and lifted the top page. "It's right here. But I'll bet you're clever enough to know where it's going now?"

"The bottom, sir."

He lifted the stack and slid the paper under it. "Will there be anything else, Alvarez?"

"Have a good day, sir."

• • •

Amara reviewed her notes from the prior two hours. No hits in the criminal databases for any of Zachary Coleman's three friends. Matias Lucero, Haley Bricker, and Liam Walker were all in their late teens, all in different high schools, and all about as ordinary as kids that age could be.

With one exception. None of them had accounts on social media. At least none she could find. She hadn't found any for Zachary either. She checked Facebook, Snapchat, Instagram, and several she'd never heard of before. Of course, they may well have been on those or any others under false names. But four teenagers who weren't active online was beyond interesting.

Especially when one of those kids had bundles of cash and missing computer drives. Too early for any theories, but not for suspicions. People didn't get cash like that by doing legal things. The three friends had the means and opportunity to take the hard drives, but so did Zachary's parents. Problem was, if either Paul or Lori Coleman was involved, why agree to the search? They had to know the missing equipment would be discovered.

It made more sense that whoever took the drives hoped their disappearance would go unnoticed and the police wouldn't get involved. If Dr. Pritchard hadn't been suspicious, Zachary's death would never have been on Homicide's radar. Maybe the parents would have eventually figured out the computer didn't work, but so what? Not enough to trigger any new probe into the boy's death.

And one more thing. If the theft—that's what it was, right?—of the hard drive was planned, why not replace it with another drive? At least not make it so obvious. No, it had to have been an act of opportunity. The thief, or thieves, had their shot and took it, meaning they were almost certainly involved in whatever Zachary was doing.

Maybe they planned to come back later and replace the drive. Maybe not. Either way, it was too late now. She stared at the three names.

Matias Lucero.

Haley Bricker.

Liam Walker.

One of them, or all of them, knew something about Zachary's death. They might not be aware of that fact, but they did. Maybe the killer was among them.

As soon as she began asking questions of one, the others would know. If all three were involved, they had their story down by now. They might think they'd gotten away with it. Time to change that notion. She scanned the names again.

Alphabetically seemed as good as anything else. Haley, then Liam, then Matias. The DMV database provided the girl's address, but before heading there, Amara reviewed the opening few minutes of the video from the water park again.

The four were all smiles as they strolled through the security checkpoint. No sign that within hours, one of them would be dead. The boys wore swim trunks, ball caps, and muscle shirts, while Haley had on a cover-up over a bikini. The guys each held a handful of water bottles, no doubt at least one of which was filled with clear alcohol of some sort, and were waved into the park. A security guard performed a cursory check inside Haley's tote bag and motioned her through.

Just a group of teenagers ready for a day of fun in the sun. None of them looked like a murderer, whatever that meant. Maybe it was more accurate to say that none of them looked capable of killing someone. No, not that either. Appearances meant nothing. Evil lived inside. Hidden from all but *Dios*.

The group paused long enough to stash their belongings in a locker. Same building Amara used. From there, they moved into the park.

A sudden impact knocked her left arm forward and she spun around. Travis Rutledge. All six foot nothing and two-sixty-plus of him. His omnipresent fedora sat high atop his head, like he'd bought it several sizes too small. Or maybe his head had grown along with his belly. Either way, the look wasn't doing him any favors.

"Sorry," he mumbled. "Guess I need to watch where I'm going. Forgot that some people don't have a desk here. Like they don't belong."

Her throat tightened. "I guess you bump into a lot of things, considering your gut arrives a couple of seconds before the rest of you." She stood and forced her hands to remain at her side. "I'd recommend you not make that mistake again."

"You're standing now? Not much different from when you're sitting, is it?"

Wonderful. Attacks on each other's appearance. Be the adult, Amara. "Listen, Travis. I get it. You don't think I belong here or you don't like me for some reason or you got tired of picking on someone else. None of that matters. What *is* important to me is getting my job done. Don't mess with me at work. Comprende?"

He poked his finger toward her, stopping an inch from her forehead. "You got lucky on Cotulla. Plenty of people in here deserve the attention more than you."

Ah. The overwhelming media blitz that surrounded the return of the missing kids. Amara, at the insistence of Police Chief Ethan Johnson, had been on all the national morning news programs at least once, and the local stations more times than she could count. Her initial enjoyment of the process transitioned to dread after less than a week. The same questions, the constant smiling, and worst of all, always having to be TV-ready. Makeup, hair done, nails manicured . . . ugh. All nice the first time. Even the second. After that, *gracias* but find someone else, *por favor*.

"You're right," she said. "There are plenty of others who deserved it, but it wasn't my choice. I didn't ask for it and I'm glad it's over. Now, get your finger out of my face."

"Or what?"

"Or learn to type without it."

He laughed and pulled his hand back. "Big words from a little girl."

She flattened her palms against her legs. "Have a great day, Travis."

"Oh, I will." He pivoted to leave, paused, and spoke without turning around. "Two months. Probably less. I might even start an office pool."

"Yeah? Let me know if you do. I want in on it."

He laughed again and drifted off in the direction of his desk. Her jaw ached and her pulse refused to slow.

Evil lived inside people. Only Dios could see it.

People were capable of anything, murder included.

She didn't want to kill Travis.

But teaching him a painful lesson was now near the top of her things-to-sign-off-on pile.

12

Amara turned right onto the residential street and slowed to look for Haley Bricker's house number. The neighborhood seemed to consist primarily of rentals. The homes were nice enough and the lawns were mostly cut, but none of the houses had the personalized touch that came from longtime residents. No decor, flags, or flower gardens. A few yards had old furniture by the curb, and a moving truck partially blocked the road farther down.

A glossy black pickup, its frame elevated high above the tires and chrome mufflers promising to push legal decibel levels, sat parked ahead. The gas mileage on that thing had to be terrible. Amara frowned and gripped the steering wheel. When had she transitioned from thinking "cool truck" to worrying about miles per gallon? She slowed and stopped behind the vehicle. A white decal in the back window proclaimed ownership. *Haley*. The girl had money. Or knew someone who did.

Amara snapped a photo of the truck's license plate and strode to the front door. A straw mat, its best days long past, lay on the concrete porch and invited guests to *Wipe your paws*. Dog lovers. Nothing wrong with dogs, certainly better than cats, but Larry was more her speed. Not so needy. Plenty moody though. She knocked and stepped away from the door. A nanosecond later, the high-pitched yips of a small dog—*please don't let it be a Jack Russell*—echoed. That was another thing about Larry. No noise.

"Dexter! Hush!" The voice from inside was loud but did nothing to slow the barking. "Who is it?"

"SAPD," Amara said. She held up her identification so it could be seen through the peephole.

The door cracked open and a girl's face appeared in the narrow opening. "Yes?"

"Haley Bricker?"

"That's me. What's going on?"

The dog's yipping reached new levels of annoying. Amara slipped her ID into her pocket. "Is there someplace quiet we can talk?"

"About what?"

"I'm trying to close the file on Zachary Coleman's death. His father mentioned you were one of his best friends and I—"

"Best friend?" She eased the door open a bit more, turned sideways, and used her foot to keep the dog at bay while she stepped onto the porch. "A few of us hung out together, but it was more of a group thing, you know?"

Amara studied the girl. A little on the thin side, blondish hair pulled back in a ponytail, and no makeup. Her oversize T-shirt had a Longhorns logo and almost hid the skimpy denim shorts she wore. A pair of neon green flip-flops completed her outfit. "Your parents home?"

"Last I heard, my mom was down in Corpus, either in jail or high somewhere. Never knew my dad. This is all legal, okay? I'm eighteen. I can live by myself. Want me to get my driver's license?"

"Nah," Amara said. "I've seen it. Could we talk in my car? I'll turn the air on. More comfortable and quieter."

"I guess so. How long will it take?"

"Not long." Amara walked to her vehicle, glancing back once to be sure Haley was following. After settling in, she pulled out her notepad and laid her phone on the center console. "You mind if I record this? It'll make things go a lot faster."

Haley shrugged. "Whatever. Why are the cops involved? I thought Zach had heatstroke."

"We think the same thing. Just waiting on the tests to come back. In the meantime, we wanted to clear up a few questions. You went with Zachary to the Cannonball Water Park the day he died, correct?"

"Me and a couple of other guys."

"That would be . . ." Amara flipped the page in her notebook and scanned it for a second. The names were embedded in her memory, but Haley didn't need to know that. "Ah. Here we go. Liam Walker and Matias Lucero, right?"

Haley shifted her position and leaned against the car door. "How'd you know that?"

"Zachary's father. He said you four went there together. He also said you're into online video games. Are you guys some sort of team?"

The girl rolled her eyes. "Yeah. Some sort of team."

"What I meant was, do you compete against each other or do you work together?"

"Mostly co-op MMORPGs, MOBAs, or FPSs."

Amara clicked her pen a few times. "Um, MMO what?"

"Massively multiplayer online role-playing games or multiplayer online battle arenas or first-person shooters."

"Yeah, that's what I thought." She scribbled a note to do more research on them. "Is that how you met Zachary?"

She shrugged. "I guess. We've all been doing MMOs for a long time and sort of found each other that way. You can tell a lot about a person by how they act online."

"How so?"

"You're anonymous. Makes it easier to be a sleaze." She stared toward her house. "Zach wasn't a creep. Liam or Matias neither."

"Did the four of you go to the water park often?"

"Not really. This was our first time this year."

"Any particular reason you went that day?"

She crossed her arms. "Yeah. It was gonna be hot."

Attitude. Nice. "So nothing special? Whose idea was it to go?"

"I dunno. We just kind of decided, I guess. Not much else going on."

"Got it." She turned the air conditioner down a notch. "The report said that none of you were with Zachary when he died. Is that accurate?"

"I wasn't with him. You'd have to ask Liam and Matias."

"Okay." She paused as an old truck pulling a trailer full of lawn-mowing equipment sputtered past. "If you weren't with Zachary, where were you?"

Haley's eyes widened. "You mean, like, what's my alibi? You think someone killed him? Why? Who would hurt Zach?"

"Like I said, I'm tying up loose ends is all."

"Yeah, well, I don't remember where I was. Somewhere in the park. Sometimes we'd be together and sometimes not."

"No problem. How did you find out Zachary had died?"

The girl's forehead wrinkled. "I remember hearing people yelling and running and I followed them."

"Did you or any of your friends carry drugs or alcohol into the park?"

"Seriously?" She turned her palms up. "Like I'd narc on anyone?"

"I'd call that a *yes*," Amara said.

Haley leaned closer to the phone on the console. "No. I did not see anyone with drugs. There might have been some vodka smuggled in, but I don't know by who."

Uh-huh. Sure. Doesn't make any difference. "Thank you. Based on your knowledge of Zachary, would it surprise you if we found drugs in his system?"

"Not really."

Amara frowned. "You know for a fact he was a user?"

"Nope. You asked if I'd be surprised and I said no. How would I know something like that?" She smirked. "Ask me if I'd be surprised if we found drugs in *your* system. I'd give the same answer."

Amara made a mental note to thank her own mother for not killing her during her teenage years. She flicked the notepad closed and forced a smile. "Is there anything else you can think of that might be helpful?"

"Not really. Can I go now?"

"Of course." She handed over a business card. "If you do think of anything, will you call me?"

"Whatever." She pushed the car door open and stepped outside.

"Oh," Amara said. "Would you mind texting me addresses and phone numbers for Liam and Matias?"

"Yeah, I'm not gonna do that. I wouldn't want anyone sharing *my* info."

"Fair enough." She pointed out the windshield. "That your truck?"

The girl gave an exaggerated sigh of frustration. "The one that says *Haley* in real big letters across the back? Ya think?"

"I like it. Do you have a job?"

"What difference does that make?"

"None. Curious is all. Gas mileage can't be good. Insurance rates sky high too. No way I could afford something like that at your age." *Or my current age.*

The girl shoved the door closed and hurried inside her house. Amara turned off the recording app and checked her photo gallery to ensure the truck's license plate was clear. Time to head back to the office and do more digging. Get addresses for Liam and Matias, though their interviews weren't likely to provide much information. Haley was probably on the phone with them now.

But the truck might be useful. The thing had to be expensive. Shouldn't take much research to get the details on the purchase and registration. See whose name was on the paperwork. Whether her insurance was current. Other things, like sources of income the girl had, would have to wait until later. After everyone else had been interviewed.

The girl remained a suspect. So were Liam and Matias and the thousands of other people at the water park that day.

Amara took a last look at the house before easing past the monster truck and toward the station. Nice place for an eighteen-year-old, at least from the outside. Couldn't be a cheap rental. Throw in cell phone bills, utilities, internet, pizzas. Tough for a single adult to afford all that, job or not.

Maybe Haley Bricker had bundles of cash under her floor too.

13

Research into Haley's truck and the other two friends would have to wait. Eduardo Sanchez had phoned and said the software vendor was on-site at the water park and working on the camera system. Sanchez said she was welcome to come out and talk to the guy if she wanted. She agreed and he told her to park near the administration building. Security personnel would wave her through.

It took forty-five minutes to get there, and by the time she made it to Sanchez's office, the July heat index was well into triple digits. She gratefully accepted the bottled water he offered.

"Cooker out there today," he said. "We'll be near capacity."

"Never understood that," she said. "I'd rather stay in the air-conditioning when it's this hot."

He grinned. "Fortunately for us, there are plenty of people who do not agree with you. If I may ask, have you made any progress in your investigation?"

"Nothing much. You said the software vendor was here?"

"Yes. Steve Marshall. Good name for someone in the security business, right? He's in the computer room. I can take you there when you're ready."

She downed the last of the water and dropped the bottle in his garbage can. "Good to go."

"It's just down the hall. Would you prefer to speak to him alone or . . . ?"

Sanchez wanted to know where he stood in the investigation. "Alone would be great."

He cocked his head to the side. "Of course. Right this way."

The computer room was a short walk down the hall, behind a locked door. Sanchez let her in, introduced the vendor to her, and asked her to stop by his office before leaving. She thanked him and agreed.

Computer room was a bit of a misnomer. Half of the space contained all manner of electronic equipment, while the rest of the area held old office furniture and cardboard boxes filled with who knew what. "Thanks for taking the time to speak with me, Mr. Marshall."

"Steve, please. No problem. Eduardo said you wanted some information on the camera system?"

"Nothing too detailed. I understand you're updating the software that controls everything? Is that because of the issues the park has been having with sporadic outages?"

He nodded. "A new version was coming out soon anyway, so we asked the vendor to bump it forward a bit to get it in here."

"A different company handles the software?"

"Yeah. That's the way the business works. Everyone does their own thing. We make recommendations to our customers, then design and install the system using products from other companies. Software is a commodity, same as a camera or monitor."

"And you're confident a software bug caused the problem?"

"Not at all." He leaned back against a stack of boxes. "But we're giving it a shot. We've run tests on the system and didn't identify any hardware concerns. No wiring glitches. Because of the inconsistency of the outages, a camera here and a camera there, it's hard to pinpoint what's causing the trouble. The easiest thing to do is swap out the software and see if that solves anything."

"And if it doesn't?"

"Back to square one, I guess."

"Are there other companies using a similar system? Have they had the same issues?"

"Yes to your first question, no to your second." He crossed his arms and paused. "Our software vendor wasn't aware of any issues, but it's possible others have had the same problems and just don't know it. Most people don't spend a lot of time checking their systems."

"Doesn't the software sound some sort of alarm when a camera's not working?"

"If you mean an audible alarm, no. I suppose it would be simple enough to set that up, but unless you're in a high-security situation, say a prison or something, most people wouldn't want it. However, the system does send an email to the customer and to us. We've been tracking Cannonball's for almost a month."

Amara shifted on her feet. "When was the last outage?"

"Been about a week if I remember correctly."

Zachary Coleman died a week ago yesterday. "So why replace the software if the problem seems to have gone away?"

"We're not sure it *has* gone away. We've seen time gaps before. Never this long though. A couple of days max. We figure better safe than sorry."

"Would it be possible to get copies of the emails? The ones you received when the cameras weren't working here?"

"Eduardo probably has them. Can you get those from him?"

She nodded. "I could, but I'd rather have the official version, you know? Straight from the vendor."

"I'd like to help, but unless Eduardo says it's okay, we really don't give out customer information. Kind of goes against the whole security thing."

Her heart sank. Eduardo would give them to her, but would

he hold anything back? She pasted on a smile. "No problem. I'll get them from him. If the cameras were intentionally deactivated, would the system report that?"

"Not directly. Either the video is active or it's not. That's what's stated. It doesn't tell us *why* the camera's down. Honestly, something like this has never been a problem before."

"Let's say a camera loses connection for whatever reason. How long before it sends the email alert?"

He held up his hand, all fingers stretched. "Five-minute delay. We can shorten it, but most people don't want to in case the power flickers during a storm or something. But the program logs any outage, regardless of length, and that data is accessible anytime. Which brings up another point. We monitor all our systems in case of catastrophic failure, such as when everything goes down for whatever reason. We can initiate contact to make sure the customer is aware and get to work on a solution if it's something on our end."

So if they could view the system remotely, potentially anyone could. Anyone with the skills to bypass protective measures. "Do you handle their network security too?"

"Uh-uh. We're more into the hardware side of things."

"Okay. One last question. When will the new software be active here?"

"It's loaded now. Once the park closes, we'll switch over."

She shook his hand. "Thank you, Mr. Marshall. You've been very helpful."

"Steve," he said. "Any time."

She retraced her path to Sanchez's office. The door was open and he sat behind his desk shuffling through a pile of folders. She cleared her throat and he looked up.

"Get what you needed?" he asked.

"A few answers and more questions. Mind if I close the door?"

"Not at all. Have a seat."

"Thanks." She pulled the chair closer to his desk before sitting. "Mr. Marshall said the camera system sent you an email whenever there was a problem. I wonder if I could get copies of those?"

"Sure. I can send them over later today." He scribbled on a Post-it note and smacked it on his monitor.

"Also, what would you say if I asked you to hold off switching to the new software?"

He rested one arm across his belly and used it to support the other while planting his chin in his palm. His gaze fixed on her for a long moment. "You want to see if the problem continues. If it doesn't, you can assume there's some link to the young man's death. But if the trouble persists, the two aren't connected." He paused. "Unless someone at Cannonball, me for example, is involved, in which case that person would continue to create the issue with the cameras so you couldn't make the connection."

She crossed her legs and smiled. "But . . ."

"But you would know that I know that you know that, so even if the problem kept occurring, you could assume I, or someone at the park, is continuing to manipulate the cameras in order to hide our involvement from you. I think." He pointed at her. "No matter what I do, you can't rule out my participation. So why stop the software upgrade?"

Good answer. "Eh, you're right. No point in holding off."

He clasped his hands on his desk. "Was that a test, Detective?"

"Just thinking out loud. No camera issues occurred after Zachary Coleman's death. Mr. Marshall said that's the longest gap since the problems started. If someone at Cannonball was involved, they wouldn't have made it so obvious. The outages would have continued for a while."

"Unless I knew that you knew that I knew—"

"Stop." She massaged her temples. Sanchez was too smart to be involved with the death. No way he'd have done it at the water park. Didn't mean he couldn't be active in some sort of cover-up, but she'd address that later if the evidence pointed that direction. Now she needed something, anything, to move her forward.

"Who handles your network security?" she asked. "An employee or, let me guess, an outside company?"

"We're an entertainment venue. Very little of our business, other than marketing, takes place online. All the attractions, shops, rides, everything is computerized. We have a tech support staff that handles all of that, including administering our network security both internally and externally."

She nodded. "Would they have the skills to dig deep into the system and identify any intrusions that weren't detected by the security software?"

Creases lined his forehead. "You think we've been hacked?"

"I think it's an option worth considering."

"If someone was after our data, why bother with anything else? That's a lot of trouble to go to just to manipulate a few cameras, isn't it? Easier to commit the crime some other place. And it went on for a month. You telling me they planned that far ahead to kill him and this was the best way they could figure out to do it?" He shook his head. "Doesn't make any sense."

Couldn't argue with that. But unless a person at Cannonball was tied to Coleman's death, or involved in a conspiracy to hide the details, then it had to be an outsider. "I think you'd agree the malfunctioning cameras are too convenient to not be part of the murder, which means remote access, either from someone at Mr. Marshall's company or the internet at large."

Sanchez held up a finger. "You said murder. Are you convinced of that? I understand I am not privy to your investigation, but if you are certain a serious crime was committed on Cannonball property, I must inform others so they can prepare to deal with the press."

She smiled again. "I'm quite certain you've already made the appropriate personnel aware, just in case. Oh, and Mr. Marshall said he could pull the dates and times on the camera outages. Would you be able to cross-reference that information with the time of the boy's death so we could see which ones were turned off?"

"I'll plot them on a park map and send them over," he said. "I would also be willing to bring someone in to check our network security logs and do whatever it is they do to find out if we've been hacked. In return, I would ask that if you determine the death was a homicide, you notify me before releasing that information to others."

"I have to tell the family first."

"Of course. And I would expect to be next on the list." He leaned forward until his stomach touched the desk and lowered his voice. "As soon as you leave their home. Before they have time to get the word out and the media catches wind."

"I can make that happen," she said. "Even ensure the press release mentions how cooperative Cannonball's security department was in the investigation."

He stood and shook her hand. "Have a nice day, Detective. I'll be in touch."

"Soon?"

"I hope so. I want this resolved as much as you do."

Doubtful. He wanted to know the extent of the park's liability and how that might play out. Nothing wrong with that. Part of his job. What he was paid to do.

But wanting answers as bad as she did? Uh-uh. He wanted to protect people.

She wanted to nail them to the wall.

14 **By the time Amara** arrived back at the office, most of the detectives were wrapping up their day. She brushed crumbs off the seat of the folding chair and settled at the card table. She needed to find the details on Haley Bricker's truck and track down addresses for Matias Lucero and Liam Walker. That would give her plenty to start with tomorrow. And with two days to go until her mother's scan, staying busy was critical. The only way to keep the worries at bay were the distractions.

She squeezed her eyes shut. Poor choice of words. Zachary Coleman was not a distraction.

She jerked as a hand touched her shoulder.

"Whoa there," Starsky said. "Didn't mean to scare you."

Her heart pounded and she swiveled around. "You're lucky I didn't go into attack mode."

"Oh yeah. I know about your workouts. Catlike reflexes and all that. No way I'm fooling around with you."

She cocked her head as his face turned from its normal paleness to a bright red. "Good info to have," she said.

"That's not what I meant and you know it."

She tightened the screws. "So you *will* fool around with me?"

He swallowed hard and glanced away. "I'll stop digging now, thank you. Just wanted to see how your day went."

"Eh, okay. Yours?"

He continued to gaze into the distance. "Nothing major. Getting ready to head out. You want to grab a bite to eat?"

"Thanks, but I don't think so. Want to get caught up on a few things and lay out my schedule for tomorrow."

"Sure." He shuffled his feet and met her eyes. "If you need to talk about your mother, or the case, or anything, let me know. I'm a decent listener."

Warmth spread through her chest and she gave him a thumbs-up. "Will do."

"Her scan still set for Thursday?"

"Last I heard. I don't expect we'll have the results for several days."

He cleared his throat and licked his lips. "I don't want to stick my nose where it doesn't belong, but will you, um, I mean, once you hear . . ."

"Of course," she said. "It'd be a good time to talk to a friend."

He placed a hand on his chest and opened his eyes wide. "I meant *me.*"

She chuckled and turned back to her laptop. "*Idiota.* Now go away and let me do some work."

She looked over her shoulder to watch him leave, then began researching Haley Bricker's truck. The DMV's database gave her the details. New model purchased fourteen months ago. No record of any violations and the registration was up-to-date. The title had always been in Haley's name. Whoever bought it had paid in full.

She ran her finger down the screen until she found the dealer's name and address. They'd be open for another couple of hours tonight, giving her time to swing by on the drive home. She didn't even have to see the paperwork. Who bought the truck, how much did it cost, and how did they pay? A flick of her badge should be enough to get the information she needed unless the business manager wanted to be a pain.

Next was finding addresses for the two other friends. By now,

Haley had no doubt filled the boys in on her visit. If they were involved, they'd certainly had time to get their stories straight.

Matias Lucero was up first. The DMV listed seven people with variations of that name in the San Antonio area. She reviewed the driver's license photo for each until she found the match for one of the boys in the video from the water park. Hispanic, dark hair cut short, and glasses. Five foot ten, weight one-seventy. She snapped a picture of the screen before typing *Liam Walker* in the search bar.

Three people by that name had a driver's license in Texas, but only one lived nearby. His photo matched the other boy in the video. Caucasian, shaggy blond hair, pointy nose. Six feet even, weight one-forty-five. Acne marks covering his face. His address was the closest to her apartment, so she'd go by there first tomorrow morning. She took a picture of the screen and checked the time.

No rush to get to the car dealer as long as she caught them before they closed. And no hurry to go home and be alone—Larry the lizard didn't count, not that she'd ever tell him that—with her thoughts.

She loaded the recordings from the Cannonball again and fast-forwarded to the final few minutes where Zachary was pulled from the water. Something about the scene nagged at her. Two park personnel stood beside the body while a third administered CPR. Within a minute, people packed the camera's view, trying to get a look at whatever was happening.

Several seconds later, Haley appeared on the right side of the screen and edged through the crowd to Liam and Matias, still thirty feet from Zachary's body. The three weren't trying to get closer to their friend. Why not? The natural assumption would be drowning or heatstroke or passed out from alcohol. No reason to hang back and act like you don't know the victim. Murder would be the last thing on their minds. Unless they knew otherwise.

Haley rocked on her heels and was breathing rapidly while Liam talked to her and gestured toward Zachary. Matias bounced on his toes and scanned the crowd. Who was he looking for? Paramedics? A killer?

Haley was shaking now. She turned from Liam and moved into the crowd, away from the body. Matias grabbed her arm and whispered something. The three maneuvered through the throng and stopped on the fringe to watch the park attendant try to revive the boy.

A medical team arrived and took over the CPR. By now, it was clear that Zachary Coleman was dead, but they continued working as the body was strapped onto a gurney and rolled to a waiting ambulance.

The video ended and she clasped her hands behind her neck. Odd that Eduardo Sanchez wasn't anywhere at the scene. Why wouldn't the park's head of security be there? Could be he was off that day. Or everything happened so fast it was over before he arrived. She made a mental note to follow up.

And the three friends. Their actions had been off, but people reacted differently to tragedies. You couldn't read too much into how someone responded to death.

She reversed the video. Who or what was Matias looking for? He ran his hands through his hair and spun in a slow circle, searching in every direction. When a young girl bumped into him from behind, he jerked and twisted to face her.

She paused the recording and zoomed in on his face. The blurry image didn't seem to show a kid who was worried about his friend. He wasn't grieving or upset. His eyes were wide and his mouth hung open. She tapped his face.

Matias was staring straight at Haley and Liam.

And he was terrified.

15 Amara kicked off the covers and flipped onto her back. Eleven p.m. and no real sleep. So much for going to bed early so she could hit the gym before it got crowded tomorrow. There were gaps in her thoughts, so she must have dozed at some point, but here she was again. Staring at the tiny blinking green light on the smoke detector on the ceiling.

Her mind refused to quiet and flopped between worrying about Mama and thinking about the Coleman case and remembering Daddy. Her father died in a car crash nearly seventeen years ago, and the pain remained. Not always. Not even often. But still there. She visited his grave around the eighteenth of every month to rest and remember.

Mama had been strong, but she'd always been better at hiding her emotions than Amara. And now that Wylie was becoming a fixture in her life, she seemed happier than she'd been in a long time. Cancer could change everything. The waiting for the scan and diagnosis and treatment plan meant tonight's lack of sleep was the new normal.

She blinked her eyes in time with the flashing of the smoke detector light. Fixating on work was at least productive. The car dealer confirmed her suspicion that Haley's vehicle had been paid in full when purchased. Thirty-six thousand dollars and some change. The business manager wouldn't provide any other details, but Amara didn't need them.

Zachary Coleman had loads of cash hidden under his floor.

Haley Bricker had enough money to buy herself that truck. No doubt the two other friends had their fair shares as well. Whatever the four of them were doing was lucrative and apparently dangerous. Nothing else in Zachary's life pointed to him becoming a murder victim.

The question was whether one of the three killed him, and why. Certainly not for his money. No evidence anyone went looking for the hidden cash. Had to be for something he knew, or something he did or didn't do. She squeezed her eyes shut. *Way to narrow it down, Amara.*

The scene at the water park played through her mind. Of the three kids, Liam seemed the calmest. Did that mean anything? And Haley obviously wanted to get as far away from the body as possible. Why? Wasn't she concerned about her friend? And then there was Matias. The kid looked scared out of his wits, the way he jerked around as he checked the crowd. He wasn't looking for help. He was watching his back.

She'd planned to go to Liam's house first, but Matias was the better option. Fear could be an excellent motivation to talk, as long as he believed he could help himself by doing so. He'd have to reach the tipping point first. That place where his desire to improve his own situation outweighed his concerns about what his compadres might think. Or do.

She pulled the sheets back up and shoved another pillow under her head. Maybe that's what got Zachary killed. He wanted to talk. If so, his death served as a strong message to the others. One they wouldn't be likely to ignore.

Frustration amped her heart rate and her limbs itched to do something productive. Not likely at this time of night. Somehow she needed to pass that information along to her brain so it'd shut down. Turning on the TV might divert her focus, especially if she watched one of those British detective shows on Netflix. They were mostly entertaining, albeit a bit slow for her taste. And she was convinced the most dangerous places in the world were the small towns in England where these detectives worked. Their murder rates had to be off the charts.

She opened her personal laptop, browsed for a show, then clicked the button to send it to her TV. Halfway through an episode of *Father Brown* that she thought she'd seen before, but only remembered as events transpired, her cell rang and vibrated on the nightstand beside her. Fifteen minutes until midnight. She clutched the device and checked the caller ID. Area code 210, so it was local, but not a number either she or her phone recognized.

She pondered whether or not to answer, decided she was awake anyway, muted the TV, and coughed to clear her throat. "Hello?"

"Hello, Detective."

Sounded like a male voice, but not positive. A tad high-pitched with a bit of static interference. "Who is this?" she asked.

"No one you know."

She paused the TV and sat upright. "I'm hanging up if you don't tell me who you are."

"You don't want to do that."

She disconnected the call, pulled her Glock from the holster attached to her mattress, and grabbed her laptop. The phone rang again and she pushed the button to block all calls from that number. Before she could type the digits into search, the cell buzzed again, this time with a different number.

She inhaled deeply and answered. "Yes?"

"We can do this all night if you'd like," the voice said.

"Who are you?"

"Is that how the police work? Ask the same question over and over despite knowing they're not going to get an answer?"

She gritted her teeth. "What do you want?"

"See? Was that difficult? What I want, Amara, is to—where are my manners? May I call you Amara?"

"No."

"Rude. Whatever. What I want, Detective, is to express my sympathy. I know how difficult times like this can be."

She squeezed the phone. "I have no idea what you're talking about."

"Of course you don't." The voice chuckled. "That's the whole idea, isn't it?"

"I'm getting tired of your game. Get to the point or I'm turning off the cell."

He sighed. "Very well. I simply wanted to say that I hope your mother is able to beat her cancer. Terrible disease, but she's fortunate to catch it before it gets into her organs."

A shock bolted through her. Who was this and how did they know about Mama? She closed her mouth and breathed through her nose to slow her pulse. "How do you know my mother?"

"I don't. But I do know she had a PET scan today, and the results, well, when her doctor sees them tomorrow morning, I imagine he'll be contacting her right away. The image from the radiologist had several splotchy areas." He paused. "I really do hope her treatments work."

She kicked off the sheet again and pivoted so her feet were on the floor. Mama's scan wasn't for two more days. Or so she'd said. "Listen, I don't know what you think you're doing, but you're dead wrong. I suggest you—"

"One thing I am not," the voice said, "is wrong. Call your mother. Ask if she had her scan. See if her doctor phones in the morning. I promise you, Detective. I am not wrong."

Suspects flashed through her mind. The techs at the hospital.

Whoever transferred the results to the doctor. But why? First thing was to call Mama and find out if she did have the scan done. "You never answered my question. What do you want? I mean *really* want."

"To prove that I can do what I say. That's all."

"And what is it that you do?"

The voice chuckled again. "Good night, Detective. Oh, and at the risk of spoiling things, I bet Father Brown catches the murderer."

16 **Amara's fingers tingled** as adrenaline flooded her system. The call disconnected and she dropped the phone. He knew what she was watching on TV. How? She snatched her gun and rolled out the opposite side of the bed, away from the open door, and went into a shooting stance. She kept her back toward the wall, edged sideways, and maintained her focus on the hallway.

The closet was just ahead on the same wall, and she slid the door open. The ambient light from the TV confirmed no one was hiding there. Her flashlight remained atop the nightstand. Too late now. She moved around the corner, paused to steady her breathing, and reached over to turn off *Father Brown*. The only sound was a low hum from Larry's room. His heater must have kicked on.

She continued her movement toward the open door, careful to limit her exposure. The TV ruined her night vision, but the LED night-light in the bathroom provided enough coverage for her to see into the area. She leaned to her right to peer into the hall and took a small sidestep. Nothing. She repeated the process until she'd completed a counterclockwise semicircle viewing arc. The space was clear.

She moved out of the bedroom and flattened her back against the wall, sidled toward the bathroom, cleared it, and continued down the hall. Time crawled as she crept through the rest of the apartment and verified no one was there except her and Larry. The doors remained locked and chained. From all indications, the caller had never been inside.

She grabbed a drink from the refrigerator, retrieved her phone from the bedroom, and plopped onto the sofa in the living room. With the Glock beside her, she popped open the can, took a swig, then dialed Starsky. He answered on the third ring.

"You up?" she asked.

"Yeah." His scratchy voice and sniffling said otherwise. "What's going on?"

"How soon can you get to my place?"

Several moments of silence followed. "Um, is this a butt dial?"

"What?"

"You know, like when someone calls and is like, hey, come on over and let's, uh, hang out for a while. Or something."

She sighed and shook her head. "First, you're talking about a booty call, not a butt dial. Second, nobody says that anymore. It's Netflix and chill now. And third, no, this absolutely is *not* that."

"Oh. Then what's going on?"

"I've got a problem," she said. She stretched her legs and twisted her head left-right as the adrenaline wore down. "Someone called a few minutes ago. He knew things he shouldn't have. At least I think he does. I need to call Mama to confirm."

His voice sharpened. "Amara, what happened?"

"Get here quick as you can, okay? Call me when you're approaching my door so I'll know it's you."

"Want me to send a patrol car? They can be there sooner than me."

"No. I'm safe, but I'm not sure what's going on. Whatever it is, I don't like it."

A loud clunk sounded through the phone. "Sorry," he said. "Dropped it while I was getting dressed. Heading out the door in about thirty seconds. No jokes about how I look when I get there."

"No problem. I'm not in much of a joking mood."

"Understood. You protected?"

She moved the Glock to her lap and rested her hand on it. "Fifteen in the magazine, one in the chamber. Anyone besides you who comes through that door is gonna have a very bad night."

* * *

Starsky made the twenty-minute drive to her apartment in barely over ten. Once there, he insisted they clear the rooms again before talking. Afterward, he checked all the windows and doors, then joined her in the living room.

"Need a drink?" she asked.

He sat on the edge of the recliner, his weapon still in hand. "No. Tell me what's going on."

She stared at his face. Normally jovial, or at least relaxed, his expression was tight. Eyes narrowed and scanning the room constantly, rapid breathing, splotches of redness across his cheeks. Anger. Because she was in danger. "I got a phone call," she said.

They spent the next half hour discussing the call. He recorded the conversation and interrogated her several times to ensure they covered everything. Toward the end, he asked the two questions she'd fixated on. Did she have any idea who might do this, and was the information about her mother correct?

"I've thought about who it might be," she said. "It could be someone I know. I think the voice was altered so I couldn't recognize it."

"Doesn't mean you know them."

"No, it doesn't. The way I see it, there are two options. This has something to do with the Zachary Coleman case, or someone involved with Cotulla is looking for payback." She brushed a strand of hair out of her face. "But I don't think it's Cotulla. Too coincidental for that to pop up at exactly the same time the Coleman investigation is getting serious. Plus, I'm out of the loop on that whole deal and it seems odd that they'd come after me for some revenge thing. Nothing to gain by it."

"Agreed," he said. "What about your mother?"

"It's the middle of the night. We can wait until morning."

He raised his eyebrows. "You sure?"

"Yeah, but I'm not going to be able to sleep. How did they know what I was watching? Might be a camera, microphone, or something hidden in my bedroom. I'm guessing not, but I'd feel better if we searched."

He stood and stretched. "What's your theory?"

"Has to be the network. It's the only way."

"The network? You mean the internet?"

"Uh-huh. I'm no expert, but if he hacked into my router, he'd be able to see what I was doing. I think. Possibly even access my personal laptop and read my emails."

He nodded. "We'll search your bedroom, but I'm far more interested in the *why* than the *how*. If this is somehow linked to the Coleman case, what does our anonymous caller gain by doing this?"

She gripped her weapon and stood. "He proves he can get to me."

17 **Starsky and Amara spent** over an hour inspecting her bedroom for any sign of hidden electronic devices without success. When they'd finished, she retrieved a roll of masking tape from the junk drawer in the kitchen and ripped off a piece to cover the camera on her laptop.

She sat on the edge of the bed, loosed a yawn, and typed on her computer. "Changing my Wi-Fi and laptop passwords."

"We could have someone from the department come in and check the place again," he said. "Better yet, the FBI owes you some favors, I'm sure. Have one of their people come scan the apartment. They can go over your network too."

She shook her head. "Not yet. I need more proof first. There's a thread here, and if I pull too hard, it will break."

"This guy, whoever he is, threatened you and—"

"No," she said. "No threats. More of a show of power. I'm willing to play along for a while. See what I can learn about him. If it gets too volatile, I'll get others involved."

"Promise?"

"Promise. But if what I'm thinking is correct, I'm dealing with kids here."

"Yeah? From your investigation?"

She nodded. "Teenagers."

"Teenagers who may have killed their friend." He leaned against the wall. "Can we go to the living room? Nowhere to sit in here, and I wouldn't mind checking out the contents of your fridge."

She glanced up from her laptop. *He doesn't want to sit on the bed.* "Tell you what. Let's go get some breakfast. My treat."

"Waffle House? I'm in."

"Nah. Breakfast Bodega. I know one of the managers there."

"Not even two a.m. yet. They open all night?"

"Yep, starting a couple of weeks ago." She grinned. "And Ronnie—that's the manager—is absolutely thrilled about working third shift."

Starsky's stomach rumbled and he gestured down the hall. "Lead the way. You can fill me in on your investigation on the drive over. But when breakfast is done, you know what you have to do."

She closed her computer and rubbed her hand over the warm metallic case. "Call Mama? No way. Not until later in the morning."

"You need to know." He rubbed his eyes and scratched his forehead. "Investigations don't have a schedule. They have an on button and an off button. That's it."

"We'll see. Breakfast first, okay?"

He moved into the hall. "Try to keep up."

■ ■ ■

Starsky poured hot sauce over his three-egg Western omelet, diced it faster than a Benihana chef, and scooped a heap into his mouth. "Delicious."

"Good," Amara said. She nibbled at her fruit plate, then used her fork to point at the rest of his food. "Told you the pancakes were huge."

"Should've got the big stack. And the hash browns."

She sipped her coffee and took another bite of cantaloupe. The Breakfast Bodega was nearly empty. Two guys sat at a table on the opposite side of the restaurant, pecking at their phones and their food. The lone waitress-slash-cook was nowhere to be seen, and

Ronnie had scurried off to the office in the back to, as he'd put it, "try to figure out what sort of owner thinks it's a good idea to stay open all night and let who knows what kind of lowlifes creep in from the dark. No offense."

She downed the last of her coffee. "So Zachary Coleman was into something. Whatever it was, it was online and generated serious money. I'm sure his friends are into it too."

Starsky dabbed at the corners of his mouth with a napkin. "What's the connection to the water park?"

"Don't know yet, but I'm willing to bet they find out they've been hacked."

"Question. Remember you're talking to a non-techie here. If someone did break into the Cannonball's network, would their security be able to tell why? What they were after?"

She pushed her plate away. "Great question. I have no idea." She slid out of the booth. "Need more coffee?"

"Sure. And if you spot the cook, can you have her throw on some hash browns? Grilled on both sides with onions. Please."

"I'm gonna have to take out a loan to pay for your breakfast." She wandered to the kitchen, placed the order with the barely awake cook, and grabbed the coffeepot. She refilled both cups and walked over to the other two customers and topped off theirs. They grunted their thanks without looking up, and she slid the pot back on the burner before sitting again.

"How long you going to wait?" Starsky asked.

She wanted to call Mama to find out if she'd had the scan yet but doing so would verify the caller's information. Info she didn't want confirmed. Plus, it was still the middle of the night. A call at this hour would frighten her mother half to death. *Several splotchy areas.* That's what he'd said. Yes, Mama had cancer, but how bad? What did that mean? And what would she say if she called her mother? *Did you already have your scan? Yes? Okay. Your doctor may be calling. If he does, let me know immediately.* No way to say those things without scaring her. And even if she only asked about having the scan done, Mama would want to know how she knew that.

"You there?" Starsky asked. "How long are you going to wait to call her?"

"I'm not calling her."

He laid his fork on the plate. "Amara, you have to know."

"I'm calling Wylie. He'll know." She searched the phone's contact list and pressed his number. After four rings, the call went to voice mail. "Wylie, this is Amara. Have to talk to you when you get a chance."

The phone beeped to signal an incoming call. Wylie.

She switched over to him. "Sorry," she said. "Didn't mean to wake you."

"Huh?" He sounded like his mouth was filled with cotton. "It's, uh, three in the morning. What did you think I'd be doing?"

"Sleeping. I need to ask you something. Promise me you'll be honest."

An exuberant yawn was followed by a few sniffles and a cough. "No."

"No what?"

"No, I won't promise anything until I know what you want. I'm retired now. Re. Tired. Emphasis on *tired*."

"This has nothing to do with police business. At least not directly."

"Hmm." He released a long sigh. A gurgle echoed and crescendoed in a loud *whoosh*.

"Wylie," she said, "please tell me I didn't just hear a toilet flush."

"You wake me in the middle of the night and complain because I used the opportunity to take care of pressing matters?"

"Fine. Listen, one question and I'll let you go back to bed." She flexed the fingers of her free hand. "Did Mama have her PET scan yesterday?"

"I can't answer that question."

She rested her forehead in her palm. "You can't answer it because you don't know or you can't answer it because she made you promise not to tell?"

"Yes."

"Wylie, this is important."

"So is keeping a promise."

"Enough said." Mama made him promise, which meant he knew, which meant she had her scan. Otherwise there'd have been nothing for him to keep his mouth shut about. And if the caller was right about this much, they were probably correct about the results too. Her heart plummeted to her stomach. Mama was sick. Very sick.

"Wylie," she said, "I'm going to ask you to do something for me. Please don't question why, okay?"

He cleared his throat. "Amara, what's going on? How did you know about the scan?"

"It doesn't matter. Listen, I'm not sure what you've got planned for today, but would you be able to hang out with Mama? Find some excuse to be with her?"

His voice took on a new intensity. "Is she in danger?"

Not the kind you think. "Nothing like that. I don't want her to be alone. Not today. And don't tell her we talked."

"Should I go now?"

"No," she said. "Let her sleep. Head over after breakfast."

"Amara, I need to know what's going on. You can't put all this out there and expect me to sit here and do nothing."

"If I'm right, she's about to have a rough day. I can't tell you why, but I can say there's nothing you can do about it except be there with her."

"And if you're wrong?"

She tilted her head to stretch her neck muscles. "No one will be happier than me."

Starsky peered at her, his eyes watery and wide. He knew as well as she did.

She wasn't wrong.

Mama's cancer was bad.

And someone used that information to prove a point to her. Her pulse quickened and she stood and dropped a pair of twenties on the table. "Wylie, you'll know when to get in touch with me." She disconnected the call and motioned to Starsky. "Let's get out of here."

The waitress moseyed from the kitchen with a plate of hash browns in her hand. "You want me to . . ."

Amara was out the door before the woman finished her sentence.

Three a.m. or not, it was time to go to work.

18

Starsky dropped Amara at her apartment and checked the place again for any sign of intruders. Once he was satisfied, he waited outside until she clicked her deadbolt.

"I'm heading out," he said. "Keep your phone and gun nearby."

She rested her palm against the door. "Will do. Go get a shower. Please."

She hurried through her morning routine, opting not to wait for the hot water to wind its way to her bathroom. Saved a few minutes at the cost of around half her body temperature, it seemed. After checking on Larry and apologizing for spending so little time with him lately, an apology he appeared not to accept, she hustled to her car and sped to the office.

The few detectives there that early mumbled their greetings, and she used her forearm to clear a swath through the crumbs on her card table desk, then plugged in her laptop.

"Alvarez. You want coffee?"

She smiled and turned to face Starsky. "How old is it?"

"Made it fresh about twenty minutes ago."

He'd beaten her here? "Half a cup. Thanks."

He grabbed a chair and headed her way with the drinks. "Mind if I join you?"

Both sat and she logged into the PD network. "You didn't go by your apartment, did you?" she asked.

"No need. Showered a few days ago. A little deodorant and I'm good."

"So you say." She sipped the coffee and let it sit on her tongue for a moment before swallowing. "Starsky, I appreciate your help last night. I do. But I'm okay. I can handle the case."

He shrugged. "Never thought you couldn't."

"I guess what I mean is, well, I want to do this by myself."

"No problem there. We've all got enough of our own work." He glanced around the room and lowered his voice. "I'm not saying this is happening, but don't let your pride get in the way of the investigation."

She opened her mouth to protest, but he held up his hand.

"Not accusing," he said. "If you need help, ask for it. And tell the LT about the call."

Lieutenant Segura could decide the case had become too personal. He might assign someone else to take over. "I'll think about it," she said.

"No. You tell him or I will. And before you say anything, I'd do the same for any other detective. Things that could affect the prosecution of a suspect need to be out in the open as soon as you know. It has to be that way."

"What if he pulls me off the investigation?"

"He'll do whatever he thinks is best. Not for you, for the case. That's his job, and like him or not, he's good at it."

She crossed her arms across her chest and frowned. "Fine."

He nodded and stood. "What's your plan?"

"Track down the two boys and—"

"Not what I meant. About your mother."

What could she possibly plan? "Wait. Pray. Cry. All of the above. Until I know for sure how bad things are and what treatments are available, I can't do anything else except stay busy."

He stared at the floor. "I'm sorry about all this, Amara."

She reached over and placed her hand on top of his. "I know you are. But Mama's strong. She'll get through this."

He wandered off and she stared at her reflection in the laptop screen. *Mama is strong. She'll beat the cancer. Fight through it and come out a survivor.*

But the truth was a lot of people didn't beat it. Not because they weren't strong or didn't try hard enough or any reason other than cancer was a disease and people died from diseases. Even strong people.

She shook her head violently to chase away the thoughts. All she could do was all she could do. And until she had more details, sitting around fretting about what might happen didn't accomplish anything. She resisted the urge to search for *cancer treatments* and instead opened the Zachary Coleman files.

Still two hours or so before the LT would arrive at work. Enough time to begin piecing together her notes into something resembling a theory. The call from last night would have to be included, but she'd play down the personal factor. Stress to Lieutenant Segura the caller wasn't threatening anyone, merely proving his point that he had access to data that was supposed to be secure.

What were they—Sanchez or the three friends or whoever—doing with that knowledge? So what if you could control the camera system at the Cannonball? Seemed like an extravagant waste of time and energy if the only goal was to hide your tracks when you killed someone. Far easier to take them out to a field somewhere and leave them where they'd never be found.

Unless Coleman's death really was a message to the others. One that said there was no place safe. The murderer had taken huge risks by doing it in such a public location, cameras or not. There had to be an easier way to accomplish the same goal.

A notification popped up in the bottom right corner of her display and alerted her to a new email. She clicked over and reviewed her inbox. Starsky had sent over the recording from earlier this morning when she'd recounted the phone call. It'd have to be typed up and included as part of the case file.

Segura would want the crime lab to dump the data from her cell and take a look at it, but that would be futile. The caller wasn't stupid. The LT might even want someone to go to her apartment and review her network configuration or check again for hidden electronics. If he did, she'd let them, but they wouldn't find anything.

The guy was smart. Too smart to leave an obvious trail. If he'd broken into her network, finding his footprints would take more than a quick once-over by the PD's IT gurus.

She plugged in her earbuds, closed her eyes, and counted her breaths. Silence crept through her brain and she pictured herself going through her close-combat workout routine. Each punch chased and scattered thoughts into a corner. Every kick brought clarity. Her muscles begged for the reality of the Muay Thai bag's worn leather surface.

The caller had seemed older. His words and mannerisms spoke of an adult. A professional. Sanchez?

Her right shoulder twitched as she visualized two quick jabs to the bag.

Not one of the teenagers. Probably. Couldn't rule them out. Either way, they were involved. They knew something.

She tightened her left gluteal muscles as she followed up the punches with an imaginary roundhouse kick.

Zach and Haley had stacks of money. Liam and Matias most likely did too. The source of the cash was illegal and online.

Her torso swiveled as a left jab led to a knee strike and a right uppercut.

A boy was dead. He must have been a threat to someone. If she applied pressure to the other three friends, would it put them in danger? And the biggest question of all. Was the caller Zachary Coleman's killer?

She opened her eyes, unclenched her jaw, and sighed. Imaginary workouts sucked. No sweat, no exertion, no pain. None of the distractions that truly allowed her to escape from the world. A couple of hours was plenty of time to hit the gym, pummel the bag, and return to the station before the LT arrived.

She drummed her fingers on the table. It was also enough time to get ahead of her paperwork, type up the transcript of Starsky's recording, and lay out her day.

Priorities.

She stretched her arms high overhead and lifted her straightened legs off the floor for a thirty-count, then clicked the play button on the audio file.

● ● ●

Lieutenant Segura arrived on schedule and Amara hurried into his office before he had a chance to start his paperwork-signing ritual.

"Morning, sir," she said. "I need to advise you of a situation that's come up in the Coleman case."

He loosened his tie, unbuttoned the top collar of his shirt, sat, and surveyed his desktop. "Go ahead."

"Last night I received a phone call from someone claiming to have, um, personal information about a member of my family."

His face tilted upward. "Personal information?"

"The caller claimed he had the details of my mother's medical situation. Details that she doesn't even have yet."

"And did he?"

"Don't know. I should be able to verify later this morning. He also knew what I was watching on TV when he called."

Segura leaned back in his chair. "Maybe he heard it through the phone?"

She shook her head. "TV was muted."

"And you think there's a connection between this call and your investigation?"

She chose her words carefully. "I think that's a possibility, but I can't be certain. My prior involvement in Cotulla could be a motive as well. And there's also the chance this was nothing more than a prank call."

"Were you threatened?"

"Not directly, no, sir."

He opened his desk drawer, pulled out today's cigar, and jammed it in his mouth. "That's a *yes* then."

This conversation was not going as planned. "Honestly, sir, it was more of an informational call. Something to show he could do what he said. I, um, I never felt like there was any real danger to me." She held her chin high and maintained eye contact, hoping he believed her lie.

"Want the techs to look at your phone? Might be able to track the origin of the call if nothing else."

She shook her head. "Not yet. I didn't get the impression this guy would make such an obvious mistake. He hid the number, so I'm certain he knows how to protect his location too."

"Maybe. Any chance your work laptop was compromised?"

"I didn't even have it turned on when the call came in. But I have used it at home before, always with the VPN on."

Segura grunted and worked the cigar side to side in his mouth. "Stop by IT and swap yours out for a new computer. Tell them your old one might have been attacked and to tag it in case we need to check it later. You don't leave the office until I see the report, got it? And whatever this situation is with your mother, if there is a connection to the investigation, you're to inform me immediately. Failure to do so would not be a good career move, understood?"

"Yes, sir. As of now, I believe the connection to be nothing more than ancillary. If there's more to it than that, you'll know about it."

He dragged the stack of unsigned paperwork in front of him and clicked his pen. She leaned forward in an attempt to see if the requisition for her desk had made it to the top of the pile again.

"Something else, Detective?"

"No, sir. Have a good day."

Amara checked the car's clock as she pulled to a stop in front of Matias Lucero's home. 9:14. A later start than she wanted, but swapping out her laptop plus typing up the report for the LT, which included a transcript of her late-night interview with Starsky, took a while. She'd hustled out of the office after laying the file on Segura's desk. Once he discovered Starsky had come over, that might open a whole new can of worms. Best case was the LT would realize she felt at least a little threatened and want more details. Worst case was he'd pull her off the investigation. No point in rolling the dice before she had to. Give him time to review the report and move on to something else.

She stepped out of her car and strode along the walkway leading to the two-story brick-and-vinyl home. This neighborhood had their driveways at the back of the houses, and she'd cruised through the alley first and confirmed a single vehicle was parked there. An older model Prius, nothing extravagant like Haley's monster truck. No guarantee the small car belonged to Matias, but at this time on a Wednesday morning, most adults would be at work. Most teenagers, especially a soon-to-be senior in high school, would still be in bed.

She banged on the door and pressed the bell several times. Down the street, a landscaping crew unloaded their mower, Weed eaters, and blower. Four guys swarmed the postage-stamp yard. Couldn't be more than a ten-minute job. Fifteen tops.

The deadbolt clicked and a groggy face leaned around the door.

Matias Lucero looking like he'd either just rolled out of bed or decided to skip sleeping altogether. The kid's license had said he was five ten. On tiptoes maybe, but she wasn't one to talk.

"Yes?" he said.

She showed her identification. "Detective Amara Alvarez. I wonder if I could ask you a few questions?"

"About Zachary?"

Haley must have told him. "Yes. I'm trying to finalize a few things."

He pulled the door open and yawned. "Sure. Come on in."

"Thanks." She tapped her elbow on her weapon to ensure it was in the hip holster. There'd never been an occasion when it wasn't, but she'd developed the habit long ago. One she had no intention of trying to break. "Lead the way."

He plodded into the living room, his bare feet slapping the hardwood floor, and slumped onto the sofa. An empty bag of chips and a couple of soda cans sat beside him on a table, with a blanket shoved to the far end against a few throw pillows. Someone spent a late night there. Maybe calling her apartment.

She sat on the edge of a leather high-back chair and opened her notepad. "Can you tell me how you and Zachary knew each other?"

"Same way we all did. Through video games. Haley told you yesterday."

Wonderful. Not surprising that Haley called him, but it certainly made things more difficult. She maintained an even expression. *Let's see how he deals with pressure.* "Got it. Were you with Zachary when he was murdered?"

His hands vibrated on his thighs and he glanced around the room. "Murdered? Who said he was—"

"Spare me the drama," she said. "You and I both know someone killed Zachary, and I'm going to find that person. You and

Haley and Liam can rehearse your stories all you want. I don't care. Know why? Because you're wasting your time. One of you will break. Guaranteed. That little seed of doubt that's festering in the back of your brain there. The idea that someone could cut a deal or conspire against you or, I don't know, see that you end up like Zachary. Your friends have the same thoughts. That seed will grow until one of you can't take it anymore. And when it does, that person will be beating on my door to talk."

He stared at her for a moment. "Are you finished? I have no idea what you're talking about. As far as I know, Zach died of heatstroke or alcohol. End of story."

"You're seventeen. A minor. You and Liam both. No guarantee you won't be tried as an adult though. Think about that. A little bit of cooperation can make a huge difference when the DA's deciding what to do. Unfortunately for you, it works both ways. Refuse to share what you know, hide things from the police, not gonna look good. Not to the DA, the judge, or a Texas jury."

"I can't tell you what I don't know."

"Yeah? What *can* you tell me then?"

He rubbed his eyes. "Aren't you supposed to tell me I need a lawyer or something?"

"You're not under arrest. What was in the water bottles? The ones you carried into the park the day Zachary died."

"Water."

She flipped her notepad shut. "Fair enough. I won't take up any more of your time." She stood and headed for the front door.

Matias scooted off the sofa and trailed behind her. "You going to see Liam next?" he asked.

"So now you get to ask questions?" She turned to face him. "I'll see Liam soon enough. Whatever this is you three have, it's not falling apart."

He swallowed but remained silent.

"Want to know why it's not falling apart? Because it's not getting a chance to. I'm ripping it down, and when I do, you'll wish you'd talked to me this morning. Murder doesn't ever go away." She cocked her head and smiled. "Neither do I."

The boy shifted his stance and leaned against the wall, doing his best to appear casual. "You believe what you want to believe, but we didn't have anything to do with Zach's death. If you think someone killed him, then you're wasting your time on us."

She stepped closer, narrowed her eyes, and stared until he looked away. "No, I don't think so. Want to know a little secret? My money's on you. You're the one who's going to talk. Know why? I saw the video."

He crinkled his forehead and peered at her. "What video?"

"At the water park. You three are standing there while they do CPR on your friend. Haley's pretty upset and Liam's trying to calm her down. But you . . ." She jabbed her finger toward him. "You're scanning the crowd. Looking for someone. Someone who terrifies you."

He shook his head. "That's not—"

"And that look on your face in the video? The one that says you're scared out of your mind?" She turned for the door. "That's the same look you had when I asked if you were with Zachary when he was murdered."

She stepped onto the porch as he closed and locked the door behind her. Once in her car, she pulled up Liam Walker's address in her phone. A twenty-minute drive. By the time she got there, Matias would've talked to him. Nothing she could do about that, but it likely wouldn't make much difference. Until she had more evidence, something pointing in the right direction, she couldn't apply enough pressure to any of them.

Her cell rang before she could pull away from the house, and she glanced at the display. Wylie.

Her heart raced and the back of her neck tingled. "Hey there."

His voice was a whisper. "We, uh, your mom and I are about to head to the doctor's office. He called and wanted to meet with her."

Her throat tightened. "Did he say anything?"

"No, just that we needed to come in today."

"How's Mama?"

"She's okay. Getting her things together now. Didn't want me to call anyone until we knew more."

She rested her forehead on the steering wheel. "I'll meet you there."

"No. You can't. She's serious about the kids not knowing. Not yet. You know how she is. All she's talked about is how she doesn't want the cancer to affect you guys. If you show up, it'll only make things worse."

She puffed her cheeks and let the air escape. "Yeah, I know how she is. I won't go, but you have to call me as soon as you get done there. I need to verify whether the caller's info was accurate."

"What caller? What info? Amara, what's going on?"

"I can't go into all that. Not now. It has to do with a case I'm working. But Mama's not in any danger from it, okay?"

"I don't like this." He grunted. "*You* in any danger?"

Good question. "No. I'm just trying to figure out if what I'm being told is true. And yes, I've reported all this to Lieutenant Segura."

"Here's the deal. Tell me what you *think* you know, and we'll go from there."

"Wylie, there's no need to—"

"You're talking to an ex-cop. I know better than to go undercover without all the facts."

She squeezed the phone. "Fine. I was told that Mama's breast cancer might be in more than one spot, but I don't know if that's true."

"Told by who?"

"Uh-uh. Can't get into all that. Please, just let me know one way or the other as soon as you can, okay?"

He grumbled something too low for her to hear. "If your info is accurate, I'll call you. Otherwise, I'm respecting your mother's wishes. You should do the same."

"Don't let her wait too long. She has to tell us."

Mama's voice popped up in the background and the call disconnected.

Amara sat back in the seat and stared out the windshield. Too much not knowing.

The cancer.

The treatments.

Her relationship with Starsky.

Why Daddy had to die.

The missing computer drive.

Travis Rutledge's problem.

Zachary Coleman's murder.

She pressed the heels of her palms against her temples and watched the landscaping crew down the street reload their gear. 9:26. Twelve minutes start to finish. Efficient. Productive. Focused.

The exact opposite of her life right now.

The trip to Liam Walker's house turned out to be a waste of time. If he was home, he wasn't answering the door. She ran the tags on an older GMC SUV parked out front with vanity tag RAJKWIT—raj k wit? r a jackwit? raj quit?—and it was registered to Liam. The boy was probably there and dodging her.

With no one left to interview, she headed for the nearest eatery with free Wi-Fi, grabbed a banana and a bottled water, and settled into a corner booth away from other customers. Plenty of research to be done. When she'd completed the report for the LT earlier, a few things niggled at her and she'd scratched notes to follow up on them. She dotted her finger on the list's first item.

The cash and missing hard drive from Zachary's house. The crime scene techs hadn't called or emailed, meaning they hadn't looked at the items yet. No surprise. It'd only been two days since the search warrant was served. Much like the requisition for a new desk, her evidence would have to work its way to the top of the pile. And calling to ask would risk bumping her down the stack. Better to hold off. Chances were, they wouldn't find anything to identify a suspect. Even if they found fingerprints other than Zachary's on the computer, so what? That proved nothing beyond showing someone had been in his room.

Next on her list was contacting Eduardo Sanchez, the security chief at the Cannonball Water Park. She clicked her tongue on the roof of her mouth several times. What to do about Sanchez? He didn't kill Zachary. That didn't mean he wasn't involved in a cover-up to try to limit the park's liability in the press. An accidental OD sounded a whole lot better than a murder. Put the blame on the kid.

She'd struggled to get a read on him. His background in law enforcement meant he knew how to play the game. He understood what would be important to her investigation, and if he wanted, he could steer her down a plethora of dead ends. Until she could figure out where his priorities lay—getting to the truth or protecting the park—he remained a suspect.

Yesterday he said he'd schedule a network specialist to come inspect their system to see if they'd been hacked. She had no idea how long it took to get something like that organized. Only one way to find out. She picked up her cell and dialed his number.

"Good morning, Detective," he said. "I thought you might be calling today."

"I wanted to follow up on our conversation yesterday. See if you'd had a chance to get an expert out there."

"We have a young lady out here now. She's from a security firm we've never done business with. Felt like that was the way to go. She began diagnosing our system yesterday."

"That's fast work." She unscrewed her water and took a drink.

"If the park has been hacked, we need to know. This is not just about your investigation."

"I don't suppose you know how long it will take?"

He chuckled. "She started explaining the process to me in great detail. I nodded a few times, pointed her toward the equipment, and left her to her work. Best I could understand, she'll be done sometime between now and never. If you'd like, I'd be happy to check with her for an update?"

"No, that's okay. Interrupting her won't speed things along. Thanks though."

"Certainly," he said. "As soon as I know anything, I'll be in touch."

"I appreciate it." Time to push him. "One thing's been bothering me. Why weren't you there when they were working on Coleman? In your position, I'd think something like a death would bring you running."

"You're asking for an alibi. An incident like this would normally require my presence. However, at the time this occurred, I was twenty miles away at a job fair recruiting new hires. I'll email you all the details so you may verify. It was at a hotel so I assume their security cameras can confirm my attendance."

If they were working. "Thank you."

"May I ask *you* a question, Detective?"

"Sure."

"When you resolve your investigation and are confident I am not involved, would it be possible for us to have dinner together?"

A wave of heat swept from her chest to her face. Flattered, but suspicious. Was that her new reality? Question every motive, no matter how innocent it might be? "I, um, let's hold off on that, okay?"

"Of course. I should not have asked. I placed you in an uncomfortable situation, and I apologize. However, please know that when you do close your case, I will ask again. I hope you will not be offended."

"That would be, um, that would be fine. Have a good day, Mr. Sanchez."

She stared at the table and took several heavy breaths. What just happened? Why did she feel like she'd cheated on Starsky? Their relationship was casual. Would he be hurt if she went out with someone else?

She downed several gulps of the water. Not now. No time for a personal life anyway. The investigation and Mama's health were priority. Keep the focus on what had to be done. Everything else could wait.

But for how long? There'd always be another case. Always something else that took priority over her personal life. She thumped herself under her chin. Sounding too much like Mama.

She opened her new laptop, verified the security software was operating, and logged onto the Wi-Fi. Sanchez had moved quickly. Made sense from a precautionary standpoint. He'd want to know if the company was vulnerable. The man was doing everything he should, which still wasn't enough to scratch him off her suspects list.

Next up was researching the games Haley had mentioned. She searched for *MMORPG* and reviewed the first page of results. The Wikipedia link seemed like a good place to start. She'd never been into video games beyond a few time-killing apps she had on her phone. Gaming consoles had been around when she was growing up, but the family could never afford them. Her ex-husband had spent more time playing games than he had with her. Looking back, that was probably best for both of them.

She reviewed the Wikipedia article and clicked several of the internal links for more information. Massively multiplayer online role-playing games were exactly what they sounded like. A bunch of people, thousands or in some cases millions, logged on to the game and became a character of their choosing. That character was free to roam the huge make-believe world alone, but most opted to join other players in a team or clan or tribe or whatever that particular game called them.

Haley had said that's how the four friends met each other. There must be a search feature that allowed you to find people who lived nearby. And you'd have to be able to chat with them to establish any kind of real-world relationship. Was it possible that the teens used the games as a way to communicate and remain anonymous? If so, how could she find out what was being said?

The companies that ran the games would be serious about protecting their players' privacy. Assuming any records of chats were kept, it would take a subpoena to see them. A subpoena and lots of time. And there was no way to be sure which game they were playing at any given minute. Haley said they played several.

Amara peeled the banana and ate half, then set the rest aside. The fruit still had a tinge of green, spoiling the sweetness. She took a long draw of the water and swished it around her mouth before swallowing. What if she started to play too? Found them in the game and befriended them? She could pretend to be anyone and . . .

And when would she have time to do that? It would take forever to learn how to play and they would be suspicious of anyone who approached. Especially someone new.

The CSI tech who'd taken Zachary Coleman's computer equipment said she played online games. Barb Something. Should've written down her name. She might be able to answer questions about how the games work and the possibility of gaining any useful information.

She dialed the crime lab and asked for Barb. After being on hold for nearly three minutes, the music stopped.

"Barb Freemont."

Freemont. She jotted it down. "Hi. This is Detective Alvarez. I met you at the Coleman house a couple of days ago?"

"Sure. But it's way too early for us to have any information on the items we took."

"That's not why I'm calling. I know you're busy, but I wonder if you'd have time to answer a few questions for me. About online games? You mentioned you played them?"

"I do when I have time." A crinkling sound came through the phone, followed by a loud crunch and her muffled voice. "Sorry. Eating some chips. First break I've had in hours."

Amara grimaced. The chewing noise grated her bones. "No problem. If now's not a good time, I can call later."

"No, it's fine." Another crunch. "What do you need to know?"

"This is all part of my investigation, so it stays between us. I have three suspects in the murder, each of them friends with the victim and in their late teens. Two boys and a girl. They said they met online while playing games, and I'm wondering if there's some connection between that and the boy's death."

"Interesting," Barb said. "In what way?"

"Not sure. Maybe they use the games to communicate anonymously? That would keep their phones clean. What about their computers?"

"Depends, but unless they saved the chat logs, I'd guess you wouldn't find anything on them either."

"So no help there," Amara said. "I assume their discussions wouldn't be visible to other players?"

"Right. You control who you talk to. You can request to friend someone, and if they accept, you can communicate. Otherwise, you're blocked by default." Crunch. "Anything else? I need to get back to work."

"One more question. How hard is it to find a specific person in a game?"

"How hard is it? Impossible unless you know their character's name. Even then, you can't be sure who you're dealing with. That's the whole idea. You become someone else and live a fantasy life. Doesn't matter if you're a fourteen-year-old girl in Ukraine or a seventy-year-old man in Samoa. You can be who you want to be. It's about escaping reality for a little while."

Amara scratched her forehead. Escaping reality sounded great, but it was a one-sided agreement. Reality never left. Never went away. Never stopped. You could do your best to forget it for a while, but it would always be there waiting when you returned. "So who are you, Barb?"

"Calina Iceguard, level seventy-two elven frost mage on *Planetary Orcs*."

"Is that, uh, is that good?"

She laughed. "Calina can handle herself. She's got some friends she runs around with and they watch each other's backs."

"The three of them said they met online. I'm assuming there's a way to search for players who live nearby?"

"No can do. That kind of thing hasn't been possible for a bunch of years. Too many issues with privacy."

"Understood. I appreciate it."

"No sweat." Crunch. "Let me know if you need any more help. I could talk gaming all day."

"Will do." Her cell beeped and she glanced at the display. Wylie. He said he'd only phone if the anonymous caller's information was accurate. "Thanks again, Barb. Got to run."

Her hands shook as she pressed the button to switch to Wylie.

"Hi," Amara said. Her throat tightened as she tried to speak. "You've got news?"

"Walked out to get the car," he said. "I've only got a second."

The weight of his voice spoke the words he couldn't say. Tears flooded her eyes. "The cancer's spread, hasn't it?"

The restaurant's din faded to the background as Amara reread Mama's text. A special dinner at her home tomorrow night. A chance to get everyone together after her PET scan that morning. Possibly, she'd have an update on her diagnosis.

Amara's chest ached with the pressure of knowing the truth. She longed to call her mother. To stop by and hug her for hours. But that wasn't Mama's way. Her health concerns paled in comparison to her desire that her kids' lives not be affected.

It'd only been a few years since she'd spent a night in the hospital with pneumonia, a fact her children discovered after spotting an insurance statement on her kitchen counter months later. When confronted, her mother said it was nothing serious and no point in troubling anyone. Nothing serious. Right. As if going to the hospital was part of her normal routine.

She danced her fingers on the laptop's keyboard, trying to think of what to type to distract herself from chasing the what-ifs of Mama's disease. Something work-related that would move the Coleman case forward. It could be hours or days before she heard from Sanchez with the results of their network inspection. No point in talking to Haley or Matias again until she had more to pressure them with, and Liam was hiding from her.

A sudden urge to squeeze the half-eaten banana into oblivion overwhelmed her as her heart pounded in her ears. Instead, she stood and carried it to the trash can, then wandered the restaurant, always keeping her computer in sight. What she wanted to do was run until she dropped to the ground. Release the anxiety and frustration in beads of sweat. Let her body rule her mind, if only for a moment.

She returned to her laptop and opened a blank document. Her thoughts were too scattered. Narrow them down to a workable process. Focus only on the next step.

4 friends. 2 had $$$. Prob other 2 also. How? Online. Illegal. What?

Online games. Relevant? (Barb)

Why kill @ water park? Cameras not working. Premeditated. To prove no place safe? To who? Other friends?

Who is anon caller & are they the killer?

Is killer one of the 3 or someone else? Sanchez (verify job fair alibi)? Unknown 4th person?

She reviewed her notes so far and highlighted "cameras not working," then underlined and bolded "online" and "illegal." If the security expert who was digging into the Cannonball's network found anything—a possibility that seemed increasingly likely—did that mean one of the teens had hacked into the water park's system? If they had that kind of skill, breaking into her home network would have been simple. And if they were good enough, they could've gotten into the doctor's system to see Mama's medical records.

But how would they even know to look? She frowned and shook her head. She'd entered Mama's appointment in her calendar, which synced between her phone and her personal computer. The caller could've easily seen that, and when he broke into the doctor's system, he'd have known Mama already had the tests done.

But why tip his hand? If he hadn't called, she wouldn't know she'd been hacked. What did he have to gain by alerting her to his activities? Surely more than proving a point. Was that supposed to derail the investigation? Not going to happen.

She touched the laptop display. Stay focused. If this was all about hacking, then what would they want from the Cannonball? Credit card numbers of guests? Employees' social security numbers? Industrial spying? Whatever they were after seemed to boil down to a single commodity. Secret information. And there were plenty of people who paid for secrets. Paid well, based on the pile of cash at Zachary Coleman's house.

But Sanchez was right. If you're after information, why bother with the security cameras? What could you possibly gain? Nothing to do except wait for the report from the network expert. Would she be able to tell what the hackers did, or only that the system had been breached?

On cue, a notification popped up in the lower right corner of her screen to indicate a new email. She clicked over and opened the message. Nothing about the Cannonball's network, but Sanchez had sent over the information on the job fair, complete with links to the hotel's website and an article in the *Express-News*. A black-and-white photo accompanied the paper's story, and Sanchez was clearly visible sitting at a table with a line of applicants in front of him.

She switched back to the document and deleted his name. If he was involved in any way, it would be after the fact. Deal with that later. The three teens remained at the top of the suspects list. If this were a movie, she'd have each of them hauled into a separate interrogation room and spend the next several hours playing them against each other until one of them broke. Gave up the information she needed. Didn't even have to be about the murder specifically.

How did you get the money?

The answer to that question would open the door to everything else.

She checked her watch. Nearly one in the afternoon. Time to go back to Liam Walker's address and try again. If she couldn't make contact, she'd head to the office and work from there for the rest of the day. Later, she'd hit the gym for a long workout. Exhaust herself before going home to Larry.

She packed her belongings, wiped the table clean, and stopped at the counter to order another bottled water and half a turkey club sandwich to go. The credit card terminal flashed its "waiting for approval" message for a few moments before she asked if they were having problems with the card reader.

The cashier shook his head and checked the display on his register. "Says your card was declined."

What? "That doesn't make sense. I pay it off every month. Can I run it again?"

He gave her a do-you-know-how-many-times-I've-heard-that look, shrugged, and reset the order. "Try it now."

She repeated the process with the same outcome, then pulled out her debit card. "Let me try this one."

After nearly a minute, the cashier shook his head.

Her muscles quivered as she slipped the card into her purse and gave the cashier a twenty-dollar bill. He glanced at her before using a counterfeit detector pen on the cash and handing her the change.

She made no attempt to smile as she snatched her food and hustled to her car. The July heat was nothing compared to the steam radiating from her neck. The tires screeched as she backed out of the parking spot and headed toward Liam Walker's house.

Someone was messing with her finances. Probably the same person who'd called in the middle of the night.

She squeezed the steering wheel with both hands and hunched forward. The emotions bubbling inside, the stress and frustration and anger and fear, begged to be set loose.

All they needed was a target.

22 **Amara parked two houses down** from Liam Walker's home. The same SUV sat in the driveway, seemingly unmoved. She pointed the air-conditioning vents away from her and gripped the cell phone. Had to chill before talking to him. She opened the app for her bank and tried unsuccessfully to log on. A message popped up advising her to contact customer service. She repeated the process with her credit card app and got the same result.

The pounding moved from the back of her skull to the front. Dealing with banks was not on today's agenda. She craned her neck and shoulders to chase at least some of the tension away. Might as well deal with this now. She dialed the number for her bank and began pressing zero before the voice could finish telling her to "please listen carefully as our menu options have changed."

"You've selected an invalid option. To check your balance, press or say 'one.' To open an account, press or say 'two.' To speak to—"

"Three," she said.

A series of beeps sounded. "You wish to speak to a customer service representative. Is that correct?"

"Yes."

Another series of beeps. "Did you know that you can make changes to your account online? For instructions, please say or press 'nine.' Otherwise, please remain on the line and the next available representative will assist you."

She counted six breaths before she heard a click and music

started playing. At just under two minutes, another click and a voice. "Thank you for—"

"Hi," Amara said. "Sorry. I'm in kind of a hurry. I need to—"

"Thank you for choosing to bank with us. All calls are monitored and recorded. At the end of your call, you'll have the opportunity to take a brief survey. If you wish to take the survey, please press 'one' now. If not, please press 'two.'"

She squeezed the phone, careful to keep her fingers away from the hang-up button. So much for calming down.

"Please hold while we transfer you to a customer service representative."

What do you think I've been doing? An acoustic version of the Beatles' "Yesterday" played as she waited. Appropriate, since it seemed like she'd been on hold since then. As the song neared its end, a click sounded, followed by silence. If they'd disconnected her, the car windows were about to explode outward.

"Thank you for calling, Ms. Alvarez. How may I assist you?"

Phone number linked to name. Things like that used to seem convenient, but with all that was going on, she could use a little more security and a little less convenience. "I'm calling because my, um, hold on."

The front door of the Walker residence opened and a young man, tallish and thin, stepped outside and shaded his eyes while ambling to the truck. Liam.

Have to talk to him before he drives off.

Unbelievable. "I'll call you back."

She glanced in the rearview mirror at the tiny vein throbbing on her temple, then turned off the car, pulled on her jacket, and hurried his direction. "Liam Walker?"

He stared at her, glanced back at his home, and took another step toward the truck.

"Hold up," she said. She fished her ID from her pocket and quickened the pace. Seconds later, she stood in front of him. "I'm Detective Amara Alvarez, SAPD. Need to ask you some questions."

He frowned and dug his hands into his pockets.

She angled herself and tapped her thumb on the Glock under her jacket. "Mind keeping your hands where I can see them?"

He pulled them out and held his palms up. "What's this about?"

Nice try. "I'm investigating Zachary Coleman's death, as I'm sure you're aware."

"Do I have to talk to you?"

"No," she said. "You are not required to answer any of my questions. However, you should think about how that would make you look. I'm trying to determine the circumstances surrounding your friend's death. If you don't want to cooperate, I have to ask myself why not."

He shrugged. "Because I don't know anything about what happened, and I've watched enough documentaries to know not to talk to the police. So unless you're arresting me, in which case I want a lawyer, I'm getting in my truck and leaving."

"What's your license plate mean?"

One corner of his mouth turned up in a sneer. "Rage quit. You're too old to understand."

Ah, the boldness of the young. And just because she didn't know what that meant didn't mean she was old. "What happened at the water park?"

"Zach died."

The way he said it made her want to smack the look off his face. Hard. She gritted her teeth and stared up at him. "You know, don't you?"

He stepped to the side to go around her. "No idea what you're talking about."

"You know your friend was killed, and you know why. That's good enough for me. Maybe you didn't actually do it, but worst case is that you go down for accessory to murder."

He opened the truck door and slid inside, then pulled the door shut and started the engine.

She tapped on the window and raised her voice. "First one to talk gets to see the DA about a deal. The other two spend their best years behind bars."

He put the SUV in gear and motioned for her to back away.

She smiled. Why not sow some seeds of dissension? "Oh, and better hurry. One of your friends already called me."

He backed out of the driveway and eased down the street before turning left at a stop sign. He'd been ready for her. His reactions came across as planned. Forceful. No indication of fear or concern. Either he was a good actor or extremely confident. Or a psychopath.

She googled "rage quit" while strolling back to her car.

Get so angry, usually while playing a video game, that you quit playing and throw your controller, often breaking it.

Fitting.

Next stop was her bank. No more pushing buttons to talk to someone. After that, swing by the Coleman residence, and if they were home, ask to take another look around Zachary's room. See if she'd overlooked anything that might hint at the victim's online activities.

A surge of depression washed over her as the truth clenched its arms around her chest and forced the air from her lungs. There'd be no clue. No *aha!* moment. Only more spinning in circles. Her chance to prove herself fading.

Maybe it was time to ask for help. No shame in that. No weakness.

That was for the best, what with everything going on with Mama. Mama.

She slapped her palm on the steering wheel hard enough that she worried she'd injured herself. What would her mother think if she knew her daughter wasn't fighting? Worse, was using someone else's cancer as her excuse? Pity party over, Alvarez.

Rage quit? Absolutely.

Her rage. Their quit.

Liam and Haley and Matias would play *her* game from now on.

23

Amara pulled into the Coleman driveway and parked by the garage. Zachary's Mustang still sat there, another of those countless decisions the parents would have to make. Sorting through the aftermath of an unexpected death took time.

Dealing with the bank and credit card companies turned out to be less painful than she expected. The local branch informed her the account was frozen as a result of her online request. No funds had disappeared. Whoever hacked her personal laptop obviously accessed her passwords too. She should have thought of that a lot earlier and changed everything. A project for when she got home tonight. After withdrawing a wad of cash, she told the bank to keep the account locked. Password change or not, no sense exposing her money to the internet until this was over.

The credit card company gave her the same information. A zero balance and the card frozen at her request. No charges authorized until further notice. She told them the same thing. Leave it locked. Probably forever.

She walked into the late-afternoon shade provided by the tall mesquites and oaks. Anywhere else, the trees would be considered small. In this part of Texas, you'd call them giants. She ambled toward the front door, taking her time to regain focus on her reason for being there. The cash was the key. Until she made progress on its origin, the investigation would continue to hover in place.

A rapid chirping from the closest tree grabbed her attention. A mockingbird. She bowed her head slightly toward the animal. *Point taken. Just trying to do my job here, okay? Positive attitude.*

She stepped onto the porch, raised her hand to knock, and paused. The cash. It was real. Tangible. Not a dollar amount on a bank statement. Somewhere, somehow, it had to be converted from the ethereal realms of the internet to paper. Whatever these kids were doing to earn the money, they needed a way to turn it into something usable. Most transactions could be done without cash but not without banks. Credit cards, checking accounts, all that. Zachary Coleman wasn't old enough to open his own accounts, and even if he was, the kind of dollars he'd hidden didn't move through banks without notice.

Digital currencies like Bitcoin were a definite possibility, especially with the apparent technical expertise of the four teens. She didn't know much about how online money worked, but the whole setup had always seemed shady to her. Like Monopoly cash, only more confusing and supposedly more real.

She knocked on the door and took a step backward. The mockingbird continued its chirping, daring Amara to turn and look. The distinct click of a deadbolt sounded and the door opened slowly. A woman, substantially older than Zachary's mother, smiled. "Hello. Can I help you?"

From behind her, a familiar male voice echoed through the house. "Who is it, Mom? Hold on, I'm coming."

Paul Coleman. Zachary's father. This woman must be the grandmother he'd mentioned. Did she know her grandson's death was under investigation? "Hi there. I'm, uh, Ms. Alvarez."

Mr. Coleman appeared behind her. "Ms. Alvarez," he said. "How nice to see you again. Would you like to come in?"

"Yes, thank you." She moved inside and waited until the older lady closed the door.

"Mom, Ms. Alvarez took care of some of the arrangements for Zach's funeral. I asked her to stop by so we can finalize a few things."

Amara nodded. "I'm so sorry about your loss, ma'am."

"Yes," she said. "Thank you. But where are my manners? I'm Eugenia Coleman. Zach was my grandson. His passing has been very difficult for all of us."

The woman's straight posture, modern clothing, and pixieish hairdo served her well, though the heavy age spots, large rings, and high veins on her hands couldn't disguise the truth. Close to eighty, probably. Amara lowered her chin. "Yes, ma'am." Was she supposed to say something more?

Mr. Coleman touched his mother's arm. "Mom, would you mind checking on Lori again? She ought to be getting up soon."

"Of course, dear."

The two waited until the grandmother was out of earshot.

"Thank you," he said. "I appreciate you playing along. If Mom found out that Zach might have been killed, I'm afraid of what it could do to her. She's already devastated and, well, you know."

"I understand. And I'm sorry for dropping by without calling first, but I was out this way"—she resisted the urge to cross her fingers behind her back—"and wondered if it'd be okay to take another look around Zachary's room?"

"I have to leave to take Mom back to her home in a few minutes. Can you be done by then?"

"Sure. And have you had a chance to get copies of the statements from your joint checking account?"

He nodded. "I'll print them and meet you in his room. I'll bring the phone records too." He flicked his hand toward the hall. "You know the way."

She strode to the room and scanned the area. Other than new blank spaces on the computer desk, everything appeared to be just as it was the last time she was in here. Too soon for the family to even begin thinking about packing their son's things. Assuming they ever did. *Things* tended to become so much more when they were all that remained.

She sat in the chair and stared at a dark spot on the wall in front of her. The now-gone computer's fan must have been pointed there. A headset, complete with microphone and heavy padding, lay beside the huge monitor. The keyboard, probably one of those that lit up so he could type at night, rested next to a mouse with more buttons than she'd ever seen. She sighed and stood. Zachary was far too computer literate to do something as stupid as leave a password on a Post-it note or any other physical evidence of online activity.

A shadow on the hall wall caught her eye and she stepped away from the desk as Eugenia Coleman walked into the room. The woman frowned and pointed at Amara. "You didn't tell the truth, did you?"

"Ma'am?"

"Lori told me. You're a detective, aren't you?"

Amara's stomach fluttered. "Yes. I'm sorry for misleading you, but your son thought it was for the best." *Where was he?*

"Why are the police involved in Zachary's death?"

"This is all routine." She glanced past the woman to the hall. Now would be a good time for Mr. Coleman to arrive.

"Young lady, I was a schoolteacher for more years than I like to remember. I know when someone's not telling me the truth."

You didn't know earlier. Amara rolled the chair to the grandmother. "Please have a seat. I'll get your son and we can chat."

"Pish posh. If this involves my grandson, I have as much right to know what's going on as Paul does."

Um, technically, no you don't. "Did you see Zachary often?"

"Changing the subject." She eased into the chair. "Hate these things with wheels. Afraid I'll fall. They say that's the beginning of the end."

"Ma'am?"

"The fall. 'Poor Eugenia. Fell out of that chair and broke her hip. Mmm mmm mmm. Beginning of the end for her.' Course, I could live another twenty years and people would still say it was the fall that got me."

Amara smiled. "Best to be careful."

"Paul and Lori have been after me for years to move in here. Scared something will happen to me. 'Won't be any bother to us,' they say." The wrinkles on her forehead deepened. "What about the other way around? I live alone and prefer to keep it that way. I can still drive if I need anything, and when the time comes, I'll move out of my cottage into the assisted living building. That's a long way off though."

"I'm sure it is. If you don't mind me asking, your son mentioned that Zachary planned to visit you on the day he, uh, the day he passed?"

The woman nodded. "He'd come by at least once or twice a week. Sometimes he'd bring a pizza and we'd pull out the TV trays and watch one of my programs. He was a good boy." She pressed her elbows into the armrests and leaned forward. "I don't know what you're looking into, but my grandson was not a troublemaker."

Uh-huh. Didn't all grandmothers think that? "Yes, ma'am."

Steps echoed down the hall and Mr. Coleman moved into the doorway. About time.

He glanced at his mother. "Lori okay?"

"She's fine. This young *detective* was just about to explain why she's here."

"Actually," Amara said, "I was about to leave. Thank you both for your time."

Mr. Coleman gave her a manila envelope. "The bank statements and phone records. If you need anything else, you'll let me know?"

"I will." She laid her hand on top of the grandmother's. "Again, ma'am, I'm very sorry for your loss. I'll leave you with your son to discuss any questions you may have. I hope you understand."

"Certainly," the woman said. "And I hope you'll understand when I phone you later to get all the details."

24

Amara spent the rest of the afternoon going through Zachary's bank statements and phone records and doing more research on the teenagers. Three hours after beginning the review, she had one additional piece of solid information. His bank account was completely normal. Regular direct deposits from his job at Target, but not near enough to explain the hidden cash. No overdrafts, nothing unusual in his spending habits. However he'd gotten the money, the answer wasn't in the bank statements.

The cell records weren't much more helpful. More texts than phone calls, but not many of either, and all of those came from his mother, father, or grandmother. Nothing on the day of his death.

As for Liam, Matias, and Haley, zilch. No arrest records. No speeding tickets. No social media. Some of those big-time commentators on TV news would say the lack of any suspicious activity was fishy enough to prove they were doing something wrong. Good luck getting a DA to sign off on that.

She stretched, performed her shut-down pack-up ritual, and headed for her car. In the parking garage, a trio of cops—two in uniform and the unmistakable profile of Rutledge—stood near the door. She angled away from them and kept her head low. A confrontation now wouldn't do her any good. Her reaction might be career-ending.

"Alvarez!"

She stopped, closed her eyes, and sighed. "Have a good evening, Travis."

"Get over here. Got some people want to meet ya."

Her neck tightened in a vise. Maybe he didn't mean it that way. Like she worked for him. Or was somehow less than he was. Nah. He did. She smiled and walked toward the group, picturing with each step where she would stand, what defensive posture she would assume, and how she would attack. Travis didn't realize it, but the fight was already over. All he had to do was say the wrong thing.

The two officers extended their hands and introduced themselves. After an awkward moment, she gave the nice-to-meet-you wave and turned back toward her car.

"Hold up," Rutledge said. "What you two boys might not realize is that Alvarez here is the Queen of Cotulla. You've heard of her, right? Couldn't miss that pretty face splashed all over TV and the paper. Goes to show you that looks can get you places."

"Yeah?" Amara said. "Guess that explains why *you* never got anywhere."

One of the cops laughed and Rutledge's face reddened.

"I earned my way," he said. "Something you wouldn't know about."

Her tension faded as she stared at him. This was too comical to deal with. Rutledge was a caricature inflated by his own self-importance. Not worth the effort. There'd be no stereotypical big bad bully taken down by righteous little girl. "Nice to meet you two officers," she said. "Detective, I hope you have a pleasant evening."

As she walked to her vehicle, Rutledge's laughter echoed through the garage. The sound was loud, grating, and alone.

■ ■ ■

She crawled into bed shortly after midnight. An almost two-hour workout and a one-hour apology session with Larry had kept her up later than planned. The lizard finally caved and accepted her apology, but not before she'd offered spinach and mango as a peace offering.

The drive home had been uneventful, but she found herself checking the rearview mirror often. Rutledge wouldn't be stupid enough to follow her or "accidentally" run into her away from work. Too much could go wrong for him. She knew that, but did he?

She scratched her nose, switched off the lamp on the end table, and scooted under the covers. Exhaustion weighed on her and the anxiety had returned. Dinner tonight at Mama's would be emotional. Questions and no answers. Fear and no relief. This was going to be one of those nights when she stared at the clock and told herself that if she went to sleep right now, she could get five hours of rest. Then four and a half hours. Then four . . .

She stirred and checked the time on her phone. 4:15. Falling asleep had been easier than expected. Her body insisted on another hour in bed, and her mind capitulated without a battle. In a little bit she'd roll out and throw on some clothes for an early morning jog but for now, a few more minutes in the quiet of her bedroom were in order.

The quiet.

Why was it so quiet? She blinked several times and propped herself up on an elbow. No whir from the ceiling fan or electrical hum from the heaters in Larry's room. No night-light reflecting from the bathroom. None of the tiny red or green or yellow lights from the assortment of devices plugged in around the space.

Great. The power's out.

She shuffled through the hall into the living room and peeked out the front curtains. Weird. Lights were on in some of the other apartments.

No.

She clenched her fists and strode to retrieve her cell phone from the bedroom. They'd had her power turned off. Bad move. Lack of sleep always made her grumpy. Today that would be taken to a new level.

The utility company confirmed that yes, someone had phoned with her account number and password to have the service turned off as soon as possible. And yes, they'd be happy to turn it back on after she paid the reconnection fee. She was welcome to do that now with a credit card or with any form of payment at any of their convenient locations around town.

Amara informed the customer service rep that she'd changed all her passwords recently. How could someone without the newest code access her account?

The rep said that if someone had her account number and the answers to her security questions, the power company would accept them as the actual customer.

The security questions? Where she went to grade school? Her pet's name? Anyone with any skill could find that info easily enough. Her hands shook as she disconnected the call. She'd seen the old telephones in the movies. The ones where the bulky object sat on a desk and a person could slam down the receiver if they were angry. The bell would ring from the force, accentuating the effect. It would not be a bad thing to bring those phones back.

Her credit card was locked by choice, so she'd have to wait until later in the morning to get the power turned on. Lucky for whichever representative had to wait on her. She'd have time to double up her morning run and work out some of the aggression before then. Or more accurately, add the anger toward the ever-growing arrow aimed directly at the three teens.

Someone was talking. Liam or Haley or Matias.

And they were doing it soon.

She smiled as the idea blossomed. If *she* couldn't apply enough pressure, she knew who could.

Three teenagers. Two living at home with their parents.

Wonder how Mom and Dad would feel about a homicide detective visiting them at work?

***

After a long run and a short shower in her dark bathroom, she waited in an all-night diner for the power company to open. The coffee was strong and bitter, the kind you drink because you need it, not because you like it. She opted for wheat toast, unbuttered, no jelly. The dryness of the bread forced her to wash it down with the coffee. She could dunk the toast and let it disintegrate, then down the whole thing in a few gulps. Combine two evils into one disgusting elixir. She shoved both away. Not that desperate. Yet.

Still an hour to kill before she could get the electricity turned on. Might as well get some work done. Track down the teenagers' parents and try to figure out if and where they worked. She followed the usual security procedures to log onto the diner's Wi-Fi, then opened her email program. First thing was to clear out the 95 percent of daily generic office communication. Reminders that if you haven't filled out this or that form for HR yet, now is the time. Tips on communicating effectively with the public or your coworkers. Should mark that one urgent and forward it to Rutledge. Links to articles with volunteer opportunities.

And an email from Eugenia Coleman, Zachary's grandmother,

sent an hour ago. The woman sure gets up early. Probably goes to bed before dark though. Sounds wonderful.

Ms. Coleman gave her address and phone number. Said she wanted to ask a few questions and wondered if there was a time they could get together today? Um, not likely. The woman was a low priority. Talking to her might reveal some insights into Zachary's life but not enough to bump her to the top of the interview list. Besides, the grandmother would want all the details about the investigation. Information Amara couldn't give, either because she didn't know the answer or the woman didn't need to know. Maybe when this was all over, but not now.

She typed a short response saying that she had a packed schedule but would touch base if she had any questions. In other words, Don't call me, I'll call you. How's that for communicating with the public? She hit the send button and coughed as a toast crumb embedded itself in her throat.

An email from Eduardo Sanchez, sent late last night, said he hoped to have the security consultant's report this morning. Once he'd had a chance to review it, he'd contact her to discuss. She fired off a quick "thanks" to let him know she'd received the message. Short and to the point. Nothing that could be interpreted as anything other than what it was.

His invitation for a dinner date once the investigation ended still hung out there. She'd have to deal with that then. Once she figured out exactly what her relationship with Starsky was. Brother or confidant or boyfriend. Everything seemed to be in place for the third option except the physical attraction. Sweet guy, great friend. Not what you'd call classically handsome though. *Nice, Amara. Shallow enough for you?*

She punished herself with another sip of the coffee and searched the internet for Bexar County property records. Each of the teenagers' homes would be listed there, along with recent appraised values and owner names.

One person, Nicole, for Liam's address. Single mom? Two names, Daniel and Silvia, for Matias's. And the owners of Haley's house had a different last name, confirming Amara's suspicions that the place was a rental. She jotted down the information to contact later if needed.

Nicole Walker's social media listed her as a physical therapist at a privately owned clinic not far from here. The facility opened a few minutes ago, though no guarantee Ms. Walker started that early. Worth the drive to kill time until the power company opened.

She slid out of the booth and dropped a ten-dollar bill on the table. Way more than necessary but best get her good deed done early.

Tonight's dinner at Mama's promised a rough end to the day.

25 **Amara studied the young man** at the receptionist desk. Midtwenties, coiffed dark hair
with blond highlights, and too-small round
glasses. His khakis, dress shirt, and tie said
professional. The cheek stubble, bloodshot
eyes, and still-damp hair said late night and early morning. She
nodded. "Is Nicole Walker in yet?"

He leaned forward and tapped on a clipboard resting on the
counter. "She is." He clenched his jaw and forced a yawn through
his nose. "Sign in, please, and I need to make a copy of your insurance card. Are you a new patient?"

"I'm not a patient. I just need to speak to Ms. Walker for a few
minutes. In private."

The corners of his mouth dropped. "I'm sorry, but policies pro-
hibit anyone except employees and patients from going beyond the
waiting area. I'd be happy to let her know you're here, Ms. . . . ?"

"Alvarez. Amara Alvarez."

He stood and took a step backward. "And will she know what
this is regarding?"

The automatic door behind her slid open as a woman, her right
knee resting on one of those rolling crutch things, scooted in line.
Amara lowered her voice. "I doubt it. She's not expecting me."

"She's not? Perhaps you could leave your name and number and
she can call you later?"

"Unfortunately, that won't work for me. I just need a couple of
minutes. Family emergency thing, okay?"

His eyes narrowed and the tiniest of frowns appeared. He didn't believe her. "I'm sorry, but as I said earlier, Ms. Walker is very busy today. If you'd like to leave your information, perhaps she can contact you on her lunch break."

Her muscles tightened. *Today just gets better and better.* Fine. Playing the cop card might work to her benefit anyway. She counted five breaths, each slower than the last, before flipping open her SAPD identification and raising her voice. "Here's my insurance card. Alvarez, Homicide. Want to make a copy of it?"

His head flinched backward and he hurried around the desk to open the door leading to the back. "Second room on the left, please. I'll let her know you're waiting."

"Thanks." She tilted her head and furrowed her eyebrows. "Uh, sorry about the scene back there. No offense."

The cold look on his face was his only response. He ushered her into a small office and strode off to find Ms. Walker. A pair of beige leather chairs with brass tack outlines sat on this side of a wooden desk. She maneuvered them until they faced each other, then sat in the one that allowed her a view of the entrance. The squeak of tennis shoes on tile floor echoed her direction and a moment later, a woman stepped into the room and closed the door behind her.

Amara stood and extended her hand. "Nicole Walker?"

"Yes." The woman closed her fingers into a fist and held it out. "Sorry. Germs and all."

"No problem." Amara gave her a fist bump. "I'm Detective Alvarez. Sorry to bother you at work, but I was hoping you could help me with a case I'm investigating."

Ms. Walker blinked rapidly and scrubbed her palms on her thighs. "What's this about? Darryl said you worked in Homicide? Is Liam okay?"

Amara motioned to a chair. "Your son is fine. Please, sit. I'll try not to take up too much of your time."

The woman sat on the edge of the seat, hunched forward with her hands clasped and her left knee bouncing. "I don't understand. Why are you here?"

"I'm trying to resolve a few questions surrounding the death of Zachary Coleman. He was a friend of Liam's. Did you know him?"

"Um, I maybe met him a couple of times in passing. Liam's friends don't come over very often. He OD'd, didn't he?"

"Has Liam ever said anything negative about Zachary? Any fights between them that you're aware of?"

"No, I, uh, none I can think of." Her leg stopped moving and she straightened. "What's this about? You think my son had something to do with that boy's death?"

Here we go. "Ma'am, has Liam made any large purchases recently? Done anything out of the ordinary? Acted strangely?"

"What? No. Of course not. I can assure you he had nothing to do with the young man's death."

No, you can't. Amara stood, handed over a business card, and walked to the door. "Ms. Walker, I believe your son has knowledge that could help me in my investigation. I'm not saying he did anything. I'm also not saying he didn't. What I do know is there are at least three people who have information about Zachary Coleman's death. Someone is gonna tell me what I want to know, and that person will be labeled as cooperating with police. The others go to the back of the line."

"Detective, please, wait. Liam doesn't know—"

"I've taken enough of your time." She opened the door and stepped into the hall. "And I have several other people to see. Have a nice day."

* * *

She stopped by the power company's customer service location to change her security questions and get the electricity turned back on, an ordeal which lived down to her expectations. Technology was supposed to make things easier. Less complicated. Uh-huh.

Afterward, she drove to a park and found a bench in the shade. Her energy level sagged as the caffeine and emotions gave way to the lack of sleep. She'd either have to stay busy or schedule a nap.

A squirrel inched toward her, pausing every so often to rear up and scout its surroundings. "Sorry, buddy. Got nothing for you." The rodent chattered and moved within a few feet before abandoning its quest and returning to a tree.

Her phone's ringing jump-started her heart. Sanchez. "Good morning."

"And to you, Detective. I just emailed you a copy of the report from the consultant. Wasn't sure if you wanted to review it before speaking?"

"Can you bottom-line it for me? Got kind of a hectic day going."

"Of course. As you suspected, we were hacked. Or, as the expert put it, there were signs of unauthorized network intrusions."

"Yeah? Could she tell what they were after?"

"She said she discovered two back doors. Ways for whoever broke into the system to easily return whenever they wanted. The initial hack seems to have been caused by an employee opening an email attachment. As for what they were after, we're not sure. The report has a lot of talk about using checksums to compare the original programs to what was on our server."

"Sorry. You said checksums?"

He chuckled. "I had to ask too. When a software developer issues a new program or update or whatever, they run an algorithm that spits out a long number called the checksum. Say you're download-ing software. You want to make sure what you downloaded is what the developer put out. Nothing lost in transmission. The checksum of the file on your computer should be identical to the checksum of the original file. If anything's different, a period missing, an extra space, an *a* instead of an *e*, the checksums won't match."

She massaged her forehead. "So the numbers didn't agree. That's how she knew something changed."

"Precisely. And that's how she was able to identify where the hacker went. Or at least what they modified. They could look at anything, and as long as they didn't make any changes, we wouldn't know they were there. For example, employee data and guests' credit card information weren't breached."

"So did she identify any specific areas of concern?"

"They obviously got into our security software. Cameras and keycards mostly. We've reset all the codes and she closed the back doors. They were also in the programming that controls our rides. We triple-checked everything and there's no evidence of any tam-pering."

"What were they after? No way this was all about killing Zach-ary. What's the point of hacking your system and then not doing anything with the access?"

"Only scenarios I came up with are either a disgruntled em-ployee or kids playing around. Breaking in for the fun of it."

"Maybe." As far as she knew, none of the three teenagers ever worked at the water park. "Is it possible they downloaded data without being detected? To sell it or something?"

"Highly unlikely, according to the consultant." He paused. "But she didn't say it was impossible. Honestly though, other than credit card data, we don't have anything someone would want to buy."

"Not even your competitors?"

"Not that I can think of. Rides are custom-built based on each park's specific criteria, and those are the only things that are unique. It's all about location and establishing the proper atmosphere to attract guests."

So we're stuck with the why. An employee's revenge didn't make sense. The water park hadn't been harmed. And breaking into their network for fun didn't add up. Who would go through all that effort just to play with some cameras? No. There was a connection between Zachary's death and the hacking. Had to be. Coincidences like that didn't exist.

One answer would explain everything. How did hacking the Cannonball turn into a stack of money under Zachary Coleman's floor? No question in her mind the link existed. Her brain threatened to lock up. She needed to reboot.

"You still there?" Sanchez asked.

She stretched her eyes open. "Yeah. Sorry. Rough day already. If you come up with anything else, will you let me know?"

"I'm working on the map you asked for. Should have it ready soon."

"The map?"

He softened his voice. "Plotting the cameras that were not functioning at the time of the boy's death. You asked for it when we met two days ago."

"Right." *Ugh. Way to look like you're on top of things.*

"I hope your day gets better."

That's not going to happen. "Yeah. Me too."

26

A visit to Matias's parents was next on the agenda. His father worked as a real estate agent and his mother was a chef at a hotel on the River Walk. No point in talking to both yet. Tell one and let them spread the news. The mom would be easier to track down but harder to get any time with. The touristy River Walk area would be packed with vacationers and convention attendees, and a hotel chef might be too busy to talk.

The father was the better choice. A real estate agent would have more flexibility. Unless he was with clients, he could talk. Or, more accurately, listen. And as with Nicole Walker, best to go in unannounced. Catch him completely off guard. She got a more authentic reaction that way. The shock value alone should be enough to trigger a serious phone call to his son as soon as she left.

She checked his listings on the realtor's website and selected a pretty starter home. Two bedroom, one bath, established neighborhood. Too cute for words, the description said. Cute. Realtor-speak for small. She scanned the photos. The place did look nice. Two identical bedrooms, one for her and one for Larry. Decent kitchen and living area. Full bath including a tub. Plus a fenced backyard with trees.

She fiddled with the online calculator. If this was correct, she could get the house for less than she paid in rent now. Of course, the upkeep added a lot to the cost of a home. Things like repairs, painting, new appliances, not to mention the time investment of yard maintenance and everything else. Something to consider though.

She dialed the number and a man answered on the second ring.

"It's a great day to buy or sell a home with Daniel Lucero. How can I help you?"

That was not very clear. "Uh, are you Daniel Lucero?"

"I am. What can I do for you?"

"Oh, hi. My name is Amara Alvarez. I was browsing online and I saw your listing for a house." She switched apps on her phone and recited the address. "I wonder if I could take a look at it this morning."

"What time? I'm showing another home in a little while, but if we could meet soon, I can make it work."

"I can be there in about twenty minutes?"

"Sounds good, Ms. Alvarez. See you in a bit."

When she arrived at the house, a large black SUV waited in the driveway. A man stepped out of the vehicle and waved. His broad smile seemed a bit too used-car-salesmanish, and she braced herself for the overly friendly greeting she knew was headed her way. *Come on, Amara. Maybe he's just a nice guy. Don't be so cynical all the time.*

She parked behind him and walked his direction. "Good morning."

He grasped her hand, a bit too soft with the grip, and shook twice. "Ms. Alvarez, I presume? I'm Daniel Lucero. You can call me Dan, Daniel, Danny, or the guy who sold you a house."

Yep. Spot on with her instincts. Everything about him reeked of slime. Instant unlikability. "And you can call me Detective Alvarez."

He placed a hand on his chest. "Detective? Always happy to serve members of our law enforcement. Why don't we get out of this heat and take a peek inside? You're going to love what you see. The home has only been on the market for—"

"Mr. Lucero, I'm afraid I haven't been completely honest with you."

His lips puckered and he took a half step backward. "I'm sorry?"

"I'm sure it's a lovely home, but I actually wanted to talk to you about something else."

He shook his head. "I don't understand."

"I work in Homicide and am investigating a case that you may be able to help me with. Zachary Coleman. The young man who died at the water park."

He donned a pair of dark sunglasses. "Zach? Matias's friend?"

"Yes, sir. We're trying to tie up a few loose ends."

"I didn't know the boy, so I don't see how I can be of any use to you. And I thought alcohol or drugs killed him."

She pulled out a notepad and clicked her pen. "Sir, are you aware of any problems between Matias and the victim? Anything that would have led to, um, a physical altercation?"

His mouth hung open. "No. What's this really about?"

"Has your son made any large purchases recently? Anything out of the ordinary?"

"I don't think I like your tone, Ms. Alvarez. Matias hasn't done anything wrong. Now if you'll excuse me, I have real clients who need my attention."

"*Detective* Alvarez." She handed him a business card. "Matias has information that will aid my investigation. Whether he's involved in the crime or not, he has knowledge of what happened. If he comes forward with that info, it can only help him with whatever happens later." She shrugged. "If not, he's on his own. That's the same offer I made to the others. First come, first served."

"The others?"

She walked to her car. "Matias will know. Ask him."

∎ ∎ ∎

Amara stopped just inside the restaurant's doors to give her eyes time to adjust to the dimness. She'd agreed to meet Starsky for lunch in an attempt to brighten her day. His car was out front, so he had to be here somewhere. She wandered to the right before spotting his lanky arms waving high, a menu clutched in each hand.

"Hey there," she said. "You bringing aircraft in for a landing?"

He handed her a menu as she sat. "Worked, didn't it?"

"So you're saying I'm as big as a plane."

"Stop. Uh-uh. Not guilting me into anything. I'm too hungry." He pointed to her glass. "I went ahead and ordered us both a water with lemon."

She unwrapped a straw and took a long drink. "Good stuff."

He squeezed his lemons into the water, added several packs of sugar, and stirred the concoction. "Free lemonade. I'm getting loaded fries with extra ranch. You?"

She scanned the good-for-you section of the menu as their waiter stepped to the table. "Small chef salad, please. Light honey mustard dressing on the side."

Starsky recited his order and shifted his attention back to Amara. "Productive morning?"

"Meh. You?"

"Got a new case. A hanging near St. Mary's."

"A hanging? Pretty rare to kill someone that way, isn't it?"

He nodded. "Ninety-nine-point-nine percent sure it's gonna end up being a suicide. Relative of the deceased is apparently part of the old money in the city. LT wants to be certain we cross all our t's just to be safe."

"Not dotting our i's too?"

"What can I say? I'm a rebel." He sipped his water, scowled, and dumped in two more packs of sugar. "Got a big afternoon planned?"

"Need to track down the parents of one of the kids."

"What's that about?"

"Don't ask. Shot in the dark. And later I'll probably head back to the station and get my notes in order."

"Might want to hold off on that."

She scooted her chair closer to the table. "How come?"

"Out of sight, out of mind. You've been on this for what? A week or so? The LT's going to want an update, and if you don't have much to show him, he might switch things up. Assign someone else to it or put the case on hold."

She gripped her fork as her stomach tightened. "I've got plenty to show him. It's not like I haven't been busting my—"

"Whoa there." He nodded toward the fork. "Put down the weapon before someone gets hurt."

"Not funny, Starsky."

"You misunderstood what I'm saying. Nobody, including the LT, is questioning your work ethic or ability. Nobody."

"That's not entirely true."

"Rutledge?" He rolled his eyes. "Ignore that creep. But, as I was saying, sometimes a homicide investigation reaches a point where all you're doing is rehashing old information hoping a clue jumps out at you. That's when you set it aside until something new pops up. A witness decides it's time, someone hears something at a bar or snitches in jail, the murder weapon is found, whatever."

Rehashing old information. Sounded familiar. "How do you know when it's time to move on?"

"Some of the detectives will tell you it comes with experience. To a small extent, there may be truth in that. From my perspective, a *lack* of experience is often as useful as anything else." He held out his hands. "Don't take what I'm about to say the wrong way, okay?"

She nodded and laid down the fork.

"You're new," he said. "So afraid of missing something that you shotgun. Scatter your focus in every possible direction. The downside is information overload. Trying to decide what's relevant and what's not." He leaned forward. "But the upside is huge. You haven't fallen into your routine yet. Your standard questions and preconceptions. That doesn't mean you're a better detective, but it *does* mean you're more likely to—man, I hate this expression—think outside the box."

"There's a reason most things are in the box," she said.

"Sure. The overwhelming majority of murders boil down to money, sex, or power and involve someone close to the victim. It's how we, as detectives, get from the deceased to the killer that differs. You'll ask questions and do things I'd never think of because my experience has, like it or not, impacted how I investigate. I know what works for me because I've seen what's successful. Hence, every investigation I do starts with preconceptions. Doesn't mean I stay there. Wouldn't be much of a detective if I did."

She squished her mouth to the side. "One thing confuses me."

"Yeah?"

"Did you really just say 'hence'?"

"It was either that or a 'therefore.' Seemed like 'ergo' was too formal."

She grinned and paused as the waiter placed their meals before them and wandered off to another table.

"Money," she said. "Zachary's case is about money. I'm sure of it."

He took a bite of his loaded fries and scrubbed a thin string of cheese off his chin. "Mind if I offer you a piece of friendly advice? You can take it or leave it. This is going to sound harsh." He stared at his plate. "Cruel even. But you've always heard you don't name the animals you're planning to eat, right? Makes it harder to kill them because it's more personal."

"Zachary wasn't an animal."

"I know that, but experience counts this time." He sighed. "Don't use your victim's first name unless you're dealing with his family or interrogating a suspect. Makes it too personal. More difficult to process internally. Trust me, you won't have any trouble remembering the boy's name."

She waited until he made eye contact again but stayed silent.

"Yes," he said, "Zachary was a real person who deserves justice if he was murdered. And yes, you want his family and friends to know the truth of how he died. But you have to remember this is your job. There will always be another Zachary waiting for you. A ninety-year-old grandfather who's killed by his greedy grandson. A three-month-old baby abandoned so the mother can run off with her new boyfriend. There's always another Zachary. Don't make it harder on yourself than it has to be."

She stabbed her fork into the salad and dipped the bite into the dressing before eating it. Starsky was right, but . . . he was right. "No more work talk." Did they have anything else to chat about?

"If you want to come by tonight," he said, "after you see your mom, I mean, I'll be up. Or I can stop by your place. Or you can just call."

"Um, we'll see how it goes. Not sure if I'll feel up to talking, but thanks."

He nodded and stared at her for a moment. "I like what we have, Amara."

Her mind rocketed and she concentrated on keeping her mouth closed and her eyes on her food. What did *he* think they had? How was she supposed to respond to that and why, of all days, would he say something like that today?

"Just wanted to say that out loud," he said. "I'm not looking for a response. I'm not sure what this is or if it's going anywhere or even if I *want* it to go anywhere, but I know I don't want to mess it up. Know that I'm on your side. I enjoy listening to you. I hate seeing you hurting. If you want to talk about your mom or the job or Larry or anything else, I'd love to listen, but there's no pressure. You don't owe me anything."

She cleared her throat and peered at him. He had the same questions about their relationship she did. That was a good thing, wasn't it? She reached across the table and placed her hand on his. "Thank you. That means a lot."

"Plethora does too."

"Huh?"

"*Plethora* means a lot." He tilted his head and arched his eyebrows. "No? Nothing?"

No hiding her smile. "Weak. I expect better from you." She grabbed a cheesy fry off his plate and dragged it through the ranch before popping it into her mouth. "Want some of my salad as payback?"

"Punishment is more like it. No thanks. If you wanted a fry, all you had to do was ask."

She snagged another one and snatched the bacon bits that fell off onto the table. "Yeah, but where's the fun in that?"

Her phone shook with a series of three short vibrations. Missed call. She checked the history. "Unknown number" left a voice mail. Great. What did they do to her this time? She pressed the button to play the message and held the cell tight against her ear.

"Detective Alvarez? This is Haley Bricker. Is there, uh, somewhere we can meet? I have to talk." The incessant yipping of her dog cut her off. "Dexter, hush! I'll take you out in a minute. Anyway, call me back, okay? Soon."

Amara slipped the phone in her pocket and glanced at the barely touched salad. Hard to call someone when you didn't know their number. No choice but to swing by her house. Could box up lunch and give the lettuce to Larry, but by the time she got home, the soggy mess wouldn't be worth eating by her or the lizard. She pushed her plate across the table. "Got to go. Feel free to finish that."

He plucked off the larger pieces of ham and turkey and dropped them on his fries. "Work?"

"Might be the break I've been waiting for."

"Good luck." He inched his plate toward her. "One for the road?"

"No thanks." She grabbed a small handful of fries and cupped them in her palm. "A dozen is more like it."

"Call me later. If you want to."

"I might." She turned and strode toward her car, knowing one thing in her day was a certainty.

She'd be talking to Starsky tonight.

27

Amara sat in her car outside the Bricker home and stared at the house. Her repeated knocks on the front door had been met with silence. No surprise since the monster pickup was gone. What now? She could hang out here and hope the girl came home soon, but who knows how long that would be? And, despite the size of Haley's truck, driving aimlessly in the hopes of spotting it would only waste gas and time.

She could issue a BOLO, but there wasn't enough cause. The girl didn't say she was in any danger. Amara watched the rearview while her finger doodled on the armrest. So where to? Could go see Eugenia Coleman, Zacha—the deceased's grandmother. Give her a chance to talk. Maybe learn something new about her grandson while letting the elderly woman move forward in the grieving process.

Amara dug out the grandmother's address and keyed it into the GPS on her phone. Twenty-three-minute ETA. Should she call first? Old people liked to take a nap after lunch, didn't they? She shook her head as she drove off. *She'd* like to take a nap after lunch.

The directions indicated she should turn left at the stop sign, but she paused. Maybe Haley was at Liam's or Matias's house. She ought to drive by and check before visiting Eugenia Coleman. That would give the woman time to rest, and if Amara did find the teenager, she could stake out the truck and wait for her to leave. Best not to try and connect with her if she was at their home. Confronting the teenagers might slam the door on the girl's willingness to talk.

A horn honked from behind and she glanced in the mirror, waved, and turned right toward Matias's house. The GPS voiced its somewhat accusatory "recalculating," and she tapped the button to stop the app, then scooted straighter in her seat. Her stomach gurgled as the cheese fries sank to the bottom of her belly. Ugh. Bad call. One she'd be paying for all day.

Traffic was heavy with the after-lunch crowds on their way back to work, and every stoplight seemed to detect her vehicle and switch to red. If Haley wasn't at either of the boys' homes, should she go back by the girl's house before heading to Eugenia Coleman's? If she didn't, she'd spend the rest of the day thinking she should have, so might as well. Driving around San Antonio all afternoon wasn't exactly productive, but it was a diversion from thoughts of tonight's dinner at Mama's.

She eased past Matias's street, slowing enough to see if any cars were parked out front. Her pulse pounded as she saw Liam's SUV behind Haley's truck. All three were here. Amara drove a large loop around the area but couldn't find a place that offered a view without also exposing herself to being seen. The subdivision had two exits onto a main thoroughfare, and she backed into a spot at a convenience store about halfway between them. Couldn't see Matias's house, but she'd be able to see when Haley left.

She'd barely shifted the car into park when the black pickup pulled onto the street and passed in front of her. Haley was driving and seemed to be alone in the vehicle. Amara watched to make sure neither Liam's SUV nor Matias's Prius followed the girl, then accelerated and tailed her from a safe distance. Better to wait until they were far away from the other two teens before trying to talk to her.

If she was headed home, they could talk there. If not, Amara could flick on her lights and initiate a routine traffic stop or have a marked unit do it for her. Ahead, the truck's right blinker flashed as Haley turned into a shopping center parking lot. Amara slowed, checked her rearview, and followed.

The girl parked at the rear of the lot, away from other cars. Amara veered off, pulled into a spot near the stores where she could observe, and opened the camera app on her phone. She zoomed in on Haley's truck and made out the girl's silhouette through the tinted windows. She appeared to be just sitting there staring out her windshield. Was she waiting for someone?

Five minutes passed.

Then ten.

Amara's muscles twitched. If it got to fifteen minutes, she'd go over. Make sure Haley was okay and try to talk or at least get her phone number. Hopefully whatever happened at Matias's house hadn't affected the girl's desire to speak.

The seconds ticked past with no change. Fourteen minutes. One more and . . . nope. She'd seen enough movies to know something bad happens in the last minute to derail everything. Not a hunch. Paranoia, plain and simple. She drove toward Haley and pulled alongside so their driver windows were next to each other.

Amara lowered hers and smiled up at the teen.

The truck window went down and Haley frowned at her. "What are you doing here?"

"Looking for you. I got your call but I don't have your cell number. You wanted to talk?"

"No. That was a mistake." Her puffy eyes and red nose stood out on her face.

"Haley, what's wrong?"

"Nothing. You need to leave. I don't want to talk to you."

"What did they do? I know you were with Matias and Liam just now. Did they threaten you? Do they know you called me?"

She peeked out the back window. "No clue what you're talking about. Don't contact me again. I have a lawyer."

Sure you do. "Understood. What's your attorney's name? I'll give them a call."

Haley waved her hand. "I'm leaving. Don't follow me."

"I'm trying to help you." She stared behind the girl at the reverse *Haley* decal. A thin, green strap hung from a hook, splitting the name in half. A dog leash. "Where's Dexter?"

"What?"

"Dexter. Your dog. He wasn't at your house. I knocked on the door several times and never heard a sound."

"He's, uh, he's not here."

No kidding. The beast's yapping would've overpowered any attempt at conversation. "So where is he? Is that why you've been crying? Has something happened to your dog?"

"I have to go."

"Haley, did Liam and Matias do something to Dexter? Why?"

The truck window started to go up but stopped halfway. The girl's nostrils flared and she swallowed hard. "Get away from me."

Amara clenched her jaw. Was this her fault? Because she'd tried to bluff Liam by telling him one of his friends had already called? "I can protect you."

Haley laughed. "This is where I say you can't even protect yourself, right? It's true though."

The truck window finished its upward path and Amara stared in her mirror as the vehicle drove off. Haley wasn't going to talk. Not now. The girl feared for her safety. And using that knowledge to threaten either Liam or Matias would only make the situation worse. At this point, her best move was to wait and give the boys' parents time to react. Hold off until tomorrow to see if any of them phoned. Gaps were beginning to appear in the teenagers' relationships. All she needed to do was jam a crowbar in the cracks and pry them open.

She checked the clock. Still plenty of time to swing by Eugenia Coleman's. If nothing else, the visit would allow Amara some low-stress minutes before the avalanche of emotions came tonight. She called the woman and asked if she could stop by for a few minutes.

"That would be wonderful, dear," Ms. Coleman said. "I'll put on a pot of decaf and get some cookies from the freezer. Would you prefer vanilla wafers or Fig Newtons? Or perhaps both?"

Decaf and thawed cookies. Why not? Her stomach had already taken a beating at lunch. Might as well make a day of it. "Your choice, but please don't go to any trouble. Give me about, um, twenty minutes maybe? Would that be okay?"

"I have to run out later this afternoon, but I'll be here for at least another hour."

"No problem. Oh, and remember, I won't be able to answer many questions. This is more to give you a chance to tell me about your grandson. I hope you understand."

"Of course. Drive safely, dear."

"You too." What? "I mean, see you soon."

She hung up and dropped the phone in a cup holder. Haley's parting words still hovered in the air. *You can't even protect yourself.* Was she referring to past events or future dangers? Both? *Safe bet she knows who's messing with my bank accounts and utilities.* Amara checked her surroundings as she left the parking lot and headed for Ms. Coleman's home. No sign that Liam or Matias was nearby.

Meet with the grandmother, then head home and check on Larry before dinner at Mama's. It'd be a late, draining night.

But tomorrow morning, if none of the parents had called, she'd find the sledgehammer that would drive the crowbar deep into the gaps that divided the teens.

28

Eugenia Coleman's home sat among dozens of cottages in the retirement community, each nearly identical to her own and differentiated primarily by the door decorations and whatever statuettes or knick-knacks the owner had spread around their manicured minuscule lawns. Ms. Coleman's door displayed a red, white, and blue wreath with a pair of small American flags sticking proudly from the top at two and ten o'clock.

Amara studied it for a moment. *Appropriate for July. She probably has a different one for every month. What would August's wreath be? Dead grass and heat lamps?* She knocked and stepped back as the click of the deadbolt sounded and the door swung open.

"Hello, Detective." Ms. Coleman stood aside. "Won't you please come in?"

"Yes, ma'am. Thank you." To the left, a newish-looking small sofa and pair of fabric recliners were angled toward a TV. Unmatched end tables, their surface areas covered with framed photos, sat on either side of the recliners. A hallway straight ahead probably led to a bathroom and one or two bedrooms. The tiny kitchen to the right, complete with a wooden dining table not much bigger than the serving tray atop it, was immaculate.

"Have a seat," the woman said. "Would you like some coffee?"

"That'd be wonderful." Amara sat on the sofa as Ms. Coleman poured the brew into a china cup, set it on a saucer, and strategically placed two fig newtons on a matching dessert plate. She repeated the process, then put everything on the wooden tray and brought it into the living room.

"Here you are, dear." She bent forward and smiled.

Amara took hers and nodded. "Thank you." She glanced to either side. No place to set these down. She balanced the plate in her lap and sipped the coffee. Weak. Very weak. "This is delicious."

"I'm glad you like it." She eased into a recliner and adjusted the tray in her lap. "I need something to catch the drips and crumbs."

"Yes, ma'am. I wonder if you could tell me a bit about your grandson? I understand he visited quite often?"

"Yes, he did." Her eyes moistened and the skin on her face sagged. "At least once or twice a week. We'd always been close. Paul is my only child, and when Zachary came along, well, you can imagine how excited I was." Her hands shook and she steadied them on the armrests.

Amara pretend-sipped her coffee, nodded twice, and waited.

Just as the silence approached awkwardness, Ms. Coleman reached beside her and lifted one of the photos from the table. "This is Zachary when he was a baby." She turned the picture so Amara could see. "His daddy always called him Zach. Not me. I liked the sound of the full name. So proper, don't you think?"

"He was a beautiful baby." Got to keep her focused. "I wonder if you could tell me about the last several months? Did he seem distracted or worried?"

The woman lifted her cup and saucer and blew across the coffee, then slurped a few drops. "Not at all. He was a bright boy. I could tell he was really going to be a fine young man. We sometimes talked about his future. College, of course. He wanted to study computers. Most of his chatter about that stuff went over my head, but Zachary did love to talk about it."

Amara's heartbeat quickened. "Can you remember anything

specific? Things he might have said about his friends or what he did online?"

"Not really. I know he played video games though. Does that help?"

Not a bit. "Yes, ma'am. I wonder if you noticed any changes in him as far as his spending habits. We, uh, found some things that—"

"I know about the money." She nibbled on a fig newton and brushed a crumb off her bottom lip. "Paul told me about it. Zachary was never a big spender. I can't remember him ever asking to borrow money. But I'm not naive, Detective. Nobody saves that kind of money working part-time at Target. I can tell you this though. However Zachary obtained it, he didn't do anything illegal. I'm certain of that. He would never do anything to hurt anyone."

Would any grandmother say anything different? "I understand, but you can see our concern and why that would make his death suspicious." She bit into her not-completely-thawed cookie. Dry and crumbly. She chased the fig newton with cold coffee. "If your grandson didn't die of, um, natural causes, the money may point us to a suspect."

"I'm afraid I can't help you there." She raised her chin. "I believe Zachary's death was related to the heat and possibly some alcohol. When the blood work comes back, you'll see."

That was one question answered. Did it matter to a grieving relative how their loved one died? It did to Ms. Coleman. Even if she was right, the money still needed to be explained. "Yes, ma'am."

"But if my grandson *was* killed, I would want to know. Now, tell me about your investigation."

Amara stalled by nibbling on her cookie. "I'm afraid I can't go into the details. We remain"—confident? skeptical? optimistic?— "curious about his death."

"Because of the money?"

"Primarily, yes."

The woman bent forward and placed her tray on the carpet, then slid it to the side with her foot. "Primarily. What else makes you think his passing was no accident?"

"Again, I can't go into those details at this time. I will say there are other reasons we suspect Mr. Coleman's death may be more than it appears."

"Other reasons." Her voice softened. "His name was Zachary. It's all right if you call him that."

Her heart sank. Remember. Sympathy, not empathy. She stood and placed her dinnerware on the tray, then half squatted so she was at eye level with the elderly woman. "Ms. Coleman, I'm very sorry about Zachary."

"Thank you, dear." Tears pooled in her eyes. "I miss him terribly."

Voices filtered through the front door, followed by a sturdy knock.

"That's my ride," Ms. Coleman said. "We're going to pick up some flowers and go visit a friend's grave. Dorothy Engers. Lovely lady. Seems I do a lot of that these days. Visiting cemeteries, I mean."

Amara squeezed the woman's hand, careful not to apply too much pressure, then picked up the tray and carried it to the kitchen. "I try to go on the eighteenth of every month to see my dad. Make sure the tombstone is clean, take a marigold, stuff like that." She placed the dishes in the sink. "It helps me remember him. Not that I could ever forget."

"I understand completely." The grandmother pushed herself out of the chair and opened the front door. "Come in, ladies. I'll be ready in just a moment."

Two women stepped into the coolness of the home and nodded to Amara.

"Oh," Ms. Coleman said. "Forgive my manners. This is Amara Alvarez. Amara, this is Patricia and Mary Ann. Give me just a moment to use the restroom and get my purse and I'll be ready to go." She wandered down the hallway out of sight.

The two visitors maintained their positions by the door and stared as Amara squirted some blue dishwashing liquid onto a wet rag and cleaned the tableware. Patricia and Mary Ann, but which was which?

After a few uneasy moments of silence, one of the women spoke. "If I may ask, how do you know Eugenia?"

Amara kept a noncommittal expression. *Twenty bucks says they think I'm her new maid.* "Friend of the family," she said. "Stopped by to check on Ms. Coleman."

"That's sweet of you," the other woman said. "We've all been worried about her. Eugenia's had a rough few weeks."

"Yes, she has," Amara said. A toilet flushed in the back of the house. No secrets in a small home. "Was she good friends with, um, Ms. Engers, was it?"

"Yes," the first woman said. "Dorothy Engers. We really only met her recently. She had no other family, at least none that we knew of. When she fell and broke her hip, we went to see her at the hospital several times. And when she came back here to do her rehab, we would go sit with her regularly. Her death was quite a shock."

"Mmm," the other lady said. "She fell again. Hit her head this time and bled out, they say."

The first woman frowned. "Tact was never your strong suit, Mary Ann. Dorothy was on blood thinners and took a tumble during the night on the way to the restroom. When they found her several hours later, it was too late."

Amara used a dishtowel to dry the dinnerware and wipe her hands. "I'm sorry to hear that."

Ms. Coleman walked into the room and glanced into the kitchen. "Oh, dearie, you didn't have to do that. Thank you." She clutched her purse in front of her. "Ladies, shall we go?"

"I'll follow you out," Amara said. "Don't stay in the sun too long. This heat is dangerous." The *for people your age* remained unspoken.

"Nonsense," Mary Ann said. "We've been visiting for six or seven weeks. A few minutes in the sun never hurt anyone."

Patricia clucked her tongue and lowered her voice. "Could you be less sensitive? Heatstroke?" She nodded toward Ms. Coleman. "Her grandson? And besides, it's only been five weeks since Dorothy passed."

Mary Ann's eyes widened. "I am *so* sorry, Eugenia. I didn't mean to hurt you."

Ms. Coleman flicked her hand. "You didn't. Five weeks? Are you certain, Patricia?"

"Of course I am. My memory's as good as it's ever been."

Mary Ann giggled. "That's not saying much."

A tinge of pink appeared in Patricia's cheeks. "I remember it well. It was the night the phones and air-conditioning and everything else quit working."

Amara crinkled her forehead. "Quit working? What do you mean?"

"Computer hiccup," Ms. Coleman said. "That's the way it is these days. Everything all tied together. Zachary tried to explain it to me, but at my age, why bother trying to remember things like that?"

A glitch in the computers? She ran a finger across the sweat beading on her upper lip. Had the retirement community been hacked too? She checked her watch. No time to follow up on it today. Couldn't be late to Mama's. "Pleasure to meet you ladies."

She waited until they were all in their car and the air-conditioning was running before striding toward her vehicle. If this place had been hacked, would their IT people know that? Was the death of Dorothy Engers somehow related to the outage? And what did all that mean to her investigation?

Her mind whirred with the possibilities. Finally, another route forward. Maybe.

But that was for tomorrow.

Tonight was about family.

29 **Amara was the last** to arrive at her mother's house, not because she was late, but because her brothers and sisters were early. Wylie was there too, of course, smiling and making small talk. Heat or not, dinners at Mama's were outside unless the rain, or on even rarer occasions, the cold interrupted. She grabbed an icy drink from the cooler, dragged a lawn chair beside Wylie, and sat.

The normal joviality of the family had given way to nervous laughs and somber voices. Even the kids seemed subdued as they half-heartedly chased each other around the yard. She ran her palm along the condensation of the drink can and glanced at Wylie. His eyes told her what his relaxed countenance didn't. This wasn't good.

The back screen door swung open and Mama walked outside. A pair of mismatched oven mitts covered her hands as she carried a still bubbling dish of enchiladas to the table. "Time to eat," she said. "Two or three of you go get everything else. Wylie, would you mind bringing me something from that cooler?"

He smiled and grunted as he leaned forward, shoved his hand to the bottom of the ice, and grabbed a can.

Amara placed her palm on his back and whispered, "Thank you."

He shrugged. "It's just a drink."

"Not what I meant, and you know it."

"Don't thank me for doing what I love." He glanced at her and his smile evaporated. "It's been a rough couple of days. She's been dreading tonight. I think telling everyone is worse for her than the cancer itself. She's terrified that y'all will have to take care of her."

"Yeah, that sounds like her. If it comes to that, we'll be happy to—"

"She asked me to marry her."

Amara's mouth fell open as a wave of dizziness washed through her brain. "What? When?"

He patted her knee. "I suppose I should be thankful you didn't ask 'why' too. We'll talk later. No mention of this to anyone, right?"

She nodded as his smile returned and he wandered off toward her mother. Could her world get more confused? Thoughts ricocheted in her mind as they jockeyed for priority. Mama's cancer. Haley Bricker and her dog. The computer problems at the retirement center. The anonymous phone caller who knew all about her. Starsky. Liam Walker and Matias Lucero. And Wylie, her new stepfather?

Her pulse quickened as the thoughts combined into a muddy mixture. She pressed her drink against her forehead and closed her eyes. *Focus. Prioritize.* Tonight was about Mama. Get the facts on her health and make sure there was a plan to move forward. *She* was the priority.

Amara whispered a prayer for peace and stood. One of her nephews bumped into her as he ran toward his designated spot at the kids' table, his "sorry!" barely audible over the cacophony of voices from those already gathered under the mesquite tree. She settled onto the only open space at the end of the bench and scooted until most of her rear was on the seat. Wouldn't be long until they'd need to add more seating, though Mama always liked it better when everyone was squeezed together. Said it made the table look full. She was right.

Wylie tapped a spoon against a glass and cleared his throat.

"After dinner, we'd like to go inside for a, um, brief discussion. Everyone is welcome, including grandchildren." He glanced at Mama. "Especially grandchildren. For now though"—he waved his hands over the table—"your mother has prepared a feast. Eat up!"

Conversations briefly faded as the clanking of forks and glasses and knives and plates overtook the area. Amara chose a chicken enchilada and added a spoonful of rice, a large dose of black beans, and some grilled corn. The meal was, as always, delicious and too much. She surveyed the others seated around her. What would happen when Mama could no longer fix a dinner like this? Would someone else step forward and take over? Should she? It would require a time commitment she wasn't sure she could make.

But the time excuse was a cop-out. She loved her family, but spending time around them drained her. Her favorite activities outside of work were primarily solo ventures. Workouts on the Muay Thai bag. Long jogs around parks. Visiting Dad's grave. All things that recharged her. Planning, preparing, and presenting a meal to her family required skills she didn't have and didn't want. Was that being selfish? She'd help Mama in every possible way, of course. Whatever it took to get her through this battle.

A poke on her arm startled her and she peered at her brother seated next to her. "Hello? You with us? Mama's talking to you."

Amara raised her head and nodded. "Sorry."

"You're not eating," her mother said. "What's wrong?"

"Just, um, just thinking about some things I need to take care of. Not very hungry anyway." She straightened and smiled. "It's delicious though."

Mama stared at her for a few seconds before standing. "Help me with something in the kitchen for a moment."

She followed her mother inside and the two stood so they could peek out the window into the yard. Neither spoke and, after a moment, Amara sniffled as tears filled her eyes. Mama pulled a paper towel off the roll and handed it to her. "I know about the calls," she said. "Wylie told me. Your anonymous one and his call to you after my appointment."

What? Why? "He wasn't supposed to. That information is confidential and concerns an ongoing investigation. If I thought you were in any danger because of it, I would have told you. Made certain you were safe."

"Confidential? You told Wylie. He's no longer a police officer."

She placed a hand on the counter. "I needed to know if the information was valid."

"Are *you* in any danger?"

How did a cop answer that? No more than usual? "No. And I don't want you to worry about any of this. The call, the cancer, any of it. We'll get through it."

Mama faced her and brushed her fingertips on Amara's cheek. "Is that what you think I worry about? My life is gathered around those tables in the backyard. You too, of course. I am blessed beyond words. Everything else comes and goes." She shrugged. "Or it doesn't. Do not mistake my meaning. The cancer is not good and I will fight, but my strength is my family. You want to help me get through this? I will tell you the same thing I am saying to the others later. If I need help, I will ask for it."

"You can't expect us to act as if nothing is different."

"No, I cannot." She gestured out the window to the rest of the family. "But there is my joy and I will not allow cancer to take it from me. You understand?"

"Mama, you're not being realistic. It's selfish to not let us help you. We're a part of this now, whether you like it or not. We can't put on happy faces and pretend everything's okay."

A long sigh flowed through her mother's lips. "I did not ask for happy faces. I understand what is about to happen. One way or another, the cancer will consume my life. The treatments may work or they may not. I cannot ask you not to worry, but you should have no guilt."

"Guilt? For what?"

"For the times to come." She hooked her arm through Amara's. "For the nights you work late and think you should be with me. For the weekends you spend home alone instead of visiting me. For the dates you go on—you do still go on dates?—and remember halfway through the meal you haven't called me in a while. That guilt does not come from me." She poked a finger into Amara's chest. "Do not allow it in there. Your life is yours. Do not change who you are or what you do. *That* is what would truly hurt me."

Outside, the family began the process of stacking plates and cleaning up. Soon, everyone would head inside. Amara squeezed her mother's arm. "Wylie told me you asked him to marry you."

"That man cannot keep a secret."

"Tell me about it. Kind of soon, isn't it?"

Mama shook her head. "Maybe for someone your age. I know he loves me."

"And you love him?"

"I would be happy to share my life with him."

Amara took a step backward. "That's not what I asked. Do you love him?"

"I think so." She wiped her palms on a dishtowel. "It's difficult. Your father was the love of my life. I will not experience that again. Wylie and I are comfortable together. We enjoy each other." She winked. "Very much."

Heat flashed through Amara's face. "Mama, are you and Wylie, you know, *together*?"

"Is that a question you truly wish me to answer?"

No. Emphatically no. "So when's the wedding?"

"He has not given his answer yet. There are things he must consider."

"Such as?"

"I do not know. Perhaps you could speak to him?"

Amara's stomach rumbled as she watched the crowd outside finish their clean-up work. She drummed her fingers on the counter and cleared her throat. "I wouldn't know what to say. I think this is something you two should settle."

Mama nodded, then pulled a slip of paper from her pocket and read from it. "I have Stage 3 breast cancer with a six-centimeter tumor that has spread to three lymph nodes. Tomorrow morning, I begin six cycles of chemotherapy, once every twenty-one days, and then my doctor will reevaluate my situation. That may mean further treatment, a lumpectomy or mastectomy, and radiation. He feels my prognosis is good."

She folded the paper and ran her hand along the crease. "That is what I am telling everyone tonight." Her voice quivered. "I expect it will be emotional."

Amara wrapped her arms around her mother. "Why are you telling me now?"

"Because it is you I worry about most. Everyone else here will go home with family. They can talk and cry and be together. You will be alone in your apartment. If that is by choice, fine. But no matter your decisions or personality or history, there are times it is not good to be by yourself. You need to learn that."

Same thing Starsky said. The two separated as the back door opened and the family filtered into the house. Amara took a stack of plates and began rinsing them at the sink as her mother piled them into the dishwasher. "I could spend the night here," she said. "You don't need to be alone either."

"That is *exactly* what I need. After I tell the rest of the family, my talking is done. Whatever Dios has planned for me, my life will change. I must come to peace with that, and I cannot if others are here."

"So I shouldn't be alone but you should be? How does that make sense?"

Mama closed the dishwasher and straightened. "I will be by myself because I choose to be. I am not convinced you can say the same." She took Amara's hand. "My sweet baby. Can you look your mother in the eye and promise her you are happy?"

Amara looked toward the ceiling to keep the tears from dripping from her eyes. "I love my job, Mama."

"I know you do, sweetheart. You are a detective. What would you say your answer means?"

That I'm being evasive. Avoiding the question for some reason. Maybe because I don't know the answer.

Or worse, I do.

30

Amara's alarm clock jolted her awake at five the next morning and skyrocketed her pulse. Her late-night desire to rise early and stop by the gym on the way to work had seemed plausible at the time. Not so much now. The discussion with Mama and the family meeting left her drained. And that was before Wylie cornered her as everyone was leaving.

He wanted to marry her mother but feared she only asked because of the cancer. Not in a selfish way, but in a "I know you want to marry me and my time might be short so let's do this" sense. Yes, he knew she loved him and he loved her too. And yes, he'd take care of her, married or not. But what if she changed her mind once the treatments were over? Everyone's emotions were out of whack and maybe it wasn't the time for spur-of-the-moment decisions. Was he being fair to her if he accepted her proposal? And what about her kids? What would they think? Would Amara put out feelers? Oh, and bounce his thoughts off her mother while she was at it?

Matchmaker or go-between or arbitrator. Whichever she was, it was a job she didn't want. Why couldn't they simply talk to each other instead of acting like a couple of middle schoolers passing "do you like me? check yes or no" notes? After finally getting away from Mama's and returning to her apartment, she'd spent nearly an hour on the phone debriefing with Starsky. He'd asked a few questions, but mostly he listened. At one point she tried to lighten the mood by wondering if this was what therapy was like. He responded by saying that he didn't know, but if it was helping her, he'd stay on the phone all night. Her talking had dwindled until the seconds of silence stretched into minutes and her yawns could no longer be stifled and they said goodbye.

It seemed as if they'd just hung up when her alarm went off. She lifted her head, paused, and let it fall back onto the cool pillow. Sleep was more important than the gym. Another thirty minutes would make all the difference. Big day today. She'd go by the retirement community to get more details on their computer problems. If, as she suspected, there was some commonality between what happened there and the outages at the water park, that would be a major lead. A connection that might point to the teenagers' online activities and source of income.

She let loose a wall-shaking yawn. Why was her bedroom so bright? She flopped her arm over her eyes and licked her dry lips. Morning breath was in full force today. She stretched and turned toward her clock. Eight thirty? She'd fallen back asleep. Her heart pounded as she hurried to the bathroom. How many years since she'd overslept?

Her reflection frowned back at her. Saggy skin and puffy eyes and Edward-Scissorhands hair. The quick shower and smidgen of makeup barely dented the damage. Might need her oversize sunglasses. And a hat.

Fifteen minutes later, after checking on Larry and telling him not to look at her like that because she had enough guilt in her life right now, she was in her car headed toward Green Horizons Retirement Community. Breakfast consisted of a dry granola bar and bottled water, an apt punishment for her tardiness.

She opted against phoning ahead, reasoning that in a facility so large, surely someone would be there she could talk to about the incident. She'd need to tread carefully though. A woman had died the night they experienced the problems, and anyone in management would be wary of potential lawsuits. If Amara spooked them by trying to tie the death to the computer outage, whether that was the case or not, there was a good possibility she'd be shown the door, or worse, referred to their legal department.

The radio hushed as her cell's ring echoed through the car's speakers. A local number popped onto the display, not that that meant anything lately. She pressed the button on the steering wheel to connect the call. "Hello?"

"Detective Alvarez?"

"Yes."

"This is Nicole Walker. Liam's mother. We spoke briefly yesterday."

The skin on Amara's arms tingled. "Right. How can I help you?"

"I spoke to my son last night. He, um, he said he doesn't know anything about that boy's death."

Yeah? He's lying. "And you believe him?"

"I do. He's, uh, got no reason to lie to me."

"Interesting. If he's involved, I'd say he has *every* reason to lie to you."

"If you have evidence to the contrary, let's hear it. Otherwise, I choose to believe my son."

Time to tighten the screws. "That's your decision. I hope you can live with it."

"Meaning what?"

"Your son is withholding information regarding the death of Zachary Coleman. I'm certain of that and I think you are too. Look, all I can do is go where the case leads me, and right now, there's an arrow pointed straight at Liam. He's not the only one, and I'm not saying he killed the boy, but he knows something."

"Even if he did have information, why would he share it with the police? You've already made up your mind that he did something. No wonder people are scared of cops."

Especially guilty people. "Are you sure it's *me* he's frightened of? If someone did kill Coleman, they're still out there. Maybe Liam is involved in illegal activity and maybe not. I'm going to find out, and when I do, I'll meet with the DA to discuss the charges. Your son has an opportunity to be seen as helpful in the investigation. That's a sign of remorse for any wrongdoing. Judges and juries like that."

"This isn't easy, Detective." A voice in the background announced that a patient was on the way to her room. "I couldn't sleep last night worried about Liam. If he *has* done something, I want to mitigate the punishment as much as I can."

"Then the best thing would be for him to come forward. The sooner the better."

"I don't want to lose my son."

"I understand. Neither did the Colemans."

An iciness crept into her voice. "I have to go."

The call disconnected. Not even a goodbye? Amara stopped as a light turned red. Had she pushed the woman too hard? Everything she'd said was true. Liam, Matias, and Haley were somehow involved. She might be a long way from being able to prove that, but the day would come. The truth always came out.

Except in the large percentage of homicides in which no one was ever charged.

The light cycled green and she continued her drive to the retirement village. Should be there in another ten or so. Right about the time Mama would be getting her first chemo treatment. The doctor said it would take around four hours and any side effects wouldn't kick in until the third or fourth day afterward.

Maybe she should take Mama and Wylie to dinner tonight. Hash out this whole marriage thing so she could cross it off her to-do list.

That would mean getting to bed later, but tomorrow was Saturday. Unless something broke on the case today, she'd let everyone stew over the weekend. Otherwise, sleep in, hit the Breakfast Bodega, and make up for the lost workouts with a weekend of exercise interspersed with quality time with Larry. And no family meal tomorrow night since they'd just done one. A chance to find two or three movies to veg out with, either alone or invite Starsky over.

Alone sounded good though. Less talking. Less human interaction. Less cleaning to do. Less emotional effort.

More excuses to avoid her mother's question.

31 **Amara pulled into a visitor's parking spot** at the main building and texted Wylie to ask how Mama was doing. Two seconds later, he called to remind her how much he hated typing texts. Her mother was fine, he said, but freezing. Cold enough to hang meat in that room. She had a blanket but would know to dress warmer next time.

Amara mentioned taking the pair out to dinner that night, and he immediately became suspicious. She assured him it was simply a chance for a quiet meal after a rough week. He hemmed and hawed, but eventually caved after she swore there'd be no discussion about the marriage proposal since that would be awkward for everyone. And to ensure she didn't bring it up, he insisted she bring a date.

A date? Fine. Starsky would come with her. Seven o'clock, quiet Italian restaurant not far from Mama's, reservations under Amara's name. And she'd text if she was going to be late. Wylie promised to call if anything changed and said he'd try to get her mother to take a nap that afternoon. Amara laughed, wished him good luck, and hung up.

She pictured tonight's dinner as she walked past the dozen or so empty handicapped visitors' spots to the door. Why had she been so certain Starsky would come with her tonight? He would, of course, unless he had other plans, which she'd never known him to have. But a tinge of guilt washed over her. Was she stringing him along, knowing he probably wanted a deeper relationship? Taking advantage of him? Was her indecisiveness keeping him from moving on to someone else? And what was up with all the inner monologues whenever she thought about him?

The building's doors swung inward as she approached. She walked inside and pressed the square metal handicapped plate on the wall to open the second set of doors. The lobby consisted of a seating area off to the right with magazines and brochures spread around. A large electronic sign cycled through a litany of upcoming events at the complex, complete with photos of smiling senior citizens enjoying themselves.

To the left, numerous offices lined the wall. Voices, ringing phones, and the unmistakable sounds of copiers and printers told her that work was already in full swing. Straight ahead, a middle-aged woman sat behind an ornate wooden reception desk, speaking several "yes, ma'am's" into her headset.

Amara smiled at her and walked closer, waiting for a free moment. The lady raised one finger to indicate she was almost done, left it there for a good minute, rolled her eyes, and offered her final "yes, ma'am" before disconnecting the call.

"I'm sorry about your wait," she said. "Part of Mrs. Vacanti's a.m. ritual. I made the mistake a couple of years ago of mentioning something about baseball. Now, every morning of the season, she calls to update me on how the Astros are doing. I don't have the heart to tell her I hate baseball."

"Not a fan either," Amara said. "But it's sweet of you to do that. I'm sure it means a lot to her." She suppressed a giggle. *Plethora* means a lot too.

"I don't mind it so much. Gives her something to look forward to. That's important, especially for folks her age."

"I imagine it is." She showed her ID and paused as a man came out of one of the offices, waved to the receptionist, and strode out the front doors. "I need to speak to whoever is in charge of your security here."

Deep lines creased the woman's forehead and she leaned forward. "Is something wrong? What's happened?"

"No, ma'am. Nothing's wrong. Can you point me in the right direction?"

The receptionist's shoulders slumped and she looked away. "You'll want to speak to Mr. Goodlett. He's over our Properties Department and they handle security." She pressed a series of buttons on her phone. "Mr. Goodlett? Good morning. You have a visitor at the front desk. Uh-huh. She's, um, with the police." She made eye contact with Amara again. "I don't know. Thank you." She hung up and stared at the monitor in front of her. "He'll be with you in a moment. There's coffee and water over there if you'd like some."

"I'm good. Thanks."

"Well, if you'd like to sit over there while you wait, you're welcome to do so."

Wow. Somebody got her feelings hurt. Amara nodded once and roamed toward the seating area, stopping halfway when she heard the steady click of shoes on tile floor. She pivoted in time to see a man enter the lobby. His dark suit, complemented with a white shirt and striped red tie, seemed more fitting in a funeral home, particularly when combined with the dour expression on his face. His too-black hair pointed to vanity, while the heavy jowls that morphed into his neck suggested maybe he waited too late to start worrying about his appearance.

The receptionist pointed to Amara, and the man accelerated toward her.

"Good morning," he said. His voice echoed in the empty space of the lobby.

She met him halfway and extended her hand. "Detective Amara Alvarez, SAPD."

His meaty palm engulfed hers. "Davidson Goodlett. How can I help you, Detective?"

She glanced at the receptionist. "Perhaps there's someplace else we can talk?"

"No problem." He gestured back the way he'd come. "My office is down here." He took off without waiting for a response.

She trailed behind him, grateful for not having to make small talk. He swiped his ID card on a reader to unlock the doors into the administration area, then repeated the process at his office.

"Please," he said, "have a seat." His desk was at least a foot too long for the space, and he turned sideways to scoot beside it before plopping into his chair.

"Thanks. I hope I won't take up too much of your time." She pulled her ID from her pocket and passed it over to him, then sat.

"Homicide?" He frowned as he returned the badge. "What's this about?"

"I understand you experienced a computer outage five weeks ago. Is that correct?"

His left eye twitched and he smoothed his hands over the desktop. "There are matters I'm not free to discuss."

"Mr. Goodlett, I'm not investigating Dorothy Engers's death. I'm here about the problems your complex experienced the evening she died."

He sank back in his chair and spots of color returned to his face. "Yes, well, we did have an outage that night. I'm afraid I can't go into detail, but the situation was resolved as quickly as possible. That's really all I can tell you."

"I'm guessing you don't have a background in law enforcement. Am I right?"

He raised his chin, though his neck flap still covered most of the knot in his tie. "If you're insinuating that I don't know how to do my job, then I think we're done here."

"Hold on." Her breathing accelerated and she flexed her fingers. "Ever see a TV show or movie with cops in it? They're mostly garbage. Fun to watch, but not that accurate. But"—she scooted her chair closer—"they do get one thing right. There is an easy way and a hard way to do things. I suspect that a man such as yourself, one with an important position in the company, would understand the implications of that statement. So I must *insist* that you go into detail about the computer issues that night."

He planted his elbows on the desk and steepled his hands as if praying. "Detective, I will not be bullied in my own office."

No? How about being bullied down at my office? She flipped her palms up and shrugged. "You win. All I wanted was information that might aid me in my investigation. You don't want to help. Hey, that's your prerogative. And if I choose to believe your reluctance to provide information means you're hiding something, well, I suppose that's *my* prerogative."

"I assure you I have nothing to hide."

"*Everyone* has something to hide. Look, my concern at this point is only with the events of that night as they relate to my case. It's quite possible your computer problems have nothing whatsoever to do with my investigation, meaning you'll most likely never hear from me again." She crossed her legs and tilted her head. "I think that's something we'd both like, isn't it? The alternative is much more complicated. For you, anyway."

He cleared his throat and worked his mouth as if this morning's breakfast was still in there somewhere. Or yesterday morning's. For a moment, she feared he was going to lean over and spit into the trash can. He nodded, rocking his whole body as he did so. "I'll tell you what I can," he said. "Which isn't much. Not because I don't know, but because our executive board prefers to keep this as low key as possible. And not because of Ms. Engers's death."

"Fine. I'll take what I can get." *And if it's not enough, I'll do what I have to.*

"On the evening in question, our computer network did experience issues. Temperature control, communications, security, elevators, and other systems stopped working. None of this was life-threatening to any of our tenants. Certainly a major inconvenience and one that created a great deal of chaos. As you can imagine, we were eager to resolve the situation quickly. Within a matter of hours, everything returned to normal."

Nothing she didn't already know or couldn't have guessed. "Why did your system crash?"

"I never said it did."

She rolled her eyes. "What caused the computer problems?"

"I'm afraid I can't get into that."

She stared until he glanced away. "Mr. Goodlett, was your network attacked?"

"There was an incident, yes. We informed the authorities and took the appropriate steps to return our operations to normal. The safety of our tenants is paramount."

Sounded like something straight off a brochure. "What authorities? The SAPD? Who?"

He rolled back from his desk, opened the middle drawer, and pulled out a business card. "Hector Canales with the FBI."

"Why not the SAPD?"

He returned the card to the drawer. "I would think you'd know that better than me. We called the police first, and they directed us to the FBI. Said they would be able to handle it quicker."

Probably true. Cybercrimes fell into a jurisdiction gray area. The

SAPD wouldn't have the experience or the access to investigative tools the Bureau had. "Is there anything else you can tell me about what happened?"

"No. We believe a crime was committed and reported it properly. Perhaps your questions would be better directed to the FBI."

"Right." She'd worked with several agents during the Cotulla investigation, but Hector Canales wasn't one of them. She stood and nodded. "I'll see myself out."

"Actually, I'll escort you." He maneuvered around his desk and walked into the hallway. "Security regulation. I'm sure you understand."

She trailed behind until reaching the lobby, then hurried past him, flashed a smile at the receptionist, and stepped outside. The morning sun reflected off the windshields of vehicles scattered in the parking lot. Beyond that, groups of cottages, most nearly identical to Eugenia Coleman's, clustered near a large pond. Fifteen or twenty people strolled at varying speeds along a paved trail circling the water. Not a bad way to start your morning. Quiet and relaxing.

The guttural din of a motorcycle's exhaust pipes broke the reverie, and she snapped her head toward the main street outside the complex. There. Except it wasn't a motorcycle. A black pickup truck, its frame sitting high above oversize tires, cruised past. The vehicle was too far away for her to make out the white splotch on the rear window, but she knew what it said.

Haley.

32

Two hours later, Amara left the station with an appointment at the FBI, a new phone, if you could call it that, and a borrowed vehicle to use for the remainder of the day. Once she'd explained as much of the situation as she thought necessary to the IT guy, he said that yes, it was quite possible hidden software had been installed on her phone. If her home network had been hacked, chances were whoever did that gained all the information needed to pose as the phone's owner and remotely install whatever they wanted. His solution was to give her one of the department's old flip phones and transfer her number to it. It was like going back to the pioneer days, but no way anyone could track it. At least they'd managed to import her contacts. She'd just have to get used to the looks from anyone who saw her use it.

Hector Canales met her in the lobby and escorted her to his office. The agent was about her age but better groomed and very GQ. If the FBI wanted to project an appearance, this guy had it nailed. His office matched his style and gave an aura of professionalism and order. Not quite the same as her card table back at the station.

"Thank you for seeing me," she said.

"Not a problem. You've got a bit of a reputation around here. Nice to finally meet."

"A good rep, I hope?"

He grinned and exposed his bleached-white teeth. "The best. Your work on Cotulla is the stuff of legend."

Overselling it, aren't we? Canales wanted something from her, personally or professionally. She forced a smile. His faux charm hinted at a man who practiced in front of a mirror. "Thanks. As I said on the phone, I wanted to get some info on the incident at Green Horizons Retirement. What can you tell me?"

"Not much, really. By the time they called us, it was over. We filled out the forms and filed it away. We don't have the manpower to work on something this small."

She pulled out her notepad and wrote the date and time at the top. "Would you mind backing up a little? I don't know anything other than they had computer problems."

He tilted his head. "Yeah? What's your interest then? I thought this had something to do with another case you were working on?"

"It might. There's a, um, tenuous connection between the retirement village and my case. Their network issues may or may not tie into my investigation. That's why I need to know what happened."

"You're Homicide now, right? You working on the old lady, what's her name, Dorothy . . . hold on, it'll come to me . . ."

She clenched her jaw. "Dorothy *Engers*. And no, I'm not investigating her death."

"Just wondered." He shrugged. "The security guy told us about it. Not our jurisdiction and didn't seem worth forwarding to you guys. Figured if the woman's family wanted her death checked out, they'd be in touch. Anyway, you want to know about the network attack. Simple enough. Ransomware. Seeing more and more of it every day."

Ransomware. Online kidnapping, except it was your data that was held hostage and destroyed unless you paid. Was that what they were planning at the water park too? "Got any details you can share?"

"Sure. Like I said, this is a local issue anyway. Until there's evidence of the crime crossing state lines, we're not gonna do anything."

He shrugged. "And even if there was proof that happened, our cyber guys have their hands full with the big-dollar attacks. The ones coming from overseas. Word is a lot of that money goes to terrorist organizations. You can understand why that would be more of a priority than this deal."

"I can. So what exactly happened?"

"Everything shut down and all the company's computers displayed a message from the hackers. Wanted ten-k in Zcash to release the key that unlocked everything. It didn't take the company long to decide that was cheap compared to the time it would take to rebuild their systems, and that's assuming they didn't lose any data. A few hours later, they paid, and within thirty minutes things were back to normal."

She scribbled a few notes. "Zcash? Not Bitcoin?"

"Nah. Bitcoin's not as secure. Word is that it can be traced, but that's out of my realm. The Bureau's got teams that work on this stuff, but to be honest, they're overwhelmed."

"Got it." Online currency was no different from Monopoly money as far as she knew. She'd have to do research on it. Figure out how you turned fake money into real. Was that where the stack of cash under Zachary Coleman's floor came from? She tapped her pen on the notepad. "How's that work? I mean, what's the process for the company to agree to pay and then get the ransom to the hackers?"

"It's actually pretty simple. Green Horizons is like most organizations. They don't want to deal with this type of headache, so they contact a service to do it for them. Look up "ransomware incident response" or something along those lines. There are dozens of companies that do that now. All of them say the same thing. Paying the ransom should be the last resort, but if it's a low-dollar amount like this one, it's usually cheaper to just pay and be done with it."

"So this outside company takes care of everything? Contacts the hackers and sends them the payment? Then takes their fee and moves on to the next one?" She narrowed her eyes and crossed her legs.

"I know where you're going," he said. "It's like the home security company that breaks into homes and goes by later to sell them an alarm system, right? But in this case, no way anyone could have known which service Green Horizons would contact, or even if they would. Plus, not only do these companies pay the hackers, they'll actually try to negotiate for a lower ransom."

"Does that work?"

"Lots of times it does. And when the company gets the encryption key, the service helps get everything back up and running."

"What if they pay and don't get the key? What happens then?"

"First of all, the money's gone either way. With digital currencies, once you've sent it, there's no way to get it back. If you don't get the data you need in return, you're pretty much toast. Not much you can do about it except get to work trying to rebuild everything. Most of the time any backups are also infected, so the process can be excruciating. But we see that in the vast majority of cases, the encryption key is returned."

"Awful decent of them."

He shook his head. "You're looking at this the wrong way. This is a business to these hackers. Businesses are built on reputation. That's why they don't hit the same place twice. Bad for future business. And if they *don't* send the key back, it reduces the likelihood the next victim will pay. And they're getting smarter by going after critical services like hospitals and government facilities. Doing that ramps up the pressure on the target to respond quickly. Usually they'll give forty-eight hours or more to respond, but if you need access to your systems now, who's waiting that long?"

"Any leads on this?"

"I'll let you know when and if we decide to investigate."

She pinched her lips together. The reality of modern law enforcement. No one had the resources to work everything, so you picked and chose cases based on impact and threat. The Green Horizons data breach would only be solved if another larger ransomware case was investigated and the culprits were tied back to this one. "Is there anything else you can tell me?"

He passed her a sheet of paper. "That's a photo of one of the monitors at the place during the attack."

A yellow background with slowly rotating and flashing red lights in each corner covered the screen, giving it a very amateurish look. A large countdown clock, 46:53:12 at the time of the photo, filled the center of the display. Text below the ticking numbers gave the details.

Your files are locked.

If you want them back, you need to pay €10.000 in ZCash within 48 hours. After the payment is received, we will give you the key to unlock your files. Click on the next button to pay.

We guarantee that you can recover your files quickly and safely.

We are TOXICftw.

"Toxic f-t-w?" she asked. "Fort Worth?"

"Maybe, but I'd guess 'for the win.' Seems more their culture. If they've done any other hacks, we don't have a record of it."

"And they specified euros, not dollars. Any relevance, you think?"

He shrugged. "As far as where they are? Who knows? Works out to, what, around eleven thousand dollars?"

If you say so. She held up the photo. "Okay if I keep this?"

"Of course. You'll let me know if you learn anything that might help close this on our end?"

Ah. I do the work, you get the credit with your bosses. She stood and moved to the door. "Thank you for your time, Agent Canales."

33 **Amara sat in her car** and went through the laborious process of locating Eduardo Sanchez's number on the teeny screen of her flip phone. How had she ever survived her teen years with such primitive technology? He answered on the first ring and she broached the subject of a possible ransomware attack with him.

Both agreed it made as much sense as anything else they could think of, and he said he'd make some inquiries as to what the financial impact would be if the park were shut down. Assuming the hackers could pick and choose when they attacked, they'd likely select a cycle of sunny days, hot weather, and high attendance. Closing for even a day during that period could be financially catastrophic. The company would probably pay and do so quickly.

The problem, as both saw it, was they had to know killing Zachary Coleman would increase the likelihood of discovering the network intrusion. So, again, why do it there? If it was to send a message, was that worth the risk of losing a substantial amount of ransom? Sanchez agreed to call back when he had some numbers on the water park's potential liability.

Starsky was next on the agenda. This close to noon, if he wasn't at a crime scene, he'd be having lunch. Maybe for the second time. She could meet him somewhere, but eating on the go was more in line with her plans, especially since an Italian dinner was on tap for tonight. A quick text would be the simplest solution. She glared at the phone. Simplest if she had her normal cell. Texting on this beast might take the rest of the day. Pushing a button three times to get the letter you wanted was a skill she'd lost long ago.

Her heart jerked as the phone sounded a series of digital notes. An old-school ringtone. The screen displayed Starsky's name and she smiled as her breathing slowed. If she didn't believe in coincidences, what was this?

"Hey," she said.

"I'm about to order some lunch. You headed back to the station anytime soon? Want me to get something for you?"

"Thanks, but I'm good. Listen, while I've got you, what—"

"You sure? I'm thinking Chinese. Either that or Thai. I could be talked into a burger though. Ooh, what about Jamaican? Jerk chicken sounds good, doesn't it?"

"None for me. Get what you want."

"Will do. No Italian though. We're having that tonight."

Her brain locked. "Uh, yeah, but how did, um, huh?"

He laughed. "I called Wylie to check on your mom. Glad to hear she's doing well. He told me we were meeting at a restaurant tonight. Seven, right? I'll pick you up at your apartment if that's okay."

"Yeah, that's fine." She didn't tell Wylie who she'd bring, did she? He assumed it would be Starsky. What if she'd invited someone else already? How awkward would that be? She sighed. Wylie knew. Who else was she going to bring?

"You okay?" he asked.

"Yeah. I'm sorry about tonight. I should have called you earlier to see if you were free. If you can't go, I understand."

"Eh, no big deal. Sure, I had to move a few things around, but I'll make it work."

She chuckled. "What did you have to move around? Your Friday nights are as busy as mine."

"Toe shaving night. Pushed it over to Saturday."

She snorted. "You say that so often I'm starting to wonder. I don't want to believe you, but there's a part of me that says you might be telling the truth."

"Remember what I told you. Everybody lies. The only variance is the quantity and quality. I'll admit that I'm a very good liar. Think about that."

She squeezed her forehead. "If you're a very good liar, you could be lying about being a very good liar and I wouldn't know, in which case you'd be a bad liar. But if you were a bad liar, ugh." She pressed against the headrest. "I just realized I don't care. Shave your toes or don't. Whatever makes you happy."

"It would make me happy to come by your place a little early and visit Larry. He's been calling. Says you're neglecting him."

She swallowed hard. "That really does make me feel guilty."

"Not my intention, but you know what they say. The guilty flee when no one pursues. Truth. It's in the Bible."

"Fine. Come early and see the lizard. And dinner's on me."

"You'll get no argument here. I'm all about equal rights. Wouldn't want to impose my ancient belief system on you. No, ma'am. Women have just as much right to pay as men do. I'm awake."

"Woke."

"What?"

"The word is 'woke.' Means you're keeping an eye out for social injustices."

"Describes me to a T."

"Mm-hmm," she said. "You really are a good liar. See you tonight."

She hesitated at the exit of the FBI's parking lot. A light lunch, salad or soup, sounded good. She flipped on her turn signal. It was a ten-minute drive down I-10 to the River Walk, where Matias's mother was in the middle of the lunch rush. Wonder if her husband told her about the SAPD's suspicions? That her son was involved in illegal activity, including murder?

Problem was that this time of year, peak tourist season, it would cost her a thirty-dollar lunch to find out.

• • •

Amara studied the menu for a moment, wishing there were an option to sort price lowest to highest. The hotel, like all the others along the River Walk, catered to tourists, convention guests, and business travelers, all people who were freer with their money. Locals only visited the area for special occasions or to crowd-watch. Not counting the ones who preyed on the visitors.

She stared out the windows at the swarms of people sweltering in the midday heat as they moved along both sides of the river. The Alamo, its underwhelming size a surprise to most visitors, sat tucked away a couple of hundred yards off. Every hotel and restaurant had outside eating areas, and all she could see appeared to be crammed full. Why anyone would choose to sit in the heat when air-conditioned comfort was a few feet away was beyond her. Scenery, maybe. Regardless, the money flowed a lot faster than the river did.

A waiter, dark pants, white shirt, narrow black tie, sauntered her way. "Do you have any questions about the menu?" he asked.

Other than are the prices in dollars or pesos? "No," she said. "I'll have the small salad with grilled chicken, please." Nineteen bucks.

"Would you like a bowl of soup with that? Today's special is a spicy chicken enchilada topped with a dollop of fresh sour cream."

For eight dollars? No, thank you. "I don't think so. Can you tell me if Silvia Lucero is working today? She's a chef."

He nodded. "She is."

"Would you ask her to stop by my table if she has time? It'll only take a minute."

"Of course." He took her menu and wandered out of sight.

What to say to the woman? She was doubtless busy, which worked in Amara's favor. Hit her hard and fast. Force a reaction. Tell her the truth. Matias was involved in something that had already gotten one kid killed.

The waiter returned with a small basket of crackers. "Ms. Lucero will be out in a moment."

"Thanks." Crackers? Seriously? Not bread? Nineteen dollars for a small salad and she got saltines?

He refilled her water, then drifted to other tables. She reached for her cell, paused, and sighed. No way to check email, news, or even play on an app. What was she supposed to do? Just sit and wait? How was that productive? All around the restaurant, other diners taunted her by using their smartphones. She bounced her legs and shifted in her seat as heat seeped into her face.

Good grief. Was she actually having phone withdrawal? She closed her eyes to focus on her breathing. Ridiculous. She could go without checking her email or texts for more than half a day. If anything urgent happened, someone would call.

"Hello?"

Amara jerked back to reality. A woman wearing a white chef's coat and holding a salad stood beside the table. "Hi. Ms. Lucero?"

"Yes." She leaned forward, moved some silverware slightly, and set the salad in front of Amara. "How can I help you?"

"Looks delicious. Do you have time to sit for just a moment?"

The woman glanced behind her. "I'm sorry, but I have to get back to the kitchen."

"It's about Matias."

Her eyes widened. "Matias? What about him? Who are you?"

Amara showed her ID. "I spoke with your husband yesterday. Did he mention that?"

Ms. Lucero took a step closer. "Spoke with him about what?"

"I believe your son has information regarding a homicide. I'm not saying he's involved in the death, but I do think Matias is participating in, let's say, questionable activities. Things that could send him to prison."

The woman clutched her chest and sat in the chair opposite Amara. "What things?"

"Things that are best discussed someplace quieter. Call him or your husband. They'll know what's going on." She checked her watch. "It's almost one o'clock. If I don't hear from you or him by three, I'll assume you're not cooperating. That's your choice. I hope you decide to do what's best for your son."

Ms. Lucero wiped her shaking hand across her mouth. "Ms., um, I'm sorry?"

"Detective Alvarez."

"Yes. What do you think Matias has done?"

Amara picked up a fork and poked at her salad. "I'm afraid I misled you, ma'am. I don't *think* he's done anything. I *know* he has. To be honest, I can't prove it yet, but I'm close. Three o'clock, Ms. Lucero. That's when anything I might do to help your son expires. If you'll excuse me, I need to eat before the lettuce wilts. Have a good afternoon, and whether you call or not, I will see you again."

The woman stood, her mouth hanging open and a blank stare on her face. She turned, pulled a phone from her pocket, and trudged toward the kitchen.

Amara tasted the salad. Delicious. The grilled chicken had a smoky flavor and fell apart in her mouth. Not worth nineteen bucks, but at least the meal was better than average. She glanced at the crackers and frowned. Not even name brand or the buttery kind or wheat or sesame. Generic saltines.

Should've brought Starsky. He could eat twenty dollars' worth of free crackers.

34 **Amara reviewed the room** a last time. Silvia Lucero had phoned forty-five minutes earlier to say that she and Matias, and possibly her husband, would be at the station no later than three o'clock. She'd updated Starsky on her investigation and he would sit in on the interview as well, not as an interrogator but as support in case he was needed. Department policy stated a preference for more than one detective to be present whenever possible.

She'd chosen the smallest available interview room and had the table removed. She wanted nothing between her and the family. A table acted as a buffer. A place to put your hands or shield your body. She wanted to be able to get close to Matias. Her proximity would ramp up his anxiety while building some rapport. It'd be better if he was alone, but that wasn't her choice. He wasn't under arrest, so she had little control.

Five chairs, three facing two, consumed most of the space. She positioned them so the camera in the corner had the best angle on the middle of the three seats. That's where the teenager would sit, flanked by his parents for support. She'd use her cell as a backup microphone for the . . . no, she wouldn't. "App" and "flip phone" were words that didn't mesh. Starsky would have to record their conversation.

He cracked the door open and poked his head in. "They're here. Ready?"

"Yeah. The father come too?"

"There's a guy with them, so I'm gonna say he did."

She nodded. "Good. I got the impression mom wasn't real happy that dad didn't clue her in about all this. I can use that."

He pulled the door open farther and stepped back. "Y'all can come on in."

Silvia Lucero entered the room, followed by Matias and a well-dressed man with a briefcase who definitely was *not* Daniel Lucero. Wonderful. They brought a lawyer.

"Thank you all for coming," Amara said.

The attorney shook her hand. "Wilson Manchester. I represent the Luceros."

Wilson Manchester? Sounded like a butler from *Downton Abbey*. His drawl dispelled any illusion of recent British ancestry. She waited until everyone sat before speaking. "Detective Peckham will be sitting in with us. Matias, I want to make sure you understand that you're not under arrest and are free to leave at any time."

The teenager nodded and looked around the room. "Where's the big mirror?"

Amara pointed to the camera. "Nobody has mirrors. TV and movies made that up. Guess it's supposed to add drama. Sorry to disappoint you."

The lawyer balanced the briefcase on his lap and pulled a pen and legal pad from it. "I'd like to go over the ground rules before we begin."

Starsky leaned forward and Amara shot him a warning glance as the attorney scribbled a note at the top of the page. "Mr. Manchester," she said, "this is not a formal interrogation. There are no ground rules. I'll ask questions and your client will choose whether or not to answer them. I assume you're paid whether you do anything or not, so you want to make certain the Luceros feel like they're getting something in return. No problem, but remember,

Matias, this is your one and only chance. If you walk out of here without telling me what I want to know, I won't help you when the time comes. Clear?"

The boy shifted in his seat and swallowed hard.

"For my benefit," the lawyer said, "assuming my client has information that would be of use to you, would you detail exactly how you plan to help him? In my experience, detectives are rarely able to fulfill their promises. Or perhaps it would be more accurate to state that they choose not to do so."

"Fair enough," Amara said. "Your attorney is correct, Matias. I can't promise you anything because I don't have the final say. The DA's office will make the decision when charges are filed."

Mr. Manchester tapped the teenager's arm. "*If* charges are filed."

"As I was saying," Amara said, "*when* charges are filed, I will explain to the DA that you were helpful in resolving the investigation. That could affect his decision on whether to charge you as an adult. I can tell you it is not uncommon, especially in cases with multiple offenders, for that to have a substantial impact on sentencing. Would you agree, Mr. Manchester?"

"I might dispute your use of the words 'not uncommon,' but yes, I have seen that occur."

She placed her hands on her knees and leaned closer to the teenager. "So the only thing you have to decide is who to trust. Me or whoever killed Zachary Coleman. Maybe I'm biased, but is that really a tough call?"

He licked his lips and pushed his glasses higher on his nose. "I know some, uh, things."

"Yeah?" Amara said. "What kind of things?"

The attorney raised his hand. "We'd like to see something from the DA in writing."

Starsky sighed loudly and rolled his eyes.

Amara frowned, both at him and the lawyer's request. "That's not how this works. Your client tells me what he knows. If he's completely honest and leaves *nothing* out of the story, then we'll talk about getting the DA involved."

Mr. Manchester scribbled another note. "We are willing to share a few details but nothing that might be used against my client. I believe that's a fair compromise, yes?"

Fair? She glared at the attorney. "This is not a negotiation, Counselor. Your client is involved in criminal activity. Any truthful information he gives will speed up my investigation. If he chooses not to say anything, that's fine. It simply means it'll take me longer to put the pieces together. Maybe another day. Maybe another week. But I *will* close the case. And when I do, I suspect Mr. Lucero here will want to know why you didn't offer him better advice."

Mr. Manchester slid the notepad back into his briefcase and clicked the latches closed. "I know a bluff when I hear it."

Amara smiled at him. "So do I."

He stood and turned to Matias. "We should go."

The teenager alternated his view between his mother and Amara. "Mom?"

Ms. Lucero twisted her wedding ring as her chest rose and fell rapidly. "Detective, I'm asking you to understand our situation. We don't know who to trust."

"But you do know who *not* to trust," Amara said. "If your son didn't kill his friend, he knows who did, or at least has useful information. Aside from all the other charges likely to be filed, nothing tops first-degree murder." She concentrated on Matias. "You and your buddies want to live and die together on this, go for it. But I saw the video at the water park. When you were standing a few feet away from Zachary Coleman's dead body? I saw your fear. Remember that feeling? How you realized you could be next?"

His mother gasped and covered her mouth. "Are you saying Matias is in danger?"

Amara kept her eyes on the boy. "Why don't you ask him?"

Ms. Lucero angled herself in the chair. "Has someone threatened you?"

He stared at his lap. "No."

His mother placed her hand on his chin and turned his head toward her. She studied his face as if for the first time, then hugged her son. "Detective," she said, "would you give us a few minutes alone with Mr. Manchester?"

"Certainly." She and Starsky stood. "We'll be just outside."

The attorney pointed at the camera. "Don't forget to turn off the audio."

"Come get us when you're ready," Amara said. "But don't take too long."

They stepped into the hall and she pushed the button on the wall to disable the audio. The video feed ran to a bank of monitors in another room, usually not supervised unless there was need to do so.

"Good job in there," Starsky said. "Think the boy would've broken if his mom or lawyer wasn't there?"

She shrugged. "If he'd showed up alone, yeah, we would've been halfway done by now. I'm guessing when we go back in there, he's going to tell us just enough to whet our appetite. Manchester will want them to hold most of the good stuff back so he can force a deal."

"I wish you hadn't said that."

"Why? You think I'm wrong?"

"Not that. About whetting our appetite." He rubbed a hand over his belly. "Three hours since lunch. I'm trying to hold off until dinner tonight, but I honestly feel nauseous. My stomach's sucking up against my spine. Do I have time to run to the vending machine?"

"We won't start without you, but hurry. And don't take food in the room, okay? Finish before we go in there?"

He half jogged out of sight around a corner. She shoved her hands into her pockets, reclined against the wall, and counted the seconds. Forty-three before Starsky barreled around the corner.

"No snacks?" she asked.

"I got something." His voice sounded like he had a mouthful of wet cement, and a peanut butter odor washed over her.

"Reeses?"

He held the back of his hand over his mouth. "Cwackers." Random bulges arose on his cheeks as his tongue worked around his teeth.

"Larry has better table manners, you know that? He wouldn't have food stuck all over his teeth."

"He has a longer tongue."

She snorted just as the door opened. Mr. Manchester stared for a second before telling her they were ready. She pressed the button to turn on the audio recording as they entered the room and took their seats.

Amara crossed her legs and fixated on Matias. "Ready to talk?"

The teenager took a deep breath. "I know who killed Zach."

35 **Amara maintained** a stoic expression. Of course the boy knew who killed Zachary Coleman. All the teenagers did. "And?"

Matias twiddled his fingers. "I, uh, there are things you don't know."

She resisted the urge to respond sarcastically. Barely. "My understanding is you're here to tell me those things?"

The lawyer cleared his throat. "My client is being forthright. There are circumstances he cannot divulge at this time."

Amara squished her eyebrows together. "Isn't that convenient? When can he divulge them? Wait, let me guess. After the DA offers a deal?"

"Yes," Mr. Manchester said. "You must understand that Mr. Lucero is taking a great risk just being here."

"I'm sure he is. No doubt he's being tracked just like I am. Nice your friends have your back, right, Matias? Tell me something. Which one of you messed with my bank accounts? Who hacked my home internet? Who called me?"

The teen's eyes widened and he opened his mouth, then closed it and stared away.

Heat rose to her forehead. "Well, Matias? No? Nothing to say? Did you three really think making personal attacks on me would affect the investigation? Maybe they did, because now I'm having second thoughts about any potential deals." She lowered her voice. "Counselor, would you advise your client he has about fifteen seconds to start talking before I walk out of here?"

The attorney held out his hand, palm down. "I think if we all take a deep breath, we can—"

"Ten seconds left." Her heart pounded. Part of her—a very large part—wanted to walk out now. The boy had his chance. Let him go down hard with the others. She was close to figuring everything out on her own. The loose threads in her brain weaved their way toward each other. Soon there'd be a connection.

"Hold up," Matias said. "I don't know about that stuff. We never talked about, um, doing anything to you."

"No?" Amara said. "Who is *we?*"

"No more," the lawyer said. "This fishing expedition of yours isn't free. Anything else is going to cost you."

Starsky grunted. "See what happens when you try to help someone?"

Mr. Manchester stared at him. "So you *can* talk."

"Yep." His tongue dug around his upper teeth.

"Matias," Amara said, "your attorney thinks this is a fishing expedition. That I'm trying to figure out what happened, and I can't do it without your assistance. He believes I'm so desperate for your help that I'll offer a deal based on what I hope you know. Here's the truth. I would like your cooperation. Not because it makes my job easier, but because it could speed up the process. That would allow me to move on to the next case in line. But please don't misinterpret this meeting as any desperation on my part."

She pulled her notepad and a pen from her jacket pocket. "Mr. Manchester here says it's going to cost me to get more information. He could not be more mistaken." She pointed the pen at Matias. "It's going to cost *you*. Think about it. I've got nothing on the line here. Can you say the same? So here's what's about to happen. I'll start asking questions. The first time you don't answer or I believe you're lying, I'm done. Walking out. You'll have no more opportunities for a deal. Oh, sure, you can still talk and I'll listen, but don't expect me to do you any favors with the DA. Got it?"

The attorney shifted the briefcase on his lap. "I'm not comfortable with this arrangement."

Starsky gestured to the door. "Then leave. No one's being detained."

Amara waited as the three people opposite her exchanged glances but remained seated. "Okay," she said. "Let's start with an easy one. Matias, where is Dexter?"

"Wait," the attorney said. He shuffled through papers in his briefcase. "Who is Dexter?"

"Tell him," Amara said.

Matias brushed his hands on his jeans. "That's Haley's dog."

"Uh-huh," she said. "So I'll ask again, where is Dexter?"

He shrugged. "I guess Haley has him?"

She rubbed a fingertip in the space between her eyebrows and sighed. "Couldn't even make it through the first question." She clicked her pen and wrote *TOXICftw*, then ripped the paper out and handed it to the teenager.

His hands shook as he read it.

Ms. Lucero craned her neck to see. "What does that mean?"

Amara and Starsky stood and walked to the door. As she exited, she turned to the mother. "It means your son is going to prison for a very long time."

■ ■ ■

Amara smacked the button to turn off the audio, and she and Starsky stood in the hallway outside the door. "Think they'll talk now?" she asked.

"Fifty fifty. Depends on how much weight they put in their lawyer's recommendations. He'll tell them to keep their mouths shut.

Not bad advice, really. I would." He rested his back against the wall. "The kid's guilty of something. Maybe not killing the Coleman boy, but something. Best thing he can do right now is not talk to the police. There'll be time for deals down the road if it comes to that. Nah, if it was me, I'd roll the dice and make you prove your case."

"Yeah, me too. You don't think he's the murderer?"

"No. Wasn't sweating enough. But I wouldn't put money on it. What did you write on the paper?"

"TOXICftw. I think that's what they call their little group online."

"F-T-W? Ft. Worth?"

She fake-sighed and flipped her hair with her hand. "You really are old. F-T-W. For the win."

"I knew that."

The door opened and the trio stepped into the hall. Both Luceros avoided eye contact with either detective.

"I know the way out," the attorney said.

"I'll walk you to the lobby," Amara said. "Required to."

"Suit yourself. No questions though. From this point forward, all communication with the Luceros is to go through me."

She smiled. "Except the arrest warrant. That'll go directly to your client. Make sure we can find him this weekend. I'd hate to hear he did something stupid like run off and hide. The extra paperwork I'd have to do. Mmm. Not to mention the fact his two buddies would be in here talking and he couldn't give his side of the story."

Matias peeked at her and quickly looked away.

"You know what?" she said. "I've got to make some calls. I'm certain your client does as well. Probably to the same people I'm phoning. You can show yourselves out. Have a nice day. Oh, and Matias? I'll see you soon."

After the group turned the corner, Amara and Starsky wandered toward their office.

"You really calling the other two?" he asked.

"No point," she said. "Matias will tell them what happened in there. They'll all know that I'm getting close. If one wants to talk, they'll call. If not, so be it. There's already a split in the group. He didn't know about the personal attacks on me. If he did, he deserves an Oscar, but I don't think so. Haley or Liam stepped out of line without running it past the others."

"Or both of them did it without telling Matias."

"No matter how you look at it, there's a wedge between them now. That can only help me."

They stepped into Homicide and walked to Starsky's desk. "Almost four o'clock," he said. "How late are you planning to work?"

She frowned. "Eight at least if I didn't have this dinner thing."

"Didn't mean to put a damper on your evening."

A knot twisted in her stomach. "Sorry. That's not what I meant. But I am dreading it. Not because of you, but this deal with Mom and Wylie."

"Yeah, I need the scoop before we go. What's off-limits and that kind of stuff."

"Bottom line is Mom asked Wylie to marry her but he hasn't answered yet because he's afraid she only asked because she knows he loves her and she loves him and the cancer forced her to speed everything up whether she's ready or not and that wouldn't be fair to her with everything else that's going on in her life so maybe they should wait even though he wants to marry her and how would the kids react to all this happening now."

"Wow. That's a—"

"But she's worried that since he hasn't answered her, he either doesn't really love her or he's scared she's only asking because of the cancer—which he is but she doesn't know that—and so she made a mistake by asking and should have waited to see if he would ask her first but he might be waiting because it's not great timing and he doesn't want to overwhelm her while she's going through all this."

He paused for several seconds. "That everything?"

"I think so. It made sense when I was talking but I might have lost something in the translation."

"So the purpose of the dinner tonight is what?"

Her shoulders sagged. "No idea. We'll figure it out as we go."

"I'm gonna need a hint as to which way you want me to push."

She sat in his chair and swiveled back and forth several times. "They love each other. Marriage now or later is their decision. I just want them on the same page."

"Okay. I don't want to be in the doghouse when this is over." He crossed his arms and stared at the ceiling for a moment. "What was the deal with the dog? In the interview?"

"Dexter? Haley Bricker had a dog. I think Matias and Liam killed it as a warning to her. She was supposed to meet me but didn't show. I found her at Matias's house and Liam was there too. She'd been crying, and when I asked her about Dexter, she wouldn't talk."

"You sure they killed it?"

"No. Why? What are you thinking?"

He stretched and yawned. "If we were talking about a domestic violence situation, maybe they did something to the dog. But not sure I see that happening here. Plus, hard to kill a pet even if it's not yours. You can hate a person enough to kill them, but an animal's different."

"You didn't know Dexter."

"Not buying it." He leaned against the desk. "You couldn't have hurt him, and you know it. *Fatal Attraction*."

"What?"

"The movie. *Fatal Attraction*? You've never seen it? Seriously? That's an omission we'll have to correct. Anyway, this married guy's being stalked by his ex-mistress, or maybe it was a one-night stand, can't remember—either way, the woman's a nutcase. She ends up taking a rabbit, did I tell you the guy is married with a kid? She takes the little girl's pet bunny and boils it on their stove. The guy's wife finds it."

She scrunched her face. "Gross. I think I'll pass on the movie."

"Your reaction. It's just a rabbit, right? So what? But it's not. It's a little girl's pet. Who could ever hurt something so sweet? Only a psycho. Liam and Matias might be criminals, but either one of them strike you as nuts?"

"No, but that doesn't mean they're not."

"True, but start with what you believe. Besides, why kill the dog? Wouldn't that make Haley *more* likely to talk? Uh-uh. My money's on a hostage situation."

He was right, but no point in admitting it. "That's one theory, though no more valid than mine."

"Sure. A bit of trivia for you. The rabbit in the pot was real. Dead, of course. Bought from a local butcher. They had to boil it guts and all to make it look right on camera. The actress said the whole set stunk horribly."

"Thanks for sharing that tidbit so close to dinnertime."

He grinned and held his palms up. "It's what I do."

"Uh-huh. So if Dexter's not dead, there's still a chance Haley will talk." She flicked her finger on her bottom lip. "I don't have to find the killer yet."

"No," Starsky said. "You have to find the dog."

36 **Amara straightened the linen napkin** in her lap
before buttering another slice of hot bread
and laying it on the small plate.

"Nervous?" Starsky asked.

"No. Why?"

"You're a slice ahead of me on the bread and the waiter's already filled your glass twice."

She lifted the goblet and drank the last of the ice water. "Small glasses. And I'm hungry."

Mama and Wylie should be here any minute. After stopping by Amara's apartment so she could change and Starsky could visit Larry, they'd ridden together to the restaurant since her vehicle remained at the station. Her muscles randomly twitched and her stomach fluttered no matter how much she ate.

"I should be at work," she said. "Looking for Dexter."

Starsky slid the basket of bread away from her. "Do you feel anyone's life is in imminent danger from whoever killed Coleman? And I don't mean the dog's."

"No."

"It's your first case and you want to get it in the books. I understand that. Trust me, there will be plenty more. Draw the line now. Guard your off time." He snatched a piece of bread and scooped out the remains of the butter bowl. "Here they come."

She looked toward the door as Mama and Wylie spotted them, waved, and headed their way. Her mother wore a full-length white dress with a pattern of large multicolored flowers, and Wylie had on dark pants with a blue dress shirt and tie. Amara grinned. Two kids out on a date.

Starsky stood and greeted them while Wylie pulled out a chair for Mama next to Amara. The waitress stopped by for the drink order, water with lemon all around, and rattled off the daily specials before walking away.

Amara placed her hand on her mother's arm. "How do you feel? Did everything go okay this morning?"

"I'm fine. It wasn't as bad as I expected. The doctor warned me about that though. The first treatment or two can be deceptive." She squeezed Amara's hand. "It'll get worse, but I'm ready for it."

Starsky tilted his head toward Wylie. "This guy taking good care of you?"

Her mother smiled. "I cannot complain. He is a good nurse."

Wylie's face reddened and he reached for the basket of bread. "No butter?"

Starsky shook his head and pointed to Amara. "She ate it all."

"Did not," she said. "Dinner's on me, okay? No arguments."

The other three nodded their approval and scanned the menu.

Amara chuckled. "You could at least *pretend* to argue about the check."

"Yep," Starsky said, "just like I could pretend I'm not ordering the most expensive thing I can find."

She kicked him lightly. "How did I know you'd say that?"

The waitress returned with the drinks and left a pitcher of water and two butter bowls on the table in front of Amara. She ordered the grilled asparagus wrapped in prosciutto and mozzarella, Wylie and Mama agreed to split the lasagna and a salad, and Starsky opted for the chicken parmigiana.

"Yours sounds delicious," he said, "except for the asparagus. I bet if you asked, they'd put the ham and cheese between a couple of pieces of this bread, butter it up, and throw it on the griddle. Now *that* would be good."

"But not healthy," she said.

He raised his eyebrows. "Because eating half a loaf of bread and a pound of butter is healthy."

"I did not eat that."

"Did too."

Mama tsk-tsked them, but her eyes shone with approval. "If I wanted to dine with my grandchildren, I would have invited them."

Amara folded her hands in her lap. No easy way to approach this. "You and Wylie getting married or what?"

Starsky held his napkin over his mouth as he coughed bread-crumbs and his eyes watered. "Subtle, Alvarez. Way to ease into the interrogation."

Wylie reached for one of the butter tubs. "Yes, we are. Haven't set the date, but it'll be soon."

"I think we'll have the ceremony in our backyard," Mama said. "Unless you have any objections?"

Amara blinked rapidly as she glanced back and forth between them. "I, uh, no. No objections. When did you . . . I thought . . . I mean, I knew you asked him, but when?"

Wylie slathered butter on a slice of bread and set it on her mother's plate. "We worked it out this afternoon," he said. "Didn't want to ruin a free dinner with all your jabber about it."

Her brain bulged with thoughts and questions. "And you're both okay with it?"

Mama nibbled at her bread. "What an odd question." She turned to Starsky. "Is she like this at work?"

He held up both palms. "I invoke my right to remain silent."

"You know what I mean," Amara said. She scratched the back

of her neck. "I don't know how to ask this without sounding weird, but would you be getting married if, um, you, uh . . ."

"If I didn't have cancer?" Mama said. "Yes. Maybe not so quickly, but"—she reached for Wylie's hand—"he makes me happy."

Yeah, but being happy wasn't the same thing as being in love. Was it? "Well, okay then. When are you going to tell everyone?"

"Already did," Wylie said. "At least as far as your brothers and sisters are concerned. Called them this afternoon."

"So everyone knew before I did?"

"Not true," Mama said. "Starsky didn't."

She rested an elbow on the table and massaged her forehead. "But everyone *in the family* knew? No offense, Starsky."

Redness filled his pale cheeks. "I, uh, might have known too."

She jerked her head upright. "Might have known? What does that mean?"

Wylie cleared his throat. "It's possible I mentioned it this afternoon when I phoned him."

She narrowed her eyes. "Why did you call him?"

"To find out if he can keep a secret? Turns out he can."

Her mother laughed and Amara's emotions rose. She leaned away from Starsky. "So you've known about this since this afternoon? And you let me sit here nearly bouncing off the walls without saying anything?"

He shrugged. "Wylie said they wanted to be the ones to tell you."

She playfully slapped his arm. "Nice to be the last to know. At least I can enjoy my dinner now."

"Asparagus is not dinner," he said. "You shouldn't have filled up on bread."

Wylie stared at Amara, then Starsky, then back at Amara. "You two getting married or what?"

Fire sped through Amara's face and her skin tingled. She couldn't look at Starsky. "Excuse me?"

"Fair question," her mother said. "You asked us, now we ask you."

She had a sudden urge to dunk her face into the pitcher of ice water. A notion surged to the forefront. Had Starsky known they were going to ask? One peek at his countenance, frozen wide-eyed, mouth hanging, no visible sign of breathing, told her he was as shocked as he was.

Wylie leaned forward. "Your mother and I have been talking. It's obvious you two care for each other. Make each other happy. Got each other's back. What else are you waiting for?"

Amara dabbed at her forehead with the napkin. "You're making us very uncomfortable, right, Starsky?"

His expression hadn't changed but a slight grunt escaped from his lips.

"Well," Mama said, "we can see it even if you two can't. Think about it. That's all we're saying. Love doesn't always come with an engraved invitation. Ah. Here's dinner."

The waitress set their plates before them, made sure everything looked all right, then faded into the background.

"Looks wonderful," Wylie said. He jabbed his fork toward Amara's food. "That's hardly enough for a baby bird. Want some of our lasagna?"

She shook her head and stared at the asparagus.

"Suit yourself." He pointed at the untouched chicken parmigiana on Starsky's plate. "You not gonna eat?"

"No." He took a swig of water. "Not hungry."

"That's a first," Wylie said. "Not feeling well?"

"I'm okay."

Amara pulled her phone out and flipped it open. "Sorry, got a call coming in. Excuse me a moment?"

"I didn't hear anything," her mother said.

"On vibrate." Do these things even have a vibration mode? She stepped out of earshot, turned her back to the group, and made exaggerated motions with her hands while pretending to talk. After what she deemed the appropriate amount of time, she slipped the cell into her pocket and returned to the table. Starsky's eyes pleaded for his rescue.

"Got a break in my case," Amara said. "Got to go."

Starsky stood and shook his head. "Always happens, doesn't it? I'll get the waitress to box up our dinner."

"I can handle this. You should stay. Finish your dinner."

He licked his lips. "We rode together in my car, remember?"

"I'll grab a rideshare. No problem."

"Yeah? Good luck."

"Why?"

He stepped forward and whispered in her ear. "Because you need the app or internet access to schedule a ride. I'm betting that gadget you call a phone has neither. Plus, I'll tell your mom there was no call."

"So? Who do you think she'll believe?"

"And that you begged for a picture of me in my Speedo."

She choked on her saliva and coughed into her fist before looking at her mother. "Starsky needs to go with me. He's getting the car while I get our food boxed up."

He nodded and jingled his keys. "Meet you out front. Throw some bread in with mine, okay?" On his way to the door, he caught their server, pointed at the table, and spoke briefly before hurrying outside.

The waitress reappeared with two Styrofoam boxes and packed their dinner, topping Starsky's off with six pieces of bread. "That look okay?" she asked. "He said to fill it up. I can get some more from the kitchen if you want."

Amara shook her head. "That's plenty, thank you." She kissed her mother's cheek and bent toward Wylie. "Take care of her." She kissed his cheek too and grabbed the flimsy food containers as she strode to the exit.

"Hey!" Wylie said.

She paused to look back.

"You said you were paying."

She cupped her hand to her ear and shrugged. "Can't hear you. Gotta run. Duty calls."

37 **Amara slid into the passenger seat** of Starsky's car and set the food containers at her feet. "Sorry about that," she said.

"No sweat. That will cover this year's aerobic workout for me." He checked the rearview and pulled away from the restaurant. "Where to?"

No point in going home. It would be hours before the dinner's flood of embarrassment receded enough for her to sleep. "Let's drive by the Lucero residence and see if we can spot Dexter."

"Sure, but even if the dog is there, so what? If the kid is holding it hostage, you plan on calling in SWAT or something?"

She glanced out the window to hide her smile from him. "I wouldn't have to tell them Dexter was a dog."

"Amara, hey. That, uh, yeah. Tell me you're joking."

She chuckled and angled herself toward him. "Sorta. But if we do see Dexter and can grab him, think Haley would talk to us?"

He cut his eyes at her. "Can I tell you how many things about that question bother me? Let me make sure I understand this. Your plan is to dognap Dexter?"

"Not dognap. Rescue."

"Semantics. So you *rescue* Dexter so you can hold him hostage to force Haley to talk? I seriously cannot wait for *Dateline* to get word of this."

"No," she said. "If we get him back, I'll give him to Haley. It'll have to happen quick though. Before Matias and Liam have a chance to react and find another way to keep her quiet."

231

"You that certain she'll talk?"

"Not at all. But if she doesn't, we haven't lost anything. Besides, the dog's probably not even there. Wouldn't make sense to have it where people would look." A flash of distant lightning lit the dark clouds overhead. "They'd want to keep Dexter on the move. Make it hard to track him down."

"You do remember we're talking about a dog?"

"Keep him mobile. That's what I'd do."

He straightened in his seat. "And I'm supposed to be the odd one. You going to give me directions or do I go straight until we're south of the border?"

"Take a right at the next light," she said. "Be a long time before I want to go back to Mexico."

■ ■ ■

Huge drops of rain randomly pelted the windshield by the time they parked down the street from the Lucero residence. The subdivision of look-alike homes on miniature lots was deserted as people abandoned the outdoors for the security of their houses. At each end of the short road, a streetlight illuminated a circle of brightness.

Starsky checked the weather app on his phone and shook his head. "Ten minutes max before the bottom falls out."

She scanned their surroundings and stepped out of the car. "Come on. We'll walk past the front of the house and then circle through the alley."

He joined her on the sidewalk. "You realize this has all the makings of a bad comedy? We're about to get drenched while going on a spy mission to kidnap a dog that might not even be there."

Her heartbeat sped and she held out her hand. "Might make us look more natural?"

His breathing accelerated as he closed his hand around hers. "Whatever it takes."

The pair strolled past several houses, some with open curtains and visible activity, others battened down as if Fort Knox's gold rested inside. The Lucero residence was one of the latter. Cracks of light seeped around the windows' edges but gave no indication of who might be home. More importantly, no yipping.

"Dexter's not there," she said. "We'd hear him."

"Maybe he's asleep." They walked past a couple more houses before he stopped and squeezed her hand, then bent toward her. "I can't believe I'm doing this."

She tilted her head upward. Was he going to kiss her?

"Hide," he said.

"What?"

He pointed to a cluster of bushes a few houses away. "Hide on the other side of those."

"You want me to hide?"

His eyebrows scrunched together and he released her hand. "Am I pronouncing it wrong? H-i-d-e. Hide."

"What are you going to do?"

He turned toward Matias's house. "*Dumb and Dumber* has nothing on us."

"Do you need backup?"

He motioned emphatically to the bushes and resumed his journey.

She strode to the chest-high shrubs and stared as Starsky hurried up the Luceros' walkway. He raised his fist, banged once on the door, and sprinted her direction.

A lightning flash lit the area for a millisecond, and he seemed to be running in slow motion, his wide-eyed, open-mouthed face cartoonish. She doubled over in laughter and sank to the wet ground.

By the time he arrived beside her, she was on her side in a fetal position as spasms of giggles overwhelmed her.

He eased his head around the side of the bush to get a view of the home. "Shh. They'll hear you."

"I can't"—another wave of hysteria arrived—"I can't breathe." She snorted and clenched her legs together. "I think I just peed a little."

He covered his mouth as laughter convulsed him. "Worst date ever?"

Warmth oozed through her chest. *Best.* "Can you see anything?"

"Curtains moved, so someone's there. Listen."

The insistent high-pitched yip of a tiny, obnoxious dog filtered through the bushes to Amara. "You found Dexter."

"*We* found Dexter." He stood and held out his hand to help her up. "What do we do now?"

Amara wiped grass clippings off her pants. A low rumble in the sky built into an explosion of thunder. "What would you do if you had a dog and it was about to rain for a while?"

"Potty time," he said. "We head around back. But remember, we're cops. No climbing fences, no opening gates, no stealing the dog."

"Observe and report. That's the mission. If we see Dexter, I'll phone Haley, and if she wants to come over and do something, well, that's her choice. But if the dog somehow gets out of the yard, we grab it."

He tilted his head and frowned. "Amara, what are you planning?"

"What? I promise not to do anything that might come back to bite us later."

He stared upward and exhaled a long breath. "Would it be okay if I, uh, if I kissed you?" He dragged the back of his wrist across his forehead. "For luck, I mean?"

She licked her lips and massaged her thumb on his hand. "For luck. Make it quick."

He bent forward, kissed her gently, and stood straighter.

She stood on her tiptoes. "One more. For me this time."

Her heart pounded as he kissed her again, longer and stronger than before. She breathed heavily and waited for the lightheadedness to clear.

"Amara," he said, "I don't want to ruin our friendship. You know how I feel about you, but if there's any chance that—"

"Don't mess this up, Starsky."

He shifted on his feet. "Do you mean don't mess up what's happening between us? Or don't mess up the dog situation?"

She tugged him toward the narrow lane running behind the row of houses. "I'm still holding your hand, aren't I? Figure it out."

No streetlights reached here, and the standard six-foot-high wooden fence darkened each backyard. Most houses had a second story with blinds or curtains blocking the windows. On cue, yipping, followed by an outburst of profanity and a door slam, reverberated through the darkness.

They strolled toward the barking and slowed behind the Luceros' home. Amara ran her hand on the fence and dragged her foot along the bottom as the dog shadowed them on the opposite side.

"What are you doing?" Starsky asked.

"Checking for holes or loose boards."

"I'll pretend I didn't hear that."

"How could you hear anything over that nonstop barking?" She stopped, took a step backward, and tapped her toe against the fence. "Here. There's a hole and the board's loose." She squatted to get a closer look. "Too dark."

"Wanna use the flashlight app on my phone?"

"No. Someone might notice." She reached down and ran her hand around the hole. "Not big enough, but I think I can loosen it."

She squealed and jerked her arm.

"Splinter?"

"No," she said. "He licked my fingers."

"That beast."

She placed her ear close to the fence and stuck her hand through the hole. Dog slobber coated her fingers within seconds and she scratched his head. "Who's a good dog? Oh, yes he is. That's a good boy." She eased her hand back and grabbed the board. A gentle tug pried the wood far enough for Dexter to escape.

"I'm not seeing this," Starsky said.

The yipping renewed with a ferocity they hadn't heard. Dexter had gone into attack mode. Amara released the board and the dog yelped as it smacked him. "See what you did?" she said. "He was almost out."

"How is this my fault? All I did was talk."

"Well, don't. He doesn't like you."

Another flash of lightning and peal of thunder sounded the alarm as scattered dime-size raindrops fell around them.

"Wait here," Starsky said. "I'll be right back."

"Where are you going?"

"To grab my dinner. That'll get Dexter out of there."

She smiled. "Good thinking."

He turned and jogged a few steps, then looked back. "You're sure that's Dexter, right?"

"Who else would it be?"

"I dunno. But if this was a movie, it would be the wrong dog."

That's true. Maybe this wasn't Dexter. After all, she hadn't seen him and didn't all small dogs sound the same? No. That'd be too big a coincidence. Wouldn't it? "Starsky, get the chicken parmigiana. And hurry."

He trotted out of sight while she continued whispering and try-ing to soothe Dexter. After several minutes-that-were-probably-seconds-but-that-yipping-makes-time-stop, she tugged the board again and stuck her hand into the backyard. The dog barked a few more times, then his wet nose—she hoped that's what it was—brushed her palm. "Good boy. Goooood boy."

Starsky returned, opened the container, tore off a piece of bread, and gave it to Amara. "What about the chicken?" she asked.

"No way. That's mine."

His voice triggered another round of dog barking and the porch light switched on. "Get down," she said.

He knelt beside her and leaned close. "If we get caught, you're writing up the report."

Several choice words echoed from the house encouraging Dexter to stop barking or he'd be spending the night in the rain.

"See," Amara said. "It *is* Dexter."

The door closed, but the light remained on.

"Keep your mouth shut," she said.

"It didn't take long for this relationship to become one-sided."

She chuckled and nudged the bread under the fence. The bark-ing stopped as the distinct noise of a grizzly bear swallowing a moose was followed by a quick cough and whine for more food.

"Dexter's a good boy," she said. "Yes, he is." She passed another bite to him, this time closer to the fence. Four pieces of bread later, the dog was in her arms. The sound of a waterfall told her they were too late. Sheets of rain would be on them in seconds. "No talking. To the car, but keep giving me food."

By the time they got into the vehicle and sped away from the scene, all three were dripping wet. Starsky kept both hands on the wheel and his attention on the road. The wipers *thwump-thwumped* as fast as they could but were unable to keep up with the volume of water now flooding the area. Small ponds covered low-lying sections of the street, and he slowed to a crawl to get through them. He mumbled and frowned.

"You say something?" she asked.

"My car's going to smell like wet Dexter."

"Strange. He said the same thing about you."

He laughed and wiped his arm across his forehead. "Where to?"

"I need to call Haley and let her know we have her dog. See if she wants to meet."

He glanced at her. "*If* she wants to meet? I thought this was a done deal."

A drop trickled down her neck and she shuddered. "It will be." She placed Dexter in the back seat and tossed the last of the bread to him. "Might have to dig into your chicken parm."

"He's going to explode if you keep feeding him."

She shrugged and flipped open her cell. "Not my car." She pressed OK to open the menu on the tiny display. *Let's see. Contacts. OK. Scroll scroll scroll scroll. Haley Bricker. OK. Dial. OK. Can't understand why people don't use flip phones anymore.*

The girl answered on the first ring. "Hello?"

"We have your dog."

Starsky laughed and shook his head.

"What?" Haley said. "Detective Alvarez?"

Starsky touched Amara's arm. "Tell her we want five thousand in unmarked Milk-Bones."

She shushed him. "Haley, we have Dexter. I was hoping we could meet somewhere and return him to you. Maybe someplace we could talk?"

"You have Dexter?"

"Uh, yeah." *Is she not listening?* "Where do you want to—"

"Nooo!"

Amara held the phone away from her ear.

Haley's scream transitioned to sobbing. "You have to take him back. Now."

You have got to be kidding me. "Whatever's going on here, we can help."

Her breathing came in gasps. "Please. I'm begging you. Take him back."

"We can do that. We'll put him in the Luceros' backyard. Is that okay?"

"No. They'll know Dexter's been gone and think I did it. You have to tell them."

Amara nudged Starsky and drew a circle in the air to signal him to turn the car around.

"Tell her that"—he waited until she covered the phone with her palm—"tell her we'll take the dog back if she agrees to talk to us."

She scrunched her face and shook her head. "That's as bad as them."

He cut his eyes at her. "She's not your friend. She's a suspect."

An empty space swelled in her chest. Was she blackmailing a teenager to force her to talk? "Haley, what happens if they think *you* took Dexter?"

"Bad things." She sniffled and her voice shook. "Tell Matias you took him or found him or whatever, okay? I can't be involved. If they think I had anything to do with it, they'll hurt him."

"We'll take care of it, but after that, maybe we can talk?"

"Whatever you want. Just hurry. Please."

"I'll call you when we're done." She hung up and scrubbed her hand over her face. "That felt wrong."

"We were taking the dog back no matter what she said." Starsky lifted a hand from the steering wheel and reached toward her, then stopped. "It's an investigation. Use whatever leverage you can gain."

"Fine. As long as it's not illegal."

"So stealing Dexter wasn't wrong? How is returning the dog so Haley will talk any different from taking the dog so she'll talk?" He took a heavy breath. "Either way, you're doing what she wants, and in exchange, you're asking her to do something for you."

Her throat tightened as she tried to swallow. Did he have to say it like that? "It didn't feel the same."

"No, because you thought you were the hero. She'd be so happy she'd talk to you. Now you're the bad guy. Doesn't feel as good."

She ground her teeth. This night had taken a turn for the worse. "Don't talk down to me."

He returned his hand to the steering wheel. The wipers continued their back and forth treks. Neither spoke for several minutes.

"I'm sorry," he said. "You can't be their friend. Not while they're a suspect. Don't trust anyone."

"That include you?"

His head twitched and he sniffled.

"I shouldn't have said that," she said. "I do trust you. I hope you know that. Sometimes, I, um, sorry, okay?"

He nodded. "I don't know if this can work."

"Me neither." Her nose ran and her voice cracked. "But I think I want it to."

"So how do we do that? Can we separate work and personal?"

She touched his arm. "I don't know if I want to separate them. That's who we are. We'll figure it out."

"I hope so." He stopped the car down the street from the Lucero house. "From now on, I'll do my best to keep my mouth shut unless you ask for help. I just hate to see you make some of the mistakes I've made."

"I want your help. I do. But some things I think I need to learn on my own."

"Like how to return a dog you just stole?"

She wiped her eyes with the back of her hand. "I think this is one of those times I need to watch and learn."

He grabbed the chicken parmigiana in one hand and the dog in the other. "What am I supposed to tell them?"

She shrugged. "I trust you."

38 **Starsky trotted back** to the car and settled behind the steering wheel. "That went better than I expected."

"Yeah?"

"Ms. Lucero answered the door. She recognized me right away. I think she was afraid I was there to arrest Matias."

"What did you say?" Amara asked.

"Handed her the dog, said I was on a stakeout and spotted him walking in the street. I left before she had a chance to think things through."

"Like how you knew which house Dexter belonged to? Or who you were staking out?"

He cranked the car and drove out of the subdivision. "Pizza, right?"

"First place you see. My treat but get it to go. I'm calling Haley and having her meet us by El Mercado. They'll be closed and shouldn't be many people around."

"Don't want to go to the station?"

"Too risky. They're probably tracking each other. I don't want anyone to know she's meeting with us."

"Good call," he said. "Of course, they could always follow her to see what she's doing."

"If they do, they do."

She phoned Haley, explained the plan, gave directions, and told her not to be late. A queasy rumble vibrated her stomach. Her mood had settled into a dark place. The fight with Starsky, brief though it was, drained the lightheartedness of the evening. And the fact that he was correct, she needed to do a better job separating herself from suspects, wasn't helping. Manipulating people was a skill—was that the right word?—she'd have to learn. Used properly and legally, there was nothing wrong with backing people into a corner to force them to talk to you. Not if it was part of a murder investigation.

Except that wasn't entirely accurate. There might not be anything technically wrong with it, but it sure did feel morally iffy. One of those "the ends justify the means" deals. What bothered her most was the certainty that if they were dealing with Liam and his cocky attitude, she'd have enjoyed the process. Savored the subtle blackmail. And if she didn't treat all suspects the same, her career in Homicide wouldn't last long.

"You okay over there?" Starsky asked.

She looked at him before turning away again. "The job messes you up, doesn't it? Makes you do things. Feel things."

"Don't let it. Look, I know it's easy to say that, but we were all you once. You learn to do what you have to do to solve the case. Want to know the difference between a good homicide detective and a bad one?"

She stared at him and waited.

"The bad ones start to enjoy the dirty parts of the job. The manipulating and pushing boundaries between legal and illegal. Soon, the only thing that matters is solving the case."

"Isn't it?"

He turned into a pizza restaurant and parked. "Yes, it is, *for the job*. Not for *you*. This career demands things from you, but that doesn't mean you have to like them. Know where the line is, and don't cross it. That's the best advice I can give." He opened the door and stepped outside.

"Starsky?"

He hunched into the vehicle. "Yeah?"

"You'll tell me if I get too close? To the line, I mean?"

He shook his head. "Can't. In this job, we all draw our own lines."

• • •

Haley, Starsky, and Amara sat around a wrought iron table outside one of Market Square's shops. The bright colors of Mexico surrounded them. Small flags rippled overhead on lines run across the walkway. Displays of piñatas and sombreros filled the store windows. Día de los Muertos, the Day of the Dead, artwork covered everything from guitars to T-shirts to ceramic tiles.

As expected, the only people around this late at night were security guards. One had tried to shoo them off but left them in peace when the two detectives showed their badges and offered a couple of slices of pepperoni pizza.

"Thanks for coming," Amara said. "I appreciate your willingness to speak with us. Do you have any questions before we get started?"

A long pause preceded her response. "I'm not sure. I want to help but, um, I don't want to."

"Understood." Time for a little nudge. "Did you know Matias came to the station today?"

Haley squinted and blinked rapidly. "For what?"

"Why do you think? He wanted to cut a deal." Amara double-checked Starsky's cell to confirm it was ready to record. "I'll make some opening introductions and explain what we're doing."

The girl nodded and placed her phone on the table. "I'm recording this too."

"No problem. Here we go." She pressed the button on the app. "This is Detective Amara Alvarez. Detective Jeremiah Peckham is

here also. We're speaking to Haley Bricker. Haley, do you understand that you are not under arrest?"

"I do."

"And do you also understand that you are free to leave anytime
you want?"

"Yeah."

"Great. Haley, I'm curious why you gave your dog to Matias.
Can you explain that, please?"

"He said it was insurance. That Dexter would be fine as long as
I didn't, uh, you know."

"As long as you what?" Starsky asked.

The girl's posture stiffened. "What am I supposed to do? If I talk
to you, he said they'd hurt him. If I steal him back, he said they'd
find him anyway and that would be worse."

Amara tapped her finger on the table. Worse for Dexter or worse
for Haley? "Who is *he*?"

"Liam. He can be cruel sometimes. I don't think he'd really hurt
Dexter, but I didn't want to risk it, you know?"

Poor girl. If she'd let them bring the dog back, they could've
found a safe place for it. "I do," Amara said. "Did Liam or anyone
else threaten you?"

"No. There's sort of an understanding between us. We protect
each other. At least we used to."

"Thick as thieves, huh?"

Haley squished her nose. "What?"

"Forget it." She scooted back and crossed her legs. "If Liam said
they'd hurt Dexter if you talked to us, why are you here?"

"What choice did I have? If you didn't take him back to Matias's
house, it could've been bad."

That'll be fun to explain if anyone ever listens to the whole recording.

Like a defense lawyer. "I have some questions regarding the death of Zachary Coleman. He was a friend of yours?"

Haley tilted her head side to side several times. "Sorta, I guess. We did some stuff together, but he wasn't like a boyfriend or anything."

"Got it. What do you believe to be the cause of Mr. Coleman's death?"

"I'm, uh, hoping it was an overdose or something."

"But you don't think that's the case?"

"I don't know."

Amara stared at her. "Haley, would you describe the events that occurred on the day of Mr. Coleman's death?"

"We all—me and Zach and Liam and Matias—we went to the Cannonball Water Park. It was hot and we figured it'd be a good way to cool off. I wasn't with Zach when he died though."

"I see." Amara interlocked her fingers. "Did you provide drugs to him? Alcohol?"

The teen glanced at Starsky, then concentrated on her phone. "No. I didn't have anything to do with it. But there might be some things that happened, and if they did, I want to help."

Vague enough? "And you understand that to be helpful, you need to tell the truth? All of it?"

She nodded.

"Sorry," Amara said. "The phone can't hear you nod."

"I have to tell the truth."

"Great. Earlier you stated you were *hoping* the death was due to overdose. You don't believe that though, do you?"

"I'm not sure."

Time to fix that. "Haley, the body was pulled from the lazy river attraction at the water park, right?"

"Yeah."

"Would it surprise you to know that Zachary Coleman was already dead when he went into the water? That a person or persons placed him there *after* he died?"

Her breathing quickened and she fidgeted with her hair. "I don't know anything about that."

"No? Okay. We'll circle back in a minute. You, Matias Lucero, and Liam Walker all visited the Coleman residence after Zachary's death. I saw you there. Did you take the hard drive from his computer?"

She dragged her arm under her nose. "I, uh, I don't think I want to answer any more questions."

Starsky pointed toward the parking area. "Like the detective said, you're free to go anytime you want. You've been very helpful. Not enough to do yourself any favors, but we learned a few things."

Haley frowned. "I didn't tell you anything."

"Of course you did," Amara said. "Maybe not in so many words, but it's clear you think Zachary Coleman was murdered. That implies you know of a reason for him to be killed. And your reaction to my question about the computer equipment might as well have been a confession. One of you three, I'm guessing you, stole the hard drive. That's evidence of conspiracy. So, stay with me here—you put those two words together, conspiracy and murder, and what do you get? Help me out, Detective."

Starsky grunted. "Let's see here. She's an adult, right? The only one of the three if I remember correctly. Twenty years minimum. That's assuming this doesn't get kicked to the federal courts. You didn't do anything outside of Texas, did you? Mm-mm. That'd make things really ugly."

"Let me be clear," Amara said. "We're not threatening you. We can't tell you what a jury will decide. Or maybe you're fine with being in your forties—if you're lucky—when you get out of prison.

Bottom line is that if you don't want to talk to us, then don't. Your decision."

Haley's shoulders slumped. "You'll help me?"

"We'll do what we can," Amara said, "but I can't promise anything. Deals aren't up to me."

Her head dropped lower. "I took the hard drive and destroyed it. I don't know what was on it. He probably had it encrypted anyway. I do."

"Thank you," Amara said. "Why did you take it?"

"There might have been, um, things on there that we didn't want people to know about."

"What kind of things?"

"Stuff he wanted to keep secret. Plans and passwords and, I don't know. Maybe details on things he did."

"And all of those are regarding TOXICftw?"

Haley's head jerked. "You know about that?"

So Matias didn't tell her the police knew. "Huh. When I spoke with your friend this afternoon, he was as surprised as you are. Odd that he didn't mention any of this to you. Wonder if he told Liam?"

The teenager shifted in her seat and stared at her fingers.

Amara flattened her palms on the table. "How did the group get into ransomware?"

"It was just something to do, you know?" She flopped her head backward and sighed. "We'd been hacking into systems for a few years, kinda challenging each other to see who could break in first. After that, I guess it sorta evolved. Seemed like a harmless way to make a little bit of money."

"A little bit?" Starsky asked. "I've seen your truck."

"We didn't take more than we figured they could afford."

And how exactly did you determine that amount? "No harm done, right? Haley, was Zachary Coleman killed because of something that happened within your group? Was it because of the ransomware?"

"Maybe." She closed her eyes. "Probably."

"Do you know who killed him?"

"For sure? No."

"If you had to guess?"

She paused before answering. "None of us."

"No?" She crossed her arms and clicked her tongue. "Then who was it?"

Haley's chin trembled and a tear streaked down her cheek. "I just know their name."

"And . . . ?"

"He, or for all I know they're a woman, they call themselves Mighty Mouse 12."

39

Amara rested her forearms on the table and leaned forward. "Mighty Mouse 12? What does that mean?"

Starsky raised a finger. "Not that I'm old enough to remember, but Mighty Mouse was a cartoon character. Don't think he's been on TV in decades, but maybe the show's in syndication and you can still watch it."

"Wow," Haley said. "Ever hear of YouTube? We went on there when the dude first showed up and watched some of the old shows. Kinda retro, you know? Anyway, no clue who he is."

"Wait," Starsky said. "If he's Mighty Mouse 12, who are you? Online, I mean."

"What's your social security number?"

He tilted his head. "I'm not sure I see how that's relevant."

The girl shrugged. "Protecting your identity, right? If I tell you my character name, you know who I am. Not gonna happen."

Amara pinched her fingers along her eyebrows. "Let's back up. This might be easier if we stick to chronological order."

Wrinkles appeared on Haley's forehead.

"Tell us things in the order they happened," Starsky said.

The teenager crossed her arms. "I know what it means. Duh."

Starsky nodded. "So go back to the beginning. Zachary, Liam, Matias, and you got together how?"

She shrugged. "We're all, I guess, maybe thirteen or fourteen and into computers. It just kinda became a thing."

Amara clasped her hands together. "Could you be more specific? Like, did you meet on a hacker forum or what?"

Haley snorted. "A hacker forum. Yeah, that's what happens. A bunch of hackers get together in chat rooms. 'Do you want to break into the Defense Department with me?' 'Sure. I'm not doing anything else this weekend. Maybe we can hack a bank after that?'"

Starsky chuckled and Amara shot a glare his direction, silencing him instantly. "Fine. How did you four first get together then?"

"Different ways, I guess. Trolling online, RPGs, whatever."

"Role-playing games," Amara said for Starsky's benefit. "Those things have thousands of players, don't they? Kind of strange four people from San Antonio happened to run into each other."

"Not really," the teenager said. "Back then, games let you sort players by all kinds of stuff, including location."

Starsky grabbed another slice of pizza. "Is that something you would normally do? Find people close by, I mean."

"Sometimes. You can spend a lot of time in these games just running around and exploring. Helps to have things to talk about. Being from the same area makes that easier. Course, you still can't be sure who you're talking to. That's why we agreed to meet in person. Only way to verify who we were dealing with."

"Understood," Amara said. "And how long after you four met did the first in-person meeting occur?"

"Not for a couple of years at least. We'd figured out by then that we had, um, common interests." She picked all the pepperoni off a slice and tossed the spicy stack into her mouth. "What you really want to ask is when we decided to get into ransomware, right? That's why we met. Exchanged IDs, took photos of each other and our vehicles, visited our homes, anything we could think of. We had to make sure we could trust each other."

"I guess that's one way to earn trust," Starsky said. "And that's when your merry band of hackers was formed? TOXICftw."

"Yeah," Haley said. "We wanted something that sounded dangerous. TOXICftw was my idea. We all came up with a suggestion and voted on the one we liked best."

"And you were the lucky winner," Starsky said.

The girl frowned. "Not really. We all voted for ourselves, so we had to use an RNG to pick a winner."

"RNG?" Amara asked.

"Are you even serious right now?" Haley said. "Random number generator. Let the computer decide."

Starsky grunted. "What happened to drawing names from a hat?"

Amara glanced at him and gave a quick shake of her head, then turned back to Haley. "What next? Did you choose a leader?"

"Nah. Doesn't work like that. We made a few rules like not doing any hacking on our own and being careful how we spend our money. Our targets were all small, mostly local. The fee was paid in Bitcoin back then."

The fee. Not the ransom. Just a normal business transaction. "Makes sense. What would you say your average fee was?"

"Anywhere from a few hundred to a couple thousand. Not like we were getting rich on it. Worked fine for a while, until we decided to go after bigger clients."

"Why change what was working?" Amara asked. "More money?"

"More challenge," Haley said. "Got bored. Too easy to hit the small companies. Yeah, a bigger payout was nice, but that's not what we were after. Not at first. Plus, hard to make a name for yourself when nobody's heard of you."

"Forgive me," Starsky said. "Maybe I'm missing something here, but why would you want people to know who you are? I mean, you're breaking the law. Isn't the whole point to remain anonymous?"

Haley stared at him for a moment before looking back at Amara. "Was he, like, around with the dinosaurs or something?"

"Close. Humor him." *And me.*

"It's a business," the teenager said. "You want to get some cred, you gotta grow. People need to know they can trust you. TOXICftw had to move on to bigger customers. It's the way things work."

Starsky rubbed his nose. "Credibility and trust for the people who are robbing you. Makes perfect sense."

"We do what we say," Haley said. "You pay, we release your files. You don't pay, good luck trying to recover them. A few times we lowered the amount after the customer explained their situation, but nothing was ever free. Do that once and word gets out. The next client might not be so willing to cooperate."

"Okay," Amara said. "I can see that. So what changed? You're cruising along, things are going good, and what? Mighty Mouse 12?"

"There was a, um, complication, I guess you could say." She slid the pepperoni-less slice back into the box. "One night a year or so ago, me and Dexter are chilling at home and Liam calls. Says there's a problem and to check out our Bitcoin address. I log on and see a message there telling us we screwed up, but it's cool."

"Screwed up how?" Amara asked.

"By using Bitcoin." Her nose scrunched as Starsky bit into her picked-apart pizza. "Turns out some governments can now track it and find out where the money goes. No big deal for us though, 'cause we figure they're looking for terrorists and mega dollars. No way they're coming after us."

Starsky held his hand in front of his mouth. "Bigger fish to fry."

"What?" Haley said. "Forget it. Anyway, this message says not to worry but might want to change to a privacy coin to cover our tracks. That's why we switched to Zcash before our next, uh, customer. The weird thing was that whoever sent the message knew our Bitcoin address. No way that could happen unless they'd been one of the people we already hacked. See, Bitcoin changes addresses after every transaction. The old addresses are still good, but you really don't want to use them more than once. Helps with the secrecy and all."

Amara rubbed her dry eyes. Way too late at night for this technical talk. "So were you able to figure out which previous 'customer' they got the address from?"

"Yeah. It was really old. One of the first ones we did, like almost two years before we got the message. Place isn't in business anymore. A pool supply store. The paper did a story—who even reads the paper?—anyway, they did a story on ransomware and this place was included. Had a screenshot of the monitor, so that's probably where MM12 got the address. Not long after that, a couple of white vans pulled into the store's parking lot and the place was gone."

"Immigration," Starsky said.

Haley sneered at him. "Thanks, Captain Obvious."

Starsky winked. "No sweat, Sergeant Sarcasm."

The girl turned away and hid her grin from him.

Amara stood and arched her back. "Write down the name of the pool store. The date too. What happened next?"

"Like I said, we switched to Zcash. Then, I dunno, maybe a week or two later another message comes in. He wants to meet with us and we're all, like, for real? But he says he can help us get bigger scores without more risk. Says we can pick the time and place to meet. Liam said not to trust him 'cause if he can really do that stuff, why not do it himself? He's got a point, you know, but Zach says we should meet him online. That way we stay anonymous."

She crunched her Dr Pepper can and held it up. "Any more of these around?"

"We'll find a vending machine in a minute," Amara said. "So the four of you agreed to an online meeting?"

Haley shook her head. "First we voted. Two to two. Used the RNG again and that's when we set up the meet. Told him we'd be on TM the next night at ten. Gave him our screen names but nothing else."

"TM?" Starsky asked.

"Dude, seriously? *Tango Murked*. The game? Hello?"

"That's what I thought," he said. "Just wanted to make sure."

"Ignore him," Amara said. "Go on."

"We're standing around in an open area and this noob comes up—we could tell he was new 'cause he still had on the basic gear—and tries to talk to us. MM12. We shoot off to a private chat room and invite him in. That's the first time we talked. Guy says he wants to be like our manager. Get better gigs for us. Course, he'd want his cut, but we'd never have to meet in person. Whole thing stays anon."

Starsky surveyed the pizza bones in the box before choosing the crust from a slice Amara had abandoned. "Did you ask why he didn't just do it himself?"

"Yeah. No skills, he said. At least not like ours. He's more of a sales guy. Finds us new customers and we go in and close the deal."

Amara glanced at Starsky as he finished the last of her crust. For most people, someone polishing off your half-eaten food would be a sign of either a close relationship or a person with no table manners. With Starsky, it could be either, neither, or both. She turned back to the teen. "Sounds like he wanted you to take all the risk. Couldn't you find your own, umm, 'customers'?"

"Sure, but it's not as easy as it sounds. Most of the ones we'd already done were small-time stuff, like the pool guy. The bigger you go, the more work involved in the hack. Problem is that if you spend all that time and then the customer refuses to pay, everyone loses. You trash their files, they lose their data, and you've wasted your time." She flicked her finger against the crushed soda can and sent it skittering across the table. "And if you want cred, you've got to eventually get your name out there. The only way to do that is with a big payday or two. MM12 said he could deliver that."

"You trusted him? How did you know he wasn't FBI?"

She shrugged. "Didn't, so we set up a test. Told him to give us the names of a couple potential customers and we'd look into them and pick one and let him know. No problem, he says, and we agreed to meet same place and time the next day. We all drop offline and, like, an hour later two company names show up at our old Bitcoin address. The four of us talk it over and choose this podunk town in Indiana. Barstow, wherever that is. But we told MM12 we picked the other option, some lawyer group in Phoenix."

"Smart," Starsky said. "If it is the FBI and they're watching for you on the network, you're not there."

"Yeah." She reached for the Dr Pepper can. "I'm getting that d-peps or what?"

He stood and frowned. "D-peps. You're just messing with us now, aren't you? Making stuff up?"

Her lips remained in a thin, straight line. "It'll catch on. How much longer is this gonna take?"

Amara sat again. "It takes as long as it takes. What was the name of the legal firm in Phoenix?"

"Why does that matter? Lawyers are lawyers. Unity Legal, maybe?" Haley said. "MM12 said to let him know when we were ready. Set the fee at thirty-five k. Way more than we'd ever been paid. After a couple of weeks, we were good to go. Had access to everything we needed in Barstow's network, so we contacted MM12."

"How?" Starsky asked.

"Same as always. His Zcash address. Send him a few pennies and attach a message to it. Told him to meet us online again and let him know that we'd be flipping the switch in five minutes, but we didn't do the lawyers. Did Barstow instead and put his old Bitcoin address on there. Money goes to him, so if anyone's tracking it, he gets nailed."

"Let me guess," Amara said. "If he sends the money to you on Zcash, you can claim you don't know where it came from. If he doesn't send the money, you're out a bit of work but that's it."

"Yep. Barstow went off as planned, so we gave him our Zcash numbers, and less than two days later, eighty-five hundred shows up in each account. He kept a thou for himself and sent the rest on. After that, more of the same. Bigger jobs, more money. Even splitting the pot five ways instead of four, pretty soon we had some decent funds."

Starsky scratched his cheek. "Define 'decent funds.'"

"A little over a quarter mil."

He held out his hand. "Divided five ways, that's—"

"Quarter mil each," Haley said. "Like I said, decent. Not that we actually got that much in payments. Value grows, you know?"

"Like interest at a bank?" he asked.

Haley released an exaggerated sigh. "A year ago, one Bitcoin was worth four thousand. Today it's close to ten. Seen some people say it'll go up to twenty within another year or two. Zcash works the same way. Of course, it's entirely possible the bottom falls out and my quarter mil is worth half that by the time I wake up in the morning."

Amara planted her forearms on the table. Sounded a lot like

playing the stock market. "Why not just withdraw it? Convert some of it to dollars to protect yourself?"

"Not how it works. There are ATMs that can do some transactions, but they have dollar limits, plus the fees are ridiculous. Oh, and can't use an ATM without being videoed. And if you convert your digital money into dollars online, it almost always has to be linked to a bank account. Can't do that, obviously. Too many questions."

Starsky held up his hand. "Can I ask a stupid question?"

Haley giggled. "Better than anybody I know."

He licked his finger and dragged a "1" in the air. "That's one for you. What good is having all this money, and I'm still not convinced it's real, if you can't use it?"

"Didn't say you couldn't turn it into cash. Just meant you have to be careful how and when you do it. Besides, who needs paper? You don't think Zcash and Bitcoin and all the others are real? My truck real enough for you? Bought it with digital funds." She stood and picked up her phone. "Everything else I could tell you is more of the same. If you want details on our customers and more info, I'm gonna need to see my deal first. I've told you everything I can at this point."

"Not yet," Amara said. "Why were the four of you at the Cannonball Water Park that day? And don't tell me it was just a coincidence you all went on the day Zachary Coleman was killed."

Her lips turned down and she stared at the table. "That was the day we were going to make the water park our newest customer."

So it *was* them. No surprise. "And you wanted to be there so you could, what? Watch it happen? Why?"

"Why not? We'd been playing around in their system for weeks, making sure everything was ready. We gave MM12 instructions and he was gonna activate the attack. Plan was to shut down a few rides, disable some of their security systems, stuff like that. Nothing that would put anyone in any danger."

"Wait a minute," Starsky said. "This Mighty Mouse character. He knew you would all be at the water park on that day. That's why you think he had something to do with Coleman's death?"

"Yeah, but I don't know how he knew who we were or what we looked like. We screwed up. That's the first time we could be connected to a physical location."

"I get that," Amara said. "But assuming he's responsible for the murder, I still don't understand why."

"Me neither," the teenager said.

"Humor us," Starsky said. "I'm certain you have some theories."

She nodded. "I've thought about it. A lot. I think MM12 was afraid Zach was going to talk. Tell the cops what we were doing."

"Why would he think that?" Amara asked.

"Because of that nursing home where Zach's grandmother lives. Should've skipped it, but it was on our list from way back. We broke their network before we even met MM12. Weren't going to set them up as a customer or anything. Just wanted to see if we could do it. Somebody, Liam I think, says we should go ahead and collect since we did the work. Zach said no way, so we voted. Two to two—I didn't want to do it either—so we asked MM12 and he says, yeah, go for it but keep the price low. Made the vote three to two."

Amara swept crumbs into the pizza box. "So Zach disagreed. Doesn't seem like a lot of motive to kill someone, especially considering you voted against it and you're still here."

The girl lifted her face. "That woman died. Zach said it was our fault. Said he was thinking about getting out. We were all cool with that as long as he kept quiet. Guess MM12 wanted to make sure."

"At the water park," Amara said, "why did you all separate? Why not stay together?"

"We were going to record it when it happened. Not for anyone to see except us, of course. We all had our assigned places where we could shoot our videos and not be seen on the park's cameras."

She clicked her pen twice. "Who was supposed to be where?"

"Um, I was Aqua Attack. I don't remember where the others were."

"Don't remember or won't tell us?"

The teenager smirked. "Is there a difference?"

Starsky nodded. "Why not shut off all the cameras?"

"I wondered about that." She worked her hands together. "MM12 said not to. Might trigger some sort of emergency response in the park." She chewed on a fingernail. "But I don't think that's why. Not anymore. If all the cameras go off at the same time Zachary dies, it looks too suspicious."

Amara scribbled a few notes. "Everyone would make an immediate connection between the death and the outage. No way law enforcement doesn't get involved immediately. But once you knew we were looking, how come nobody deleted the video?"

"Wouldn't matter," she said. "The footage backs up locally and off-site. We'd have to break the other company's network too. Could do it but didn't have the time. If we'd known up front this was going to happen, then sure."

"Has there been any contact with MM12 since Zachary died?"

She nodded. "We met him in the game the night of the funeral and told him what had happened. If Liam and Matias had suspicions about him, they never said anything. He said he was sorry to hear about our friend, but nothing needed to change. Keep doing what we do. Take a break and we'll start back up in a little while. Contact him when we're ready."

"And, assuming we didn't get involved, that was your plan?"

"Our plan?" She frowned and looked around her. "Our plan is to do what he tells us to do."

Starsky put his hands on the back of his chair and leaned closer. "You're afraid of him."

"You don't get it, do you?" The teenager scooted away from the table. "He owns us. We're not anonymous anymore."

"We can help," Amara said. "There are worse things than losing your anonymity."

"No, Detective. There are not."

40 **Amara sat on the edge** of her bed trying to gain the energy to get the day started. Last night's interview with Haley had gone about as well as could be expected, and the investigation should continue to pick up steam. Despite that, sleep had come in fitful bursts. Fifteen minutes of dozing followed by chasing feelings for a random amount of time. Repeat for seven hours.

The guilt had arrived. As she'd settled into bed the prior evening, she'd congratulated herself on a productive day. Stayed busy. Got things done. Made progress.

And barely thought about Mama.

That her mother wanted it that way made little difference to Amara's conscience. Easy for Mama to say not to worry or don't feel guilty. She wasn't the one who had to do it.

Great, Amara. Mama has cancer and you're justifying how your life is now harder than hers. Throw another brick on the mound of guilt.

She trudged to the bathroom and turned on the hot water in the shower. What she *wanted* to do today was continue her investigation. What she *needed* to do today was go see her mother. In a matter of minutes, those two options would switch places as they had throughout the night.

In a way, the guilt was a relief. Having it meant she didn't have to feel guilty about not feeling guilty. The fact that she put that in the plus column meant she needed guidance. A way to balance things so everyone's demands were met. Including her own. Maybe.

The morning called for a therapy session.

● ● ●

Forty-five minutes later, a stack of pancakes sat in front of her, barely touched. After taking a taxi to the station—no smartphone meant no Uber—to get her car, she'd arrived at the Breakfast Bodega later than usual and the crowd was thicker. She'd waited until her usual booth became available, smiled at the waitress when she brought coffee, and watched the other customers as her breakfast grew cold and thoughts chased each other around her mind like a cluster of hummingbirds fighting over a feeder.

That booth—the one right there—was where she'd first met the Reyeses and stumbled into the Cotulla investigation. Life had transformed in the short time since then. Better and worse. She watched Ronnie, the weekend-slash-third-shift manager, head her way, slide across from her, and thunk his empty coffee mug down. He studied her plate and his rotund belly pressed against the table as he exhaled.

"What's wrong with the pancakes?" he asked.

"Nothing. Just trying to watch what I eat."

"Then why did you order them?"

"I always order them. You know that."

He studied her for a moment. "There are other things on the menu."

She nodded. "But I always get the pancakes."

The waitress walked by and Ronnie motioned toward his coffee cup. "When you get a chance, please. No rush." He turned back to Amara. "This isn't about pancakes, is it?"

She pushed the plate to the side. "No. Well, sorta. Ever feel like there's not enough of you to go around?"

He patted his stomach. "Not lately. Wanna talk about it? Might help."

"Not really. I just need to figure out where I'm going with all this, you know? It was complicated enough before Mama's cancer and—"

"Wait, your mother has cancer? Honey, I'm so sorry. I don't want to pry but, uh, how is she?"

"Breast cancer. Just diagnosed and started treatment. We have to wait and see how the cancer responds." She swallowed the lump in her throat.

"You'll tell me what I can do to help. We have a room in the back we can set aside whenever your family needs it. Food's on us. Anything we can do. I mean it."

She reached across the table and patted his hand. "Thank you, Ronnie. I'll let you know."

"Promise?"

"Promise," she said. "Anyway, Mama doesn't want us to act any different. Can't say I'm surprised since I'd do the same thing."

"If you even told anyone."

True. "So here I am trying to do my job and focus on my investigation while that's going on, and then feeling guilty because I'm doing what Mama wants. And forget any personal time, right? All I do is think about my case and my mother."

The waitress arrived and refilled both their cups. "Pancakes no good this morning?"

"They're fine," Amara said, "but I think I'm done with them. Thanks."

Ronnie waited until the waitress left. "You've still gotta pay for those even if you didn't eat them."

"Wouldn't have it any other way. But at least I don't have to work them off. Oh, that's the other thing. When am I supposed to exercise? Go for a run? Sleep? There's not enough time in the day." She plopped against the back of the bench. "And don't tell me to cut something out, because if you do, it's got to be my personal life. Everything else is too important."

His chest rose and fell several times before he answered. "More important than you?"

"Of course. Don't you feel the same way about your family and job?"

"This is where I work. Where I earn a paycheck. I do that for my family. And for me if I'm honest. I like a few luxuries in life. And before you say that your job is not the same as mine, I know that. Just like you knew what you were getting into when you switched over to Homicide. Can I give you a piece of advice?"

"Sure." She held the coffee to her mouth and let the steam flow across her lips. "Something your daddy's daddy told you a long time ago?"

He chuckled. "Not likely. But when I get overwhelmed like you are now, there's a thing I do to help me stop worrying so much. See, you don't have to figure it all out. Don't have to wonder about how to pull it all together or what the future holds. You only have to answer a single question. What should I be doing *right now*? Not tonight or tomorrow or next week or next year. Right now. And when that's done, ask the question again and again as many times as you have to."

"Hard to keep things organized when you do that."

"Not really," he said. "Turns out a whole lot less things need organizing than you think. So, Detective Amara Alvarez of the San Antonio Homicide Division, what should you be doing right now? After paying your check, I mean?"

"Going to visit my mama. Then going to—"

"There is no 'then.' Go visit your mother."

Ronnie's simple concept seemed sound. Workable. And would last about five minutes. Her mind didn't work that way, and she had no desire to try to rewire her brain. But she did feel better and, if nothing else, knew where her next stop would be. "Thanks, Yoda." She smiled at him and dropped a twenty on the table as she stood.

"No problem. I'm just sorry you didn't want to talk about what was bothering you."

Her grin widened. "Same time next week?"

"Yeah," he said. "Be on time. Don't like to keep the other patients waiting."

41 **The visit with Mama** lasted barely twenty minutes. She'd played the fake-annoyed routine that her daughter had better things to do on a Saturday morning than stop by to see her mother. Amara followed suit with the fake-annoyed routine that her mother should show some appreciation for her daughter stopping by on a Saturday morning. Both knew the game well enough that it was over in a few seconds. Amara tried to bring up the cancer treatment but was quickly tsk-tsked into silence.

"Not now," Mama said. "I feel fine."

Amara nodded. Don't waste the good days. There would be plenty of time later to dwell on chemo and radiation and whatever else was headed their way.

The goodbye hug lasted longer than usual, or at least seemed so to Amara. A tighter squeeze too. As if the gesture was an understanding that, cancer or not, one of these hugs would be the last they ever shared. When they separated, a tear made its way down Amara's cheek, slowing long enough for Mama to wipe it away and tsk-tsk her again.

As she drove off, she pondered her next move. Exercise could wait. The interview with Haley had opened new areas for investigation. Whichever route she went, they'd all end up in the same place. Mighty Mouse 12. She probably had enough now to go to a judge for search warrants for the three teenagers' homes, specifically their computer equipment. What good would that do though?

The drives would be encrypted and useless. Nothing there would help point to a killer.

And if she went to the LT about a possible deal for Haley, he'd want her to lay out the whole case before he'd go to the DA. And right now, that consisted of little more than the ME's suspicion combined with the chatter of a teenage girl. Neither of those added up to the stack of cash found at the Coleman house. Didn't mean it wasn't true. Just meant that she was a long way from proving it. And the LT wasn't going to go to the DA with smoke. She needed fire.

First thing was to get her hands on the rest of the security footage from the water park the day of Coleman's death. All the videos that *didn't* show any of the four teenagers. If nothing else, she was a hundred percent sure the killer was on there somewhere. Maybe she'd spot someone paying a little too much attention to the group of teenagers, particularly the victim. Still didn't explain how MM12 knew what the four looked like, but one step at a time.

"Call Eduardo Sanchez."

No response from her cell.

She ground her teeth. Of course not, because her phone was from the 1920s. She grabbed the device off the passenger seat and flipped it open, alternating her view between the road and the cell. Texas law said she couldn't do that, and if she was in uniform or a marked car, she wouldn't. Not because of the statutes, but the new reality for cops. Some random, uh, *citizen*, with nothing better to do than snap a photo of an officer doing something wrong and splattering it all over social media.

A horn sounded behind her and she glanced in the mirror. What? The vehicle swerved and eased past her, slowing to give a stare. Oh. Thirty in a fifty-five zone. She frowned and pulled into a strip mall parking lot. Quicker to do it this way anyhow. After trudging through too many button presses and squinting at the tiny screen, she found Sanchez's number and dialed him. As head of security at the water park, chances were he'd be at work on a Saturday in July. Had to be one of their busiest days.

He answered halfway through the third ring. "Ah, Detective Alvarez. I'm glad you called. I have you on my list for today."

"That mean you've got some news?"

"Yes, but not sure how helpful it will be. You asked what the financial impact would be if the park were shut down. The numbers I got said somewhere between twenty-five and fifty thousand per hour. Depends on the weather and the crowd size. On the day the Coleman boy died, I'd expect a figure on the upper end of the range. And that only counts lost revenues. There'd be ancillary expenses to add to that number."

"Such as?"

"Dealing with potential refunds, increased marketing to cover any bad PR, probably a dozen other things. It would be a nightmare scenario for us."

Perfect way to generate a huge payday for TOXICftw. "Any thoughts on whether or not the company would pay a ransom to get their systems up and running?"

"Absolutely they would. Hold on a sec." His voice muffled as he spoke to someone in his office. "Sorry. Busy time of the morning. Anyway, yes, we'd pay and we'd do it quickly. Turns out that two years ago, our legal team added an amendment to the park's insurance to cover—let me make sure I have this right . . . here it is. 'To cover costs and fees associated with the intentional disruption of the insured's network with the specific purpose of disabling the insured's operations, to include all monies required to bring the network to a functioning status within a reasonable amount of time.'"

"So the insurance company would pay the hackers to bring the system back online?"

"Not necessarily," he said. "A lot of variables would come into play, but basically, the insurance company is going to do whatever is cheapest for them. If that means paying the ransom, so be it. And let's be honest here. Not like they won't get their money back in the long run by raising the rates they charge."

She stared out the windshield as an old Toyota parked near a Pizza Hut at the corner of the strip mall and a middle-aged man stepped outside, yawned and stretched high enough for his T-shirt to expose his belly, and wandered inside the restaurant. Ransomware insurance. Too perfect. The whole thing was a business, everyone said. Build credibility. Make a name for yourself. Follow through on what you say, whether that's releasing the data upon payment or abandoning the customer to their fate if they refuse. An insurance company is going to take the path of least resistance. Pay now, raise their rates, recoup their losses, and go about their day.

And someone smart, like Mighty Mouse 12, would understand the best way to get the biggest, quickest paydays would be to know who has the insurance. Take the personal out of the transaction. Let it be an issue between the hacker and the insurer. Why not? The customer has the policy in case this happens, and guess what? It happened. Now pay up so I can get my business back online.

"Detective?" Sanchez said. "You still there?"

The man strolled out of Pizza Hut, his arms loaded with three boxes and a couple of two-liter somethings. "Yeah," she said. "I'm still here. Can you email me the name of the insurance company? And sorry to ask, but I need all your video from the park on the day Coleman died."

A low whistle echoed through the phone. "That's a lot of data," he said. "I already gave you everything I have with the teenagers on it. If you're looking for someone else, maybe you could give me a photo and I could have someone search for them."

"No." Now that she finally had a string to tug, no way she was going to risk someone else getting their hands on it. "I'll make it simple and get a subpoena. That work for you?"

"Detective, I meant no offense. You must understand we have an obligation to protect the privacy of our guests. I will happily provide other items you need as long as they don't jeopardize that concern. And I am only trying to help."

Don't. "Mr. Sanchez, you've been very helpful. I'll be in touch about the subpoena. In the meantime, please ensure none of the video from that day is destroyed."

"I will have a copy available."

His tone had stiffened. Did she hurt his feelings? Did she care? Didn't feel like it. "Thanks. I'll be in touch." She snapped the phone closed and tossed it into the passenger seat. Felt kinda nice. Not like tapping a button to hang up. Skip the "goodbye," click the cell shut, and move on. Not as much fun as slamming down the receiver on one of those old rotary dials, but close enough. An expression of emotion. A reaction to events.

Not sterile, like tapping a button on a screen.

Maybe the old ways weren't so bad.

42

After exchanging the usual pleasantries and head nods with a few other detectives, Amara settled in at her card table. The place was relatively quiet. Either everyone was out chasing bad guys or gone to lunch or didn't have a case that demanded weekend work.

She scribbled three names on a notepad.

Barstow, Indiana

lawyer/Unity Legal?/Phoenix

Cannonball Water Park

The first two were the options given by MM12. If both of them had ransomware insurance, that would be a strong lead. And if all three had the *same* insurer, that'd be a giant arrow pointing the way.

If Haley was being truthful.

Amara tapped her pen on the pad. The girl seemed sincere enough, but that didn't mean much. She'd been genuinely upset about her dog. Or was a really good actress. None of that was relevant anyway. Not yet. Even if she was being honest, her truth may not equal reality. The world was filled with examples.

Facts mattered. They could be proven. Hold up in a court of law. Convict the guilty. All she had to do was get enough of those facts together to convince a DA to prosecute. Easier said than done when you had to assume everyone was lying to you.

No one could be trusted.

Even Sanchez seemed suspicious again. Not because of anything he'd said or done, but because she'd found a new focus. A spot she could pry into and peel back until facts revealed themselves and accelerated toward Zachary Coleman's killer. Find the first absolute, undeniable truth and the rest would follow.

She circled "Barstow, Indiana" on the paper and looked up the city. Small town, around twelve thousand residents as of the last census. Farming community. No one famous ever born there, apparently. Their surprisingly modern website displayed panoramic drone footage as the machine swept over downtown into the surrounding fields. A message at the top of the page reminded everyone it wasn't too early to register for this autumn's Miss Soybean pageant, being held in the Methodist church this year. The town's mayor, chief of police, and volunteer fire department captain each had their own page, along with a generic "here's everybody else you might need to contact" list. All in all, nothing popped out as special. Nothing that made them a target for hackers.

But maybe that was the idea. Haley said they were supposed to demand thirty-five thousand in ransom. Sure, it was a lot of money, but barely a blip to an insurance company. Might make more sense to do a bunch of small jobs rather than a few big ones. Keep a low profile so the insurers didn't catch on. And thirty-five k would be low enough that any town would jump at the offer, especially if they had coverage. Anything was better than having the city's computers shut down. Customers couldn't pay their water bills. Tax records would be offline. The mayor and cops and whatever other workers Barstow employed couldn't get their paychecks.

She clicked back to the mayor's page. Powell Vandenberg. Might as well start at the top. She dialed the number and he answered almost immediately.

"Mayor Vandenberg?" she asked.

"Yes?" The voice was clear and alert. "Can I help you?"

"Yes, sir. My name is Amara Alvarez and I'm a detective with the San Antonio Police Department. In Texas."

"Is there another San Antonio?"

"Uh, no, sir. Not that I know of." *Great. He thinks that I think he's some backwoods—*

"What can I do for you, Detective?"

"I'm working on a case and was hoping you could give me some information about an incident that occurred in Barstow recently. Your computer network was attacked and, I guess, the town's insurance took care of things?"

"Well, there was a bit more to it than that, but you've got the gist. Why? Happening to you in San Antonio?"

"No, sir. At least not that I know of." She drew a star next to the town's name on her pad. "Can you tell me what company handles your insurance?"

"Carbonis." He spelled it for her. "Specialize in that area. Our normal carrier wanted too much, and we want to be careful how we spend tax dollars. Still cost us ten thousand for the deductible, but Carbonis paid out the other twenty-five. Just glad they didn't ask for more."

"Why is that?"

"That's all our policy covered. Insurance would pay the twenty-five k max. Anything over that came from the town's budget. On top of the deductible, of course."

She wrote *$35k* and circled it. Convenient that the hackers asked for the exact amount insurance would cover. "Whose decision was it to pay the ransom?"

"Mutual, I guess. They were clear that we could refuse, but no telling how long it would take them to get our systems back online. And even if they did get things fixed, they couldn't promise we wouldn't lose data. Quickest and cheapest thing to do was pay and hope the people who did it would provide the key to unlock everything, which they did."

She jotted *Carbonis* and a dollar sign on the pad. "What would the company's responsibilities be if you didn't agree to the payment?"

"You'd have to talk to Mitch Conrad, he's the city's legal counsel, for the details, but as I understand it, they'd be on the hook for all expenses associated with getting things back to normal. New computers, any lost revenues, extra labor costs because of working overtime to fix things, even potential lawsuits. I'd say they have a pretty strong reason to pay."

"Uh-huh. Why did Barstow purchase the insurance? Forgive me, but that doesn't seem like the type of thing a small town would even think about. Did Carbonis initiate contact?"

He chuckled. "No, ma'am. Actually, it was Drew's suggestion. He handles most of our technical stuff. Did a great job on our website if you get a chance to look at it. Anyway, I guess it's been almost two years now, Drew gave a presentation at one of the city council meetings and answered a few questions. He does his best to keep us up-to-date with technological issues that might affect the town."

"And did he recommend purchasing insurance?"

"Not really. That's kind of beyond his scope."

"Got it. Can I get Drew's last name for my records?"

"Vandenberg. Same as mine. Drew's my eleven-year-old son, so that would make him, what, nine when he gave the presentation. Earned him a merit badge for Scouts, though don't ask me which one. At the next meeting, we decided to purchase the coverage. Premiums were cheap enough, though we still had a couple of hours of arguing. Don't suppose there's much debating going on now, but I suspect we'll see a hefty jump in the premiums next year. That's all insurance is. A gamble, but the company always wins."

True enough. No company was in business to lose money. "Do you happen to know how much your premiums are now?"

"To the penny? No, but it comes out to somewhere between two and three thousand a year."

She wrote the number on the paper. "Thank you for your time, Mayor. If I have any other questions, would it be okay to call you again?"

"Of course," he said. "And if you're ever out this way, be sure to stop in and say hello. Be a pleasure to meet you."

"Will do." A sudden image flashed in her mind of her standing in front of a church wearing a Miss Soybean sash and a tiara. She grinned and hung up the phone. No visits to Barstow anytime soon.

But the mayor's comment about insurance did stir some thoughts. Was it a gamble? For the customer maybe, but for the company? Not really. If it wasn't profitable, they wouldn't be selling it. Say Barstow pays three grand a year for the policy, and they've had it for two years. That's six thousand the town has paid, and if their network is never hacked, the insurance company pockets the money.

But they *were* attacked, so Carbonis is out twenty-five k, minus the six Barstow paid them. Nineteen thousand dollars out of pocket, while the town is out the cost of the premiums plus another ten thousand for the deductible. If the ransom amount was typical for towns and companies that size, Carbonis would have to . . . She scribbled the numbers.

19000 / 2 years = 9500 per year cost to Carbonis

If the premiums were three grand a year, the company needed to sell the same policy another three times to recover the money they'd spent. And they most likely had thousands of customers, the vast majority of whom would never experience a ransomware incident. And that didn't include the increase in premiums everyone knew was coming. Oh, and the more attacks, the more publicity, the more sales of cyber insurance.

A win for the criminals. A win for the insurance companies. And the customer thinks they came out on top too. Almost seemed like a victimless crime, so why not pay the ransom? It was good business, which meant the crime would continue to grow until enough people refused to pay or the risk to the hackers increased dramatically.

But this crime wasn't victimless. Zachary Coleman died. His family grieved.

Justice demanded a response.

She demanded answers.

Anything else would be bad for business.

43 **Amara reread the email** from Sanchez. Sorry, but the water park's attorneys insisted on a warrant for anything else she needed. He probably didn't even ask them. Whatever.

The video would serve as proof that the suspect, once she identified them, was at Cannonball the day Coleman died. There'd be time to deal with that later, once she put a face to MM12.

The bigger issue in the email was the info that the park used a different insurance firm than the town of Barstow. A company named LockShield handled their policy. Nothing was simple. Didn't mean there wasn't a connection.

She searched for an Arizona legal corporation close to "Unity Legal," the name Haley thought it might be, and found the unlikely title United Divorce Group in Phoenix. Their website said they were a collection of attorneys specializing in making certain "you get what you deserve" from the dissolution of your marriage.

Amara wanted to spit in her garbage can. If she could find it. Her own divorce ten years earlier had been quick, though a couple of years too late, and cheap. Had she got what she deserved? She did have Larry, but he was a gift to herself after the final hearing. Definitely a step up from her ex.

A recording stated they were closed for the weekend, but she could leave a name and contact number and they'd be in touch first thing Monday morning.

She fidgeted on the keyboard. Easy enough to find a phone number for one or two of the lawyers in the group, but chances were that's not who she needed to speak with. If the company was big enough, there'd be someone who handled things like that. Not a divorce attorney. And if they weren't big enough, they'd have an insurance agent who did it for them. If she ran out of things to do before Monday, she'd start down that trail. If not, her time was better spent elsewhere.

Over the next half hour, she researched Carbonis and Lock-Shield. Both claimed to specialize in network restoration with an emphasis on getting the client back up and running as quickly as possible. Each also stated that paying ransomware was the final option, but in rare cases may be necessary. Fear not though, since they would handle everything from negotiation to file recovery. Of course they would. Once they determined what was cheapest for their company. Both websites were filled with alarming statistics surrounded by photos of smiling customer service representatives and urgent requests to call now for your free quote. Testimonials cycled through from individuals with last initials only and un-named companies.

She flicked a finger on her bottom lip. Hackers who wanted to go big would surely target organizations with this kind of protection, wouldn't they? A better chance at a quick payout since, by the time they got involved, the insurance company would be eager to settle quickly. Otherwise, they'd be on the hook for substantial costs if the victim opted against paying the ransom.

MM12 had access to the files. It made sense. He knew the companies that had insurance. And once she figured out how he gained that knowledge, she'd have him.

The obvious solution was that he worked at one of the companies. Since both LockShield and Carbonis were based in Connecti-cut, it was possible he'd moved from one to the other at some point and taken a customer database with him. Wouldn't be the first time something like that happened, especially if he was in sales and was hired with the promise of bringing some of his clients with him.

There were other possibilities. MM12 could be working with someone from the other company or might be part of an entirely different outfit that happened to service both companies. Communications, cleaning, banking, whatever. The only way to figure it out was to get going.

She dialed the 800 number for LockShield and heard the message telling her to please listen carefully as their menu options had changed. The most secure job in America had to be changing menu options for companies. Every single corporation she'd ever phoned had recently changed their menu options.

She punched 3 for all other inquiries and listened to elevator music—was that "Stairway to Heaven"?—while debating whether to ask for security or legal or HR. Maybe go straight to the CEO. Like they'd be at work on a Saturday. And even if they were, how could she be sure they weren't MM12?

A beep sounded and she pulled the phone away from her ear to check the display. Incoming call from Wylie. Her mind sped through dozens of possibilities in a nanosecond but, as usual, settled on the worst-case scenario. Something was wrong with Mama. She pressed the button to hang up on LockShield and switch to Wylie.

"What's going on?" she asked.

No response. She glanced at the phone. Stupid thing hung up on both of them. She redialed Wylie and listened as his voice mail kicked on. She clenched the cell until her knuckles hurt. "Wylie, it's Amara. Call me back."

After hanging up, she began dialing him again and a tiny icon appeared at the top of the screen notifying her of a new voice mail.

She scrolled through the menu to find the option to check messages. Her heart pulsed against her chest and she slapped her free hand on the desk to release the frustration. Didn't work.

Wylie's name popped up on the display again and she answered before the first ring could finish. "What's happened?"

"Get to the hospital," he said. A siren echoed in the background. "Maria's had some sort of reaction. The EMTs said to hurry."

"Hurry? How serious is—"

"Go, Amara. I'm calling the rest of the family."

She slowed and killed the siren as she neared the ER parking area. The twenty-five-minute drive took her fifteen. She ran Code 3—lights and siren—the entire way. If the SAPD had a problem with that, let them. Halfway there, she'd dialed Starsky, put the call on speaker, and dropped the phone into the center console. Both hands on the wheel when running hot. She'd shouted, "Mama's on the way to the hospital," and he'd said something, but the combination of external noise and internal focus shoved his voice away. Regardless, the call disconnected.

She parked outside the ER, careful to leave room for other emergency vehicles, and jogged inside. Selina, one of her younger sisters, paced toward her. The woman's damp eyes, rapid breathing, and trembling chin were all it took. Tears overflowed and streamed down Amara's face as the two hugged.

"What happened, Selina? Is Mama—is she okay?"

Her sister squeezed tightly before stepping back. "She's, um, she had a bad reaction to one of the drugs. They're working on her."

Amara turned toward the double doors blocking access to the ER. "Working on her? What does that mean? Where is everyone else?"

"Wylie rode with them. He's back there with her and they said only one family member. I was the first to get here, but everyone else should—"

"Amara!"

Her heartbeat slowed minutely. Starsky. He must've run Code 3 too. She spun around as he hurried to embrace her. After a moment, they separated. His hands fidgeted and he shifted on his feet.

"How is she?" he asked.

"We don't know. I just got here too. Selina said they're working on her and Wylie's back there. They won't let anyone else see her and no one has given us any update."

He glanced around the area. "Wait here." He trotted past the semi-crowded waiting room to the admitting desk where a brief, animated conversation took place. At one point he'd shown his badge. In return, the nurse at the desk showed her ID. His slumped shoulders and slower pace gave the battle results.

"Thanks for trying," Amara said.

"Yeah." Wrinkles creased his forehead. "Officially, Wylie's not family, but I didn't want to, uh, you know."

"He's where he should be. Selina, could you text him? Let him know we're here and to call when he can?"

She nodded and wandered a few steps away.

"You want to sit?" Starsky asked.

"I'm okay. I saw her this morning and she said she felt fine. If it was a reaction to the chemo, wouldn't that have happened yesterday?"

He frowned. "I don't know. We'll have to wait and see what the doctors say."

"Uh-uh. I'm going back there now. We don't even know if she's still in danger."

"He's coming out," Selina said. "Wylie, I mean."

Seconds later, he walked through the double doors, spotted them, and hurried over. Most of the color was gone from his face, and his stubble and messy hair aged him twenty years. Amara's throat tightened. Even when Wylie had been shot and laid up in the hospital, he hadn't looked this bad.

He raised both hands. "She's going to be okay."

Amara wrapped her arms around Starsky as sobs of relief poured from her. He cupped one hand against the back of her head and waited until she had nothing left. A few quivering deep breaths later, she pulled away and used her finger to trace a circle around the large wet spot on his T-shirt.

"Sorry," she said.

"No." He sniffled and wiped his eyes. "Don't say that." He blinked several times, then exhaled and ran his hand under his nose. "Of course, this was my favorite shirt."

Her grin faded as quickly as it appeared. "What happened, Wylie?"

"The nausea was bad when she woke up this morning. She took a pill but it didn't help, so we called the doctor and he phoned in a prescription for a different kind. Less than an hour after she took that one, she was having trouble breathing and her lips were tingling, so I called 911."

He swallowed and wiped under his eyes. "The doctors said she had an anaphylactic response to the drug. Like if you're allergic to bees and get stung. Extremely rare, they said. The paramedics gave her a shot of something and put her on oxygen. By the time we got here, she was lots better. Told me not to tell anyone about it. I said it was too late. Now she's mad at me, I think. Can you believe that?"

"I can," Amara said. "But for future reference, you call us regardless of what she says. If you don't, I'll put you in the hospital myself."

"I'll call, but don't kid yourself," he said. "I'm more scared of her than I am of you. They're moving her to a room soon and keeping her overnight for observation. Switching her meds too. The nurse said no visitors until she gets out of the ER. Probably another hour. But she wants to see you, Amara."

TOM THREADGILL

"The nurse?"

He shook his head. "I bet you fit right in over at Homicide. Your *mother* wants to see you." He gestured toward the woman at the admitting desk. "I'll tell her."

After a brief conversation, the woman nodded and waved Amara back. A click sounded on the door as the lock released, and she stepped into the maze of doors, curtains, beeps, antiseptic, and scrubbed personnel. A young man leaning against a wall and punching something into a computer tablet pointed her in the right direction.

She peeked around a curtain to make sure she had the correct location and was spotted by a man taking her mother's vitals.

"Family?" he asked.

"Oldest daughter," Mama said.

Amara cringed and waited for the "she's single" comment any decent sitcom mom would include. It never came and she moved to her mother's side and grasped her hand. "How are you feeling, Mama?"

"I'm fine. All this fuss because I had a little trouble. Ridiculous."

The shaky tone of her voice failed her bravado. Amara fought to maintain a steady expression. A new pain weighed on her heart as her extremities went numb. Mama was scared. She'd thought she was going to die. All the focus on attacking the breast cancer and she nearly lost before the battle even began.

"It's okay," Amara said. "I'm here now. Selina too, and the rest are on their way. I'll sleep in the room with you tonight and won't leave the hospital until you do too."

"Hush." Mama waited until the nurse jotted down some notes, checked her IV again, and left the room. "That's not why I wanted to see you. I need you to do something for me. You have to promise."

"If I can."

285

Her mother nodded once. "I'm not going to win," she said.

"Mama, don't say that. You'll be okay."

"Let me talk." She sighed and squeezed Amara's hand. "I'll beat the cancer, or I won't. Even if I do, who's to say how much longer I'll be here?"

"You've had a scare, but you'll be back to normal soon."

She let her hand slide from Amara's grip onto the bed. "My time will come. My prayer has always been that none of my children would go before me, and Dios has granted that so far. Do you know what frightened me today? Not death. More like the goodbye, I think. We've seen that pain in the ones left behind."

Daddy. He'd died of a heart attack when Amara was fifteen. The day of her *quinceañera*. "Mama, you should be thinking about yourself. We're fine. All you need to do is concentrate on getting better." She gently rubbed her mother's arm.

"I love you, baby. You know that, right?"

"Of course."

"I can't say things like this to your brothers and sisters. But you'll understand. You've always been that way. Do you remember Izzy?"

"Yes." Their pet chihuahua.

She smiled. "I hated that dog. But you kids loved her. Your dad did too. You must've been around twelve when she died. She'd been throwing up, not eating, whining all the time. We knew something was wrong."

"I remember. We buried her in the backyard. Had a little service and everything."

"She had cancer, Amara. We knew for almost three months before she died. The vet said we should put her down, but your dad and I couldn't do it. Not if there was a chance. We didn't want to see our kids hurt, so we opted for some experimental medication." She let her head sink into the pillow. "Mmm. For a dog I hated. It cost us thousands and accomplished nothing except prolonging Izzy's suffering and your grief."

Where was she going with this? "I didn't know all that, but if you're trying to make some comparison between Izzy and you, that's not even realistic."

"No? What do you think Izzy would have told us to do?"

Amara wiped the back of her hand across her forehead. Did they turn on the heat?

Her mother smiled. "A day or two after we buried Izzy, your brothers and sisters had already moved on. But not you. I'd catch you in the backyard putting a flower or bone or toy on his grave." She paused for nearly a minute. "He's not there, you know."

Her father. Every month on the eighteenth, or as close to that as she could, Amara visited the grave. "I know. I just go there to clear my mind."

"And there's not a thing wrong with that as long as you understand you're doing it for you, not your daddy. I'll fight the cancer. Hard as I know how. But whether it's this or something else, when it's time for me to go, let it happen. Nothing would ease my heart more."

Amara's heart sank. "What exactly are you saying, Mama?"

"I've lived my life and I'd love to live another fifty years, but if the treatments don't work, I won't chase a cure. One good year with my family is worth more than a dozen years of hospitals and nursing care and"—she flicked her hand toward the curtain—"and this. Do you know what your father used to say to me? 'That girl's going to be just like you.' He was right."

How? Mama loved cooking and socializing and a big family. Long hours solo at the gym or working on a case were more her speed.

The nurse poked his head through the curtain, announced that

Mama would be wheeled to her room within the next couple of minutes, and disappeared just as quickly.

"I'll go with you to the room," Amara said. "When we get there, I'll call the others and let them know where we are. They're anxious to see you. But I'm staying. No argument."

"The sixth," Mama said.

"What?"

"Your dad and I were married on May sixth. I go visit his grave every month on that day. You were there once so I didn't stop. I sit and remember. So I'm asking you to promise me that when it's my time, you'll think about what you would do if you were in my place."

An orderly swung the curtain back. "Ready to go?"

Amara kissed her mother's forehead. "Ready."

45 **Amara rolled her shoulders** and stretched her head every possible direction. While the recliner in Mama's room had been surprisingly comfortable, it would never replace her own bed. The night had been uneventful, and her mother seemed to be fully recovered from the reaction. Just after eight, Amara went home to shower and get some work done. Mama had insisted, since the flow of visitors hadn't decreased and she'd be released at any moment.

After spending some quality time with Larry while getting laundry done and cleaning out the fridge, she'd headed to a local soup-and-salad restaurant and unpacked her laptop. No sense going to the department today. A shooting at a bar on the River Walk last night left two dead and several injured, including a couple of tourists from Japan. Homicide would be buzzing and she didn't need the distraction. Too easy to get drawn into someone else's case, especially one with that much visibility.

The chatter of the Sunday lunch crowd blended into background noise as she checked old newspaper stories to confirm Haley's statement about the pool company. Sure enough, a short article, complete with a photo of the store's monitor, verified what the girl said. Next up, she resumed her search for a connection between LockShield and Carbonis. Forty minutes later, the only thing she'd learned was her chicken tortilla soup was a lot better when it was hot. If there was a link between the two companies, she wasn't going to find it online. And of course it was a weekend.

Everything happened on weekends, when you couldn't get in touch with anyone. Everyone except tech support and customer service, both of which were probably handled by people reading from a script, would be off until tomorrow.

She spread her fingers and dragged them through her hair. An employee directory for both organizations would be nice, particularly one dating back several years. Or a list of customers. Better yet, a database of all payouts in the last decade with details on ransoms that had been paid. That info could be sorted and dissected for possible ties to the teens.

"Idiota!" The outburst caused several patrons to stare at her for a moment before returning to their meals.

She squeezed her lips together and exhaled several hot breaths through her nose. Great detective work, Amara. We want to build our credibility, Haley said. Make a name for ourselves. Customers have to know they can trust us. And the FBI said the same thing.

She typed TOXICftw into the search bar and the page filled with links. The top few were sponsored ads for ransomware solution companies, meaning the search engine's algorithms had enough information to be aware of the hacking group. The first nonadvertising link took her to an article geared toward protecting yourself from online attacks. TOXICftw's network intrusion on a tax-preparation office four years ago was used as an example. The owner of the company complained that it cost him almost three hundred dollars to get his data back, but that was cheaper than losing all his work and buying new equipment.

Three hundred dollars. TOXICftw had come a long way. She read through each of the links on the first page, several of which were different pieces about the same events. In every case, the business paid the ransom and had their data promptly restored. A credibility boost for the hackers. Good advertising for the insurance companies. The most recent stories, at least the ones that shared specifics, confirmed the dollar amounts had grown dramatically. Details about whether the victims had coverage, and if so, with whom, were missing from all but one article. It included the name of the customer's insurer, Carbonis, and a quote from their chief information officer, Vincent Blume, about the importance of organizations having a procedure in place to deal with these incidents.

Mr. Blume would be a good contact. And maybe a good suspect. A CIO would know the ins and outs of network hacks and insurance and how to mesh the two into a profitable venture. She searched for information on him and found his name mentioned in several magazine and newspaper stories. Most were of the industry up-and-comers variety, though a few did have more in-depth interviews, none of which revealed anything important. Like did he ever work for LockShield?

A search for his employment history pointed her to LinkedIn. No looking without signing up. She completed the enrollment process and ignored the prompts to update her bio—what would she say? Cop. Single. Iguana roommate. Then she scanned Blume's details. No mention of LockShield, but he was passionate about people. Said so right there under his picture. Loved living in Hartford, Connecticut, the insurance capital of the world. A few jobs since he'd graduated college twenty-some years ago. At Carbonis for the last eight years. No phone number. She hovered the cursor over the *Message* button. Not yet. The first contact should be a live conversation. See how he reacted to her questions without time to think.

She closed the browser tab and clicked to the second page of search results for TOXICftw. More of the same. Most of the links led to information about the same hacks she'd seen on the first page. One link pointed to an article giving a broad overview of how ransomware worked and why it would be difficult to eliminate without removing some of the privacy protections of the internet. The piece included a list of known hacking groups and there, close to the bottom, was TOXICftw. She bookmarked the page and clicked the writer's name. Shelby Rymer, a journalist for the alliteratively appropriate *Hartford Hardline*, which was an "independent news source specializing in all things Connecticut."

Amara enlarged the woman's photo. Why did she look familiar? Early thirties maybe, though who knows with all the editing that could be done on pictures these days. Brunette hair tied back in a ponytail. Round glasses a tad too big for her face, just enough of a smile to show she was a serious journalist but had a fun side too, and a nose ring through her left nostril. Amara settled in her chair and stared.

Where had she seen the woman? She scratched her forehead, but the itch was deeper. Had she been on one of the videos from the water park? Maybe, but wouldn't there be plenty of people who looked like her? The only photo she'd seen was a headshot. A standard image used for her work.

For her work. This time the *idiota* remained unspoken as she clicked through the links she'd already visited. Of course she'd seen Shelby Rymer before. The woman's photo was on three of the other items she'd read. Didn't mean she couldn't be a suspect, particularly if she had access to confidential information from insurance companies. Client lists would be worth their weight in Zcash to a hacking group.

She shook her head as the woman's name fell atop the mountain of data pressing against her skull. What're you doing? Look long enough and you'll come up with a thousand suspects. Narrow the scope. Wrong target? Pivot to someone else. Put away the shotgun and pull out the Glock. Aim for what you know. Center mass. Keep firing until the threat is eliminated. Four options to choose from.

Haley Bricker, Liam Walker, Matias Lucero, and Mighty Mouse 12. She'd spoken to all but one. Time to change that.

People chose their online names for a reason, didn't they? So why "Mighty Mouse 12"? Wikipedia said the character debuted in theaters in 1942 and moved to Saturday morning TV in the '50s, with the last revival of the series airing back in the '80s. Also a comic book . . . spoof of Superman . . . blah blah blah . . . girlfriend Pearl Pure-heart . . . archenemy a cat—very original—named Oil Can Harry.

Nothing that indicated why anyone would want to choose the name for their online persona. But why the twelve? Maybe there were eleven other Mighty Mouses. Mighty Mice? She typed the alias into Google and received a list of comic book sellers offering the twelfth edition of the comic. Near the bottom of the page was something different. A link to player stats for *Tango Murked*.

Mighty Mouse 12 had exactly zero wins. Zero losses. Zero kills and zero deaths. Every category was a nada except duration—53:41. MM12 had spent less than an hour in the game. No shocker, but it did lend credence to Haley's statements. The guy only showed up when he had a new customer or when they needed to discuss something.

How to find him? No way to be notified when someone came into the game. You could set up an alarm when friends joined, but MM12 would have to accept her request. Not gonna happen. And even if she did see him online, so what? Not like she'd get anywhere near their private chat room.

She closed her laptop. MM12 would have to wait. The other three wouldn't be as fortunate. She packed up her belongings and strode to her car.

They like playing games?

Let's play.

Winner take all.

46

Barb Freemont, the CSI tech who'd inspected Coleman's computer, grinned at Amara. "So what do you think?"

The woman's three-bedroom two-bath home could've been cut from the pages of *Better Homes and Gardens*. Beautifully furnished in a southwestern motif, but not with the Texas kitschy overkill. No longhorns over the fireplace or cow-print sofas. Tasteful with an understated elegance. That's what a magazine would say.

Until they got to the last bedroom. A pair of black desks, both anchored with a huge monitor, faced each other. Multicolored keyboards, padded headsets with microphones, mice with neon outlines, and an array of peripherals, some which Amara recognized, some she didn't, filled any open space. Blackout curtains prevented any outside light from creeping into the darkened area. An assortment of backlit images lined the wall, all cartoonish drawings of what she assumed were computer game characters.

"Wow," Amara said. "This is, um, wow. I've never seen anything like it."

"Thanks," Barb said. "My hubs drew the pictures. He's a natural, isn't he?"

"They're very nice." Not her style, but definitely creative and colorful. "Is he an artist?"

"Nah. Programmer." She pointed to one of the drawings. "Recognize her?"

Amara stepped closer for a better look. A tall, thin woman, her long brunette hair cascading over her shoulders, stood on a snow-covered hill. She wore a blue dress that sparkled with flashes of white and silver. Her arms were extended and wisps of a much lighter blue flowed from her fingertips into the frigid air.

"That's you," Amara said.

Barb grinned. "Technically, it's Calina Iceguard, my elven frost mage. But yeah, that's me." She matched the pose in the photo. "The color coming from her fingers is arctic blue. Hubs thought that was pretty cool."

"Love it." *But do you have to call him Hubs?* "I really appreciate you taking the time, especially on your day off."

"Not a problem. Even if it doesn't help your investigation, maybe you'll get sucked into the world of online gaming." She rolled a second chair to her desk and motioned for Amara to sit. "Always looking to get more women involved. *Tango Murked*, right?"

"That's what one of the suspects said. They meet in the game to make plans."

An assortment of whirs and clicks sounded as the computer booted. "Don't suppose you know their character names?"

"One. Mighty Mouse 12."

"I'll do a search once we get in the game, but I'd be surprised to find anything. Public visibility is turned off by default, so unless a player activates it, or you're on their friend list, you'll never see them."

"Any thoughts on how we find him?"

The monitor filled with the *Tango Murked* logo and flashed to a screen full of options. "We don't," Barb said. "The only way would be if we were randomly matched with him, but that's remote. You're talking about hundreds of servers, each with thousands of players. The chances of being on the right server at the right time? Astronomical."

"One of the suspects said she found friends by searching for players who were close to her."

Barb nodded. "Used to, could do things like that. Not anymore. Too many privacy issues."

"I guess that's a good thing. Not for my investigation though."

"It's a very good thing, but meaningless in the bigger picture." She swiveled her chair toward Amara. "I'll give you the short version of my usual rant. The privacy battle is already over. Guess what? We lost. Mostly because we didn't even fight. At this point, there are two options. Move as far away from civilization as you can and live off the grid, or trust that whoever has all the data isn't going to use it in a way that harms you. I know which option I choose. Hubs feels the same."

A bit dramatic, isn't it? Watched *Terminator* a few too many times? But someone had *her* data. They knew about bank accounts and Mama. "But you're hooked up to the internet now, aren't you?"

"Yep. But even if I wasn't, it wouldn't matter. Everything we do is recorded online somewhere. Banks, work, traffic cameras, my phone. Did you know there are major cities in the US considering the installation of facial-recognition devices in all public areas? That if you walk around London for an hour, it's estimated you'll be captured on video by nearly three hundred security cameras? Listen, I'm not talking about wearing tin foil hats and that nonsense, but think about it. Technology is a wonderful thing." She waved her hand around her. "We love it when it makes our lives better. But nothing is free. There's a cost to all this."

The woman certainly had passion. "I have to ask," Amara said. "I'm assuming you'd choose to move to the end of the earth if you could. Where would you go to get away from technology?"

"Can't tell you."

"Can't or won't?"

Barb smiled and turned back to the monitor. "Okay. You want to watch me play and I'll explain as I go, or would you rather create your own character?"

"I'll watch you." Being online didn't seem as appealing as it had moments ago.

The woman clicked several buttons and the screen zoomed to another section. "*Tango Murked* is a team-based multiplayer first-person shooter. First person means you see what your character sees, but don't see yourself. Like in the real world. I mean, you'll see yourself in mirrors or your arm if you raise a gun or sword, but, eh, you get the idea. You can have up to six players on a team, and they all work together to protect their base and attack their enemy's home."

"Capture the flag," Amara said. "Try to get theirs while they're trying to get yours."

"Exactly. You've got a choice of, like, forty different characters, and you can customize them by buying unique skins, clothes, voices, and other stuff. I've actually got three other characters in progress so I can be someone besides Calina if I want to. She's my highest level though. They get stronger as you win battles and gain experience. You can also find various weapons and armor to help. And it's free to play."

"Free? How do they make money? Selling fake clothes for pretend characters can't be profitable."

"This game generated nearly three billion dollars in revenue last year."

What? For stuff that wasn't even real? "I don't know how to respond to that," Amara said.

"Lot of money for sure. It's entertainment, just like movies or books. Some people say it's an escape. I call it an adventure. A chance to be someone you could never be in reality. You should try it."

"Maybe one day. I've got enough adventure in my life right now. Can you show me how the chat works?"

"Easy enough." She clicked the *Friends* button, and a list of twenty or so names appeared. "These are all people I know, but not necessarily in the real world. There are two ways to get on this list. One is to exchange identities outside the game. Obviously, in that case you'd be able to tie the real person with the character. The other way is by chatting at the end of a match."

She moved the cursor about a third of the way down the screen. "See her? Freya Stormbringer. No idea who she really is. Or if she's even a she. I got randomly paired with her in a game and liked her playing style. Chatted with her afterward and we agreed to match up again. After a few games, I added her to my list and she added me to hers. The red light means she's offline."

"So how do you let her know that you want to play?"

"I can ping her by clicking her name and the game will send her a message letting her know I'm online. Of course, she can disable that option. Let's see if I can find your buddy." She exited her friends list, clicked the *Find Players* button, and typed *Mighty Mouse 12*. No hits. She tried multiple variations of the name with no luck. "We're not going to locate him this way."

"Couldn't be that lucky." She leaned back in her chair. "So if you just wanted to talk to your friends without playing, how does that happen?"

"By talk I assume you mean chat? You can use voice but most of us older players don't. Easiest way to communicate as a group is to go into a training server. They're set up so teams can practice together. One player pops in, then invites the others. Nothing to it."

But you had to be invited. Frustration funneled through Amara's chest. "Is there anything you can think of that might help me figure out who MM12 is? Or a way I can get any useful information from the game? Something that would aid in my investigation?"

Barb shook her head. "You need more. The way the system's built, you're not finding anyone unless they want you to. Either that, or you get someone on their friend list to work with you."

MM12's list probably had only three people on it. Haley, Liam, and Matias, though their real names wouldn't be used. "Here's what I know. My suspects are using this game to plan illegal activity. I'm certain of that. But you're telling me there's nothing I can do about it?"

"Pretty much. I'm sure you could go the subpoena route with the company that runs the game, but good luck. I'd bet that goes nowhere. Your best chance is to convince one of your suspects to cooperate and let you watch while the meeting takes place. Of course, proving in court who those people actually are is a whole different issue."

Wonderful. "Thanks, Barb. I won't take up any more of your time. Okay to call if I have questions?"

"Of course." She nodded toward the desk behind her. "Sure you don't want to stick around? We didn't even play the game yet. I'll set you up on the hubs's rig and get you going. I know you'd enjoy it."

Nope. "Sounds great, but I've got a full schedule. Maybe some other time."

Never gonna happen. Couldn't because she knew how every game would end.

If her team didn't win, it could be ugly.

Rage-quit ugly.

47

Amara stretched out on the living room rug in her apartment and whispered "Who's a good boy" repeatedly as Larry responded by flicking his tongue toward her. Midafternoon on Sunday and a clear schedule. Mama had been released from the hospital and was now at home surrounded by family. Larry had explored the area for a solid hour before finding a spot of sunshine creeping through the curtains and planting himself firmly in the center. As the day progressed, he inched along with the sun, basking in its rays.

She rolled onto her back and adjusted her sweatpants so they weren't twisted at the waist. Her fingernails looked iffy. Needed to do some work on them tonight. She stretched her legs to get a peek at her toes. Ugh. Worse than the fingers. Might have to dig out the pumice.

In a little bit, she'd head out for dinner and free Wi-Fi. Check her email one last time before bed. For now, her work laptop was connected to her TV and running the videos of the teenagers from the water park. She'd seen them numerous times, start to finish. The group entering the park, splitting up, coming together, on camera, off camera. Watching the backgrounds for anyone paying unusual attention to them. Someone who might be MM12. Several trips by each to the locker to get water and/or alcohol and check their cell phones. Haley grabbing and returning her tote once. Bathroom run probably. All the way until the three teens left after their friend was hauled off in the ambulance. A bunch of disjointed clips, none of which were helpful.

She flipped onto her stomach as the next scene began. Crowds entering the water park. The four teenagers shuffling through the ticket line to the security guards. Haley being delayed while her tote was searched, then hurrying to catch the others. Coleman glancing back at her, grinning.

She clicked the mouse to pause the video, sat up, and rewound the clip a few seconds. Liam and Matias moved into the park while Coleman slowed. Letting Haley catch up to him. When she was beside him, her smile broadened and she casually brushed the back of her hand against his.

Amara paused the video again. It might have been a while, but she still knew the signs of flirting. Zachary Coleman and Haley Bricker were a couple. The touch happened so fast. Seemed innocent enough that if Liam or Matias had noticed, they'd have thought nothing of it.

She grunted as she pushed herself off the floor, grabbed a pen and notepad, and sank onto the sofa. Larry opened one accusing eye and scooted toward the shifting sun. "Sorry, boy. Didn't mean to disturb you. Mind if I hang out here the rest of the day?"

He shifted himself so his face absorbed the light, then flicked his tail her direction.

"I'll take that as a no," she said.

. . .

By the time Amara arrived at her card table early the next morning, she knew that, despite the girl's prior statements, Haley and Coleman were either dating or headed that direction. She'd documented nearly twenty instances of physical contact between the two. A gentle tap on the arm. A too-long hand on the back. Always safe. Never blatant. But there. Adults didn't touch like that unless there was some familiarity. Intimacy.

Time for another talk with Haley. The girl lied, or at least misled, in her statement regarding her relationship to the deceased. What else had she lied about?

So much to do today. Ronnie's suggestion to not think so far ahead was a non-starter. Scheduling her day would take a chunk of the morning. Sanchez had finally sent over the park map detailing which cameras weren't functioning at the time of the boy's death. At least he hadn't demanded a subpoena for that. Plus she needed to track down the lawyers in Phoenix, the ones Haley said were the other option MM12 gave. And somewhere in there was talking to the girl. Too early to start calling Arizona, and confronting Haley might work better if she'd been awake for a while.

She opened the PDF of the water park map and zoomed in. The color image was speckled with dots. Black ones were working cameras, red were not functioning. Each camera had a tiny arrow beside it to indicate the direction it pointed. Not good enough. Without knowing how wide the angle of coverage was, she couldn't verify what was or wasn't within view. Surely he knew that.

"Alvarez."

She looked over her shoulder at Travis Rutledge. "Morning, Detective. Can I help you?"

"Whatcha looking at there? Some sort of map?"

Go with sarcasm or play nice? "Yeah, some sort of map. All pretty colors and big pictures. Makes it easier for idiots like me to understand."

He grunted. "Still waiting for my apology."

"For what?" This should be good.

"Parking garage the other day. Trying to make me look bad in front of other cops."

You don't need my help for that. "If that's what you thought I was trying to do, I'm sorry. Good enough?"

"It'll do for now." He adjusted his fedora so it slanted a bit more left. "Tell you what. We got off on the wrong foot, yeah? How about I talk to Segura? Arrange for you to ride shotgun with me for a few days. Let you see how it's done."

Her anger hid behind a smile. "I'm sure I could learn a lot from you, but I'm really busy."

"Your loss. I know you don't like me, Alvarez, but you need to understand that respect is earned, not given."

"Works both ways, Rutledge."

"That's where you lose me. See, I don't care whether or not you respect me. Your opinion means nothing around here."

"And I suppose yours does?"

He chuckled. "What do you think?"

"I could give you the whole psychoanalysis of your needy behavior toward the new girl, but I'll do us both a favor and throw out the short version. You're ten pounds of guano in a five-pound sack."

His breathing grew loud and heavy. "You want to start with me?"

Behind him, Starsky hurried her direction. "Everything okay over here?"

She frowned at him. "Morning."

"What's up, Starsky?" Rutledge asked. "Coming to protect your girlfriend?"

His face instantly reddened. "One. Not my girlfriend. Two. She doesn't need my protection."

Rutledge nodded. "Yet here you are."

"Yep. Here I am." He rocked back and forth on his feet, both hands in his pockets. "So what's up?"

"Both of you go away," Amara said. "I don't have time for this today."

"I'll talk to Segura," Rutledge said. "Set you up to shadow me for a few days. Maybe even a week or two."

"You do that," Amara said. The big man walked away, probably to find someone else to annoy. "Go away, Starsky."

"You know he's baiting you, right?"

"I don't need you interfering. Makes me look weak. I can handle myself."

"No doubt in my mind." He leaned forward and lowered his voice. "Just don't do it here. Nowhere public. Too many cameras around."

She smiled. "Maybe I should have it on video for posterity."

"That's why you're giving me a heads-up before it happens. Oh, and the not my girlfriend thing. I, uh, when I said that, I didn't mean I didn't want to be, uh, well." He turned away. "Have a good day, Alvarez."

"I'm trying."

48 Amara responded to Sanchez's email with a request for more information about the cameras. Either the range and angle of coverage for each, or if it was easier, the areas that were blind while the system was down. She'd give him an hour, then call. In the meantime, she'd contact the United Divorce Group in Arizona. See what they had to say about ransomware, especially whether they had insurance and if so, with who?

After forty-five minutes of upbeat hold music punctuated by brief interludes of "I don't handle that but let me transfer you to someone who does," she had a name. Walter Dreysdale, a broker, took care of insurance for the attorneys. But no, they would not authorize him to release any information without a subpoena. Haley was right. Lawyers are lawyers.

She phoned Mr. Dreysdale and identified herself.

"San Antonio, you say? What can I do for you, Ms. Alvarez?"

Detective Alvarez. "I'm gathering some information, Mr. Dreysdale. I was told you're the man to talk to about ransomware insurance?"

"I am indeed," he said. "May I ask who referred you to me? I always like to thank anyone who sends me new—oh. You're not interested in buying any, are you? Sorry. Sometimes my mouth runs ahead of me. I do sell ransomware insurance, in addition to burial, homeowners, life, death, auto, boat, motorcycle, you name it."

"I understand if you can't go into specifics," she said, "but could

305

you tell me if you've ever been involved in a payout on a ransomware claim?"

"I have not. Very rare, but unfortunately, as I'm certain you're aware, becoming more common. The good news is that now's a great time to buy. Rates are low."

I'm sure they are. "I spoke to one of your clients. United Divorce Group. They told me you handle their coverage?"

"Yes, that's correct. I set them up with LockShield. Big company in Delaware. Hundred-thousand-dollar policy. Cheaper than you'd think."

So much for confidential information. "Um, are you sure about that?"

"Positive. They're scheduled for renewal soon. I just looked over their details, and between you and me and the fence post, I'm going to try to talk them into doubling the amount. Wouldn't make sense not to."

Not to try to talk them into it or not to double it? "I see. Well, thank you for your time and I wish you luck."

"Thank you, Ms. Alvarez. Insurance is all about taking care of the client. Building relationships and trust. I hope if you ever move to Arizona, or perhaps have relatives or friends currently here, you'll allow me the opportunity to review your existing policies and show you how I can do better."

"Of course."

"Do you? Have relatives or friends in Arizona?"

"No. Sorry."

"No problem. Hold on. Okay. Is the number you're phoning from a good way to reach you?"

Nope nope nope. Don't need your Texas buddies calling me. "Have a nice day, Mr. Dreysdale."

She wrote *$100k—United Divorce Group—LockShield* on her

notepad. Way bigger payout than the thirty-five thousand they'd received from Barstow. Probably at least another ten thousand deductible on top of that. Too bad for TOXICftw. She circled the $100k and dotted her pen around it.

And LockShield again. If they were one of the bigger companies providing this insurance, was that a surprise? Certainly didn't prove anything. The Barstow, Indiana, payout had been handled by Carbonis. MM12 gave the teens two options, unrelated as far as she could tell.

She pressed her palms against her ears to shut out the background noise. Barstow. 35k. Lawyers. 100k. Something about those numbers annoyed her. She closed her eyes.

Thirty-five thousand dollars. Eighty-five hundred to each teen plus a thousand to MM12. The numbers added up. Haley had been certain of that.

Numbers and dates and names swirled through Amara's brain, and she grabbed at each of them, desperate to combine them into anything that might ease the chaos. Open a door. Offer a solution.

Explain why MM12 knew to ask for thirty-five thousand dollars.

She opened the recording from the interview with Haley. There. The girl said, "MM12 said to let him know when we were ready. Set the fee at thirty-five k. Way more than we'd ever been paid."

Amara stood and pushed her chair away with the back of her legs. Too much energy to sit. She rewound the recording to find the section she wanted. "The four of us talk it over and choose this podunk town in Indiana. Barstow, wherever that is. But we told MM12 we picked the other option, some lawyer group in Phoenix."

Uh-uh. MM12 would want more from the lawyers. $100k plus deductible at least. Instead, he'd asked for a much lower amount. The exact sum Barstow could pay. That had to mean he knew they were targeting Barstow, despite Haley's statement. MM12 had insider knowledge.

One of the teens was feeding him information.

There was another explanation though. One that either complicated or simplified the investigation.

Liam, Haley, or Matias was MM12.

The more she thought about it, the more sense it made. If Liam, Haley, or Matias was MM12, they'd get a bigger share of each ransom. More voting power when decisions needed to be made. They'd be the wizard behind the curtain, controlling everything while the others remained clueless.

It meant that one of the teens had broken into the insurance companies' networks, but so what? They had the skill, and as long as it didn't become too obvious, the firms would be blind to the activity. Scatter the attacks around the country, vary the ransoms, whatever. All while being anonymous.

If true, they'd have to be online in the game with two different computers, one for themselves and one for MM12. How hard could that be? It wasn't like they couldn't afford a second computer. The others would be none the wiser. No way to know their friend was MM12.

And then Zachary Coleman died. But there was MM12, hovering in the background, waiting for the group to hit another customer. No doubt if that didn't happen soon, he'd contact them to insist they get back to work. And why not? What had changed? MM12 was a very real person. And now, the teens knew, a very real danger.

She needed to talk to each of them again, but not without more information. This time she'd have the upper hand. Knowledge the others either didn't have or didn't know *she* had.

A notification popped up on the bottom right of her screen. New email from Sanchez. It would take a long time to get that kind of report together, he said. He'd look into it and get back with her ASAP.

Not happening. A face-to-face might speed things along. She typed a quick response of "See you in 30" and sent it. No more waiting.

· · ·

"Looks like you'll have a good crowd today," Amara said. The monitors lining the security chief's wall were full of people.

Sanchez made no effort to acknowledge the attempt at small talk. "My time is limited. Tomorrow morning would have been better."

For you maybe. "I promise I'll be out of here as soon as I can. Plus, this will work better with a lot of people around. Make the times more accurate."

"I would like to state again, for the record, that the park is voluntarily cooperating with the SAPD."

She nodded. "A fact I will emphasize when we file charges."

He raised his eyebrows.

"Depending on what we see in the next few minutes," she said, "I'm certain I'll present the case soon. You'll be able to let your people know to prep for our press release. Of course, if anything were to leak early, the PD would take a dim view of the park. Could alter how Cannonball is presented in our statement. Neither of us want that."

"I understand," he said. He grabbed a handheld radio off his desk. "Cesar, ETA to lockers?"

"Should be coming onto camera now."

The bottom left monitor showed a young man stop in view of the camera and hold his radio up. Behind him, a steady stream of guests rented lockers for the day.

Amara walked to the display. "Third row, six down on the left. The big one."

Sanchez relayed the information and Cesar stooped and pointed at the locker. "This one?"

"That's it," Amara said. "That's the one they used."

"E62," Cesar said.

Amara jotted it down. "Perfect. Have him go to Day's End Cove, where we think Coleman died. Anywhere in the area is fine. You can kill the cameras when he gets there."

Sanchez stiffened and paused, then directed Cesar to the appointed area. "It will take him several minutes to get there."

She moved to the large park map pinned on the wall and tapped the image of the locker building. "Got to be a dozen ways to get from here to there." Her finger traced a direct line to the Day's End Cove. "For now, let's keep the focus on the moments around the death. The first time we see him on the lazy river—"

"Crooked Creek," Sanchez said.

"The first time we see him on Crooked Creek is one-oh-eight p.m. about here." She rested her finger on the map. "You said this is the camera that first saw him, right? Can you have Cesar stop there and ask him to walk along the water's edge toward the cove? When he drops off that view, we'll have the first possibility for where Coleman went in the water. Have him mark it somehow. Then you can shut off the cameras in the area that weren't functioning the day of the death."

Sanchez relayed the message, and Cesar said to give him another few minutes.

Amara tugged at her bottom lip as she studied the map. "I appreciate this, Sanchez. I know you're busy."

"Yes," he said. "As I mentioned several times."

"If you need to go, I understand."

"In that case, tomorrow morning would—"

"Just get someone else in here who knows how to operate your cameras. I can handle the radio."

Impossible or not, she felt the heat from his glare burning holes in her back. *Guess he won't be asking me on a date when this is over.* No loss. Besides, if he truly wanted her gone, all he had to do was tell her to leave and that he wasn't providing any more help.

"There's Cesar," Sanchez said. He pointed to the monitor. "The five displays on the top row are around Day's End Cove. We have extra personnel stationed there until we're done. I need to release them to their normal positions as soon as possible." He clicked his mouse and the five monitors went blank. "Cameras are off. Okay, Cesar. Start walking. I'll tell you when to stop."

Guests and empty inner tubes floated past Cesar as he worked his way upstream. The water's edge transitioned from concrete wall to sandy beach as he neared the side of the screen and dropped from view.

"That's good," Amara said.

Sanchez keyed the mic. "Mark that spot."

"10–4," Cesar said. "There's a palm tree here. I'll tie some caution tape around it. That work?"

"Close enough," Amara said. "If we learn anything, it'll all have to be done again by CSI anyway."

Sanchez clicked the radio. "From there, loop around the cove. Stay close to the water. I'll let you know when to stop."

"Heading that way."

"10–4," Sanchez said. "Make it quick." He stood and touched one of the monitors. "That should be where we see him first."

The stuffy atmosphere grew more awkward as they stood in silence and stared at the display. A few guests wandered around the cabanas, eating early lunches or taking a break in the shade of the tall palms. This section of Crooked Creek was still sandy beach, and a multitude of people lay out on colorful towels. Why come here if you were only going to broil? You could stay home and do that. And had none of them heard of skin cancer?

Her heart fell as her mind pivoted to her mother. No news today, but none expected. That was good, right? A couple more weeks until the next chemo treatment. How soon before they knew if it was working?

"Stop," Sanchez said.

She blinked several times. Cesar was back in view on the monitor.

Sanchez returned to his seat and spoke into the radio. "Back up a few steps and mark that spot too."

Amara nodded. "Best guess. Was this the largest area of the park without coverage when Coleman was killed?"

"Possibly. There were a couple of other spots with multiple camera outages clustered together."

She crossed her arms and worked her mouth side to side. Coleman was the only one of the teens in the area at the time of his death. MM12 had to be among the hundreds of other people moving in and out of the space during the camera outage.

She checked her notes. 12:11. That's when Zachary Coleman was last seen alive on camera. He'd walked across a bridge over Crooked Creek toward his death. Why? Haley said the ransomware attack was scheduled for around twelve thirty. Surely Coleman was supposed to be somewhere busier if he planned to video? There were no rides other than the lazy river in that section. Nothing to attract crowds. Just a spot to relax and get some semblance of peace before venturing back into the chaos of the park. So why go there?

What would make a teenage boy go anywhere?

A teenage girl. Haley.

"Okay," she said. "You can turn the cameras on now and let those people return to work."

With another click of his mouse, the security chief activated the cameras and the five blank displays returned to life.

"Mr. Sanchez, I hate to ask this. I really do. But I may need a bit more of your time."

He tilted his head back, closed his eyes, and did a bit of deep breathing, then picked up his desk phone and dialed three digits. "Gabriela, you're in charge for the rest of the day. My afternoon just got kidnapped."

50 **"Start when they're all together** at the lockers," Amara said. "I want to see every time Haley's not on camera. Where she disappeared and where she showed up next. Question. Is there a way to identify the credit card she used to rent the locker? See if it was used on anything else in the park?"

Sanchez rested his chin on his hand. "You want to give me some idea where you're going with this? Might make things quicker. And less of an interrogation."

Valid argument. He could easily force her to get a subpoena. Slow down the investigation by weeks or longer. A little cooperation from her was in order. "Zachary Coleman was murdered at Day's End Cove sometime between 12:40 and 12:55. None of the three people who came with him to the park were seen entering or leaving the area during that time. My assumption was there was a fourth person. Someone I couldn't identify."

"Was?"

She nodded. "There's another possibility. One of his friends somehow managed to get into the blacked-out area without being spotted."

He stood, put his hands in his pockets, and jingled his keys. "Hold up. You can turn off any camera you want, but don't make yourself invisible from start to finish? Why?"

"Work backward. The death has to appear accidental. And if anyone gets suspicious, a trail of disabled cameras would point right to a suspect. Whoever did this put a lot of effort into the planning. Wanted to make it look like Coleman was alone when he died. Or at least with none of his friends."

"Why the girl?"

"Haley? I think she and the deceased were in a relationship. A fact she failed to mention when I spoke with her. Good a reason as any to start with her. So, can you get the credit card info off the locker?"

"I can't do it, but I guarantee there's a way. Somebody over in financials can probably pull some sort of report. Most likely won't get the whole credit card number though. Maybe last six digits or something, but it should be enough."

"How long?"

"Don't expect it today," he said. He leaned over his keyboard and typed, paused to read the message, then clicked the mouse. "Okay. I'll let you know. And instead of the girl, let's start with the victim. Like you said, work backward."

He sat again and brought up the last clip of the boy. 12:06 to 12:11. Carefree and smiling. Ball cap, shirtless, water bottle. Dead within the hour.

Amara motioned to a dry-erase board, blank except for the myriad of faded words forever planted there, victims of a permanent marker. "Mind if I use this?"

"Go for it."

She grabbed a red marker and wrote a barely legible 1. "Got any that aren't dried out?"

He opened his desk, pulled out a new marker, and flipped it toward her. Panic surged through her body. *Catch it, Alvarez.* The marker bounced off her fingers and fell to the floor. She stooped to pick it up, keeping her face turned from Sanchez. Don't give him the satisfaction. She wrote the times of the clip along with a short summary.

"Can you go to the clip before that one?" she asked.

He fiddled with his mouse for a few seconds. "Yeah, should be . . . here we go."

The corner of the display showed a time of 11:32 and she jotted it on the board. Nothing about Coleman seemed different. Same grin. Same clothes. Pausing to watch people, leaning on a railing and watching guests shoot out the bottom of a giant water slide, and walking through a contraption that sprayed mist over everyone. At 12:01, he dropped out of the camera's view again.

11:32–12:01—ZC on camera

She left room to fill in the blanks and added the last video clip.

12:06–12:11—ZC crosses bridge, dies ~12:40–12:55

Sanchez clicked the rewind button until he came to the next clip with the teen. 11:18–11:26. More of the same. Maybe this was going nowhere. With his death near, surely by now there'd be some indication if one of the other three was involved.

"Rewind to the next one," she said.

"Wait. You see it?" Sanchez asked. "No water bottle."

She hadn't. "So sometime in the, what, six minutes between clips, he bought water. We'll need to identify possible locations in—"

"Didn't buy it here. Blue wrapper. We don't sell that brand. I assumed he got it from his locker, but he couldn't have. Not enough time and we'd have seen him."

"Jump to when they first got to the park. All of them carried water bottles in. See what color they were."

He dragged the timeline to the beginning. "Blue." He paused the video. "But I bet I could watch the footage from that morning and see a hundred people bringing that same brand in."

She pulled her notepad from her pocket, flipped back several pages, and scanned her notes from the day before. "At 11:16, Haley took her tote bag out of the locker and returned it at 11:58. Forty-two minutes. Plenty of time to meet him." She pulled her chair close to his desk and sat. "Go to that segment. Let's see if where she goes matches to Coleman."

He flexed his fingers and squinted at his laptop. "Give me a second. Do do do . . . fast forward to . . . there. Top left monitor."

Haley Bricker squatted, keyed in her code, and pulled her tote bag from the locker. One of the boys' bottled water rolled onto the floor and she stuck it back inside and stood. The locker door swung shut automatically as the springs in the hinges took over. She hooked her thumb under the bag's strap and hitched it higher on her shoulder before moving into the crowds. She paused to study the menu at a snack bar, then strolled through groups of people.

"Not in any hurry," Amara said. "She heading toward the cove?"

"Not directly, but the way the paths are laid out, you'll eventually get wherever you want no matter how you go."

For the next three minutes, Haley seemed to stroll aimlessly. Then, at 11:20, she was gone. Stepped out of the camera's view beside one of those rolling ice cream stands.

Amara walked back to the board.

11:18–11:26—ZC on camera, no water

11:20—HB off camera w/tote

11:32–12:01—ZC on camera, water

12:06–12:11—ZC crosses bridge, dies ~ 12:40–12:55

"How close is she to Coleman at this point?" she asked.

"Close enough. You've got two cameras off there. The boy goes into the opposite end of that zone six minutes later. Plenty of time for them to meet."

"Can you fast-forward to when she reappears?"

He sped the video, jumping past all the clips of the other three teenagers in that time frame, and stopped when Haley was back on screen. "Same place," he said. "11:56. Off camera for thirty-six minutes."

"Circumstantial, but good," she said. "Coleman's out of sight for six minutes. Means Haley probably was close to where he came into the zone. Question is, after she handed him the water bottle, what took her so long to get back to the lockers? She'd have at least twenty minutes that's unexplained before coming in view. Keep running the video on Haley."

After returning her tote bag to the locker, the girl made a beeline back the way she'd come, once again dropping out of view near the ice cream stand.

"12:03," Amara said. She wrote the time on the board. "And we don't see her again until she appears near where the body was pulled from the water at 13:08. Theoretically, she's got an hour to meet her boyfriend, kill him, and get as far away as possible, all without being seen." She walked to the map. "Aqua Attack. Where is it?" The teen said that was her assigned spot.

"On the left about a third of the way down. One camera disabled there." He walked beside her and traced the potential routes from Day's End Cove to Aqua Attack. "Too many working cameras. We'd have spotted her."

"Where did she and Coleman meet?"

He drew a circle and jabbed his finger in the middle. "Somewhere in here."

Food vendors, benches, and a souvenir shop. "Beach Bum Louie's," she said. "What do they sell there?"

"Suntan lotion, flip-flops, T-shirts, you name it."

"Got cameras inside?"

"No," he said. "The store is open-air, like a Jamaican market. No walls. We didn't want to air-condition the place. Too many people would come in to escape the heat for a while. Makes theft prevention a nightmare, cameras or not. Between the employees and the exterior surveillance equipment, we've done okay. Surprisingly little product loss. That's good, I suppose, but makes it a hard sell to add more security."

"Do me a favor," she said. "Fire off another email about the credit card. Forget everything else for now. We need to know if she used it at that store between 11:20 and 11:56."

"And did what? Put whatever she bought in the tote bag? The boy didn't have it and her hands were empty after she left the locker."

Good point. "Could she tell them to hold it? That she'd get it later?"

He returned to his desk and began typing. "She could." He looked up and smiled. "We've been looking for the wrong girl, eh?"

"Right girl," she said. "Wrong clothes."

Red hat with wide floppy brim. Check.

Oversize *I conquered Safari Surf* T-shirt. Check.

White sunglasses, round and hiding half her face. Check.

Same neon green flip-flops she'd worn into the park. Check.

"That's the last video," Amara said. "If you don't count the blacked-out areas, proof that Haley went from the lockers to Day's End Cove to Aqua Attack. No question it's her, but hopefully she used the same credit card to buy the stuff. Never hurts to have more evidence."

Sanchez nodded. "And simple enough to ditch the shirt, glasses, and hat once she's at the final spot." He paused. "Care to venture any guesses as to what's in the water bottle? Clearly she wanted to conceal the fact she had it. Otherwise, why take the tote bag? Easier just to grab the bottle and go. No need to return to the locker."

"No guesses," she said. Water or alcohol and whatever killed Coleman. Good luck proving that. If the tox report came back with any hits, at least she could show a means of delivery. "We're not finished. Not until we repeat this process with the other two teenagers."

"Thought as much," he said. "Want to grab a quick snack before we start?"

"I'm fine, thanks."

He pulled a pack of peanut butter crackers from his desk. "Me too."

It took nearly two hours to go through the videos again, this time with a focus on Liam, then Matias. If Haley was charged with murder, her defense attorney couldn't claim either of the boys was near the scene of the killing. The timing just didn't work. Unless they had a jetpack hidden in the park somewhere, they couldn't have been there when Coleman died. Didn't mean they weren't involved, but that could be worked out later.

"Pretty thorough," Sanchez said. "Only one problem as I see it."

She nodded. "None of this proves anything other than she *could've* done it. That's a long way from a murder conviction." But close enough to put a target on Haley Bricker. The girl had some serious explaining to do. Not yet though.

Amara stood and shook hands with Sanchez. "Thanks for your afternoon. Sorry it took longer than I expected."

"I'd say our time was productive, wouldn't you?"

"I would," she said. "And I'll be sure the park gets credit when the time comes."

"Thank you. And don't forget, Detective. When this is over, perhaps we can meet for dinner?"

Oof. Hate this stuff. "I'm flattered, Mr. Sanchez, but I'm seeing someone." *I think.*

"Oh? My apologies. You did not mention that before."

She paused, decided not to respond, and turned and left the office.

■ ■ ■

Amara scanned the physical therapy clinic's waiting room while she stood in line at the reception desk. Knee brace, walking boot, no idea, bandage-wrapped arm, oooh, another knee brace. The woman in front of her shuffled to an open seat and Amara stepped forward. Goodie. Same guy as last time. Eyes still bloodshot, cheek still stubbly, blond highlights could use some touching up.

"Darryl, right?"

He nodded. "Yes, ma'am. How can I . . . oh."

"Yep. I'm the cop. Wanna go tell Ms. Walker I need to speak with her again? Only take a second."

He leaned to the side to see the man in line behind her. "I'll be right back, sir. Thank you for your patience."

The man grumbled. "Why even make appointments? Doesn't do any good. They're never on time."

She smiled and glanced over her shoulder. "Tell me about it. You know what it is? Rude. No respect for your time."

"Exactly. Every week, same thing. You'd think they'd figure it out, but no. Let me show up five minutes late and they'll be sending me a bill."

She chuckled. "Can't win, can we?"

The door opened and Darryl motioned her to come back.

The man behind her grunted. "How come she gets to skip the waiting room?"

Darryl ignored him and pointed. "Second room on the left. Same as before. She's coming now."

Amara stepped into the room with Ms. Walker right behind. The woman closed the door and leaned against it.

"I told you, Detective. Liam had nothing to do with that boy's death."

"Yes, ma'am. And I believe you. Doesn't mean your son isn't involved in other illegal activity though. He most certainly is. But I didn't come here to discuss all that. You'll see Liam later today?"

Wrinkles creased her forehead and she checked her watch. "I suppose. I'll be home in about an hour. If he's not there, he usually shows up in time for supper. Why?"

"I need you to give him a message. I'd do it myself, but honestly, I want you to see how he reacts."

"I'm not sure I understand," she said.

"No record of a Mr. Walker," Amara said. "At least not recently. I didn't do the research, but I'm guessing you're a single mom? Raised Liam pretty much on your own?"

The woman shrugged but remained silent.

"Don't let all that work go to waste. You know your son, Ms. Walker. You can't protect him from what he's done. He'll have to pay. But there are ways to mitigate the cost." She sighed and frowned. What she said next would devastate this woman's world. "It's Monday afternoon. By the end of this week, if not much sooner, charges will be filed against Liam. I can't tell you anything else. Probably shouldn't have told you that."

Ms. Walker's palms pressed against the door and she struggled to speak. "Charges? For what?"

Amara handed her another business card. "The message, ma'am. Just give him this message. Tell him Mighty Mouse is about to take a nasty fall. If he wants to talk, I'll be at the Quarry shopping center. South parking lot, between six-thirty and seven-thirty. Last chance."

"Mighty Mouse? Like the cartoon?"

"He'll know. Seven-thirty, Ms. Walker. No later."

∎ ∎ ∎

Amara fiddled with her newly purchased digital recorder. A hundred bucks for the thing. The store had cheaper units, but she didn't want to chance getting something that didn't work. The sales guy said this was the one most people got. Sure. He probably worked on commission.

Straight up seven o'clock. Parking in the center of the lot, Whole

Foods to her left, Bed Bath & Beyond to her right, made her antsy. Like there was no way to put her back against a wall. She rested her hand atop the Glock in her lap.

Most other vehicles clustered much closer to the stores. She didn't blame them. Who wanted to walk across asphalt in this heat? She'd done her environmental duty and turned the car off when she arrived. For about three minutes. She couldn't do her part to save the planet if she died of heatstroke. At least she had a decent view of any approaching cars. Whatever that was worth. Liam's SUV, other than its vanity tags, looked like a gazillion other SUVs.

Near the lot's entrance, a sedan—copper? bronze?—cruised up one row and down the next, getting closer with each pass. Could be Ms. Walker's car. Maybe Liam didn't want to risk being spotted. It wasn't paranoia if it was true. Six more up-and-downs and the sedan slowed in front of Amara. She lowered her window and leaned so her face was clearly visible. The vehicle stopped, backed up, and swung into the spot beside her.

She gripped her weapon but kept it out of sight as the sedan's driver-side window came down. Ms. Walker. So Liam was a no-show. The woman's eyes were puffy and her nose red. She knew her son was in trouble.

"Good evening, Ms. Walker."

"Detective Alvarez, I wonder if we could, uh, if we could go for a drive? There's someone I'd like you to meet."

Liam or someone else? "That wasn't the deal." She tightened her grip on the Glock. "But I'd be happy to follow you."

The woman reached to the passenger side of her car.

"Please," Amara said. "Keep your hands on the steering wheel."

Ms. Walker straightened and slowly raised her right hand to show a tissue. "Been going through a lot of these in the last hour. The, uh, person I'm taking you to see says they can help, um, help you catch the mouse." She blew her nose and tossed the Kleenex to the side, then cut her eyes toward the back seat several times.

So Liam did come. Amara raised her window, shut off her car, and stepped into the heat. She made no attempt to hide the gun in her hand as she walked around Ms. Walker's vehicle, opened the passenger door, and peeked into the back seat before holstering the Glock and sitting. A pile of used tissues sat at her feet and she nudged them aside. "Hello, Liam."

The boy remained on the floor. "I'm here because of my mom."

"Your mother's a smart woman. Where are we going?"

Ms. Walker pulled out of the parking spot. "Nowhere specific. Just driving and talking. That okay?"

"Works for me," Amara said. "Might want to make sure your tank is full. We've got a lot to discuss."

52 By the time they exited the Quarry's parking lot, Liam was in the seat behind his mother. Amara angled herself so she could make eye contact. "I'm recording this conversation. If there's a problem with that, take me back to my car now. And you understand you're not under arrest?"

The teen brushed hair out of his eyes. "Yeah. I get it. But you gotta go first. Tell me what you know. Only way this happens."

Amara chuckled. "Sorry. Didn't mean to laugh but, come on. You can't seriously think I'd do that? Lay out my case for you?"

He used his T-shirt to wipe sweat off his face. Could count his ribs. Almost see his backbone. Kid needed to eat better. Unless he was like Starsky. Quantity and quality of food had no bearing on weight. Not natural.

"Don't gotta tell me everything," he said. "Enough so I'll know you're not fishing."

The fact that she knew about MM12 wasn't enough? Fine. "You're into ransomware. Got a nice little stash of money somewhere. Cash, Bitcoin, whatever. Had a good thing going right up until Zachary died. Now you're in a bad way because Mighty Mouse 12 knows who you are. As Haley put it, he owns you."

"What else did she tell you?"

"Less than you think," Amara said. *More than you know.* "What's the deal with her dog?"

"Insurance," the boy said. "We knew she'd talked to you. She said she didn't tell you anything, but Matias and me figured we'd make sure she kept her mouth shut. Nothing means more to her than that stupid dog. Why'd you bring him back? She tell you to?"

"Yes," Amara said. "Afraid you'd hurt him."

"Nah. What would that accomplish? Better to take him to the middle of nowhere and turn him loose. Let her believe we have him hidden somewhere. If she thinks he's dead, we lose control over her."

Kid has no idea who's actually controlling who. "Sounds like you thought it through."

Ms. Walker glanced over. "Does that girl have a deal with you?"

Uh-uh. The questions come from me. "Liam, you want to know anything else, you're going to start answering some questions. If not, we have nothing to discuss."

The boy made eye contact with his mother in the rearview and she nodded.

"Sorry about calling," he said. "Only wanted to, I dunno, scare you, I guess. Stupid, I know."

"Calling me? What are you talking . . . that was you?" The anonymous caller who'd hacked into her home internet. She clamped her mouth shut and glared.

"Yeah, I did it. You should really do more to protect your network. Didn't take me very long."

Is he bragging? "My bank accounts? Shutting off my power? You did all that too?"

He nodded. "Didn't steal anything though. Could've." He turned away and stared out his window. "Sorry about your mom. Cancer sucks."

Ms. Walker braked hard as a light changed to red. "Liam's dad died of lung cancer eleven years ago. Never smoked a day in his life."

"I'm sorry," Amara said. But this wasn't turning into a personal conversation. "Why were you at the water park the day Zachary died?"

"We were shutting the place down. Biggest payday yet and wanted to see it for ourselves." He shifted in his seat and leaned against the door. "MM12 was supposed to trigger the attack. Didn't work out that way."

Same thing Haley said. "No, it didn't. Has there been any contact with MM12 since then?"

He shook his head. "Once to say sorry about Zach and let him know when we were ready to go again. Surprised he hasn't messaged us. Never got the impression he was the patient type, you know?"

When he found out who MM12 really was, his world would be rocked. A valuable life lesson she still struggled with. Not quite the *trust no one* mantra of Starsky. More along the lines of you never truly know people. Not like you think you do. Her ex was proof enough of that.

For the next forty-five minutes, they cruised the streets of San Antonio while Amara grilled the boy. Very little of what he said was new to her, but it did match what she'd already learned. While he wouldn't confirm either the amount or whereabouts of his money, he did admit his involvement.

"Anything you haven't told me?" Amara asked. "Now's the time."

"No," Ms. Walker said. "It's not. I don't understand half of what you two are talking about, but I know Liam's in serious trouble. If you want more answers, we need to get an attorney involved."

"Like I said earlier, your son is not under arrest. He's free to stop talking anytime he wants."

"I think now is good," the woman said. "I have to make some calls. Find us a lawyer. Then we can meet again. This time at our house."

"Mom," Liam said, "that's not a good idea. If the others see cops at the house, I, uh, I don't know."

"What?" Ms. Walker said. "If they see cops, what? Detective, you've been to the homes of the others, I assume?"

"I have," Amara said. "I'll taxi to your place. Kinda getting used to that anyway. I have to remind you time is short. I'm not waiting for you."

"Nine o'clock tomorrow morning," Ms. Walker said. "My house. Bring whoever you want, but I'd appreciate it if a bunch of uniformed officers didn't swarm our neighborhood."

Nine o'clock? Did she have a lawyer on retainer already? No. But she knew where to get the cash to pay for one. "I'll be there. Depending on a few things, I may bring another detective with me. No one else." Unless something happened between now and then to change the situation.

The lights of the Quarry shopping area were within sight now. "May I remind you of something?" Ms. Walker said. "Liam says he can build a mousetrap. Granted, a lot of this is beyond me, but that seems like something you'd want. Something you'd have a hard time doing yourself." She turned on her blinker to enter the parking lot. "In fact, I doubt the SAPD could handle it. Is that correct, Liam?"

The teen grinned. "FBI maybe. On a good day. SAPD? Nah." He held up one finger. "I can give you what you want."

"And what is that?" Amara asked.

"You want in the game."

Did he mean the game as in the reality of what was happening or the game as in *Tango Murked*? She needed no help on the first.

His mother nodded. "A mousetrap like that has got to be worth a lot. When you come in the morning, please bring a document from the district attorney confirming my son will not be charged as an adult. Oh, and all the stuff he did to you, the personal things I mean, you won't pursue."

Was that all? "Ma'am, I appreciate what you're saying, but—"

"I think I *am* in a position to make demands," she said. "That's what you were going to say, isn't it?" She pulled into the spot next to Amara's car. "My boy had nothing to do with his friend's death. You're Homicide, aren't you? If you want to catch the murderer, you need Liam's help. If I've misjudged things, I expect I won't be seeing you in the morning."

Amara flexed her fingers. Misjudged things? Yep. Her tolerance level. "Ms. Walker, this is not a negotiation." She unbuckled her seat belt and stared at the woman. "Regardless, here's my counter-offer. Your son has been somewhat cooperative. If he's been honest with all he said, I'll ask the DA not to prosecute Liam for his personal attacks on me. Put in a good word for him. In exchange, he will continue his cooperation by arranging a meeting with the others who are involved in his criminal activity."

"Not good enough," the woman said. "We'll get a lawyer and take our chances."

"Getting a lawyer is an excellent idea. The retainers can be outrageous, especially for a good one. You are getting a good one, right? Mmm. That puts you in quite a predicament, doesn't it?"

"We can afford it," Liam said.

"I bet you can," Amara said. "But, see, here's where things get complicated. I can arrest you right now."

Liam leaned forward. "You said I wasn't under arrest."

"You weren't. But you could be now."

"I'm not an idiot," the teen said. "You didn't read me my rights."

Amara shrugged. "Didn't have to. You weren't under arrest."

"You have a warrant?" Ms. Walker asked.

"Don't need one. Your son confessed to multiple felonies. Texas says that's good enough. So I take him in now. No phone. No computer. No way to access certain online accounts. Of course, I could be completely mistaken. Maybe he's got mountains of cash in the house. Tough to explain where that came from though. Or he could've put all his money in a bank. Have to be eighteen to get an account, so you would have had to be on there with him, in which case you surely would be aware of the balance. If Liam's money is there, that would raise a lot of questions about your involvement too."

The woman pulled another tissue from the box and dabbed her eyes.

Amara shook her head. "No, I don't think Liam would put you in that position. So his money's online somewhere, but he won't be able to touch it. Not unless he tells you how to do it, and whoops, there we are again. You're an accomplice."

"If I had any money," Liam said, "and I'm not saying I do, there are other ways."

"Tell your court-appointed attorney?" Amara asked. "Not likely. Any decent lawyer is gonna know we'll come after them if we suspect they're involved in receiving stolen money. Phone a friend? You trust them that much? Even if you did, hard to call them if you don't have a phone."

"I know my rights," he said. "You have to give me one call."

"Yeah? Learn that on TV, did you?" She sighed dramatically. "Sorry to disappoint you, but there's no law saying that. Up to me. I can give you one call or a dozen calls. Or none."

Ms. Walker clasped her hands in her lap. "What happens now?"

"Set it up, Liam. *Tango Murked* or however you meet. All four of you. I want to be there when it happens."

"They'll know," he said. "No way I can bring a noob in with me."

"I don't want in the game. Only to be standing beside you when it happens." She opened her door. "You don't follow through or anything looks iffy to me, you're done. You'll be going offline for a very long time. Oh, and you'll be the noob in prison. Comprende?"

Amara stepped out of the vehicle. "Thank you for a lovely ride, Ms. Walker. Twelve hours. I don't hear from you by then, I'll assume you've made your decision."

53

"This should be good," Barb said. "I don't get to see this side of things very often."

Amara stood behind the woman's chair. "Keep an eye on everything he does. Don't worry about what he says. I'll handle that. If I'm unsure of something, I'll ask."

Liam looked back over his shoulder. "I can hear you, you know?"

"I know," Amara said. "So hear this loud and clear. Your deal depends on my satisfaction with what happens tonight. If I get the slightest inkling you're hiding something, we're out of here and you're going with us. Take a good look around. Could be the last time you see your room."

The teen's bedroom had been hurriedly reorganized to accommodate the group now hovering around his computer desk. To his left, a tripod-mounted camera recorded the boy, keyboard, and monitor. A CSI tech stood beside the device, ready to film with a handheld camera if needed. Behind him, Ms. Walker jockeyed for a better view in the limited space between the others and the walls. Barb sat to Liam's immediate right, her excitement palpable, and the Walkers' attorney, Davis Yandell, stood behind and to the side of Amara.

Ms. Walker had phoned at five-thirty this morning, well before the twelve-hour deadline. She'd probably been awake all night making arrangements. "We'll do it," she'd said. "Liam already set it up. Nine tonight. Everyone will be there."

Amara's day had been swallowed by preparations. Running

the plan by Lieutenant Segura. Getting CSI's agreement to be there. Walking Starsky through everything. The hardest part was finding the owner of Haley's rental home and convincing him to cooperate. Haley was a good renter, the man said. Always paid on time. Never complained. Finally, after the umpteenth assurance from Amara that a cop would go with him and he wouldn't be held responsible, the owner agreed. Twenty minutes ago, Starsky texted Barb to pass the message that he and the man were in position down the street.

Eight fifty-five p.m. Less than five minutes from now. That's when the three remaining members of TOXICftw would be online. MM12 had confirmed he'd be there as well. Amara shifted her weight from foot to foot. The investigation didn't exactly hinge on the next few moments, but what occurred could shove the filing of charges from an indeterminate future to mere seconds from now.

The boy still had no clue what was about to happen. Hard not to feel a little bit sorry for him. Or his mother. Both would have to deal with the consequences of the teen's multiple felonies.

"Here we go," Liam said. The *Tango Murked* logo filled his screen and he cycled through the menus until arriving at the designated site. Here, isolated in this battle realm, he and his team could practice their moves. Learn to work together. And plot their crimes.

"You're sure they can't hear us?" Amara asked.

Barb shook her head. "The mic's disabled."

The speakers on either side of the display dinged as a character appeared on the monitor. A tall girl, blonde pigtails, heavy armor, toting a huge axe, walked toward center screen.

"That's Haley," Liam said.

Almost instantly, another ding announced Matias's arrival. A giant of a man carrying some sort of multibarreled weapon strode toward them.

Barb let out a low whistle. "Their gear is pretty high level. Wouldn't mind matching up against you guys sometime."

"Don't think that's going to happen," Amara said. "Is MM12 usually on time?"

Liam nodded. "Yeah. We start on time so we don't stay online too long."

The teens exchanged a round of "hey" in the chat window.

"Hold up," Amara said. She pointed to the screen. "Haley is Lady Ren Darkcloak, Matias is Burwulf the Usurper, and, um, you're the *Mailman*?"

"Liam backwards is mail. Had the username since I was old enough to type. Where I go, it goes."

"Don't people, I don't know, make fun of it? I mean, it's not like it fits with the other names."

Barb shook her head. "Doesn't have to fit. It's who he is online. If he wanted to change it, he would. Names mean a lot. They're part of us."

Liam half turned his head. "My dad gave me the name."

Amara's heart sank through her chest. Way to go. "Sorry."

"We usually don't chat much until everyone's here. Sometimes we mention a movie or TV show the others might want to check out, but that's about it." He turned toward the camera and leaned so he was centered in its view. "How old is that thing? You recording on tape or what?"

"Sit back, please," the CSI tech said. "Don't block your monitor."

The final ding sounded and Mighty Mouse 12 popped into view. Short with a long white beard, a sword in his hand.

Barb scoffed. "That's a mountain dwarf. I mean, a sword's okay but they're much better off with a hammer or spear."

Amara laid a hand on the woman's shoulder. "Noted. Might want to remember everything's being recorded."

Liam glanced over. "She's right, though. Noob doesn't know what he's doing."

MM12 made his way toward the others and messaged "sry again about Zach."

The others replied with "thx" and waited.

"Can you enlarge the chat window?" Amara asked.

Liam complied until most of the left-bottom side of the screen was a see-through grayish box with flashing cursor. The other three players stood there and the game initiated each character's standing-around motions. Scratches, yawns, tapping weapons on the ground, generally looking bored. "What do you want me to ask?"

"Who usually starts the conversation?"

He shrugged. "Used to be Zach mostly. Until he got outvoted on the nursing home. Now it's whoever."

"Do whatever you need to as long as it's in line with what you've done before. Nothing to alert them we're watching. No code words or anything like that."

He rubbed his fingertips on the keyboard. "This is harder than I thought it would be."

He thinks he's betraying his friends. "I'm going to tell you something," Amara said. "But you have to keep your emotions under control. Understand? At least one of your so-called buddies is cheating you. Getting far more money from your customers."

His reflection showed a frown and narrowed eyes. "I doubt that."

"Of course you do," she said. "What kind of friend would you be if you didn't? But here's the thing, Liam. You know how on the internet you can never really be sure who you're dealing with? The real world's no different. Ask your mom. She'll tell you the same thing. Sorry, but you trusted the wrong people."

"Even if I did, that doesn't make this right."

Tension squeezed Amara's neck and she clenched her fist and

bent forward. "Oh, you do *not* want to go down that road with me. Why don't you talk to Zachary's family about what's right? Or your mother? You've destroyed her life. Do you realize that? I'm about ten seconds from pulling the plug on this. Wonder what the DA will say about your deal then?"

The boy's head barely nodded. "Been there. Rage quit, right? Can't tell you how many controllers and mice I've trashed. One monitor too. Best thing to do is walk away for a while."

Walk away? Her hands threatened to take on a life of their own and wrap themselves around the boy's throat.

"Here we go," Liam said.

A message appeared at the top of the chat window and the discussion began in earnest.

```
>Lady Ren: every1 up 2 this?
>Burwolf: rdy as ill ever be
>Mighty Mouse 12: got one ready. You in Liam?
>the Mailman: yep. we r splitting 4 ways now?
>Burwolf: :-(
>Mighty Mouse 12: unless someone has another
idea?
>Burwolf: only way to do it
>Lady Ren: agreed. what's the target?
>Burwolf: what about those lawyers in arizona?
>Mighty Mouse 12: not now. got a better one.
```

Amara flicked her bottom lip. Of course Haley didn't want to hit the lawyers. Not after she'd told the cops about them.

```
>Mighty Mouse 12: Port of Pascagoula on the Gulf
Coast. $200k min.
```

"You need to respond," Amara said. "Tell him that sounds good."

```
>the Mailman: sounds good.
>Lady Ren: details per usual?
```

Liam touched the screen. "He'll send the info in a Zcoin transfer. Then we'll get to work on the hacking."

```
>Mighty Mouse 12: yes. Anything else?
```

"Liam, tell MM12 you think there's a problem with the police," Amara said. She dialed her phone. "Starsky? Thirty seconds or less. Not until I tell you."

"Yes, ma'am," he said. "We're in position."

"Stand by."

```
>the Mailman: might be a problem with the cops
>Lady Ren: ???
>Mighty Mouse 12: what kind of problem?
```

"Now," Amara said. "Starsky, do it now."

54

Amara held her breath and locked her gaze on the monitor. There. Two of the three visible characters disappeared and a message popped up in the center of the screen.

```
Lady Ren Darkcloak has left the game.
Mighty Mouse 12 has left the game.
```

"Where'd they go?" Liam asked. "What just happened?"

The homeowner cut the internet line. *Think, Liam. What's the real* question? "What does it look like?" Amara asked.

"Haley, um, she was there but her connection dropped?" He scratched his ear and peered at her. "That doesn't make sense. How could they both, uh, at the same time?"

```
>Burwulf: ??!!
```

"Answer him," Amara said.

"What should I say?"

"Doesn't matter. I got what I needed." She held the phone to her ear. "Still there?"

"Yep," Starsky said. "Sure you don't want me to go inside?"

"Yes. Wouldn't do any good. She's smart enough to have already wiped the hard drives. I'm headed your way. Just make sure she doesn't go anywhere."

"Will do. I'm cutting the home's owner loose."

"10–4. See you soon."

```
>the Mailman: dude.
>Burwulf: u think MM12 got 2 haley?
>the Mailman: maybe. im unplugging
>Burwulf: me 2
```

The teen exited the game and swiveled his chair to face Amara. "Zach was the best of us. At what we did." He rubbed his reddening eyes. "If she's MM12, I mean, the money's one thing, but Zach?"

Murder was on a level by itself. "I can't tell you anything about the investigation."

Mr. Yandell, the Walker's attorney, spoke. "You're finished with my client?"

"For now," Amara said. "Not for long though."

"Fine," the lawyer said. "Mr. Walker, please don't say another word."

Liam wiped his face with his T-shirt. "You going to Haley's house now?"

The attorney nudged his way forward. "Mr. Walker, please."

"Yes," Amara said. "I'm headed straight there."

"Mind giving her a message?"

"If I can."

Liam smiled. "Tell her I know and that effective immediately she's banned from the team."

"Sure." Don't think it'll be breaking news to her.

The teen cocked his head. "You don't get it, do you? All she has left is that stupid dog and that won't be for long. She's alone now."

There's nothing worse than losing your anonymity. That's what the girl had said. But Liam was right.

Being alone was far worse.

● ● ●

Amara stood to the side of Haley's door and knocked hard again. "I know you're in there. I'm not leaving and neither are you. We can sit here until someone shows up with a search warrant if that's what it takes."

"What do you want?"

"Detective Peckham and I just want to talk. Get your side of things."

"I don't know what you're talking about."

The grand jury will. "Haley, it's nearly eleven o'clock. Are we going to talk through a door all night?"

"No."

"Meaning?"

No response came.

Amara tapped on the door. "Whose idea was it? MM12. You come up with that by yourself?"

Again, no response. Give her somewhere else to point the blame.

"Liam and Matias know you're MM12, by the way. Oh, and Liam said that Zachary was the best hacker of you all. That true? I bet he's the one that broke into the insurance networks, wasn't he? Pretty sweet. You two make a little extra on every job. Who's to know?"

Nothing.

"Only one thing I'm not sure of," Amara said. "Was it real?"

After a moment, "Was what real?"

"You and Zachary. A couple. Boyfriend and girlfriend or whatever you call it these days."

The door opened an inch. The girl's wide eyes showed no sign of tears. "He loved me. I know he did."

"Feeling wasn't mutual, huh?"

"Maybe a little. Made things too complicated."

I'll bet. "Hold on a sec." She backed up a step and yelled for Starsky to come around front. "Okay. You were saying things got complicated? In what way?"

"The way things do."

Evasive enough. "Let me guess. You told me he wanted out after the nursing home, well, let's call it what it is. After you all committed the felony at his grandmother's place. And you didn't want him to quit. That sound about right?"

"Maybe."

Amara nodded. "Surely you weren't afraid he'd snitch? Especially not on you."

"Not on any of us."

Starsky walked beside her. "Everything okay?"

"So far," Amara said. "Still gonna make us stand out here, Haley?"

The door opened a smidgen farther. "We're doing okay like this."

"Uh-huh," Starsky said. "You tell her we're not standing out here much longer?"

"Couple more minutes. You can call then."

"Call who?" Haley asked.

Starsky crossed his arms. "Why do I have to call? You do it. Your case, your paperwork."

Amara inched forward and lowered her voice. "See, when we get search warrants and stuff, the forms are a pain."

The girl cut her eyes between the two detectives. "Get a search warrant. I don't care. You're not going to find anything."

"You're probably right," Amara said. "All that computer stuff's wiped clean by now. Nothing else to find here. Gotta go through the motions though. Hey, Starsky, she says her boyfriend would've never snitched on her."

He chuckled. "That right? I guess we'll never know."

"Says their relationship was, what was the word you used, *complicated*. Ever hear of such a thing? A complicated relationship?"

He tilted his head and rubbed his chin. "I think I'm in one."

Amara gave him the look. "So anyway, Haley here was telling me she wanted to break it off or he did or maybe it was both of them."

"I never said that."

Starsky tapped his watch. "It's late and I'm hungry. Can we speed this along?"

"Hear that, Haley? He's hungry. You gonna tell us what we want to know or are we going to have to do the paperwork? I'm feeling generous—been a real solid night—so you cooperate and I'll put in a good word for you." She bent closer. "Unless you killed your boyfriend. Mmm-mmm. Juries hate that. So tell me. Did you kill Zachary Coleman?"

"Get your warrants." The girl backed away to close the door, and Amara jammed her foot in the opening, then shoved it open.

"You can't come in here!"

Starsky stepped inside. "Too late. You want to do the honors, Alvarez?"

She moved toward Haley. "Hands behind your back. You're under arrest."

The teen edged away. "For what?"

Amara grabbed the girl's arm and spun her around. "You'll be notified of the charges at the proper time." She clicked handcuffs on the teen's wrists, then pulled a card from her pocket and Mirandized her. "You understand these rights?"

The girl nodded.

"With these rights in mind, do you wish to talk to us now?"

She shook her head.

"I'll take her to the station," Starsky said. "Meet you there?"

"Yeah. I'll get started on the search warrants for all three of them. And an arrest warrant for Matias Lucero."

Haley looked back. "What about Liam?"

"Oh," Amara said. "Look who's the snitch now. But you did remind me of something. Liam sent a message. You've been kicked off the team."

"So what? That supposed to bother me?"

"It will one day," Starsky said. "Maybe not until they're both out of prison while you're still sitting in your cell trying to get good behavior so you can play solitaire on the library computer."

Amara arched her eyebrows. "Good one. Me, I'd have gone with some play on solitaire and solitary. But, hey, you've been doing this a lot longer than I have."

He took hold of Haley's arm and headed toward the door. "Grab some food on the way to the station. Vending machine was almost empty."

"How about some cash there, chief?"

He paused. "Tradition. Rookie buys when they close their first case."

"Surprised I never heard that before now. And this case is a long way from closed."

"Perfect. My stomach's a long way from full."

55 **Amara leaned against the wall** and stared across the hall at Starsky. He looked as tired as she felt. She lifted the coffee cup to her mouth, but the smell roiled her stomach. The stuff was just a prop at this point. Any more and her guts would revolt against the bitterness. The adrenaline had worn off hours ago as she'd muddled through the phone calls and paperwork to get everything taken care of.

A couple of hours ago, around six, Matias Lucero had been arrested and now waited in a holding cell. All his electronic equipment had been seized and turned over to CSI, who would process it sometime in the next millennium. Wasn't going to be anything on it anyway. She'd requested a full search of the house to look for any hidden cash or other items, but the judge felt the scope was too broad. And Liam was supposed to turn himself in before noon today. A patrol car sat outside his home to ensure he didn't try to flee.

"Ready for this?" she asked.

He tapped the back of his head against the wall several times. "Sure. She's not going to talk though. Not if she's as smart as I think she is."

"Maybe not, but if I stand out here much longer, I'll be asleep on my feet." She moved into the room and nodded to Haley. The girl slouched in her seat, a scowl on her face. A single empty chair, off to the side so it didn't block the camera's view, was the only other item in there. Amara sat and waited for Starsky to settle against the wall. He shifted several times. Left leg bent and foot on the wall. Nope. Feet spread wide and arms crossed. Nope. Right leg bent and foot on the wall. Yes. No. Slide to the corner and—

"Go get a chair," Amara said.

He pressed his back against the wall. "I'm good."

She turned to Haley. "Before we get started, I'm going to read you your rights again." When finished, she returned the card to her pocket and set her coffee on the floor. "Get you anything?"

"You can get me out of here," the teen said.

"Probably could, but I won't. You understand your rights? You don't have to talk to us."

"When do I get a lawyer?"

Amara crossed her legs. "If you have an attorney, I will arrange for you to contact them. If you don't, sometime today or tomorrow you'll have your bond hearing. You can request that the court appoint counsel for you then."

"Do you know how much my bond will be?"

"No," Starsky said. "Typically it's very high in first-degree murder cases. Add to that your hidden money and I can see why you might be considered a flight risk."

Amara nodded. If the teen managed to make bail, no way was the judge going to appoint an attorney. If she could afford one, she could afford the other. "Once the DA decides what to charge you with, he'll take it to the grand jury for an indictment. After that, you'll get your arraignment to have the charges against you officially filed. Then come the pre-trial motions, discovery, blah blah blah, and finally the trial."

"I want a lawyer. I'm not saying anything else until I get one."

Starsky straightened and yawned. "Works for me."

"So I'm clear," Amara said, "you have no attorney and will ask the judge to appoint one. Is that correct?"

"Yeah."

She planted her hands on the armrests and grunted as she stood. "Works for me too. I'll get someone to return you to your holding cell."

The detectives stepped into the hall. "No surprise," Starsky said. "You got a meeting set with the prosecutor yet?"

"This afternoon. The LT's going to be there too. Does he always go?"

"Nah." He covered his mouth as a yawn erupted. "But you're new. He wants to see how you handle yourself. What are you doing until then?"

"Home for a shower and some sleep. Not in that order."

"Need a ride?"

She shook her head. "I'll drive my car. Why not? Everybody who'd mess with me is either in jail or on the way. Should stop by and get a new phone, but I just don't have the energy to deal with that."

"Get some rest," he said. "I'm gonna go crash too. Good luck this afternoon with the DA's office."

"Think I'll need it?"

His tired grin lit up his face. "Just remember that prosecutors like to win. The stronger the evidence, the more likely they are to take the case to the grand jury."

"You didn't answer my question," she said.

"No. You won't need luck. Just patience."

"Patience? Why?"

"So you don't hurt someone if they tell you they need more evidence."

■ ■ ■

The wall clock echoed its ticking through the prosecutor's tiny office. Lieutenant Segura tapped his armrest in time with it while

Amara tried to keep her focus. Hard to do considering it'd been nearly twenty minutes since anyone had spoken.

Harold Beckerstreet, bowtie and all, was nothing if not thorough. He read and reread each page and cross-referenced the information with the notes he'd taken during her presentation. The guy reminded her of Dr. Pritchard, minus the ME's semi-endearing quirks. And personality.

Would it be okay to excuse herself for a few minutes? Step outside and call Mama? See how she was doing today? Maybe if Segura wasn't here. He'd remained mostly silent, speaking only to clarify a point here and there. That was a good sign. Wasn't it?

Beckerstreet glanced up, opened his mouth to say something, then thought better of it and returned to his notes. At the rate he was moving, they'd have to release Haley before getting around to charging her. Finally, he dropped his pen.

"Nice work, Detective," he said. "There are some holes, but that's not unusual. There will be time to address those. Maybe get the two boys to testify against Ms. Bricker. We'll see. The issue of the ransomware is easy enough. We'll have to prove the attacks originated in Texas and the victims were also in the state. All the others we'll turn over to the FBI after we're done. Or possibly use the threat of federal charges to gain more cooperation from the three."

Amara clasped her hands. "Have you decided on other charges?"

"I assume you mean ones relating to the death of Zachary Coleman?"

She nodded.

"As it stands now, the state will not file on that issue. There's simply not enough evidence to show a murder occurred. We'll wait for the toxicology report from the ME. If the results point toward the possibility the boy was indeed killed, the state will reconsider its position."

Her heart pounded. Careful, Amara. "I respect your opinion, however—"

"Thank you," Lieutenant Segura said. "If we obtain new information that's relevant to the case, we'll be in touch. Please keep us informed as it moves through the system. Detective Alvarez and I are available when you need us."

Beckerstreet stood and shook hands with Amara and the lieutenant. "Thank you both," he said. "And again, well done, Detective. I appreciate your efforts and look forward to presenting our case to the grand jury."

Segura guided Amara out of the office toward the elevator. "Not now," he said.

Not now for talking to him or not now for asking the prosecutor why there'd be no murder charge yet? "Yes, sir." She pressed the down button. "If I may, though?"

He sighed, pulled a partial cigar from his jacket, and stuck it between his teeth. "Let me ask you, Alvarez. Yes or no. Can you prove to me that Coleman was murdered?"

"I can demonstrate motive and opportunity," she said.

"Can you now?" The doors opened and they stepped into the empty elevator. He pressed the button for the lobby. "So what? There's probably hundreds of people in San Antonio that have motive and opportunity to murder someone. Depending on how you want to look at it, *everybody* has motive and opportunity."

"I would argue that, in this case, the circumstantial evidence points toward a murder."

The doors opened and they walked into the lobby. "There's the problem. *You're* not arguing it. Mr. Beckerstreet is and I'm confident he has far more experience in these issues than either of us. Would you agree?"

"Yes, sir. But that—"

"Nope. There is no but. Haley Bricker killed that boy. You and I both know it. You've done your job, now let him do his. We wait and see what the tox report shows." He pulled the cigar from his mouth and pointed it at her. "That would be evidence a grand jury could see. Something tangible. Until then, we move to the next case."

What if the tox report was clean? How was she going to prove Zachary Coleman was murdered? She froze as her mind spun. Something tangible. Like photographic evidence. "Sir, what if I had proof Haley was with Zachary when he died? Maybe not enough to confirm she did anything, but enough to show she was there?"

"If you've got something like that, why haven't I seen it?"

"I don't," she said. "Not yet. But I think I can get it."

He stuck the cigar back in his mouth. "You planning to share how that's going to happen?"

"Once she's charged with a crime, it becomes public record. We can use that."

"As it relates to the charges, yes. But you are not to go to the press and accuse her of murder. That's a headache I don't need."

"Understood. I'm simply going to ask a few people if they might have knowledge of her whereabouts on the day of Coleman's death."

He frowned. "How many is a few?"

"Hundreds." She smiled. "Thousands."

56

It took less than ten minutes for Amara to recap her plan for Mr. Beckerstreet. Talk to Haley again. Explain to her that the SAPD and Cannonball Water Park were posting notices on their websites and on social media asking anyone who was at the park on the day of Zachary Coleman's death to review any video or photos they might have taken. Police had someone they wanted to speak with. The notice would include two large pictures of Haley, one in her disguise and one not.

There would be proof. No question. Wannabe detectives would scour the background of every picture they'd taken. At least one would give them what they wanted. Evidence the girl had been with the boy near the time of his death. Maybe even ones showing her handing him the water bottle. Better yet, images that showed her at Day's End Cove with him.

The DA would have enough to pursue murder charges, but Haley had an option. Confess to the killing prior to that, give all the details, and in return the prosecution would reduce the charge from capital murder to first-degree. The death penalty would be off the table. She'd spend a long time in prison but could be eligible for parole somewhere down the road. She would have until twenty-four hours after her bond hearing to decide. By then, she'd have a lawyer one way or another.

Beckerstreet signed off on the plan. Make sure the conversation was recorded. Mirandize her again prior to the discussion. Keep

351

him in the loop. And don't do anything to jeopardize the rest of the case.

Just over an hour later, she sat across from Haley in the same interrogation room they'd used earlier that day. "Don't say another word," Amara said after reading the girl her rights. "Not unless it's to explicitly indicate you're waiving your right to have an attorney present. I'm not going to ask you any questions, but I do want you to be aware of what's about to happen."

She recapped the plan for the teen, who responded with a smirk and shrug.

That smug look would disappear soon enough in prison. The tough-girl routine wouldn't last a day. "Final thing I'll tell you and then you can return to your cell. We have the preliminary tox report." She placed her hands on her knees, afraid she'd slip one behind her back to cross her fingers. "Be another week or so before we get the details, but we do know Zachary's death was no accident. That part of the story is over."

Haley sat in stony silence.

"That's what my boss was most worried about. Oh, he knew you killed Zachary, but it's the jury who matters. We could prove you had the motive to do it. Opportunity too. But proving his death was actually murder? That was the hard part. Kudos to you. Wanna know a secret? How this whole thing got started?"

The girl's shrug had lost most of its intensity.

"His fingers and toes weren't wrinkled." Amara turned her palms up. "Dr. Pritchard caught it. He's the medical examiner. Isn't that the weirdest thing? That's how we knew someone killed him. You're in the water that long, your toes ought to be wrinkled." Amara stood. "I suppose this will be the last time I talk to you. Don't worry. You'll have plenty of opportunities to make new friends."

"Wait."

"Uh-uh. No talking, remember? When you get your lawyer, if you want to speak after that, fine."

"What about Dexter?"

Her dog? "I suppose he'll be taken to a shelter. Check with your attorney if you want something else done."

"Will you take him?"

Uh, that's a hard no. Even if Larry wasn't in the picture, the dog wasn't coming anywhere near her home. "Haley, I don't have room for Dexter or time to take care of him."

A tap on the door interrupted the conversation. "Give me a second." She peeked into the hallway. A man stood there holding a piece of paper.

"Just got this back," he said. "Figured you'd want it immediately."

The document contained ten fingerprints, Haley's according to the form. But not Haley Bricker. Amara's blood chilled. The prints matched a girl who'd run away from home four years ago at age seventeen. Haley Bricker was actually Haley Bronson, twenty-one years old, and from New Rochelle, New York.

Everything was a lie. Her ID, school records, all fake.

"Can I keep this?" she asked.

"Yep," the man said. He smiled. "Have fun in there."

"Thanks." She moved back into the interrogation room and remained standing. "Changed my mind. I do want to ask you some questions. You remember your rights?"

"Yeah, and I'm still not talking. Come on, do the decent thing. Take care of Dexter for me."

"We'll talk about that later. After you get an attorney. Right now I've got to go do a bunch of paperwork on your case. Thought I was done, but that was before I found out you were really"—she read off the paper—"Haley Bronson from New Rochelle, New York. Nice job on your accent, by the way."

The girl chuckled. "Took you long enough."

"I'll have someone return you to your cell."

"Take him and I'll talk."

"What?"

"Dexter. Take him and I'll talk."

Seriously? Liam said she didn't care about anything except her dog. Maybe he was right. "I can't make deals. You've stated you don't want to talk unless your lawyer is present."

The girl waved her hand. "Forget all that. I don't need an attorney for this." She stared into the corner camera. "I know my rights and I'm agreeing to talk."

Amara returned to her seat. "You understand that at any point in this conversation you can stop speaking?"

"Yes. So you'll take care of Dexter?"

A line.

Starsky had said that we all draw our own lines. That wherever she drew hers, she shouldn't cross it. Ever.

She could lie about the dog. Say she would take him despite the fact there was no chance that would happen. Perfectly legal.

But it felt wrong. The girl had one thing left. Dexter. She wanted to know her dog would be taken care of. That even though she might be in prison, somewhere out there Dexter was having a good life. Haley would never know otherwise, if Amara lied. Dexter might be living in a shelter, or worse, but the girl could dream of her dog. Know that he was safe.

The line. Amara would know the truth. That she'd lied about the one thing in the world that mattered to Haley Bronson.

She reached for the girl's hands and held them in her own.

"Yes, Haley. I'll take care of Dexter."

57 **Amara watched Wylie refill** the three coffee cups, then sit beside Mama on the sofa. She didn't know how long she'd been here. Didn't care. Haley's confession had gone until nearly eleven last night. After some sleep, more restless than she'd hoped, Amara awoke early and worked out at the gym. Today would be a comp day so the SAPD could recoup some of her overtime costs. Sounded good to her.

Mama said she felt good. More tired than usual, but good. And Wylie had been a huge help around the house.

Amara asked about their marriage plans and they'd both laughed. Casual affair in the backyard. Just waiting for the temps to drop a little.

Wylie insisted on knowing all about her first Homicide case, and she'd complied, surprised at how much his approval meant to her.

Fentanyl. That's what killed Zachary Coleman. Well, technically, fentanyl mixed with alcohol, though the opioid was deadly enough on its own. Effects similar to heroin and up to a hundred times stronger than morphine. Death would have been nearly instantaneous. Dr. Pritchard said there was a possibility the tox report would come back clean. That in a lot of these cases, the death occurred so quickly the drug never had a chance to metabolize.

Haley Bronson's confession, spoken, then written, gave the details. None of it shocked Amara. MM12 was the girl's idea. After a few tries to break into the insurance companies herself, she'd given up and brought Zachary, the better hacker, into her plan.

She denied their relationship was merely a ploy to convince him to help her, but Amara doubted that was true. Why would it be? Nothing else was. He'd broken into the two insurers before deciding he wanted out. The girl couldn't let that happen. No one, Zachary Coleman included, was going to jeopardize her life. If he didn't want what she wanted, what use was he?

The two had been sitting at the lazy river's edge when she killed him. Neither wanted sand in their suits, so they dragged empty inner tubes to shore and sat in them. Shoving the boy into the water was easy.

In the end, it all came down to greed. The girl manipulated those around her to get what she wanted. In a way, her confession did the same thing by reducing the murder charge.

"Why Mighty Mouse?" Mama asked. "Was there a reason she chose that name?"

"Yeah. Guess what else used to be in New Rochelle? An animation studio. That's where Mighty Mouse came to be. Oh, and her parents, both still very much alive, worked there. She grew up surrounded by artwork from the place."

"What about the dog?" Wylie asked.

"I told her," Amara said. "When she finished her confession, I told her Dexter would be going to a no-kill shelter unless someone took him first. No way he was living with me and Larry."

"So you lied to her," Mama said. Not in an accusing way. No judgment as far as she could tell. Not even surprise. Just facts.

"I did what needed to be done." The line had moved, but not much. Not once she added the Coleman family into the equation. Haley Bronson's desires were irrelevant compared to those whose lives she'd ruined. And no one needed to know she'd called the shelter twice and confirmed Dexter had already been adopted. Good luck to whoever took the beast.

Wylie held up his coffee cup. "Congratulations on solving your first case."

Amara raised hers in response. "Solving isn't the same thing as a conviction but thanks."

"True," he said. "But sometimes it's all you get. What's the rest of your day look like?"

"Going to see the Colemans after lunch. Let them know Haley confessed."

"I thought you were off today," Mama said. "You should be relaxing. Can't someone else do it?"

"They could," Amara said. "But this belongs to me."

• • •

Zachary Coleman's parents and grandmother sat on the leather sofa facing Amara. None of them seemed nervous or anxious. Simply tired. Like the weight that pressed on them was the new norm and nothing could take it away. Would her news that their son had been killed change the burden?

"Thank you for meeting with me," she said. "I have an update on Zachary's death. If any of you don't feel up to hearing it . . ."

"We're okay," Mr. Coleman said. He touched his mother's hand. "Mama, you okay?"

Eugenia Coleman raised her chin. "I'm ready."

Zachary's mother made eye contact and nodded.

"We've made an arrest," Amara said. "One of your son's friends has confessed to the killing."

The grandmother buried her face in her hands and sobbed. Didn't sound like tears of relief. No closure here.

Mr. Coleman rocked back and forth for a moment. "Can you tell us which one?"

"Haley, um, Bricker. I'm sorry I can't give you more information than that now." They'd get the details soon enough. Their son was a criminal. Bad choices led to his death.

She stood and tugged her jacket straighter. "If I can help . . ." No point in finishing the sentence. She couldn't help. She'd done her job. Now it was time for others to take over. Three teenagers would work their way through the criminal justice system. Four families had been forever tainted by their actions. None as much as the Colemans.

Would any of them visit Zachary's grave every month?

● ● ●

She pulled into the first parking lot she saw and called Sanchez to let him know she'd spoken with the Colemans. The SAPD would issue a press release later that day or in the morning. The Cannonball Water Park could expect questions from the media at any point after that.

For nearly half an hour, she sat in her car and rotated the phone in her hand. No joy came from closing the investigation. Solving a murder. Satisfaction maybe. But no joy.

How could there be when the inevitable next case waited for her? A day, a week, a month. Sooner or later, her name would arrive back at the top of the list and someone would die.

She flipped open the phone and dialed. "Starsky? I need to go out tonight."

"Thought you might," he said. "Can we meet at your apartment? And is it okay if I bring a friend?"

● ● ●

A trio of live oaks in the rear corner of the park provided the shade for dinner. Burgers for the people, collard greens with a touch of banana for the lizard.

Starsky wiped ketchup from his chin and pointed to Larry. "He likes his cage. Told me so."

"Mm-hmm." Amara used her napkin to dab at the new mustard stain on her shorts. "What else did he tell you?"

"Not a thing. Larry is a lizard of few words."

She snorted, coughed hard several times, and gulped down her drink. "Don't do that. Not while I'm eating."

"Just wanted to hear you laugh." He took a huge bite. "Always makes my day better."

"Glad I could help." She closed the wrapper around the remaining half of her burger. "I expected to like it more. Homicide."

He nodded and stared at Larry for a moment. "The job can suck, Amara. We're always too late. We see things we can't unsee. The worst of what people can do." He draped his arm around her. "Not everyone is cut out for it."

She glanced at him.

"You are," he said. "Know how I know? No excitement. No yearning for your next case. No celebrating."

She placed her hand on his knee. "Can I ask you something?"

"Anything."

"Did you just say *yearning*?"

This time, he laughed. "Our secret, okay?"

"I don't know if I can date a guy who talks like that."

"You breaking up with me?"

She tilted her head upward and kissed him lightly. "Figure it out, Detective Peckham."

58

Amara spent the better part of Friday morning getting her smartphone back and her paperwork finished. With her comp time caught up and no unsolved cases in her file, the LT was most likely going to assign her to ride along with another detective. The odds of it being Rutledge were slim unless he'd followed through on his threat and asked to train her.

Every time Segura walked out of his office, she cringed at her card table and tried to shrink her profile. Fear of the unknown was usually far worse than the reality that awaited. Usually.

Her cell rang and she answered quickly. No sense drawing attention. "Amara Alvarez," she said. *Detective Alvarez* sounded too snooty. *Homicide, Alvarez* sounded too TV-ish. Maybe drop the *Amara* though. Go with *Alvarez*. Simple. Efficient.

"This is Gregory Griffin in CSI. Wanted to let you know we processed the cash you found at the Coleman house. Total came to $34,608."

"Really? Thought it would be more." Like nearly thirty-five thousand wasn't a ton of money to her.

"Lots of ones and fives. Can't ever tell by looking."

"Guess not. Thanks for letting me know."

"There's more. Might want to come by and pick up the report. You'll need it."

"Will do." Extra to add to the ever-expanding file. "Wait. There's more? What?"

"The bundles were secured in plastic wrap. We ran it for prints and found two sets. Zachary Coleman's, of course. No surprise there."

She squeezed the phone. "Who else?"

"Got to be a relative. Eugenia Lamore Coleman. Ran the prints through the state and got a hit on the teacher database."

Zachary's grandmother? Uh-uh. No way. "You're sure about that?"

"I'm paid to be sure," he said. "Her prints were found as much as the victim's."

"I'll be there in a few." Her afternoon just got a whole lot busier.

* * *

Amara stood to the side of the front door and knocked hard. After several moments, the deadbolt clicked and Eugenia Coleman blinked into the bright afternoon sunlight.

"Detective? I was taking a nap. Is everything all right?"

"No, ma'am." She handed a folded piece of paper to the elderly woman and gestured to the uniformed officers behind her. "This is a search warrant. We need to take a look inside."

The woman scanned the document. "I don't understand."

"Please have a seat on your couch there," Amara said.

"Of course. May I fix myself some tea first?"

"No, ma'am. It'd be best if you did as I asked." She turned to the closest cop. "Check the kitchen cabinets closely."

The woman shuffled to the sofa and sank onto the end. "Zachary was a good boy."

Amara sat across from her and remained silent as the cops went about their business. The warrant gave them the right to inspect all areas of the tiny home. If there was anything here to connect the woman to criminal activity, they'd find it.

Ms. Coleman shoved a pillow behind her back. "Nearly twenty-two years now."

"Ma'am?"

"Since my husband died." She shifted on the sofa. "You'd think in that time I'd find someone else. Never did. Don't get me wrong. I loved that man, but twenty-two years."

"Long time," Amara said.

"So you can understand why Zachary was so special to me. Someone I could love." She smiled. "Kids are nice enough. Grandkids though. They're something special."

"Back here!" The cop in the rear bedroom.

The officer in the kitchen walked over and stood by the front door.

"Be right back," Amara said. "Ms. Coleman, please wait here."

The short hallway led past the woman's bedroom, the lone bathroom, and a second bedroom. Inside that, stacked floor to ceiling in places, were various electronic devices. All appeared new and unopened. Phones, laptops, drones, even a few huge TVs. Every gadget released in the last couple of years. She checked some of the items and each had Eugenia Coleman's name and address on the shipping label.

So this was where the cash came from. Zachary must have bought it online with his digital currency and had it shipped here. Then he or she sold it and turned pretend money into real dollars. No banks involved. All nice and untraceable. A perfect setup right until the boy paid with his life.

And his grandmother knew. Had to. Maybe not the depth of the crime or the danger involved. But that she was helping her grandson do something illegal? One hundred percent. She knew.

Proving the boy had been murdered made things worse for the woman. A simple overdose could be explained away. Those happened all the time. Tragic for the family. But knowing that you might have played a hand in it? Intentional or not, that had to be a pain that drilled into your soul. What would the justice system do to her that was any worse than what she'd done to herself?

She walked back to the living room and stood in front of Eugenia Coleman.

"Zachary was a good boy," the woman said again.

Amara pulled the Miranda card from her pocket and began to read.

EPILOGUE

"Alvarez," Lieutenant Segura said. "In my office. Now."

She followed him and stood in front of his desk. Monday morning, her first day back to work since Eugenia Coleman's arrest. Too soon for a new case. This was it. Her assignment to shadow another detective.

"Got something for you." He held up a piece of paper. "The requisition for your desk. Finally made it to the top of the stack." He scribbled his signature across the bottom and slid the document over for her to take a peek.

"Thank you, sir."

He grumbled something and held out his hand for her to pass it back.

She stared at the paper for a nanosecond, then tore it in half and dropped it in the trash. "If it's all the same to you, sir, I kind of like where I am now. Just get me a file cabinet and I'll be—"

"Out." He stabbed his unlit cigar toward the door. "Out of my sight."

She gritted her teeth to prevent the smile that wanted to erupt. "Thank you, sir."

"Wait. Almost forgot." His smile outshone anything she might have attempted. "You're with Rutledge until further notice."

GO BACK TO THE BEGINNING WITH DETECTIVE
AMARA ALVAREZ IN TOM THREADGILL'S
COLLISION OF LIES . . .

1

Thirty seconds.

If they were still arguing, she'd call the cops then. Let the professionals deal with them.

Amara Alvarez leaned her athletic frame outside the diner's booth to get in the man's line of sight. He glanced up and she shot her best death stare his way. Clenched jaw, narrowed eyes, the works.

No effect. The man and woman continued their argument or breakup or whatever was happening. He bounced between whispers and shouts. She alternated between screaming and sobbing.

The couple, both appearing to be Hispanic and around thirty years old, had been at it for nearly an hour. Of all the restaurants in San Antonio, did they have to come here? Today? Her initial empathy toward the pair had faded a long time ago. Most folks would've recognized the impact of their outbursts on others. Not these two.

As a result, Amara's mood had risen to level-ten irritation. Her Saturday morning ritual of a quiet meal at the Breakfast Bodega was ruined, thanks to them. Was it so much to ask? That people keep their personal matters *personal*?

Ronnie, the heavyset weekend manager of the diner, had stopped by their table twice with little impact on the theatrics. Most of the other customers had shoveled their meals into Styrofoam containers and fled the scene. Not Amara. This wasn't her first battle of wills.

The red second hand on the wall clock hit the 12. She grabbed her phone, sighed, and laid it back on the table. Five more minutes. If they were still going, she'd call the police then.

Her heart leaped as a metallic bang echoed throughout the area. Something in the kitchen, dropped or thrown, clattered a few more times, followed by muffled shouting, which may or may not have been sprinkled with a few choice expletives. The door from back there flung open and Ronnie made a beeline for her, his face steaming. An image of herself as a matador sprang to mind and she shook her head as he sat opposite her.

"Uh-uh," she said. "Don't come over here with that attitude."

He gestured over his shoulder at the contentious couple. "They're killing our business. You going to sit there and do nothing?"

She raised her phone. "Getting ready to call the cops."

"You *are* a cop."

Yeah, and she mostly loved the job. But her Saturday plans didn't include arbitrating personal conflicts. Armed robbery, home break-in, even a shoplifter couldn't ruin her day off. But this was asking too much for too little. She shrugged and bit into a thick piece of bacon. "A little overcooked today. Tell Ruby there's a difference between crispy and charcoal."

He slapped his hands together into a praying position. "Please? I'll bring out some fresh pancakes for you. And the meal's on the house this morning."

She leaned to the side and studied the couple. The woman wept while the man held her hand across the table.

"You know the rules," Amara said. "Can't take anything free. I'll leave the usual and you can do what you want with it. Give it to Ruby for bacon-cooking lessons."

"Deal," he said. "Just go now, before we lose more business."

"Next time, call the cops." She tapped her elbow on the weapon in her belt holster and walked to the couple's table. "Everything okay here?"

The man glared at her before turning his attention back to the woman across from him. "Sorry. My wife's a little emotional this morning."

Yeah? Well, me too. She focused on his spouse. Her dark shoulder-length hair had faint traces of blonde highlights, and bright red lipstick expanded her full lips. Swollen bags under her eyes added to the pudginess of her face. "Ma'am, everything okay?"

"No, it's not." Tears trickled down her face and she pulled her hand from her partner's, then dabbed her cheeks with a napkin.

The man straightened. "Now, honey, let's not—"

Amara held up her hand. "Let her talk."

The corners of his mouth dropped, and he shifted his body to face the newcomer. "Who do you—"

"Detective Amara Alvarez. San Antonio PD." She showed her ID. "I don't know what's going on here and, honestly, don't need to know. As long as I'm certain your wife's not in any danger, I'll let you get back to your breakfast. But you have to keep the noise down."

"In danger?" the woman said. "From who?"

Amara tilted her head toward the husband. "From him."

The woman's mouth hung open and she blinked several times. "What? No. I mean . . . no. Why would you think that?"

"Police, remember?"

The woman cleared her throat and sipped her water to compose herself, then slid over and patted the seat. "Would you mind sitting for a moment, Officer? I'm Marisa Reyes and he's my husband, Enzo."

"Detective. And I really don't want to get involved unless this is a police matter."

Mr. Reyes crumpled his napkin and deep wrinkles lined his forehead. "It's not."

His wife's shoulders spasmed as another wave of hysterics neared. "How can you say that? Of course it is."

"Honey, you have to let it go."

"Do I?" The woman's voice shook. "*You* sure let it go in a hurry, didn't you?"

Amara's shoulders sagged, and she sat and angled herself toward Mrs. Reyes. "Tell me what's going on."

"She got a text this morning," the husband said, "and it has her all stressed out. I told her to ignore it. Either a prank or wrong number. Not worth getting all worked up over."

His wife brushed her hand under her eyes. "How can you be so sure? You can't know it wasn't him."

Amara turned to face the woman beside her. "Tell me about the text."

"A message came about two hours ago from a number I didn't recognize. 'Help me, Mom.' That's all it said. When I tried to respond, my phone said the number was no good." She flattened her palms on the table and took a deep breath. "I know it's from Benjamin, our son. I can't explain it, but the text is from him."

Amara dangled her arm across the back of the seat. "Have you called your son to see if he's okay?"

"Detective"—Mr. Reyes grabbed his wife's hand and squeezed—"there's no point. Benjamin's been dead for three years."

Sunday mornings in the office weren't good for much besides playing catch-up. Amara shuffled through the paperwork covering her desk. The Reyeses would be coming by sometime this morning. Meantime, she planned to get her notes from the prior week into the computer. A rash of burglaries in Leon Valley consumed her working hours. Lots of paperwork, lots of interviews, lots of angry homeowners, and zero leads.

Another thirty minutes or so and it'd be time for a late breakfast. Mama's leftover vegetable enchiladas, covered in chili sauce to jump-start her taste buds. Her stomach rumbled in anticipation and she hunched forward, covering her belly with her arms in a futile attempt to disguise the sound.

One of the other detectives eyeballed her. "Hey, Alvarez. Do you mind? Trying to work over here."

"Whatever, Dotson. Not like I haven't heard any noises from your direction. Keep it over there, okay?"

He chuckled. "More room on the outside, right?"

She threw a paper clip at him. "What are you, like, six? Grow up already."

Another detective joined in. "She's right, Wylie. Lay off the latenight burritos, for all our sakes."

Dotson stood and hitched his pants up around his waist. "And risk losing this figure? No thanks. After my tours, I promised myself that when I left the service, I'd eat whatever and whenever I wanted.

Oh, and Alvarez, fifty-eight years young come next Thursday. Be sure and buy me something nice."

"Case of Pepto?"

He laughed and plopped back into his chair. "Eh, I'll settle for whatever you brought for lunch."

"Sorry to disappoint you, but no leftovers from last night." *At least not enough for both of us. And if he gets to the food first . . .*

"Uh-huh. Never known Mama not to send food home with you. Everybody must've been extra hungry."

She shrugged. "The nieces and nephews brought friends. I was lucky to scavenge enough scraps for Larry."

He leaned around his monitor to get a better look at her. "I can't believe you took care of your iguana instead of me."

"Larry's nicer to me. Smells better too."

Dotson rubbed his chin and nodded. "Point taken. What have you got going today?"

"Got to head out to Leon Valley later. Paperwork till then. You?"

He scratched the back of his neck. "Got a B&E at a Best Buy over by North Star."

"They get much?"

"Don't know yet. Probably a bunch of VCRs and stuff."

She grinned and turned back to her computer. "VCRs. Yep. They're the hottest thing on the black market these days. Hey, while you're there, see if they've got any good deals on record players. Honestly, you're the lead detective. You could at least make an effort to stay in the right century."

Her desk phone buzzed and the lobby receptionist announced that Enzo and Marisa Reyes were here. Great. She shouldn't have offered to meet with them, but it seemed the polite thing to do at the time. No surprise that they'd taken her up on the suggestion. The pain of losing a child must be unbearable. Whether cruel joke or wrong number, the text message flared new hope in the mother, and the woman would do anything to turn that hope into reality.

She asked the front desk to escort the Reyeses to a meeting room and tell them she'd join them in a moment. Mama's enchiladas would have to wait a bit, unless Dotson found them first. After a stop in the break room to hide her breakfast under a container of some sort of pasta that had transitioned to a science experiment, she took the stairs down two flights and paused.

Keep it short. No commitments. She pasted on a smile and stepped inside. "Mr. and Mrs. Reyes. Thank you for coming in."

Enzo Reyes stood and extended his hand. "Thank you for meeting with us, Detective."

"Of course. Mrs. Reyes, how are you feeling today?"

The woman clutched a tissue in her hands. "About the same. Sorry to be such a problem yesterday."

"Nonsense," Amara said. "I understand completely. The death of a child is—"

"He's not dead," Mrs. Reyes said.

Her husband placed his arm around her shoulders. "Honey, you're making this worse on yourself. Don't dredge it all up again. We have to keep moving forward. You know Benjamin wouldn't want you to suffer like this."

"He texted us, Enzo. Why can't you accept that?"

Amara shifted in her seat. "Mrs. Reyes, your son was one of the children killed in the accident down in Cotulla, isn't that right?"

"Yes. I mean, no. We thought he was, but then we got this text and . . ." She dabbed at her eyes, took a deep breath, and stared at her hands.

Amara pushed a box of Kleenex across the table and waited for the woman to recover. Cotulla. Seventeen kids on the school bus. All dead. The train had been traveling at full speed, and if the impact didn't kill them, the subsequent explosion and fire did. Counting the bus driver and two engineers on the train, twenty people dead.

The president called the incident a national tragedy when he visited the site. For the families of those who died, "tragedy" seemed far too weak a word. Mrs. Reyes was a living testimony of that fact.

Amara cleared her throat. "Ma'am, every detail of the incident was scrutinized to the nth degree. DNA tests confirmed the remains of all the children on the school bus, including Benjamin's. Remember?"

Mrs. Reyes pulled a clean tissue from the box. "Mistakes happen."

"Sure they do." Her heart ached for the woman, but giving her false hope would only add to the pain. "There's overwhelming proof Benjamin died that day along with the other kids. There's absolutely nothing to indicate he didn't. I'm sorry. I wish I could help."

"What about the text message?"

Mr. Reyes squeezed his wife's shoulder. "Wrong number. Cruel prank. Who knows? You have to let it go, baby. You have to."

"I can't. If there's the tiniest hope, I'll always wonder."

Amara clasped her hands together. "Mrs. Reyes, your son was six years old at the time of the accident. Would he even know your phone number?"

"He knew our full names, address, and phone number. We used to make him recite them to us. The school recommended all parents do that in case their child got lost, or worse."

Smart. Sad, but smart. "I see." Amara studied the mother as her thoughts battled one another. *Don't offer. Don't.* "Tell you what. How about I get our tech guys to take a look at your phone? See if they can figure out anything on the text. Would that make you feel better? Maybe put this all behind you?"

Mrs. Reyes reached her hand across the table and clutched Amara's. "Would you do that? We'd be so grateful."

"We would," her husband said. "I know how busy you must be."

"It's no problem. Really." Amara forced a smile. *This is going to be a huge problem.*

The woman slid her phone across the table. "How long will you need it?"

Amara rubbed the back of her neck. "A day or two probably. Will that be an issue?"

"No," she said. "Of course not. Anything for Benjamin."

"Okay. We won't answer the phone or any texts while it's in our possession. Did you disable the lock screen?"

Her husband grunted. "It's always disabled. I tell her that's not safe, but she says it's a headache to always have to unlock the thing."

Amara stood and tucked the phone in her pocket. "Well then, if there's nothing else . . . ?"

The Reyeses glanced at each other and shook their heads.

"Fine. I'll get this right to the lab and give you a call when I hear from them. Oh, one more thing. The cell provider will contact you to get your signature on a couple of forms. You'll be giving us approval to look at the history of your incoming calls and messages. Are you okay with that?"

"Certainly," Mrs. Reyes said. "Thank you again, Detective. I can't tell you what a relief it is to have someone working on this for us."

Working on this? The poor woman must think we're opening an investigation. Hard to do with no evidence of a crime. She placed her hand on the mother's arm. "Please don't get your hopes up. I don't want to mislead you. I'm assigned to the Property Crimes Division. I typically do burglaries, robberies, that kind of stuff. I'm happy to help, but I firmly believe your son passed away. I'm not investigating his death. I'm simply seeking an explanation for the text you received so you can have peace about it."

Mr. Reyes placed his hand under his wife's elbow and guided her to her feet. "We understand, don't we, honey? And Detective Alvarez, *gracias*."

"*De nada*." She held the door for the couple and pointed the way out of the building. "I'll call you when I know something."

She remained staring as the couple wandered from view. Had the pain of their son's death faded at all over the past three years? Or at least moved into the realm of acceptance? And now, the grieving would begin anew. Emotional scars would be ripped open and nothing she did would heal them.

The dead remained dead.

Hope couldn't change that.

Tom Threadgill is a full-time author and a member of American Christian Fiction Writers (ACFW) and the International Thriller Writers (ITW). The author of *Collision of Lies*, Tom lives with his wife near Dallas, Texas. Learn more at www.tomthreadgill.com.

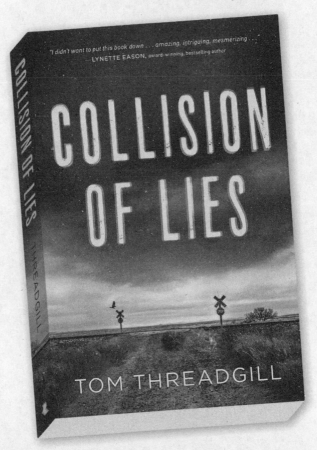